Purple Gold

Also by Jenn Shell

Wet Confetti

Purple Gold

JENN SHELL

iUniverse, Inc.
Bloomington

Purple Gold

iUniverse books may be ordered through booksellers or by contacting:

iUniverse
1663 Liberty Drive
Bloomington, IN 47403
www.iuniverse.com
1-800-Authors (1-800-288-4677)

ISBN: 978-1-4502-7899-7 (sc)
ISBN: 978-1-4502-7901-7 (dj)
ISBN: 978-1-4502-7900-0 (ebj)

Printed in the United States of America

iUniverse rev. date: 12/28/2010

Dedicated to Jeanmarie and Tom,

For their steadfast belief, support and encouragement.

And always to…Theresa, Annette, and Annmarie

ACKNOWLEDGEMENTS

Heartfelt thanks to...

M.Sgt. Antonio for his friendship and for his military service in Iraq to help insure my freedom to write.

Kelliann and John for their never ending encouragement and confidence in me.

Brandi for her warmhearted enthusiasm.

Mary Ann for her friendship and quiet, reassurance.

Bev for her constant belief in my endeavor.

Friends, too numerous to mention, for their moral support.

And forever, to my best friend and husband, John Butler, for always being there for me.

Purple Gold

Blessed is the influence of one, true, loving human soul on another.
George Eliot (1819 – 1880)

Chapter 1

The Twins, 1959, Twenty-Three Years Earlier

Rebecca and Lance entered the office with concealed apprehension. "Here we are again, Doc, two for the price of one." His attempt at humor didn't fool anyone, least of all the worried doctor. Wasn't it just this morning that he had promised the young parents that the twins would be fine? Wasn't it just a few weeks ago that their world had seemed just right? But now their boys, not yet one-year-old, were going to die and he could do nothing more.

Fear and helplessness washed over both as they watched the doctor work on their sons. Gently touching their sluggish little bodies, the doctor knew this examination would serve only to give the distressed parents a measure of relief, a chance to calm down.

"Tell me, what happened between this morning and now?" he asked, "Are there new symptoms?"

"Yes, Doctor." Rebecca was quick to answer. "One minute they were fast asleep, the next they were screaming bloody-murder. Seconds later, they seemed to have trouble breathing. I checked them over. I didn't find anything wrong, no open pins, nothing." She tried to control her panic. "Now their erratic breathing petrifies me."

"I'm sure it does, Mrs. Miles," he said compassionately.

"What do you think it is, Doctor?" she asked, "What's going on with our boys?"

"I wish I had answers. I don't know." Shaking his head he explained, "The test results came back negative. There is no logical explanation. We have done all we can."

"Take more tests." Trying desperately to reason with him, Rebecca missed his pained expression as she talked faster and louder. Biting her lip, so close to tears, she added, "I don't understand any of this."

Rebecca wasn't the only one whose confusion increased. Nervously, Lance jumped in. "Can you take more tests, Doc?"

"Mr. Miles, we ran a battery of tests. I don't know of any others. Considering the circumstances, I don't want to give you false hope."

"Circumstances, what circumstances?" Unwilling to accept this doctor's dark picture, Lance lashed out. "Is that all you have to say? What about a second opinion? Somebody somewhere must be able to help."

"Mr. Miles," the dedicated man of medicine spoke gently, "I truly wish I knew the answer."

Then as Lance's anger faded, he went quiet. Sweat beaded on his forehead and his stomach clenched as he gradually grasped the reality of the doctor's bombshell. Totally unsettled he asked, "What do we do now?"

"Go home. Continue making your sons as comfortable as possible and," he added softly, "just enjoy them."

Rebecca, beside herself, raved in disbelief. "What are you saying? This isn't happening. It's just a bad dream. I don't believe you." Quickly, she scooped up her lethargic babies and rocked them as tears mingled with moans of despair poured out. Just as quickly, Lance was at her side.

"Rebecca, please calm down. Here, let me help you. Give me one of the boys."

"I'm okay now, Lance. I just want to get out of here. I want to take our boys home."

Watching the color drain from her face, he turned to the doctor for one last shred of hope.

"Doctor, please. Call us if you find anything, anything at all." The somber doctor nodded and watched them drowning in their sorrow. He couldn't even toss them a hint of a lifeline. If only he knew what was behind this tragedy.

This nightmare started about a month ago, when David and Dennis out of the blue, turned suddenly very ill. Their chipper personalities changed drastically. Irritable, they cried almost non-stop, turned a jaundiced yellow color and ran high fevers off and on. They even gave up on their favorite food, silver dollar pancakes with whipped cream. Now breathing problems added to the boys' strange symptoms.

Frantic with fear, Rebecca and Lance turned once again to the best medical advice available. Unfortunately, this latest visit, like the last few left the doctor totally mystified and extremely troubled. He had no answers. All he could do was send this family home, where they could enjoy their time together.

Chapter 2

~

Rebecca, 1982, New Jersey

Confess: to tell or make known (as something wrong or damaging to oneself)

-Merriam Webster

Rebecca had to confess. Her lifetime masquerade of lies, which soothed her as she came to believe in them, could now expose her daughter to a lifetime of turmoil. She had no choice. Rebecca had to unmask. Her daughter's future depended upon it.

Slowly she moved the paisley veil away from her face. Her reflection looked back at her the same as always. Her lies were too deep to see. No matter, the cab would be here soon and the journey would begin. She needed to finish getting ready.

At forty-four, Rebecca hid her prematurely graying hair with champagne blonde highlights. This was yet another lie. At least the results were to her liking. Rebecca finished combing her hair and began touching up her face. Mascara lengthened her lashes and accented her deep set, indigo blue eyes. A bit of blush to her high cheek bones, a matching soft shade of pink on her lips, and she was as ready as she was going to be.

Rebecca stood and patted the navy skirt that hugged her to the knees. A sky blue sweater, still smelling faintly of cedar, emphasized her well-proportioned slender figure. Statuesque at five foot ten, she happened to like this true feature about herself, too. She knotted the patterned scarf around her slim neck just as the cab arrived.

The pouring rain slowed the ride but not her thoughts. Watching the droplets stream endlessly down the window, Rebecca rested her head against the seat and began to think. Innocence created the deceit. Life perpetuated the lies. Now she had to travel back before she could move ahead.

Nervously twisting her wedding band brought thoughts of Lance. She thought, too, about her teenage idol and how, after all these years, Lance still reminded her of that handsome James Dean. Remembering the amusing remark she and her teenage friends shared, made her chuckle. At the mere mention of his name, they conceded, James Dean could park his shoes under their beds any time. That invitation, seductive and bold, triggered any nun within hearing range to race for the nearest bar of soap and mouths would sting. Smiling in amusement, just thinking about that risky challenge made Rebecca's face redden.

Closing her eyes, she focused on Lance, visualizing the man she loved complete with receding hair line and all. It didn't matter that he carried a little more paunch around his middle now. That's just more of him to love. No, she thought, Lance isn't perfect. But what man is? How many times do I remind him to twist the toothpaste cap on tightly or to switch off the bathroom light? Then there's that matter of car grease forever under his nails. If only I could convince him to take the car to the shop. That will never happen. His fear of heights, the reason he bought our rancher instead of a two-story house, is kept under wraps. The topic is closed to discussion. Even with his flaws, I consider myself darn lucky. And, he is so supportive sticking by me through thick and thin. Like now, here I am grasping at straws and, he doesn't waver. He's behind me one hundred percent. Okay, James Dean belonged to all the teenage girls. But Lance belongs to only me. What would I do without him? Wait a minute. Don't even go there. She shook her head to rid it of that unacceptable possibility and simply cleared her mind. Nonchalantly fingering her scarf, the faint scent of Lance's after shave lotion emerged. Inhaling deeply, she recalled the warm goodbye hug responsible for how the scent got there in the first place. She tingled in the flashback. I can almost feel his face nestled still on my neck. How I do love his hugs. His arms are so strong, and yet, so gentle.

Sitting there basking in the pleasant, lingering aroma, her head filled with delicious thoughts of her leading man. She was reassured of her grateful conclusion. Yes, my Lance will always be my James Dean. And yes, she smiled. He can park his shoes under my bed any time.

She reminisced about the peaks and valleys of their marriage, glad that it held more peaks than valleys. But, the loss of two of their three children almost destroyed it.

In a devastating nose-dive, it plunged them into the depths of despair. Sadly, and without warning, two boys died before their first birthday. Rebecca thought about that horrific loss and how the hole in her heart, mending slowly, would never completely heal. She remembered accompanying each son's tiny coffin to the cemetery, and the heart-wrenching anguish clawing at her insides. Why? It made no sense. How did it happen? We asked all the right questions; saw all the right doctors and still didn't get any right answers. The boys just died.

Rebecca shook her head to rid her brain of the deep seated images lodged there. With the boys gone, now from here on, it's all about dear Emily. Oh, Emily, you grew up when I wasn't looking. Yesterday you were my little girl playing with dolls. I blinked and just like that, you're all grown-up planning your wedding. It's hard for me to believe in less than a year's time, you'll be married. That doesn't leave me much time.

Even so, Emily, don't you worry. Your babies will be safe. This time, I will get to the bottom of this long before you have children. It won't happen to you. I'll find out what caused your brothers to die, I promise.

Rebecca looked at her watch which had been given to her at graduation long ago. All these years, she thought, and this treasured gift still works. She delighted in its warm reminder of the special friend who had given it to her. Then realizing that time was of the essence, she tucked the cozy feeling away until another opportunity. Now, with the wedding coming so quickly, it was time to carry out her mission. *Odd how it seems everything else is moving so slowly,* she thought. *Even this taxi seems to be crawling.*

Sitting up, she tried searching for familiar landmarks. *Darn, I can't see a thing through this steamed-up window.* Closing her eyes, she considered, again, the reason why she was in this cab in the first place. Simply put, it was because of her love for Emily. She thought *that is the distinctive stimulus driving me into action. Love started this whole process.*

I must focus on the responsibility and obligation that rests solely on my shoulders and the challenges I face. Lance can't help me with what he doesn't know. It's all up to me. That's down-right scary. What if I fail? Stop it. Failure is not an option. Yet, there's so much to learn and so little time. I don't know if heredity played a role in the death of the boys, but I have to investigate every possibility. I'm going to find out. Lance's family is fine. That much I do know. It is my family that is of major concern. First off, I have to get my parents' health records. Considering I don't even know who my biological parents are, that's not going to be easy. After that, I'll have to confess. Then there goes my secret I swore I'd take to my grave. I'll have to tell. And everybody will know. Everybody will know that I'm an orphan and a fraud. But if that's what it takes for Emily, so be it. Phew! Why am I sweating?

Damp with perspiration, Rebecca wiped the moisture from her forehead with the back of her hand and blamed the cabbie for the problem. It was, after all she surmised, his fault for turning the heat on too high.

I know they're in here. Fumbling in her purse, she soon found them. *Thank goodness.* Inhaling deeply, she savored the cigarette's coolness before letting the smoke slowly escape. Finished, she snuffed it out in the ashtray as the pounding in her heart and the words in her head grew louder and louder...*And Everybody Will Know.*

Chapter 3

The truth of the matter is that Rebecca Harden Miles' imaginary past, created in her best interest, is catching up to her. But facing unknown intimidation possibly hidden in her roots is a challenge she planned never to pursue. That is not until now. There simply is no alternative, as circumstances catapult her in the direction she has adamantly refused to follow. That is, again, not until now.

Over the years, she convinced herself of her contrived scheme's success. But deep down, she knows. Eventually it will come back to haunt her. It is inevitable. Still it doesn't matter. That's not today's worry. It is always for somewhere down the road. So for now, she continues deceiving everyone; most especially, herself. Will there be consequences? You bet. They lurk just around the corner.

Growing up in an orphanage, part of her life was lived in a make-believe world. She had no choice. It's called survival.

Her background is counterfeit. That's all there is to it. Created in innocence, it isn't meant to hurt anyone. Intended only to spare Rebecca heartache, in time it naturally grows to protect her loved ones, as well.

Living in a fantasy world was just easier back then. But somehow, along the way, like Pinocchio's nose, what started out as a little lie grew and grew into a full blown deceptive monstrosity. There simply was no stopping it.

For herself and later for the benefit of her husband and daughter,

Rebecca proclaims her father to have been a decorated hero who died in World War II bravely serving his country. She portrays her mother as a gentle, loving, mother who sadly died of cancer not long after her father's death. That is her story and she stuck to it with no intention of ever backing down. There was never a need. That is, not until recently.

Emily's approaching wedding is the catalyst that finally forces Rebecca to change her tune. No doubt about it, learning her true beginnings is going to create a whole new ball game. And, somewhere within its confines, hopefully, she'll hit a homerun.

Life in an orphanage, considering you don't know of any other existence, is not all that bad. Rebecca is proof of that. She didn't turn out too badly. Although, looking back, she had to admit to her share of rough times.

Chapter 4

Finally, the vehicle came to a stop. It took forever to get here, she thought. She paid the cabbie and stepped out of the car. Pulling the belt on her raincoat snuggly, she stood for a long moment watching the yellow cab drive away. Okay, now what? She asked herself. I'm all alone and I can't afford to lose my nerve. I can do this. Just go.

Her eyes followed the wet sidewalk that led to the front steps of the once familiar red brick building. For a long time, I called this place home. Funny, I've been away for over forty years and yet, it still looks pretty much the same. How strange and, darn why am I so nervous?

Oh, gosh. A minute ago I was hot. Now I'm actually shivering. Rubbing her fingers to stimulate heat, it hit her. Who am I kidding? It's not only the wet, autumn weather causing me to tremble. Face it. It is fear, plain fear. This is so bizarre. Here I am facing my past and my future. Guess that gives me the right to be scared. Okay, enough of this, she chastised herself. Pull it together. Here goes.

Fear does strange things. Walking up the entrance steps, her legs felt like lead. They lacked cooperation. Taking the steps at a slower than normal pace, she felt concerned. What's happening here? I don't know. She both asked and answered her own question. I just have to coax myself. She did and she made it one step at a time. Finally, she thought. I'm here.

She rang the doorbell tentatively. Her insides were shaky as she mustered up courage. If I want to resolve all those haunting issues of my past, now is not the time for me to chicken out. Inhaling, she took a deep breath. Okay. I'm ready. Good thing, because I hear someone approaching.

The latch turned. Slowly, the door opened. There before her stood a petite nun. Mostly concealed by the religious habit she wore, at first, Rebecca couldn't tell her age. But then a few winkled furrows on her exposed face betrayed her. Holy Hannah, Rebecca surmised, sure looks like she's been around the block a few times. She's absolutely ancient. Now, that was cruel, Rebecca, she silently chastised herself.

The folds in the nun's garment were sharp and crisp from daily ironing and she gave off a scent of roses and lavender.

I don't believe it. I recognize that soap's aroma. I grew up with it. How about that? Guess, in this place, some things just stay the same. That phenomenon is remarkable. I wonder how many other surprises await me in this place to remind me of years gone by.

"May I help you?" Whoa! Guess I can't waste time thinking about that now. Gee, could your high-pitched voice get any more shrill? I know that tone. Don't think for a minute that I don't. I've been around nuns too long. You really don't want to help me. It's just the way you were trained. Sound helpful, act nice and blah, blah, blah.

Rebecca took a deep breath and released a trembling sigh to force a steady voice. Thank goodness, it came out loud and clear. It had to. Rebecca had to make it count.

She couldn't let this woman know how nervous she was, nor how close she was to turning back. To fight the urge, Rebecca gave herself a quick pep-talk. All right! I'm a grown up. All I have to do is present myself in a composed manner. Sure. But that's easier said than done. Darn all those years fearing this type nun. Well, not this time, little lady. You don't scare me. Now, that sounds pretty good, she thought. All I have to do is convince my jittery insides.

"Good afternoon, Sister. My name is Rebecca Harden Miles and I would like to talk with Mother Superior. Is she available?"

"Do you have an appointment?"

"I don't." Apologizing, she continued in the sweetest of tones. "But, I assure you, it is essential that I talk with her. You see, Sister, I was a resident of Holy Comforter Orphanage years ago. I have a serious problem and I need her help."

Rebecca could tell from the look on her face she was not getting very far with this old nun. Obviously, my touching plea got lost on her. I can tell she's not the least bit sympathetic In fact, if looks could kill, I would be a goner.

The old nun didn't say a word. She just stood there glaring. Although her training forced her to hold her tongue, it didn't apply to her thoughts. Free reign ruled in her mind allowing her to have a field day with her resentments. Silently, she aimed her harbored grudge directly at this annoying woman. Listen, she thought, don't think you are getting in this place without an appointment. I won't permit it. You think you can just walk in willy-nilly and expect the nuns here to jump thru hoops for the likes of you. Forget it.

We're all old and tired in this place. We paid our dues. We earned our quiet. Now go away and let us rest.

Holy Comforter, no longer an orphanage, nor school, now served as a retirement home for the nuns who had given their lives and talents to raising and educating unwanted children. Suddenly, the old nun began pushing the door shut announcing sternly, "I told you, you cannot see Mother Superior without an appointment."

"Wait please." Pleading, Rebecca quickly put her foot in the door to sabotage the nun's hard-hearted intent, all the while thinking, what in the world did I do to deserve this treatment? Why is she so rude? Well, she's not getting away with it.

"Young lady, remove your foot." The nun's commanding shrill voice was earsplitting, all the while mustering her shoulder into action leaning into the heavy door.

Ouch! This curmudgeon means business. I don't believe it. Bet under different circumstances, this would be hilarious. We must look ridiculous. Pushing and pulling. Why I outweigh this old fuddy-duddy. I'm Goliath and she's David. There's no way she can win. Oops, wait a minute. What am I thinking? Clever, little David won that battle, didn't he? Holy Hannah, I better push harder.

Left to their own devices, she would never know the outcome of their comical skirmish. Their struggle ended abruptly with the help of none other than Mother Superior herself.

"Sister Maria Donata, what in the world is all this commotion?"

"Mother Superior, I am sorry for this disturbance," lamenting, the old nun began explaining. "This woman doesn't have an appointment and still insists on seeing you. I was trying to get her to leave when you saw us. But she has other intentions."

Walking with an air of dignity, and self-assurance, the seasoned Mother Superior approached. Seeing the determined woman standing there dripping wet, with one foot solidly entrenched on the inside leaving its mate lingering hopelessly outside, she motioned for Sister Maria Donata to step aside.

"Come in, miss. Come in out of the rain. I am Mother Martha. Do follow me into my office." Speaking in a soft but authoritative voice, it was obvious she was used to having her orders obeyed. Well, Rebecca thought, I'm not a stranger to that demanding, blind obedience, either. How could I be after all those years of indoctrination?

"Thank you, Mother Superior." Rebecca thought and I better hurry before she changes her mind. Rushing past the disgruntled, old nun, halfway out of her raincoat, Rebecca moved quickly through the vestibule following the Reverend Mother to her office.

"Now, who are you and what is it you want with me?"

"It is a long story, Mother, I'll try to make it as brief as possible."

"Don't worry about time. What is your name?"

"Rebecca. Mrs. Rebecca Harden Miles."

"Well, Mrs. Rebecca Harden Miles, since I have no other appointments today, sit here. Start at the beginning and take your time. I'm not going anywhere until Devotions and that's not for another hour." With that, stretching out her arm in a sweeping motion, she pointed to the seat selected for Rebecca, then sat straight in her own imposing chair. Watching Mother Superior sitting so stiffly in her huge, leather, desk chair, Rebecca felt obligated to mimic the old nun's posture. Naturally, Rebecca thought to herself, she gives me the hard, uncomfortable ladder back chair.

Observing Mother Martha listening attentively with hands folded neatly on the edge of her large desk, reminded Rebecca of the nun's make-up. Serenity, that's it. Look at her sitting there with that quiet calmness about her. Come to think of it, most nuns possess that comforting quality. Not all, and, absolutely for sure, not that huffy Sister Maria Donata.

Right now, I'm glad for Mother's tranquil countenance. It puts me at ease, especially since this is a difficult topic of discussion for me. I need all the help I can get.

Well, it's now or never. Taking a deep breath, she went on. "You see, Mother, when this place was the Holy Comforter Orphanage, I lived here. For sixteen years, it was my home."

Pausing, she thought, my surrogate home and, for too long, the sum total of my existence. How pathetic. I'm going to cry. Holy Hannah, I can't afford to do that. Not in front of Miss Stability herself. She doesn't even know me and I'll be darned if I'll let the past encroach on my present.

Blinking rapidly, Rebecca managed to suppress the urge, hopeful that the nun didn't notice. Unfortunately, she did. In her usual take-charge manner, Mother Superior jumped to conclusions and assumed she knew what brought Rebecca to her office today. She also did not hesitate to chastise her.

"So you are looking for your true identity. Most orphans want to know who they are, sooner or later. That is not unusual and certainly no need for foolish tears."

Holy Hannah, Rebecca thought, she doesn't miss a trick. Now that was an unexpected kick in the head. Well, so much for her aura of serenity.

Wearing a sweet smile, Rebecca masked sour thoughts. Okay. For making me feel stupid and small, guess what, Reverend Mother? You just got yourself kicked out of that exclusive club. Now you're lumped right in there with old grump Donata's category. Yeah, like that will knock the wind from her sails. Never once did the nun unfold her hands nor, did she change the tone of her voice. Lacking the slightest hint of interest, the woman's requirements were uttered in a monotone.

"You will need to tell me about dates and whatever you remember to help me find your records."

"Of course, Mother." Rebecca answered positively, all the while harboring negative thoughts. She just couldn't shake the feeling that this woman wasn't working with her. She even questioned the validity of her compassion. After all, she had been taught that all nuns had the corner on that market. Darn it, Rebecca. Be honest. You let this nun scare you. Think about it. She is just a woman hiding behind that habit, right? Right, and who am I kidding? Okay. But I know for sure that I did not come this far just to be stopped by fear. I have questions to ask, and I want answers. Big talk when it's just in my head. Mustering up her courage, Rebecca gingerly followed her intention.

"Mother Superior, for years I yearned to know who I am, who my parents are. But time has a way of healing and over the years, my pain lessened and I've grown far less inquisitive. It is just not as important anymore. I am here for a different reason."

If that statement made an impression on the nun, she hid it well. Now what? I'm sure she heard me. She's too quiet. What in the world did I say to warrant this cold shoulder? I don't believe this. One thing for sure, if anyone needs an attitude adjustment, she's the top candidate. Maybe she didn't like me being so blunt. Maybe it's just a matter of pride.

I better be careful. If I create irreconcilable differences, it would mean total disaster. I just wish I could read her better. Trouble is she changes direction too quickly. I don't have a chance. She's just unpredictable. I can't figure her out.

Naturally, I don't know where I stand? Now what in the world is she pondering? I can tell from her eyes that something's up, like she has better things to do? I wish she would give me some clue, a smile, a smirk, a nod of approval. Now that would be really helpful. Stop kidding yourself, Rebecca. This nun will never let that happen. I still have to go for it. I'll make it as clear-cut as possible and hope for the best. Besides, all this thinking is like mental gymnastics. I'm jumping all over the place and it's starting to give me a migraine.

"Ahem!" Clearing her throat, she took a deep breath. Proceed with caution girl. Lord knows what's on her mind. Aw, come on, you butterflies. Give my stomach a break.

"What I need from you, as soon as possible, Mother Superior, is my health records and any information there may be on my biological parents." There. I got it out. I wonder if I should tell her the reason for my urgency. Should I mention the boys and Emily's wedding? No. It's none of her business. Besides, I don't think she really cares. She's like a yo-yo. One minute she seems friendly, then the next minute, she's all business and she's taking her sweet time. I don't care. I'll wait for as long as it takes. Like I have a choice? With that Rebecca filled the room with silent determination.

That Mother Superior was wrong in her assumption for Rebecca's visit did not offend the nun. Rebecca's audacity in pointing it out did. Scowling, finally she spoke but, unfortunately, in a less than friendly tone.

"Mrs. Miles, would you really have me believe that you don't care who your parents are?" Not waiting for an answer, she went on berating sarcastically, "If so, you are unique. You would be the first orphan I ever met who didn't want to know."

Oh, great. Now, to top it off, she thinks I'm a liar and this, when I'm actually telling the truth. Can it be any more ironic?

"If health records are what you are seeking, I'm afraid it will take time to locate them. With my heavy schedule, I just don't know."

This nun's colossal ego bruised, she was ready to dismiss the entire project before it even got off the ground. Glaring at Rebecca, she announced cynically, "That is more of a task than just learning your heritage and I am not sure when or even if I can get them."

Her reaction left Rebecca confused. What's her problem? She wondered to herself. I'll say this. She's good at throwing me off balance. Wait a minute. Aha, I've got it and it didn't take long for Rebecca to connect the dots. I'm such an idiot! Now I've done it. Holy Hannah, I could just kick myself, and after all those years of training. How could I have forgotten? It's so simple. It's all about rank. Just never underestimate the seriousness of the title. This Mother Superior surely doesn't. Well, there's no time to wallow in my mistake. I won't let her turn this into a Titanic moment. I'll just play by her rules. Give her the power. Okay, Miss You Must Be Right, I remember now.

"Forgive me, Mother Superior. Of course you are so very right. I did not mean to be disrespectful. It's just that there's a lot riding on my findings and I just got carried away. By all means, I definitely would like to know who my parents are. You are totally right. I don't know what I was thinking."

Meant to placate the indignant nun, for Rebecca, the apology unexpectedly held an element of surprise; a measure of truth. Okay, she thought, so that wasn't my primary concern. Then why do I feel a nagging? Maybe the nun is on to something. Maybe I do want to learn who I am. Imagine what a bonus that would be. One, I would hope, filled with its own rewards.

Look at her. She still doesn't look moved. She's one tough cookie. I think I better grovel a little and it couldn't hurt if I eat more humble pie.

"Mother Superior, again forgive my impertinence. Any assistance you may provide would be most appreciated."

Smugly, the nun relented. "I will do what I can." Bingo. Rebecca almost jumped for joy. She thought this nun just needs assurance that she is at the helm. So let her steer the ship. As long as it gets me where I want to go, do I care?

"Now how far back are we talking here?"

"Forty-four years, Mother Superior. I was born Rebecca Harden in

1938, and I lived in the orphanage for sixteen years. I'm afraid that's all I know." Gosh, Rebecca thought, talk about feeling insignificant. But then how can I be expected to provide adequate family information on a family I never had. That's why I'm here. Isn't it?

"Mrs. Miles, may I call you Rebecca?"

Sounds like the tough captain may be mellowing. Anyway, her rough edges seem to be smoother. Good. This puts a whole new spin on the conversation. "Oh, yes, Mother, by all means, please do."

"Well, then, Rebecca, let me work on your case. Let me see what I can do. Unfortunately, since your records go back so many years, I will have to get a special dispensation from my Bishop to retrieve your files from the orphanage's archives. That will take some time."

How much time? The question roared loudly in Rebecca's head and hung on the tip of her tongue. I'm dying to ask, but I dare not. I'm not taking any chances. No. I'm not going to push it.

All I can do now is wait. Of course, that's no skin off her nose. Look at her calmly taking her sweet time while my insides are churning faster and faster. Rebecca held back the temptation. She so wanted to yell hurry up before I go batty. Finally, the waiting was over.

"Rebecca, would you be able to return in say, about three weeks? I should have what we need by then."

Whoopee! She said we. That's a good sign. Maybe she endorses my problem after all. Maybe she'll give it immediate attention. Maybe I better not put the cart before the horse. But really, her being on my side would be a great start.

"Give me your telephone number in case there is a change in plans and write down your address, as well."

Curb your excitement, girl. Don't go over-board. She probably wouldn't toss you a life preserver anyway. She's happy having the upper hand. That's all she needs. So let her have it. "Three weeks will be just fine, Mother." Taking out her pocket calendar, Rebecca circled the date exactly three weeks from this meeting. Mother Martha followed suit on her large desk calendar.

Boy, that's encouraging. I feel better already. Following protocol, Rebecca waited for Mother Superior to stand first. Then Rebecca presented her address and phone information. Extending hands, wishing each other well, this meeting was adjourned.

That went relatively well, so to speak, Rebecca thought. Dare I ask for one more favor? Feeling like a guilty schoolgirl, she figured, aw, come on, why not? What do I have to lose? All she can say is no. I'm going for it. Her hand on the doorknob, she turned and faced the nun. "Reverend Mother, I know this place has changed but would it be okay with you if I looked around just the same? I bet the walls are bulging with memories."

"Be my guest Rebecca and here is a hall pass." A hall pass? Rebecca wasn't sure she heard correctly. But there it was in her hand with the nun's granted permission. "A brief journey through this special building may be pleasant."

"Thank you, Mother Superior, Rebecca said aloud but, thought to herself. Yeah, special places make lasting memories all right, whether you want them or not. Draping her coat over her arm, she smiled. Bringing with her a certain energy and passion, and with mixed emotions, she headed out into the halls she once haunted. I feel like a kid again.

Let the tour begin. But first, I better get to the lavatory. Wow, what a dork I am. Every time I get nervous, this happens. For heaven's sake, it's called a bathroom. Imagine that! After all those years, I'm still brainwashed. Sister Philomena. It's her fault. She was mean and ugly as all get out. She's the one who pinched my earlobe, for being so unladylike when I accidentally called it bathroom. Wincing at the thought, Rebecca gently tugged at her ear to help rub away the unpleasant memory. Great, now I've done it. Here I go thinking about that bad-tempered nun. Behind her back, the kids all called her, Sister Philo-just-plain-mean-o. That's funny now. It was, and it wasn't back then.

Continuing her tour, Rebecca walked to the next room. Immediately she recognized it. The music room, of course, but it's a lot smaller than I remembered it. Goodness gracious, I learned to play the piano right here in this very room. Okay, so I didn't become a concert pianist, but thanks to the patient nuns, I still play for my own enjoyment. That's one treasure I took away with me.

Ironically, there was an upright piano resting against the west wall exactly in the spot where it belonged. No, that can't be the same one. It looks old but it has to be a more recent acquisition. Gone, too, is the beehive of activity. It's so quiet in here. Except for those few old nuns snoring away in that sitting area, you could hear a pin drop in here.

Wonder how they manage to sleep sitting up? Maybe it's an acquired benefit of old age. Quietly walking into the room, Rebecca found a nicely cushioned chair. Too bad Mother Superior's office isn't equipped with these.

Chapter 5

1944

Closing her eyes for just a moment was all it took. Clearly, in her mind's eye, she could see the little girl in her plaid orphan's uniform sitting on the high piano bench. She could not have been more than six or seven-years-old. Her legs, too short to reach the foot-pedals, dangled. No mistaking it. There she was on music lesson day.

"Middle C. This is middle C, Rebecca, remember? It all starts with this key. If you know where middle C lives, all your other fingers will find their homes, too. Now, start your piece over and concentrate. You know how to play this one. I know you do." Sister Lucille Frances used a soft tone as she taught, but to make her point, loudly tapped her pointer on the resident key of middle C.

"Yes, Sister, I know middle C. I just forgot." Rebecca's little heart was breaking. Of all the sisters in the orphanage, Sister Lucille Frances was one of her very favorites. The tapping sounded like thunder to Rebecca's little ears. Her feelings were crushed. It was all she could do to keep from crying.

She had let Sister down and to top it off, she was embarrassed. It was almost too much for the little girl to bear. She so wanted to earn a star on her music page for today. She botched her chances for that. Rebecca's doleful eyes looked up at the sheet music held captive by the piano's small, creviced ledge. She tried again. Concentrating harder than ever before, this time, her thumb found middle C. Wonder of wonders, the rest of her nervous fingers magically landed on the right key just like Sister had promised. So intent on pleasing Sister Lucille Frances, she played the piece she was learning with no mistakes. To her, Johannes Brahms' Lullaby never sounded so good.

"Well, there you are little one. I knew you could do it. You focused and gave all your attention to the keys and timing of the melody. You played it beautifully."

In her delight, the music teacher not only gave Rebecca a well-deserved star for her second attempt, but a warm hug, as well. Rebecca basked in the sunshine of that unexpected bonus.

"Thank you, Sister." With that, the music student happily climbed down from the piano bench and headed off to her next class. The lullaby's melody stuck with her all day and if its intent was to make her sleepy at day's end, it didn't work. The warmth of Sister Lucille Frances' approval wouldn't let it. How she loved being hugged. At this institution she called home, hugs were at a premium.

At four feet tall, Rebecca, a second grader, was small for her age. She had no way of knowing that just around the corner, her sprouting years would take root. She was fair-skinned with wavy blonde hair which left to its own devise, by now would have fallen down past her waist. Too bad it had to be cut into a short bob. But that, or short pig-tails, was the haircut all the girls sported, not by choice but by mandate of the powers to be.

Her deep blue eyes sparkled when she smiled and her rosy cheeks matched her disposition. On one hand she was quiet, on the other, a tad impish. The tow-head was most of the nuns' sweetheart.

Math class over, the recess bell rang and all children, headed outdoors in an orderly fashion. In a single-file, boys formed one line; girls the other. Running was unacceptable.

"Come on Theresa, hurry," Rebecca challenged. Both girls scurried toward the massive old oak tree. "Annette and Annmarie are already there waiting for us." Theresa, Annette, and Annmarie were Rebecca's best friends in the whole world. Apparently, the four girls as babies arrived at this institution at about the same time. When they were four or so, they began playing together. Their little personalities clicked and, from that time on, they were inseparable or as much as was allowed within the rules and confines of this orphanage.

"It's your turn, Annmaire, go ahead." Theresa practically yelled in her anxiousness to get started. They sat in a circle on the ground. None had family and yet all liked hearing whatever the others had to say about theirs. Enthusiasm was contagious as they took turns telling their stories. Sometime in the process, embellishment set in to include wonderful birthday parties and fantastic Christmas celebrations, and the like. At least this way, everybody had a background, a family tree and one that they could pick and choose.

Lies? Fantasies? Or were they just a way for every hopeful, little, orphan girl to hang onto elusive dreams? After all, as far as they could tell, everybody had family. Why even Mother, Father, Dick, Jane, Sally, Spot and Puff were in their very first Reader.

The first part of recess was always spent in storytelling time. Games were played later, time permitting. As young as they were, their sisterhood was treasured. All four girls loved hearing the stories, old and new told over and over. It gave them a feeling of genuine belonging. It gave them an exciting past. It gave them hope for a happy future.

After all, there is no expiration date on dreams. Plunging into her creative, imaginative journey, Annmarie jumped into her adventure. "Okay, here goes." Sitting Indian style, all attentive eyes focused on her, clinging to her every word.

"My mother and father loved me very much." Imagination is such a gift. It didn't matter that she was just a baby at that time and couldn't possibly remember. It didn't matter that her parents abandoned her or that maybe they were dead. What mattered was she felt the story in her heart to be true and so, to her, it was. "We lived in a big, white, house high on a hill and our backyard was filled with toys and swings just for me." Inventing as she went along, she added. "And my Mama always made the best picnic baskets." "Oh, what was in them?" interrupted Theresa in awe. The daily food served in this place, after all, was not exactly inspiring. It was food. It was unanimous. It was not picnic basket food, for sure.

"Lots of good things were in those made-up baskets, like chocolate cake with thick chocolate icing and candy and lemonade. Sometimes, there was home-made vanilla ice-cream." She closed her eyes, licked her lips as if to savor the flavor, and inhaled deeply. "Everything was sooo delicious." Of course, exaggerating her words made the food sound more alluring.

"Then what happened?" asked Annette, wide-eyed and delighting in the story, eager to hear more.

"Well then, my Mama and Daddy both got sick so they had to leave me here."

Annmarie always ended her tale with the same hopeful words. "And they are coming to get me, just as soon as they get better." That she had never seen her parents did not matter. She was confident of their return and used the same ending just the same.

Sometimes the stories had to be short. It all depended on how good they were in class as to how much recess time was given. Today, apparently, Sister did not think their behavior deserved a generous interlude and so they knew they would have to speed up their story telling.

"Your turn, Annette," Rebecca decided. "Better hurry. Remember Sister Constance said we were not very good today."

"Okay. I'm going to tell you about my birthday party. The cake was…."

"Sshh," Theresa broke in, "Here comes Sister Constance."

All four girls knew the routine. They went right into their cover-up, sing-song game, reserved for just such an intruder. Whatever was spoken in this group belonged only to them. It was their secret and none of the nuns could know. On cue and with appropriate saluting hand motions to match the words, the girls sang:

"A sailor went to sea, sea, sea, to see what he could see, see, see, but all that he could see, see, see, was the bottom of the deep blue sea, sea, sea. A sailor went to…"

When the nun walked out of ear shot and there was no longer a fear of discovery, Rebecca held up her hand. "Stop, Sister is gone. Okay, Annette, let's hear about your party."

"It was so much fun. There were pony rides and ice-cream and cake and there was a clown with fuzzy, red hair and a big, red nose to match. I liked him the best. He made balloon animals and wore big, floppy shoes, and…"

"Sorry. Annette your party sounds wonderful but we're running out of time. You can tell us more about it next time. Okay?" asked Theresa. Theresa wanted to tell her story and Rebecca still had hers to tell.

"Sure." Living in an orphanage, one was more prone to share.

"When I was little," Theresa began, "my parents would put me in a bright, red wagon and pull me to the park. Then we would feed the pigeons peanuts that my father bought from a man who cooked them right there in his cart." Pausing, Theresa turned to Rebecca. "There's more but you better get some of your story in. I think Sister is starting to walk toward the bell."

"Here goes." Rebecca's eyes widened with a sense of urgency. Trying to get in as much as she could in the short time allotted, in a staccato pattern, she spit her words out faster and faster.

"My mother was the most beautiful woman in the world and my Daddy was as handsome as a prince and we lived happily in a big house with, oh darn. There's the bell."

It meant it was time to go back to class. It meant her story would have to wait. It meant immediate, mandatory silence.

Chapter 6

~

1944 – Holy Comforter Orphanage

Holy Comforter Orphanage, the refuge that seemed to be forever, actually began on a cold winter's night in 1890, when a recently widowed woman about to deliver a child was taken in by the Sisters of Hope. The baby survived. The widow did not. Encouraged by their Bishop, the Sisters took care of the child and opened their doors to all neglected or abandoned infants.

Situated high on a hill in the small New Jersey town of Summit Falls, it was not just about brick and mortar even though construction was an achievement all of its own. Standing three stories tall, this huge, red brick building overflowed with deserted youth trying to find their way.

The girls' dormitory was on the third floor, the boys' on the second and the main floor was divided into two wings. The left wing housed the chapel, classrooms, infirmary, library and cafeteria while the right wing was dedicated to the nuns' living quarters, the convent.

The cellar held a gymnasium with limited exercise equipment, a small swimming pool and locker rooms. The laundry room and a section devoted to the coal bins were also housed in this building's underground story.

Getting to one's destination in the cellar, with all the tunnel-like hallways linking one area to another, was like walking through the catacombs. A little scary, and a lot musty, it was the least favorite area in the orphanage.

Not all the nuns, who ran this place they called home, came to this community for the same reasons. They all, however, were aware that there was no padlock on the door and no wall, not even a fence around the convent. Unlike the orphans who had no choice, they were free to leave.

Most nuns were dedicated. But there was still that small faction of miserable nuns, and not always just the elderly, who suffered from burn-out or, who refused to admit that, for them, entering the convent was a pathetic mistake of gargantuan portions. To add to their misery and to save face, they insisted on staying with the only way of life they knew.

Some of these women entered the convent as a way to run away from life only to learn that living in a confined hideaway did not satisfy their need to run. The fact of the matter; life was still there and yet, running was no longer an option. In this place, they learned quickly. A nun runs into her worse enemy. Crash - right into herself. If some nuns felt like prisoners, it was of their own accord.

Astute children learned early on just who these nuns were and how to stay out of their way. They were easy to spot. They were the ones who never laughed or smiled or spoke unless it was deemed compulsory. They walked around all day with their heads somewhat bowed yet constantly looking for scapegoats. Someone had to be blamed for their wretched plight. They were the ones who did not hesitate to dole out punishment at every given opportunity. Many a squeal followed an unexpected, quick, yank of a pig-tail or slap to the rump. Labeled behind their backs as Grumpy Curmudgeons, the children avoided these dreadful people like the plague.

A secret list separating the sweet nuns from the grumpy ones was jointly made up by the four friends. Rebecca, Theresa, Annette and Annmarie were in agreement. The nice nuns were Sisters Constance, Lucille Frances, Perpetua and Regina. They were always ready and eager to help.

And then there was that plump Sister Philomena. Abusive, malicious and nasty, definitely, she won the prize for grumpiest. She was the one who made Rebecca eat all of her tapioca pudding. Knowing full well that Rebecca hated it, she made her eat all of it, just the same. Dubbed Sister Philo-just-plain-mean-o, she lived up to her well-earned nick-name.

Sister Regina related well to the orphans. Now she was a loveable nun. Rebecca liked her best. Later in life, Rebecca would learn just what a true benefactor she had in this kindhearted nun.

To top it off, Sister Regina was not afraid to show her human side to her charges, either. That, from time to time, a curse word would slip out of this saintly nun's mouth, endeared her to them even more. Although she had a disciplined spiritual life, she had little self-discipline. She figured, while growing old is mandatory, growing up is optional, so she would join in games and put off her chores as long as she could. She was in her early thirties, although her exact age was not known by the ones who loved her so. Whatever it was, she did not act it.

Rumor had it that one day Sister Regina got angry with God for some unknown reason. But anyway, it was reported that she actually threw a slipper in the direction of the crucifix in the Community Room and used unrepeatable language. Word of her unbelievable human actions spread like wild fire through both dormitories and the resident ragamuffins raised her esteem among them a peg higher.

Sister Regina, not only taught school, she also was the orphanage's secretary and worked in the office several days a week. Today, she was assigned to clean out the files with implicit instructions coming from Mother Superior, herself, to keep only pertinent papers found within each file. Space was at a premium. Anything thicker than ten single sheets of paper was destined for the trash basket. No exceptions.

The tedious job would have been monotonous had Sister Regina allowed it. She hummed to herself and turned the work into a game perusing and tossing and learning more about her charges. There was nothing of real consequence in these dusty files. That is until she came to Rebecca Harden.

Bulging, it stood out from the rest. Sister Regina, like a sentry on duty, snapped to attention. Gingerly, she ran her fingers over the reason for the swollen area. With her discovery, her humming stopped and out came a soft whistle in amazement.

Inside a small envelope yellowed with age, she found a beautiful necklace. Delicate in appearance only, the herringbone chain was solid gold. The protective chain held tightly onto an exquisite, heart-shaped gem.

Sister Regina was familiar with the stone. It was the same one as was worn by her Bishop. Only his was made into a ring. It was a radiant, royal purple amethyst with pink flashes in between and she knew it was expensive. Once, when she was filing, she came across an old paid invoice for the Bishop's ring and she was shocked at the price tag.

She remembered asking God's forgiveness for her ill thoughts against the Bishop.

At the time, she could not help but think the money spent on his ring would have fed a quarry-full of orphans. So annoyed with the amount of money that was spent on his stone, she remembered doing research. Why did it cost so much? She had to know. She learned that amethyst was featured in the British Crown Jewels and was in demand by royalty of other countries. It was supposed to have healing powers and bring the wearer increased spirituality. For some, it was claimed to bring love and good fortune. Sister Regina learned, too, that Amethyst is the birthstone for the month of February. She let the striking necklace run through her trembling fingers. It was precious and so was the one in whose file it was found and whose birth date was recorded as February 5, 1938.

It did not belong in the file. It took up too much space. It was to be thrown away as dictated by The Reverend Mother. There were to be no exceptions. Each file was to be no thicker than ten single sheets. The decree was ordained. The necklace had to go.

Again, Sister Regina would have to ask for God's forgiveness in her evening prayers. This time she would have to answer for her sin of disobedience. There was no way that she could throw away this gem.

She would have to take her chances. Of course, she had no intention of being caught in the error of her ways. Just the same, tonight, in her time of meditation, she would use a mantra. That way she would be forced to spend the entire evening in continuous silent chanting. In her mind, Alleluia was the word of praise she had chosen for repetition. Repeating it over and over, would be her avenue of petition seeking forgiveness for her transgression.

Returning the necklace to the safety of its original home, she sealed the envelope's flap with a strip of sticky tape. With shaky fingers, she turned it over and carefully wrote the name of Rebecca Harden on the front. Like tumultuous thunder, her heart pounded loudly as she then quickly slipped it into her habit's deep-creviced pocket. It was to be held there until she could hide it in the safety of the dresser drawer in her cell. Returning to the work at hand, she was more anxious than ever to learn about Rebecca and whatever, if any, story went with the newly found treasure.

Reading through Rebecca's entire file, she was disappointed. Not much had been written about the necklace. Just when she was about to give up; it jumped out to her. On the very last page, she found a short but meaningful message. It simply read – "Please give this heart to my daughter Rebecca on her twelfth birthday. Tell her I love her."

For just a minute and with a tear in her eye, Sister entertained the idea of its confiscation, as well. Finder's keepers, she wondered? Just as quickly, the idea vanished. After all, she reasoned, this sentimental message was written on a piece of paper that did fit in the file. So that eliminated that idea. Instead Sister Regina tucked the message away in her mind. She knew she would never forget such a poignant, communiqué. Just the same, she committed it to memory.

She made a mental note of Rebecca's age, too. It was 1945, and Rebecca was seven-years-old. In five years, on February 5th, she would be twelve. In five years, on that date, she would be the recipient of an extremely exquisite and meaningful piece of jewelry. She could not help but wonder, with some trepidation, what would have happened had she not been assigned to this task today. Sister shivered at the thought of possible consequences. Rebecca's twelfth birthday would have come and gone without the fulfillment of a loving mother's wishes. No one was tracking the time. No one knew it was necessary. What if Rebecca never received her necklace? Again, Sister shuddered at the thought. Just, what if?

Chapter 7

1948

All night long silently, and majestically, the snow came fluttering down. Falling rapidly, the trees were soon snowcapped. Mini snowdrifts, created by the blustery wind blowing smooth heaps of snow against the schoolyard fence, abounded. Truly, this was an inviting virtual winter wonderland.

It couldn't have happened on a better day. With the exception of the early church service, Sunday, was practically all free time.

Snow beckoned and they so wanted to answer its call. Inside the church, it was hard for the four, little, urchins to concentrate. Thank goodness their perfunctory responses had become ingrained.

"Dominus vobiscum," (the Lord be with you) – Father Duffy's deep baritone voice filled the chapel. In unison, voices of children responded with the familiar, "et cum spiritu tuo."(And with your spirit)

Dutifully singing, Annette nodded her head in the direction of the outdoors and winked. Theresa got the message. Shifting her feet, she checked to see if Sister Perpetua was watching. The coast was clear. Catching their attention, Annmarie and Rebecca read Theresa's lips as she mouthed the words, 'Meet at the oak tree.' Lucky for all of them, the Choir Director paid full attention to the music and Father Duffy, facing the altar, had his back to the assembly.

The ten-year-old girls liked singing in the choir. Standing in the choir loft high above the congregation gave them a feeling of being special. After all, not everybody who auditioned was chosen. Today, however, with all that snow waiting outdoors, singing was not foremost in their minds. Their attention diverted, anxious to get outside, it seemed this Mass would never end.

"Gee," Annmaire piped up, "finally. I thought Father Duffy would never stop talking. Wonder what his long sermon was all about, anyway?"

"You didn't listen?" Theresa asked in disbelief.

"And you did! Miss Goodie-Two-Shoes?" retorted Annmarie.

"Come on. Forget it." Annette stepped in squelching the little debate before it escalated. "Let's see who can make the best snow angel." With that challenge, the little dispute was quickly forgotten. Trusting completely in its softness, one by one, each fell backward onto the freshly fallen snow.

Lying straight on their backs with legs out-stretched, down fluttered tiny snowflakes landing on them every which way. Closing their eyes, giggling as the fallen flakes tickled their upturned faces, they crinkled their noses. And sticking out their tongues catching the feathery snow crystals, made it tough to hold still.

Tucking their arms in close to their bodies, with a sideway flapping motion, slowly extending their arms, they pushed away unnecessary snow. And in the process, wings were formed. To make the angel's robe, opening their legs wide and pulling them tightly together again did the trick. That was all there was to it. But in order to maintain a flawless angel, they had to be as still as possible while getting up. Otherwise, the luckless angel was doomed in its ruin. Getting up gingerly, the girls delighted in their success. Rewarded, lying neatly under their favorite oak tree, were four perfect snow angels all in a row. Of course, the next action was inevitable. Rebecca started it. She threw the first one. Splat! It landed smack dab on its target, the center of Theresa's back.

"Oh, no you don't." Squealed Theresa and the battle started. Quickly fortifying herself with a gigantic snowball, she launched it in the direction of its intended destination. Wisely, and just in the nick of time, Rebecca ducked out of its way. Before long, snowballs and giggles were flying in all directions.

It was unanimous. Words weren't necessary. Celebrating snow was an entertaining escapade they wished would last forever. But, it could not be avoided. All good things come to an end. Soon it would be time to go in. Was there a consolation? You bet. Tomorrow the snow would harden and magically create an imaginary land full of wonders in its own right. It always happened that way.

The sun would cast its brightness and the snow covered yard would glisten like thousands of sparkling diamonds. Long icicles would hang from the tree branches like so many crystal swords. Walking quietly, the girls would listen in awe to the crunch, crunch, crunching sound of their boots. Yes, when reluctantly, it was time to go in, there were always the promises of tomorrow.

"Oh, nuts, that's the dinner bell." Annette announced through chattering teeth "It's time to go in, let's go. My hands are like ice."

"Mine, too." The others chimed in.

"I'll be glad for Christmas and new mittens." Theresa managed in a shaky voice. It was tough sharing the only pair of mittens fit to wear. Worn over sock-covered hands, there was no long-lasting warmth. They shared their one and only wool hat, too. During the course of the year, mittens and hats had a way of getting lost. So they made do with what they had. But they didn't mind the time spent practically gloveless and hatless. Not really. Sure it was cold. But they wouldn't trade their fun for all the wool in New Zealand, nor its sheep, for that matter.

One thing for sure, they could depend on. Sunday night's vegetable soup was old reliable. No matter it was always served lukewarm. As cold as they were, it would taste piping hot and they could hardly wait to wrap their frosty hands around the warm mug.

It did the trick. Warm again, the meal over, the cafeteria chores done, the orphans were dismissed. They had just enough time for evening prayer before being ushered off to bed.

And still, there were twenty minutes left before lights out. Sitting on their cots, the girls were as chatty as magpies.

"I can hardly wait," Theresa gleefully announced. "Christmas is only a week away."

"I wonder what class will decorate the tree this year?" asked Annette.

"Well, I doubt it will be ours." Annmarie spat out in a huff. "Remember, we did it last year."

"Oh, right," Annette replied somewhat let-down. "I forgot. Just the same, I can't wait to see what gift Father Duffy has for us this year."

No matter that they were orphans. Kids were kids and Christmas was Christmas. They knew there would be a delicious turkey dinner with all the trimmings. It was the feast of the year and the food was actually very good. They knew, too, there would be a Christmas tree and presents and, until it got here, indeed, visions of sugar plums would dance in their heads.

* * * * *

In its time, Christmas arrived complete with Christmas carols and celebratory spirit. Father Duffy's present turned out to be a holy card with a picture of His Holiness, the Pope on it. He instructed the marker be used in their catechisms. A gift is a gift and expressions of thanks were heard. The nuns make sure of it. Manners of utmost importance were never to be ignored.

Everyone sang Happy Birthday to Baby Jesus then ate wonderful food until they could eat no more. Sitting in the cafeteria with satisfied tummies, they could hardly contain their excitement that mounted as the favorite segment of their Christmas program, for which they had waited for all year, made the scene.

Members of the local churches always got together and donated small, wrapped gifts, clearly marked for either a boy or a girl. Then tearing off the holiday wrap, amid laughter and squeals, the recipient found a treasure. No doubt about it. To the orphans' way of thinking, they made out like bandits. It was so exciting. They loved even the smallest of trinkets.

Mostly, there were handmade mittens, hats and scarves. Really needed in the cold of winter, still they did not get top billing. The toys, Ah! Now that was a different story.

There were metal toy whistles, little cars with wheels that rolled, little rubber dolls no bigger than three inches tall dressed in pretty crocheted dresses, brightly colored yo-yo's, small, bright, red balls, jump ropes and #2 pencils. There were the practical items, too, toothbrushes, toothpaste, combs, hairbrushes and the like.

But, best of all, there was always a bag filled chock full of delicious hard candies for everyone. Candy. Yum! Now that was always a first-rate prize of a gift. It was one that could be enjoyed long after Christmas was over. To an orphan, learning to ration comes early. Doled out carefully, the allotment of the limited supply could be made to last a good, long time. Candy belonged in that category. It was a long-term, savored, treat.

That night, truly, the orphans went to bed happy. Truly, they were blessed. Truly, with the exception of parents, they felt they had more than most.

The following week ushered in the New Year and each year, thereafter, held the same holidays and schedules of events. There were classes and free time and an occasional in-house Disney movie and always, there was Mass. Nothing really changed except the dates and seasons, as time marched on and, the fact that the girl friends were growing older.

Chapter 8

1950

On the first of each month, like clockwork, birthdays were celebrated. After the evening meal, every person with a birthday in that particular month would be called to stand up in the front of the cafeteria.

There, proud of themselves, amid smiles and giggles, they were honored with the traditional singing of the Happy Birthday song followed by thunderous applause.

Then everyone in attendance was treated to a delicious slice of a decorated birthday cake. Except for a birthday card, made in art class especially for this red-letter event, presents, per se, were non-existent. It was just the way it was.

That it was February first, and Rebecca's birthday was not for another four days, did not matter. The established practice did. It was the designated time for commemoration of the occasion. This occasion happen to mark her twelfth birthday.

After resting in its hiding place for four years, the time to present the special envelope finally arrived. It had been with Sister Regina for so long that just knowing it was securely tucked away in her dresser drawer gave her a sense of comfort. Knowing it was soon going to its rightful owner, gave her joy.

She was anxious now to talk with Rebecca and to witness her reaction when she received this priceless gift.

"Rebecca, I need to talk with you. Would you kindly stay after class?"

"Yes, Sister," Rebecca answered immediately, all the while wondering what in the world have I done this time? The question came naturally, especially since this was the class that seemed to best bring out the imp in her. She loved history and the way Sister Regina brought the old guys from years ago, to life. Plays involving historic characters were the best. One time, Rebecca got to play Cleopatra. She was thrilled. She remembered thinking, me as Queen of the Nile. Rebecca went around acting like royalty for days after the performance. It was clever Annette who, tired of her majesty, finally brought the curtain down on Rebecca. It was easy. She simply reminded her of how Cleopatra met her end. Her manner was dignified. After all, she was addressing a Queen. She didn't even crack a smile.

"Be careful your Majesty. Don't get bitten on your asp, oops, I mean *by* an asp." It was funny. It was appropriate. It did the trick. Queen Cleopatra reigned no more.

Sister Regina's history class promoted make-believe while learning. It was right up Rebecca's alley. In this class, she could let her hair down. It was here, too, that her funny and sometimes mischievous sense of humor reared its silly head. No wonder she was anxious. She just didn't know what she was guilty of this time.

The room cleared of students. Only Rebecca remained in her seat. Quietly, and anxiously, she waited for Sister Regina to speak. The suspense was killing her. Finally, Sister was ready.

"Come sit next to my desk, Rebecca. I have something to show you." Nervously, Rebecca obeyed as she sat in the seat usually reserved for trouble-makers. How appropriate, she figured. Now I'm really in for it. But what could Sister possibly have to show me? Uh-oh, don't tell me. Bet it's the note I passed to Annmaire. Yikes! When I said Sister Phil-o-just-plain-mean-o was ugly, I meant it. But only Annmaire was supposed to read that. Holy Hannah, I'm going get detention big time. Wish I hadn't written it. But she made me eat Tapioca pudding again today. It's her fault. Her and her ugly mole made me mad.

Oh, no. Sister Regina is reaching into her pocket. Here we go. Wait. That's a faded envelope and it has my name on it. Odd, it's not my note. What is it? Puzzled, Rebecca's first instinct was to grab it, tear it open and find out what was inside. Protocol, of course, didn't permit that. Darn rules of conduct. Rebecca had to wait for Sister to make her move.

This is a mystery. Although Rebecca held back yanking it from Sister's hand, she couldn't hold her tongue. Besides, Sister didn't tell her she had to be quiet, now, did she?

"Sister, why is my name on that envelope? What's this all about?"

Sister did not answer immediately. She couldn't. Not until she had just the right words. This moment had to count. She had to use the best explanation in order to pave the way not only for acceptance but more importantly, forgiveness.

"Rebecca, listen carefully. What I am about to tell you is of paramount, life-changing importance."

Okay, Rebecca thought. Now you're scaring me. I've got butterflies tickling my stomach. Wait, get hold of yourself. Sister likes plays. Maybe she is just being dramatic like one of her characters in history. I've been known to be guilty of that myself. Okay, that must be it. Wish she would hurry and tell me.

It has been said, the difference between anxiety and excitement is three deep breaths. Sister inhaled her share and went on to revel in the hope and gladness of what she was about to do. Snapping her body straight, she looked directly into Rebecca's eyes and placed the envelope in Rebecca's hands. Speaking with authority, she said. "This belongs to you. Happy Birthday! But before you open it, you must know that it is not from me."

Gee, Rebecca thought. Add confusion to my fright, why don't you? Sister didn't have anything else to say. She simply sat back and watched as the dear child opened a present far greater than any she had ever received before and waited for Rebecca's questions.

Even with fumbling fingers, Rebecca easily unsealed the envelope. The glue, aged over the years, started to lose its hold. Turning the envelope upside down, its content was finally released from confinement. Surprised, Rebecca's eyes opened wide, as they took in its beauty. Her mouth dropped open, too. Momentarily, she sat transfixed.

"Ooh! It's the most beautiful necklace I have ever seen." That, other than in magazines, it was the only necklace she had ever seen, did not matter. That is was magnificent and that, apparently, it belonged to her, did. It was hard to believe.

"It is really mine, Sister? Is it?"

The joy it brought to the girl was even more than Sister had hoped. Touched, she simply nodded and whispered, "Yes."

Deriving much pleasure from the girl's thrilled reaction, Sister smiled. In her heart, she knew she had been right. In her heart, she knew despite her single act of disobedience, God had to be pleased with the happiness provided this little orphan. In her heart, she knew she had been forgiven. The truth was easy to predict.

"Oh, Sister, this is the first birthday gift I have ever received in my whole life. Look how the heart sparkles. I love purple. It's my favorite color." She ran her fingers over the gold chain. "The chain Sister, it's gold. Look here."

The student instructed the teacher. Forgetting that the teacher, the one who instilled knowledge, was already educated as to the gold content in the chain. Even so, Sister let her have her moment. She just smiled and nodded acknowledgment.

"Let me put it on for you, Rebecca." Quickly, Rebecca turned her back to the nun and held up the necklace so Sister could better reach the clasp. Mission accomplished, Rebecca held her hand over the precious stone to keep it from bobbing up and down as she raced to the classroom window and its mirror image reflection. Removing her hand revealed the prettiest necklace. The sight of which would remain with her forever.

"Purple gold, Sister Regina, that's what it is. It's my purple gold and I will treasure it always." She stood there just admiring her purple gold and reveling in her discovery. She was absolutely convinced. "It is the most perfect present in the whole, wide world."

"I'm happy for you, Rebecca. Now if you can pull yourself away, kindly sit down again." Knowing full well that what she was about to give Rebecca would top even her perceived most perfect present, Sister eagerly encouraged her. The crowning glory was yet to come.

"Let me tell you a little about your necklace." Reverting to her teaching mode, she asked, "Do you know anything about amethyst?"

"No, Sister. What is it?"

"Well, it's a gem. The heart on your necklace is made of it." With that, Sister supplied Rebecca with all the nuances of amethyst. But the part Rebecca liked best was that it was purple, it was her birthstone and it was hers. When Sister finished with her mini lesson, Rebecca had plenty of food for thought.

Suddenly, curiosity hit home. "If this isn't from you, Sister, then, who gave it to me?" Aha! Sister thought. Those few words did it. The door was opened and Sister walked right into the opportunity. She did not mince words, but came straight to the point.

"Your mother."

"My mother? How? When? Is she here?" Rebecca quickly looked around searching hopefully. Just as quickly, she was disappointed in finding the room empty. Suddenly, Rebecca's world was made up of more truth than she had ever expressed in her make-believe family stories. She had an honest to goodness for real mother. How she yearned for answers. Thank goodness, Sister quickly complied.

"I'm afraid your mother is not here today. But she was, a long time ago. She wanted you to have the lovely necklace."

"How do you know that?" Rebecca wanted to believe with all her heart. Yet, she could not help but feel doubtful. Maybe Sister played the make-up family stories, too. If she did, she was good at it. Boy with this one, she took top prize.

"I found your purple gold," referring to the necklace in the term of endearment christened by Rebecca. "It was hidden away in your permanent record file folder. There was a note with it."

"Rapidly becoming a believer, Rebecca could hardly sit still. "What did it say?"

Embedded in her mind, Sister had no trouble recalling exactly what it said and spoke the message in the affectionate tone she felt was intended.

"Please give this heart to my daughter, Rebecca on her twelfth birthday and tell her I love her."

Unless you walk in orphans' shoes, there is no way you could know or appreciate the full impact of what just happened. A mother's love revealed; a daughter's miracle realized. It doesn't get much better than this. Floating on a cloud in seventh heaven, Rebecca could hardly contain herself. A mother! She thought. I have a mother and, not only that, she loves me. Imagine that! She was anxious to share the unbelievable good news with her friends

"Wait until my friends hear about this, and I can't wait to show them my special purple gold. Won't they just love it?"

"Oh, no, Rebecca," this was harder than Sister thought it would be. Too bad she had no choice, and it wasn't long before Sister popped Rebecca's bubble. "This must remain our special secret. You and I will talk about it any time you would like. But you can't let anyone else know. Not even your best friends. You must promise me that."

"Huh? Why? Why can't I tell my friends? I don't understand?"

"Because if anyone finds out, Rebecca, you stand to lose your purple gold. It will be taken away from you. We don't want that to happen, do we?" Saddened and disappointed, but certainly not wanting that to happen, Rebecca shook her head.

"No. I don't want to lose my beautiful necklace, ever. It's just that it would have been so good for my friends to know about. It's not fair." Tears rolled down the little girl's face. Here she was twelve-years-old, no longer a baby and here she was crying just like one. She couldn't help it.

"There, there, now. Rebecca. Hush. Don't cry." Taking out her handkerchief Sister tenderly wiped away her tears, and hopefully, the sadness, too.

"You know what? I'll keep it safe for you and you may see it any time you want to, okay? Remember your mother wanted you to have it on your twelfth birthday and you did. Remember, too, the best part. She said she loves you. You can wear that in your heart all the time."

Nodding, hesitantly, Rebecca whispered softly. "Yes Sister. But um, well um…"

"What is it? You can tell me."

The words catching in her throat, she asked sadly, "It's just, well, um…If my mother loves me so much, where is she? Why isn't she here now?"

That was the heart-breaking question that had plagued Sister Regina since the day she first arrived at this orphanage. Like a malignancy, it grew and gnawed at her insides. How she prayed for all the lost sheep in her flock. Where, indeed, was Rebecca's mom? For that matter, where were all the other mothers who deserted these precious orphans?

She did not have an answer and thought, no Rebecca, life is not fair. "God knows, Rebecca, and maybe, someday so will you." That was all the good Sister could say.

"I hope so, Sister. I really do." Reluctantly then, Rebecca complied. She stopped crying, well kind of, and turned so Sister could remove her beautiful purple gold. She hated to let it go. After all, she didn't have it for very long. She fingered it lovingly, gave it a kiss goodbye and then gently placed it back into the safety of its home in the yellowed envelope of yesteryear.

In a childish way, she whispered to it. "Don't worry. We'll see each other again and again. Just wait and see and maybe someday, like Sister said, I will see my mother, too. We both will."

"I'm so proud of you, Rebecca, happy birthday." With that directive, the birthday girl was excused. Just before she left, Rebecca felt the overwhelming sudden urge to hug this good nun. Truly, she had changed her life today. Holding onto her, she spoke quietly.

"Thank you, Sister, for everything, it was the best birthday I ever had."

"You are more than welcome." That was the response of the surprised and pleased nun who returned the hug, and perhaps, held the dear girl just a little tighter.

Chapter 9

Farewell Father Duffy

Mournfully, the church bells tolled. Their beloved Father Duffy was dead. It was all too sad. The kind and generous heart of this highly respected surrogate father figure; the heart that had given to so many, simply stopped giving to him. At least he had died peacefully in his sleep, if this could be of any small consolation.

He, and his love for his little charges, would be missed. They would remember him with fondness. They would remember his warm smile, his easy going manner. They would remember his unique Christmas gifts. So hard to believe; all would be no more.

It was his funeral service that assembled them here in the chapel today to bid him a final farewell. All the statuaries were covered in purple out of respect and, there on the altar in his honor, was a vase which held only a single red rose.

Never a man of pretense, never ostentatious, this gentle, simple, man's funeral, at his request, was to be the same. Respecting the intentions of this plain and down-to-earth man, this Requiem Mass held a sober quality of calmness and dignity. In fact, there was only one priest celebrant and his chasuble, the sleeveless outer vestment worn over the alb, was also purple.

For most of those in attendance, this was their first funeral, their first experience with the inevitable, death. It just never happened to them before. Having no prior reason for rehearsal of a ceremony for the dead, the choir was unprepared. The youngsters, as a body, could only sing a few of the Latin responses, the ones with which they were familiar. Arrangements were made so that the majority of the Mass was sung a cappella by the choir director, Sister Perpetua. Then as a special tribute to the beloved priest, a duet was presented by Sister Perpetua and the music teacher, Sister Lucille Frances. The nuns lifted up their sweet-sounding voices and filled the church with the God-honoring hymn, *How Great Thou Art,* so loved by this humble priest.

The information stating that in 1935, it had been translated from its original Swedish into English by Stuart K. Hine, was printed at the top of the hymn. No matter when a book was read or music sung, the honest Father Duffy taught his young charges to give credit where it was due. With words so powerful, this inspirational hymn never failed to move those who heard it, some to the brink of tears. The nuns' rendition, presented in sweet, angelic voices, along with the old pipe organ, was both consoling and reassuring.

Rebecca sat in the pew reflecting on all that happened. It was all such a shock. When she had heard of Father's death, she cried her eyes out. First there was disbelief followed by total devastating sadness. Surely the world would end. In essence, the only one known to the orphans did. She and her friends cried for a long time.

"It can't be true. It just can't." Rebecca had just awakened and was getting ready for school when the sad news raged through the dormitories like wildfire.

"What happened?" The ever inquisitive Theresa begged to know. "They say he just died in his sleep." Annette sadly replied. Annmarie interrupted with her common sense.

"Hurry, let's go to breakfast and find out what we can from Sister. She'll tell us." They never made it to the cafeteria. An announcement in a dolorous sounding voice came over the loud speaker confirming their fear. It was true. Their esteemed Father Duffy was no more. The rest of the time before the funeral was pretty much a tear-filled blur. This dark cloud that had stopped over the orphanage and darkened every crack and crevice, made everything vague and muddy.

The processional seemed endless as the orphans silently filed past the casket. Opened, the body inside was met by youngsters who had never seen the work of the Grim Reaper. This thing called death, so final and permanent could not be changed.

Their friendly Father Duffy with his ghastly, wax-like, pallid face appeared as a stranger. Some were scared. What if his eyes popped open? Some would even have nightmares.

When it was Rebecca's turn, it was his clothing that made her mind flashback to the time Father Duffy had monitored their Bible Study Class. Dressed simply today as he was then, she saw him in her mind's eye, in the classroom holding the bible talking about the story of Jonah. She knew all about what happened to the biblical character. Bored, her mind was swallowed up with the clothes he was wearing.

On his head, he wore a black biretta. It was a hard, square hat with four vertical projections with a funny looking pompom centered on top.

He always wore the same black cassock. It reminded her of a topcoat only it was longer and the close fitting garment reached from his neck to his shoe tops. Vaguely, she heard his words, something about a storm and a whale. But she was fascinated with the way the garment buttoned all the way down the front. There were so many. While standing directly in front of her, she saw them so clearly and she just couldn't resist. She counted the buttons, all thirty-three of them.

Now looking down at the lifeless face of Father Duffy, remembering that day with a twinge of guilt, tears flowed as she silently asked his forgiveness. I'm sorry, Father for not paying attention to you when you were teaching the lesson about Jonah.

Filing past, Lord knows what went through the minds of others;

each with their own special interaction remembrance, each missing him already and each wishing him to rest in peace.

The simple service did not last long. Befitting the man, it was dignified. Concluded, the funeral ended the era of their beloved Father Duffy and marked the beginning of a new regime.

Chapter 10

1953

Changes, changes, and more changes! Everything was changing. Or at least it seemed that way. To say that the new administrator, the young Father Thomas Larkin, wasn't well liked was an understatement. He wasn't Father Duffy, now, was he?

His new charges saw him as cold, demanding, and far too strict. Jeez, they weren't allowed to do anything. Yeah, like they had done a lot before. But that wasn't the point.

Anyway, they had no way of knowing Father Larkin didn't like them all that much either. His was too absorbed in his grandiose aspirations. High hopes, his ambition and drive headed him in the direction of advancement. No way was he going to be just a priest forever. He hungered for a high ranking position, one with power and prestige. He had his sights set on becoming a bishop.

Naturally, it would take time. That was for down the road. First he had to lay the foundation and earn the recognition of his bishop. Out to make a name for himself, this orphanage was his stepping stone, his building block, his ticket. With that goal and, in this place, his word crystallized into law.

Amid complaints of new rules that simply fell on deaf ears, the orphans rebelled. Their efforts futile, he didn't bend. He wasn't about to have his carefully thought out plans derailed. Let them complain.

To the orphans, some rules were just plain stupid. For instance, there was his rule on food. Everything on your plate had to be eaten whether you liked it or not. Everything, including those disgusting, miniature, cabbage-like heads, Brussels sprouts.

No matter that they were yucky. They had to be eaten. Grumbling didn't help, either. Dispensations, quite simply, were never granted. C'est la vie.

Bottom line was simple enough. No waste equaled money saved. So what if there were a few stomachaches? Coming in well below budget, now that's what counted and that's what got noticed. The books never looked so good.

Raising scholastic ratings was yet another of his endeavors aimed at hitting the Bishop's eye. Slowly but surely, change by change, the Bishop would recognize the potential leadership of this young, up and coming, priest. Nothing would derail this stubborn man's plans. His plans on track were absolutely not subject to change and, most certainly, not by ticked off complaining students.

Not only was he good at coming up with unfair rules, but enforcing them as well. After all, they were made to his advantage. His latest brainstorm focused on his idea of punctuality. Either you were prompt to the second or you paid the consequences. Arriving just thirty seconds after the bell cost you detention. At the rate of one half hour per thirty seconds tardiness, the students balked. The stiff punishment was totally unfair. Father Duffy would never have done that. But then, he was no longer here, was he? The new rules and regulations were, and like it or not, they were here to stay.

Unhappy but resilient, the youngsters eventually recovered and adjusted. They were not strangers to tough times and knew how to roll with the punches. If they wanted to survive, they had to snap back. That's all there was to it.

Chapter 11

The evening found the girls studying quietly except for poor Rebecca. Frustrated with her homework assignment, she just knew she would flunk tomorrow's test. All this studying and preparation surely would be in vain and she was loud and clear in letting that be known.

"Aah! This homework is driving me insane. I hate Latin and, cover your ears God. I hate Father Larkin, too. And I hate his new policy. Who does he think I am, Einstein? I'm only fifteen. How much brain power does this man think I have? There's no way that I can learn ten new Latin phrases each night. I just can't and I'm going to flunk the test. I know I am." Ticked off, she tossed the Latin Grammar Book clear across the room. Good thing those in harm's way ducked.

"Hey! Watch what you're doing." Annette protested loudly. "You just missed my head."

"I'm just so darn mad. Sorry Annette."

"What's your problem?"

"This blasted rotten assignment. It's hopeless. I'm hopeless and I'll never learn all these darn foreign phrases." On the verge of tears, ready to surrender before beginning the fight, lamenting she conceded, "I just won't and so much for my test tomorrow."

"Yes you will. Come on and stop being a sniffle baby. I'll help you. It's not all that hard"

"Sure. It's easy for you, Annette. That's because you're an excellent Latin student. I'm not."

Retrieving the accursed book, Annette insisted. "Okay, then, I'll teach you. Now, just cool it. It's not like you have to grow a brain." Such a Good Samaritan, Annette opened the book to the assigned page, and began

"Repeat after me, Cogito ergo sum. I think, therefore I am. Say it again and this time, think about it. Concentrate." Rebecca did her best. "Okay. Now try this. It's an easy one. You like history, so just remember history class and, what Caesar said when he defeated the Gauls in the Gallic War. Veni, vidi, vici, meaning I came, I saw, I conquered."

"Hey, I think I'm getting it."

"See, I told you. Okay, try this. Magna cum laude, meaning with great distinction like the one you're going to get when you graduate."

"In my dreams, maybe."

"Oh, Rebecca, you are too funny."

"Anyway, Annette, I appreciate your help. I never thought to study by association."

"It works for me. It will work for you, too."

The night went on. Over and over, backward and forward Annette drilled the words into Rebecca's head until, in self defense, they decided to stay there and until it was time for lights out.

At lunch the following day, sitting at the table Annette could hardly wait for Rebecca. She popped up from her seat when she saw Rebecca come into the room.

"Over here Rebecca. And, hurry up about it. Well?"

"Well what?"

"Rebecca, if you don't tell me right now, I'll scream."

"Oh, you mean the test?" She intentionally asked nonchalantly. "Duh?"

Holding back her excitement for just the right minute, Rebecca happily punched the air and yelled. "I nailed it."

"Way to go, girl."

Chapter 12

Wonder of wonders. No more boy cooties. No more icky girls. How could that be? Actually attracted to each other? How did that happen? They didn't know and quite frankly didn't care .They only knew they were tickled pink in their confusion.

When a big rush of puppy-love hits, it's terrific for the giggling, starry-eyed girls, and a wee bit scary for the, still wet-behind-the-ears, boys pretending to be macho. Dealing with all the nuances of puberty can be awkward but, they wouldn't have it any other way. Emotions they didn't even know they had, opened up to them. Bottom line, they were on a journey to adulthood and, having a lot of fun getting there.

Much to the nuns chagrin. It was that time, again, when the place was virtually filled with budding Romeos and Juliets. Boyfriend, girlfriend relationships grew rampant and, like the teenage girls, blossomed. Just what the nuns needed. As if they didn't have enough to do, they thought, go ahead. Just add sentinel duty to our already responsibilities over-load. Watching their young charges like hawks, the nuns did the best they could. It wasn't easy and nearly drove them nuts. They were very much aware that where there's a will, there's a way. It had been like that forever and with each passing year, the adolescents grew more ingenious. This year it was up to Rebecca's class.

It was Saturday. Their chores finished found Theresa and Annette sitting on the front steps enjoying the sunshine's warmth. Keeping a keen eye out for nuns within ear-shot, they were talking about boys. Lately, that seemed to be the topic of most discussions.

"Isn't Andy handsome?" Theresa wrapped her arms around her legs and pulled them to her chest. Gently rocking back and forth, she could just see him. "He has the dreamiest blue eyes, ever."

"Well, I don't know about that. I mean Allen would give him a good run for his money." Annette was not being intentionally argumentative. It was just that she had really fallen for the red-head who sat behind her in math class. In fact, they had planned to sneak out to the park this very night. No one knew. *Dare I tell Theresa?* She debated. *Of course, what are friends for? Besides, I'll need her to cover for me.*

"You're going to do what? Are you nuts?" Instantly, Theresa's daydream vanished. Just as quickly she let go of her legs and snapped up straight. "What if you get caught? No, Annette, you can't do it. It's insane."

"Stop with the dramatics, Theresa. If Andy asked you out, you would go in a flash. Who you kidding? I'm going and that's that. As they say in Latin, Carpe diem. Well, I am. Only it's the night time that I'm seizing. What's the difference?"

That night and every Saturday night for the rest of the year, weather permitting and under cover of darkness, Annette and Allen spent a few hours together in the park. Thank goodness for the fire escape and for Theresa. Reluctantly, she agreed to cover for her friend's daring scheme. Secretly shaping a pretend body of pillows securely wrapped with blankets on Annette's bunk until her return and, keeping an eye out for trouble, became the weekly drill. Annette's luck held out. She never did get caught. Poor Theresa, on the other hand, didn't have the courage to try. She was sure she would have had fun, but sneaking out was just too risky for her. It wasn't in her make-up. The time spent with Andy was restricted to the classroom and occasionally sharing the same lunch table in the cafeteria. She was glad for that peace of mind arrangement.

Science class was held directly after lunch. It was a time classroom couples looked forward to, more correctly, looked forward to being taught by Sister Mary Margaret. There was a reason why she was, by far, the young peoples' favorite teacher. And talk about ingenuity!

"Remember, everybody no noise." Andy delivered the mandate to the entire class just before Sister Mary Margaret entered the room. She always came armed with her wooden clicker. This gadget was about eight inches long and worked on the order of clip clothespins. She used it to save her voice. Whenever she wanted quiet, she simply repeatedly snapped the two wooden pieces together producing a definite clicking,- pay attention-be-quiet, sound. The darn thing made them laugh but at the same time, when pressed into action, accomplished its goal.

According to her students, Sister was old. Really old and that, alone, made her a boring teacher. Not that all old teachers are boring. But this archaic lady happened to fit that bill. She was both. However, there was a definite plus side. That their class met right after lunch was another bonus. With her stomach satisfied, this seasoned senior needed a daily nap. In short order, all needed elements were in place. Sitting quietly in their seats, listening to the old nun's voice trail off, they watched anxiously for the required signal. It didn't take long. There it was. Her head began to nod and before you knew it, rested on her folded arms on the desk top. Terrific! Going as planned, she would be good for at least fifteen minutes. These young romantics thought of everything. A guard was posted at the door just in case that Father Larkin might decide to pay an unannounced classroom visit. And they took turns keeping an eye on Sister, too, just in case.

Next came the awaited part where their astute cleverness paid off. Swiftly and quietly, people switched seats. After all, in order to neck, you had to have the right partner sit close to you. On the average of fifteen minutes a day, for five days a week, making out time added up to a lot of class time well spent.

That was some science class. Experiments abounded. But none of the ones Sister taught. The cuddling and kissing lasted right there in the classroom until the assigned look-out quickly extinguished all amorous moves with the simple alert words. "She's waking up." That's all it took.

They knew the drill. In nothing flat, like a quiet cyclonic whirlwind, everyone hastily scampered back to their original appointed seats.

Sister's eyes opened. Their shenanigans never detected, she couldn't help but think what well behaved and attentive students she had. Yes, she was, at all times, in total control. Too bad the school year was rapidly coming to an end. But then, she was pleased to see how many of her students had signed up for her summer class. Yes, indeed. It made her many years of imparting scientific knowledge worthwhile. And she applauded herself for a job well done.

Chapter 13

1954

"Rebecca. Please come to my office when you are finished in here." The request came from Mother Superior herself. Rebecca had been practicing for her piano lesson when Mother came to her. Sitting on the piano bench, finally reaching the foot pedals, somewhere along the way she had grown tall.

I cannot for the life of me think what Mother could possibly want with me. Oh, no. Don't tell me. I bet I'm getting collared for hemming my uniform too short. These darn, long legs. I wanted them and now they're getting me into trouble. My stockings no longer go up as high as they used to. That's it. I'm going to get it for showing too much knee. Jeez. I'll have to quick think up a good excuse.

She need not have worried about excuses. It wasn't the short hemmed uniform that was on Mother's mind. Sitting in her office, the topic of her intention was soon learned and it totally floored the young, long legged Rebecca.

She sat anxiously waiting for the nun to talk. In the meantime, her eyes scanned the room and she scrutinized her surroundings. She made it a quick and inconspicuous observation.

This office is opposite from Mother. She is firm but warm and this room is plain and bare-bones. The walls need color and except for a crucifix hanging on the wall behind her desk, the walls have nothing on them. There's only Mother's desk and chair and a visitor's chair in here. This austere room is cold and gives me the willies.

Rebecca didn't know quite what to expect and then, suddenly, without buildup or even light chit-chat, the nun in charge came straight to the point.

"Rebecca, there is a family in town that is interested in having someone work for them. Both the husband and wife are employed and they have a nine-year-old daughter. She is in school but needs supervision after school hours until her parents get home and light housekeeping is required as well as, assisting the cook. I have chosen you for the position. You will, of course, live there."

Whoa! What a bomb to drop on a sixteen-year-old orphan. Shocked, she could not believe her ears. "Huh? I mean, excuse me, Mother? What did you say?"

"I'm giving this opportunity to you Rebecca."

Opportunity? Opportunity? Lips pinched and trembling, Rebecca's mind ran the gamut of emotions. Sad, pleased, excited, apprehensive and mostly, baffled. That was it. Confusion sat at the very top of her list. Rebecca took a deep breath then inundated Mother with questions that begged immediate answers. Like a Gatling gun, automatically and rapidly, one right after the other, the list erupted.

Expecting her reaction, the nun just fell into a waiting silence and let the young girl release all her anxieties before addressing them. She knew, of course the girl was nervous. This whole concept was strange to her. Nothing like this had ever happened here before. The older orphans were accustomed to the usual procedure. Turn eighteen and you had a choice. Stay or go? It was that simple. Schooling was over. This place was done with you. The handful who decided to stay, worked for their keep. In return for room and board, they were housed in the old maintenance building behind the main campus and helped keep things running. At the end of each month, they were given a pittance for their efforts.

Those who chose to head out into the real world were given a small stipend to cover bus fare and some meals, directions to the local YMCA or YWCA and the classified section of the local newspaper. Other than that, they were on their own. C'est la vie! Rebecca hadn't even given thought to the options. What sixteen-year-old, did? It wasn't exactly at the top of their priority list. Jeez, anyway, two years was way down the road.

Mother Superior was so pleased that Rebecca's future was secure. To think she wouldn't even have to make a decision. Why, this is the best thing Father Larkin could do for her. Such a good Christian, that man is.

Poor nun had no way of knowing. His devious plan was clever. So clever, even she had been duped. How could she know that Father Larkin's main interest was Father Larkin? His latest undertaking was simply to make his life easier while making quite a name for himself. Little by little, in one way or another, one by one, he managed to push the older students out at an earlier age. He filled the place with younger and younger orphans who didn't eat as much and blindly followed his every word. As for thinkers and protestors, who needed them? No, he made sure there would be no trouble of any kind at this institution he was running. The quarterly reports to his Bishop would shine. You could bet on it.

Years later an obituary would catch Rebecca's eye.

FATHER THOMAS LARKIN

Trenton, New Jersey, The Rev. Thomas Larkin, 72, died Friday, April 3, 1995. Born in Long Island, N.Y., he was Director of the former Holy Comforter Orphanage in New Jersey. Instrumental in implementing numerous improvements at that institution, he is accredited with helping orphans in their walk of life. Predeceased by his parents, he will be remembered fondly for his zest for life, his love for the orphans, his church family, and friends.

Having devoted years to the betterment of orphans, he left the orphanage after being called by the late Bishop Kean, himself, to serve in the capacity of Administrative Assistant to his Excellency. His work exemplary, he held this position for many years. His ability and qualifications so great, he was about to be elevated to the position of Bishop himself when, unfortunately, he suffered a fatal heart attack.

Called to his heavenly home, today the Catholic Church mourns the loss of Father Thomas Larkin, one of the Lord's best advocates. His earthly life, marked by long hours of hard work, and his burning love for his Lord and Savior, is ended.

Mass will be celebrated at St. Anthony's Catholic Church in Trenton at 10:00 a.m. on April 6, 1995. Friends may call at the McCarthy Funeral Home.

* * * * *

Rebecca remembered the man but not with a real fondness in her heart. She did, however, think it was a shame that he did not make Bishop. And that ended her thoughts of the man who basically changed her life. She had no way of knowing his life-long ambition. She had no way of knowing the man just missed grabbing hold of the brass ring.

* * * * *

But for now, sitting in Mother's office, Rebecca was beside herself.

"I don't understand. Mother, out of everybody here at Holy Comforter, why was I picked?" Although, she had to admit, she felt kind of special to have been chosen and for a fleeting moment, the idea of getting out of the orphanage held a certain appeal. Then reality and anxieties set in and she bombarded Mother Superior.

"How in the world will I take care of a little girl? What qualifications do I have? And how do I keep an entire house clean? I have trouble just keeping my small space clean. How do I leave this place, my home? How do I leave my friends? I can't do this Mother, I just can't."

"Nonsense, Rebecca. You'll find your purpose in life long before the others. You can't just sit and twiddle your thumbs. You are perfect for the job and the job is perfect for you. As far as your friends are concerned, you can keep in touch. Just write them."

"Can I come see them, too?"

"No, dear, that's against the rules."

Feeling trapped in the teeth of despair, her eyes filled with tears. Looking bleak and abandoned, she could say no more. The truth be told, now, she was scared out of her wits. The unknown has a way of doing just that. Dabbing away her tears, the distraught girl could not, for the life of her, see anything even remotely positive about what she was sure would be a catastrophic change.

"Look at the bright side.'

Bright side? Rebecca glared at the nun and wondered what bright side? It couldn't get any darker. I feel like I just got kicked in the stomach. I've got to get out of here. I can't take this. Without batting an eyelash, Mother just babbled on or at least that's what it sounded like to Rebecca.

"You can do it all. That's why Father Larkin and I have chosen you. It's time for you to go out into the world. Your future is waiting for you out there. Rebecca, you are mature, polite and capable. All the years spent around here working in the cafeteria and infirmary and doing laundry and cleaning qualify you. Believe me. You are more than ready to meet the challenge."

No. You're not listening, thought Rebecca. She wanted to shout out to the highest heavens. You just don't get it. I don't want to leave. With tears streaming down her cheeks, she knew there was no way out, but just in case, she gave it another shot from a different angle.

"Maybe, Mother, someone else would do a better job." It was a suggestion with undertones of pleading.

"No. Rebecca. The job is yours." All mine? She thought, and tried yet a different approach. "But what about taking care of a little girl? How do I do that?"

"I've watched you, Rebecca." Undaunted by Rebecca's resistance, the nun explained. "I've seen how you treat your peers and how you help the younger girls. You help them carry their trays and I've seen you wipe their tears. I've watched, too, how you hug them when they fall. You've bandaged a knee or two. Rebecca, stop fretting. You can do this. You are ready. Now here is the best part? It will make you feel much better. This couple has agreed to your continued education. They have already arranged for you to enter the public high school. There Rebecca, just think about it. That in itself is a whole new world opening up to you. God is good. You leave in three days."

That was that. The conversation was over. She had no choice in the matter. Mother Superior stood up and dismissed her. Rebecca was leaving.

Well, thought Mother, Father Larkin will be pleased. He is working so hard to get the girls out on a work program and Rebecca will be his first. He is forever thinking of their good.

Rebecca couldn't run out of there fast enough. She almost mowed down several girls heading for class in the opposite direction. Theresa jumped aside in time.

"Whoa, girl, where's the fire?"

"Sorry, Theresa." Was all Rebecca could get out.

"Rebecca, are you crying?"

"I guess I am, a little"

"Looking at you, I'd say a lot. What's wrong?"

"It's um...um..."

"Tell me. Now I'm really worried."

"Cover for me please, Theresa; just tell Sister I can't come to history class today."

"Why? What do I tell her?"

"Anything. Tell her I have cramps. I just can't face anybody right now, okay?"

"Tell you what. I'll tell Sister that if you tell me what's going on. I've never seen you like this." Taking Rebecca by her arm, Theresa headed them in the direction of the library. There were still a few minutes before class and the library was safe. Practically no one used it and especially not at this time of day.

"Sit down. Come on, Rebecca. Tell me. Jeez, girl. Get hold of yourself. You're shaking like a leaf."

Rebecca blew her nose, took a deep breath and tried to calm down.

"I'm leaving."

"What do you mean you're leaving?"

"It's that darn Father Larkin and his rules. I just know he's behind all this, somehow."

"Behind what? Rebecca, for heaven's sake, you're not making any sense."

"I have three days. Then Theresa I have to leave Holy Comforter and work for these people in town. I have to help with the housework and get this. I have to help take care of a nine-year-old. *Me!*"

"For how long? When are you coming back?"

"That's just it, Theresa. Never." The floodgates opened again.

"No, Rebecca. I can't believe it. And, why only you?"

"I'm not sure but Theresa, oh, Theresa, how can I go? I can't leave our friends. It's too hard."

"It's not fair, either. How about we get up a petition? Will that help?"

"I doubt it. You know how Mother is and if Father Larkin is in on it, you can forget it. He's so stubborn. It's probably some kind of another new policy of his, anyway."

Theresa was beside herself. "Say it isn't true." Both girls hugged like it was the end of the world. With their group splitting, it may as well have been.

"Go to the dorm and get some rest, Rebecca. I'll tell Sister you don't feel well. Then I'll help you tell the others after school, okay? Tomorrow, you can tell Sister Regina. Jeez-oh-man, she'll have a fit. Wait and see. I still say maybe she can help."

"I doubt it. Nothing anyone can say now would help. It's a losing battle."

Rebecca did go to bed. She was sick. It wasn't cramps but her head was pounding. She had a whopping headache.

In the midst of her misery, she finally managed to fall asleep. It didn't take as long as she had expected. Good thing. Sleep was the escape she needed. It saved her head from exploding. She wasn't sure how long she had been asleep but she heard them come in.

"There she is. Come on." It was the best-friend gang being led by Theresa. She hadn't told them much. Mainly, because Theresa, herself didn't know specifics. She just knew she worried about her friend all afternoon. Now, so did the others.

"You look lousy." Leave it to Annmarie, always honest, never diplomatic.

"Good grief, Annmarie. Did you have to be so blunt?"

"Yes, Annette. I call it like I see it and there's nothing wrong with that."

Rubbing her forehead, Rebecca sat up in bed with a king sized hang-over. Her eyes swollen and red looked sore.

"Does anybody have an aspirin? Oh, my head hurts."

"Here." Rummaging through her purse, Annette found one. "I'll be right back with some water, okay, Rebecca?"

"Yep. Thanks." The girls sat with Rebecca wherever there was space for them on the bed.

"Now, what's going on?" Annmarie insisted Rebecca wait no longer. "Tell us."

"Um…well, you'll never believe this. It's even hard to talk about."

"Try anyway."

"Okay. It happened this afternoon. Mother Superior called me into her office and told me that I have to go work for some couple in town taking care of their house and their young daughter."

"Can you come back at the end of each day?" Annette wanted to know.

Shaking her head tears welled up in her eyes. It was hard to answer. "No. That's the catch. I have to live there. I'm out of Holy Comforter forever." Like the calm before the storm, dead silence reigned before Annmarie exploded. "That stinks! It's just not fair. I'm going to talk to Sister Regina. I bet she can do something about this."

"No sense trying. Mother Superior said I'm going and that's that."

"You know," Annmarie, still shocked, surmised, "I bet it is part of Father Larkin's secret plan. Now I know what I overheard some of the other girls in class talking about. At first, I wasn't sure, but now with this happening, I know what he is up to. He wants to get rid of the older students as fast as he can. I'm not sure why, but he does. That's all."

"But why," Annette asked? "What good would that do?"

"For one thing, he would save on food." Rebecca jeered sarcastically.

"Don't talk like that Rebecca. You'll burn in hell, for sure."

"Oh, Annette, you are so naïve."

Sighing heavily, Rebecca reluctantly summed up the sad situation. "Bottom line, I have to leave in three days and I'm going to miss you guys like crazy." That did it. All four cried as they converged on Rebecca hugging her tightly in a group hug. They held on for a long time before Annette made an attempt for all to see the bright side. That is if such a thing existed. "Just think, Rebecca, You won't have to sneak out anymore and you won't have to listen for those darn curfew bells anymore."

That did bring a smile to Rebecca's face as she made her point. "Annette that was never my problem, it was yours." That did it. Finally, they all giggled.

"Oh yeah, I forgot. Anyway, you still won't have to listen to them."

"You poor thing, Rebecca, I can't believe you have to leave this place and on top of that, move into a stranger's place. That has to be the worst thing in the world."

"It is hard for me, Theresa. I feel like I'm getting a double dose of misery."

Her heart breaking for her dear friend sent Theresa into a tirade. Clenching her fists, she shouted her anger. "What's wrong with Mother? She couldn't wait for just two more years? Why is she breaking us up? I'm just so mad I could spit. But hey, wait a minute. I just got an idea. Let's go straight to Father Larkin and plea our case. We belong together. He can't be as mean as she is. He just can't." Theresa's lips drew thin and tight across her teeth as she spit out words of desperation; knowing full well, they didn't stand a chance with him. Especially, since Rebecca already told them she felt he had his hand in it and if Rebecca was right, then he already was the culprit.

Annmarie's plan of resolution was to introduce her own brand of levity to the situation. Maybe nonsensical joshing would help. After all, you can only cry for so long.

"Just think, Rebecca," she said. "You won't have to look at Sister Philo-just-plain-mean-o's ugly face with that long beak of hers, anymore."

"Don't forget that beastly-looking mole on her chin," Annette chimed in adding her two cents. "And, you won't get stuck washing those darn, huge soup pots. And, you won't have to wear hand-me-down shoes. And, you won't have to wear these ridiculous uniforms anymore." And--

"Okay, Annette," Theresa interrupted, "she gets the picture."

"Well think of it this way." This time Annette was quite serious. "At least you know where you are going. None of us have any idea where we will wind up."

"Your point is well-taken, Annette. I didn't think of that." Rebecca had to admit as cloudy as her future was, at this point she still had more clarity about it than any of them.

"I have an idea." With that, Rebecca went to their shared desk and pulled out sheets of paper, enough for all. Then, carefully, she wrote down her new address and handed one to each friend. "This is the place where Mother says I will be living. Let's always keep in touch no matter where we wind up. Let's make a pact. Let's promise to write as often as we can but, absolutely for sure at Christmas."

There was just enough time to place Rebecca's new address in a safe place before curfew sounded. Lights out followed.

Rebecca desperately tried to camouflage her fear of the unknown. She clung to the promise of her friends. Just knowing they would forever keep in touch helped catapult her somewhat over her apprehension.

Nightmares! Intrusive nightmares! Darn robbers. Like bees swarming in a hive, Rebecca's head buzzed with threatening worse-case scenarios. Her future filled with what ifs? It was scary and, she was downright scared.

Intertwined in the center of it all was her precious purple gold. Teasing, it dared Rebecca to tell the whole world about the gift from her mother. Yes, from her mother. Tell your friends. Shout it from the rooftops. Tempting, that course of action was so very tempting.

But way back in her psyche, even in her sleep, her mind just wouldn't permit it. As great as all that would be, she just couldn't chance it. What if, somehow, Mother Superior found out? Worse yet, Father Larkin, and he wouldn't hesitate. Then, what if they took it away from her? That would mean sheer disaster for sure.

She shot upright in her bed. Beads of sweat hugged her forehead. Get a grip! She tried convincing herself. Finally, somewhere in the wee hours of the morning, she came to terms with her struggle. She would not tell her friends, in keeping with Sister Regina's insistence, and sage wisdom, from the very beginning. It would remain a secret. Rebecca thought about Sister Regina and how much she would miss her. She decided to talk to her later in the morning. The very thought of losing her mentor and friend made her feel sick to her stomach and she was sad when the time arrived.

"Good morning, Rebecca." The uninformed nun was her usual cheery self. "I hope you are feeling better today. Sorry you missed class yesterday, but I have your assignment for you."

"Thank you Sister. I'm better. Um…May I talk with you at recess?"

"Of course, just stay indoors."

If a watched pot doesn't boil, do hands on a watched clock stop moving? That seemed to be what was happening to the time here. It moved so very slowly. Rebecca did not care about her missed assignment. It was no longer needed. Finally, she heard the sound of the long-awaited recess bell and the quiet of the empty classroom.

"Now Rebecca, what is it? Do you need some extra time to finish yesterday's assignment?" Until Sister Regina looked into Rebecca's troubled eyes, she didn't have a clue. Then seeing the look on the dear girl's face was cause for immediate concern.

"What's wrong?"

"Oh, Sister everything," Rebecca leveled with her, "Mother says I have to move out on some work program and I'm scared. I'm really scared. In a way I want to go and in another, I want to stay. I'm so confused, too."

"I haven't heard of any such program. Are you sure?"

"I am." Rebecca managed to get her story out despite her shaky voice and shaky insides.

"I'm so sorry, Rebecca. I don't know what to say. I'm stunned."

Rebecca felt somewhat comforted as the sympathetic nun's sentiment echoed in her choice of words. "I will miss you and our talks." Taking Rebecca's hands into her own she told her, "When you can, Rebecca, try to think of this as an opportunity to find your elusive dream. Maybe that will help. Immediately, she knew Sister was referring to the discussions of an earlier event, the day she showed Rebecca her necklace and the significance of her mother's message.

"My purple gold, Sister," Rebecca questioned its fate, "what about my purple gold?"

"I have kept it for you long enough. It is time for the changing of the guards. Wait here." The nun left and returned in short order. Reaching into her deep pocket, she pulled out a box and gave it to Rebecca.

"I put it in this little box, Rebecca. It's more secure than the envelope. It is yours. Take it with my blessing. Remember, too, with or without this necklace, your treasure will always be where your heart is."

"Thank you, Sister. I'll remember and I'll never forget you, either."

"Now, go with my good wishes and if you ever need me, I'll be right here."

Sister had to quickly get this precious girl out of her classroom and out of her life. It was not going to be easy. She had to hurry. Her composure was about to crumble. She so wanted to cry but for Rebecca's sake, as much as for her own, she held back. With tears in her eyes, Rebecca tried to smile with genuine gratitude. The young girl and the respected nun and friend hugged for the last time. Sister wondered why she liked hugs and it dawned on her now. She liked hugs because they are returnable and, with that in mind, the two held each other just a little longer.

If Rebecca thought this goodbye was heartbreaking, saying goodbye to her best friends, Annmarie, Annette and Theresa, would be sheer torture.

But Rebecca's friends managed to be strong for her. They got her through it. Without a lot of tears but with a ton of hugs, they sent her on her way. "Write."

It was a word exchanged over and over, even as Rebecca stepped into the waiting car.

Officially, she left her three friends standing there on the front steps. Filled with anger and pain, her forever supporters waved frantically until the car drove out of sight

Chapter 14

~

The man driving the car and his wife sitting beside him were pleasant enough. Yet, as far as Rebecca was concerned, everything was still up in the air. She sat quietly in the back seat next to the cute, chatty, little girl.

Clinging to her laundry bag containing all her worldly goods, gave her a sense of some security. Just holding it on her lap knowing her purple gold was safely tucked inside, made her feel a little less anxious.

Rebecca smiled at the little girl all the while her thoughts grimaced. It happened so fast. What could I have done? Nothing, and here I am ready or not, resigned to an unknown fate. Riding down the lane, with a smile painted on her face, the sad scenario of recent events played over and over again like the rerun of a make-believe movie film. Only, unfortunately, this was for real.

Chapter 15

~

Life at the Driscoll House

Well, it was different, this new way of life. Parts were pleasant. Parts were ordinary and parts deviating from the familiar were very strange. On Rebecca's part, it took a good deal of adjustment.

For starters, she had come to terms with the Driscoll family's way of keeping on schedule. Gone were the bells. They actually depended pretty much on a clock. She learned that she controlled the light switches and was even the deciding factor as to when to click them on or off.

The hardest adaptation was getting use to having a private room. Hers alone, as was the bathroom, neither had to be shared. Lying in her soft bed basking in the warmth of its thick, sheep's wool blanket, she could not help but feel a twinge of guilt. She thought of her friends high on the hill shivering under threadbare cotton blankets anxiously awaiting the morning wake-up bell to warm oatmeal, and the image left her chilled.

When she first arrived, it was little Annie who delighted in showing Rebecca to her room. Introductions made, Mrs. Driscoll commandeered Annie into action.

"Annie, be a dear and show Rebecca her room."

"Okay, Mommy."

Mommy! Now that's a strange yet melodious sounding word to my ear. Never really had been in my vocabulary, Rebecca thought, as the little tyke took her hand and enthusiastically, led Rebecca to her bedroom. The child had a reason for her immediate co-operation. She was so excited. She had a surprise for Rebecca. There it sat propped up against the pillows right in the middle of the huge, double, bed.

"This is for you, Rebecca. I picked it out all by myself but Mommy helped. Do you like it?" Little Annie could hardly contain herself. "His name is Mr. Cuddles."

If nothing else, the dear, little girl certainly knew how to pull on Rebecca's heartstrings. There, sitting like a king surveying his kingdom, sat a cute, fluffy, chocolate brown teddy bear wearing a bright red bowtie.

As is the case with most children, patience was not Annie's forte. She did not wait for an answer. In a flash, she jumped up onto the bed and bounced her way to reach the bear's arm. Successfully, she pulled the bear off the bed and ran directly into Rebecca's arms.

"Here, feel his fur. It's sooo soft," she declared gleefully. "Isn't it the softest teddy bear you ever had?"

Following instructions, Rebecca did as she was told. Running her hand over the stuffed animal's body, she replied honestly, "Ooh, you're right, Annie. His fur is soft."

The little girl was about to pop with excitement. "Do you like it, Rebecca? Do you?"

This time Annie waited for an answer.

"Yes, Annie. I really do. Thank you very, very much." With that Rebecca leaned down and gave the dear, thoughtful child a big hug. It was received with the child's biggest of smiles amid a roomful of giggles.

Oh, Annie, how could you know, she thought? Of course, this is the softest teddy bear I've ever felt. It's also the only one I have ever felt. There were no stuffed animals at the orphanage. Such coddling was not in the best interest of the youngsters. Just ask Father Larkin. Later, in the stillness of the night, clinging to her very own teddy bear, she mourned that loss of tenderness. Crying softly into her pillow, the sad realization hit her hard. The joy of holding a stuffed animal, a right of childhood, is simply lost to all at Holy Comforter.

Reaching for a Kleenex, she clutched her bear closer. "Well, Mr. Cuddles, the saying goes, you don't miss what you don't have. And to that I say boloney! If that's true, then how come I miss my mother? Yikes! Now I'm talking to a stuffed toy. Guess that's okay as long as I don't expect an answer. Anyway, little guy, we can't change the past so let's get some sleep. Tomorrow's another day. We'll soon find out what it holds."

The sun rose and, with a little help, so did Rebecca. The unexpected knock so early in the morning had her sitting up. "My goodness, Annie, you'll an early bird. Come in, the door is open."

"It's not Annie. It's Beverly." And a middle-aged whirlwind of energy came bounding into Rebecca's room. Rushing about obviously in a hurry, she opened the drapes then stood at the foot of the bed shifting from one foot to the other.

"It's time to get up. Sorry I wasn't here yesterday when you arrived. Allow me to introduce myself. I'm Beverly Haltzsman, chief cook and bottle-washer. Come on, sleepy-head. I need your help in the kitchen." With that rapid-fire informal introduction, Rebecca didn't know it at the time, but she just met the woman who would prove to be the best candidate for adult friendship in this household.

"Good morning, um…"

"Beverly. Just call me Beverly." And, with that she was off and running. In the kitchen, she indoctrinated Rebecca. "Now here's the rundown. First off, you don't start school until tomorrow. That's good. It gives us time to get this show on the road." Holy Hannah! She doesn't even stop to take a breath.

"In the mornings, during the school week, you get up, make sure Annie is up and dressed for school. You come down and help me get breakfast served. Then you walk Annie to school. I'll tell you how to get there in a minute. Then you'll go to school. But not today, she repeated. After class, you meet Annie and walk her home. Help her with her homework and then help in the kitchen to get supper on the table. Make sure Annie gets to see her parents for a short visit and then you get her ready for bed. Saturdays, you clean and Sunday you go to church. After that, the rest of the day is yours. Got that?"

Gulp! Swallowing hard, Rebecca shoulders slumped as she reminded herself not to panic. You'll get the hang of it. You just have beginners' jitters and in the back of her mind, she remembered reading somewhere– 'Life is tough. Get a helmet.' Yikes! Just point me in the direction of the nearest cycle shop. Quick!

Instructed of her duties and as the days went by, a routine was slowly established. It wasn't as hectic as Beverly had made it sound. Thank goodness. It held structure for which Rebecca was glad. Although not as stringent as in her last place, it gave her direction. The anatomy of this household systematically filled with rules and order, actually made Rebecca's life a tad easier. Although, still exhausted at day's end, she still fell into bed to await the start of a new day. Except for Saturday and Sunday, each day was almost identical to the one just finished. Rebecca ate all her meals with Beverly.

Heaven forbid the help should be invited to break bread with the heads of household.

Anyway, Rebecca liked this arrangement just fine.

Sharing the evening meal and listening to Beverly chatter about her day, Rebecca gave thought to the make-up of this kitchen commander-in-chief. The longer she listened, the more she became convinced. Beverly's bark was louder than her bite.

There was something soft about this tough-nut. Maybe it was her smile. If I were to guess, I would say she is about the age of my mother. I don't know how old that is exactly, but I kind of like the idea of just sitting around talking to a mom. Unaware of Rebecca's wistful thinking, Beverly's simply talked on. "--And then I had to run to the market because we were completely out of it."

While living in the orphanage, and in self-defense, Rebecca developed an unusual talent. Just by catching a few key words here and there, she could listen with one ear to keep up with the conversation at hand; while at the same time, be at liberty to entertain whatever other thoughts popped into her mind.

Besides, she thought, it's my choice. If I want to picture my mother as a good natured, slightly plump woman with endless energy, who's going to stop me? So what if I don't know my mother. I remember at the orphanage when it came to family story-telling time, my imagination ran circles around the others. Look how upbeat this woman is, eating and talking a mile a minute. It must be nice never being depressed. Beverly's ongoing chatter gave Rebecca a chance not only to further check her out, but to compare her with the woman she held so close to her heart. She put her on a par with her unseen mother. I'd like to think my mother wears her hair pulled back and fashioned in a bun, too, and that her hair is black with the same hints of grey. My mother's apron would be a permanent accessory, too. Except for color and pattern changes, like Beverly's her apron would deny a full view of her fresh housedress. Pretend games remained Rebecca's favorite.

Feeling warm and fuzzy, Rebecca simply embraced Beverly as her surrogate mother. Beverly, of course, was not privileged to the knowledge of Rebecca's silent acquisition.

"--So what would you have done? Rebecca, didn't you hear me? I asked what you would have done at the market if the checker had been that rude to you."

"Oh, yes. You were absolutely right. I would have done just what you did, Beverly."

"Good. I'm glad."

What exactly you did, Rebecca wondered, I'm not sure. But thank goodness the bits and pieces I heard got me the right educated guess.

"Let's finish up here. It's almost time to get the little one ready for bed. In fact, Rebecca, I spent so much time bending your ear, you go ahead. I'll finish up."

Whew! Saved by the bell. Well saved by Annie, anyway. Rebecca felt grateful for the absence of actual bells in this place.

Putting the pots away, Beverly had time to think about the young girl. She's so sweet and yet so naïve. She has a lot to learn and her with no family. That's such a pity. Well, then, it's up to me to keep her straight, all right. Somebody has to and silently, amidst the noisy clanging of her stacking pot and pans, she made a vow. I'll take Rebecca under my wing. It will be my mission. There. Now, I feel so much better and from then on, their time spent together was fruitful. Beverly was only too eager to teach Rebecca the ways of the world. Her ways, of course, but nevertheless, she imparted wisdom on this innocent babe in the woods.

This arrangement was good, too, for the somewhat isolated Beverly who had always hidden her loneliness. After all, she didn't have a family of her own either. She had been the Driscoll's faithful cook and housekeeper for over ten years. She liked her work and the people for whom she worked. But that's where it ended. From the beginning, the Driscoll's made it perfectly clear that she was not a family member. Periodically, without hesitation, they reminded her that she was retained as nothing more than their domestic help. In other words, basically, she was their servant and they made sure she kept to her station in life.

Beverly knew her place. Despite living in a household of three, she was mostly alone and always lonely. As Beverly saw it, Annie, bless her heart, was so sweet but being young, needed her parents. She really didn't need Beverly in the way Beverly yearned to be needed; nor was that interaction encouraged. From time to time, a justified depression would befall her. At least that's how Beverly thought of it. So many times she would think about her life and how she ended up here. This morning, while in the process of washing the breakfast dishes, was just one of those times of remembrance. Sadness popped into her head as she thought about it. Nobody knows what a lousy life I've lived. For that matter, nobody even cares. How I wish I could forget the past and all that I have been through. But, it won't go away. All I can do is keep the regrettable parts of my life secretly locked within my heart. I would die if anyone found out, especially the Driscoll's.

Going through the motions, she put the clean dishes neatly in the cupboard as she gave more thought to her pathetic life. Whoever said a person jovial on the outside is masking sorrow on the inside must have lived the sorrow. That's me, all right. Laughing on the outside; crying on the inside and hiding it pretty darn well.

She wished she could dry up her memories like the dishes she had just wiped. Then she could just tuck them away. At least, she thought, there is something good going for me now. The pleasant orphan girl is a bonus and couldn't have arrived at a better time.

Beverly poured herself a cup of coffee and sat at the kitchen table trying to enjoy the hot drink. She thought about Rebecca who didn't even know she was a godsend. She thought, too, that lately her depression had taken a turn for the worse. For some unknown reason, Beverly couldn't shake it. Now she was convinced the good Lord sent Rebecca to pull her out of this miserable slump.

She's like having a daughter of my own. Finally, I have something important to live for. If the good Lord sent her to help me then it's up to me to look after her. Why, she's still wet behind the ears. Lord knows, too, how qualified I really am to educate her in the ways of the world. Staring into the cup of steaming liquid, her mind drifted back to a time when she was just about Rebecca's age. She remembered it well. It was the time of her schooling. She graduated at the head of her class all right. Too bad it was from the school of hard knocks. Talk about depression bait. There she was sixteen-years-old, and pregnant out of wedlock. Disowned by her family, her train conductor boyfriend did the right thing. He married her. Their puppy love never grew. She had a miserable marriage. To add more tragedy, the baby was born dead and they never had another. Adding insult to injury, several years later her husband was killed in a tragic train crash and she was forced to make it on her own ever since.

What she lacked in book smarts she made up for by the abundance of knowledge she had learned firsthand. At this point in her life, she was very well-versed in the shrewdness needed to live in what she perceived to be a cruel, unfair and inequitable world.

Shivering with a chill of resentment, she was more determined than ever to guide her new charge, her young student, her new focus, down the straight and narrow. On my mission she promised herself, Rebecca will never be permitted to repeat my costly mistakes. That Rebecca had no say in the matter, never even occurred to the headstrong woman. Her quest, plain and simple was to keep Rebecca safe. Opinions of other people, including Rebecca, didn't hold water.

Beverly went so far as to even inspect Rebecca's daily choice of clothing. Well aware of Mrs. Driscoll good fashion taste and that she selected and paid for Rebecca's outfits, didn't matter. She needed to check them over just the same. She couldn't take the chance of her Rebecca somehow winding up with an inappropriate style or the wrong color combination or, most importantly, sporting an indecent hem line. After all, how much would a girl uniform-bound all her life know about today's teenage fashions? Now, if Beverly had just thought past her prejudice, the question would more likely have been how much does a middle-aged cook know about teenage fashions of the day?

Her intentions were good. No one would laugh at her Rebecca. Not if she could help it and she could. Meal times spent at Beverly's table became Rebecca's academy of life.

Chapter 16

1954 – Summit Falls High School

...Sleep opens within us an inn for phantoms. In the morning we must sweep out the shadows.

Gaston Bachelard (1884-1962)

Tossing and turning, she chased fleeting hints of sleep. Her mind held too many rooms with too many uninvited spirits and the scary apparitions haunted her far into the night.

Punching down her pillow, she soon gave up trying to make it more comfortable. Sitting in the dark, she also reconsidered her initial thought of turning on the light. What was the chance it would drive away the dreaded illusions in her mind anyway? She wondered, too, why this night was lasting forever. I can't believe I'm scared to death of going to high school tomorrow. It's not like I haven't gone to school before. Okay, so I don't have any friends. So what? Like Beverly says, I'll just make new ones. I'm still a pretty good student, too and that has to count for something in my favor. Then why do I still feel like I'm about to walk the plank?

She punched her pillow again. Right, she thought, beating up my pillow will straighten out my life and went on mentally battling her thoughts. I'm just as good as the public school kids. I am. Almost convinced, and maybe even getting closer to getting some sleep, her mind slipped. Racing with worrisome questions, she caved. What if I don't dress right? What if I can't find my classrooms on time? What if nobody likes me? What if everybody laughs at me? Yikes! Girl, get a grip. It can't be all that bad. It just can't.

Once again, she tried resting her head on the soft pillow. Miraculously, this time, the phantoms were evicted and she managed to sleep the remaining few hours left until morning. If Beverly noticed her nervousness, she diplomatically looked the other way. Keeping things on an even keel, trying to put Rebecca at ease, she didn't push a heavy breakfast.

"Don't you look nice today, Rebecca. Would you like a little toast?"

"No thank you, Beverly. I'm fine. I better get Annie and start off to school. I don't want to be late. Not on my first day."

"You are absolutely right, Rebecca. You and Annie go and have a good day. I'll be right here when you get home I can't wait to hear all about it."

Just like that, Rebecca found herself walking her little charge to school and then heading to Summit Falls High School and her initiation.

Walking into the Principal's office, a twinge of anxiety mixed with a ton of nervousness, and uncertainty, along with a smidgen of fear, walked in with her. Did I just hear a bell? Finally, there's a reminder of home. For a second, it felt good. That is before she thought it through and had to correct herself. I meant my last home.

Given a brief welcome, her daily schedule and a short orientation, Rebecca was sent on her way to face her new world. As it turned out, the task wasn't exactly easy but not too tough either. Manageable, it took her through the day interacting with strangers as best she could in this great, big, building with its way too many classrooms. Timidly learning her way around, her calculating plans included an easier tomorrow. At home at day's end, Rebecca found Beverly chomping at the bit. "Well, how did it go? Pull up a chair and tell me all about your first day. Come on, before I pop and don't leave out a single detail."

"Okay, but first let me get Annie a cookie and some milk. I'm starving, too."

"We'll be eating soon, Rebecca so don't spoil your appetite." Of course it wasn't Rebecca's appetite Beverly was concerned about. It was the time wasted waiting.

"I won't." Finished, she rinsed the glasses, wiped off Annie's milk mustache and gave the little girl drawing paper and a pencil. "Here, Annie, and when you finish drawing a nice picture, wash your hands and get ready to eat. Okay?"

"Um-hum."

Finally. Rebecca sat next to Beverly and began to satisfy her curiosity. "Today wasn't bad. Here, look at this. It's my schedule and, look at this, too."

"A map?"

"Yep. Can you imagine a place so big that they actually had to give me a map? Good thing, too. Turned out I needed it."

Thumbing through the papers, she said, "Looks like a doable schedule." But Beverly's interest was not in schedules or maps. To this end, she had cleverly run her plan with mastery, lulling Rebecca into a sense of calm security. Now she could jump right to her point while Rebecca would simply remain clueless. "Did you make any friends?"

"Not really. I did talk with a few people, but no one in particular. It's only my first day. I really didn't expect much."

Friends, the magic word Rebecca thought. Now why did Beverly have to go and spoil it? That's all it took. She thought about Beverly's soon to be filled bountiful table.

Suddenly and without warning, Rebecca's thoughts turned to the ones she had to leave behind. Seeing the bread basket overflowing with freshly baked rolls didn't help her cause. Rather, it reminded her that soon they would be sitting down to their meal too. Only their table would be sparse and she hoped today would not be one of those days when there wasn't enough bread to go around.

Here at Beverly's table, the variety of food would not only be served in abundance but, beautifully presented and piping hot. Hard as it was for Rebecca to believe, the meal would end with a mouth-watering scrumptious dessert. In fact, dessert was on the menu each and every night. No wonder Rebecca had a hard time adjusting to the frequency of this luxury. She had grown up believing dessert was absolutely restricted to Sunday nights.

This invasion of memories would not permit interruption. They seemed to be locked on other times, so she let them have their way. How many times, she thought, because of petty infractions of illogical rules, had she been sent to bed without supper? She wasn't alone on this belittling putdown.

Suddenly, sitting at this food laden table, it hit her. She knew the reason for that maneuver. Contrary to what she and other orphans believed, it was not done out of meanness; rather, it was in a strange way, an act of kindness. It was quite simple, really. The fewer mouths to feed at one meal meant the more food to be stretched for another. That would account, too, for the nuns fasting so often.

She couldn't count the number of times her friends came to her rescue. Hiding their own meager slices of bread in their pockets, she remembered, sitting in her bed after lights out, and under cover of darkness, hungrily devouring every morsel they shared. She closed her eyes for a moment and prayed. Please don't let my friends go hungry tonight. Like the savory roast beef she was slicing, Beverly words cut into Rebecca's thoughts. She passed the seasoned mashed potatoes, waited until Rebecca scooped a spoonful onto her plate then pressed ahead with her first degree.

"Rebecca, did you meet anyone at all who was at least interesting?"

"Not really."

Relieved, Beverly thought good, saved for now. If you only knew how very well versed I am in these matters. If you knew how I live an extremely reality-based life and how I know from experience what getting mixed up with boys will do to unsuspecting girls like you, then you would understand.

Rebecca swallowed a mouthful of delicious, creamy potatoes and wiped her lips with her white, linen napkin. Holy Hannah, she thought, yet another nonexistent perk in the orphanage. We were lucky if and when we got paper ones. She wondered how many uniform sleeves catered to food stains in their absence.

Her stomach full simply left no room for the butterflies that hounded her all day. Much calmer now, she was able to share more of her day with Beverly. Although, she had to admit just thinking about her friends made her feel melancholy. Of course, the dumb stunt she pulled in class didn't help her feel any better. Embarrassed, she almost kept it to herself, but for the anxious look on Beverly's face, she would have.

"I did something really stupid in class."

"Oh, and what stupid thing would that be?" The painted smile never left Beverly's face, while her mind raced with negative thoughts of personal guilt. This better not involve boys.

"Well, um… being new, I'm not familiar with all classroom procedures. It's so different in public school. I was in my Problems of Democracy class and was called on to answer a question."

"What was the question?" Not that she cared. What mattered was that whatever did happen did so in a classroom full of people. Safety in numbers, Beverly figured.

"It was regarding the conduct of man's inhumanity to man, in certain social situations."

"Wow. That's a bit deep. Wouldn't you say? Did you know the answer?"

"Yes. We already covered that in my last school. But that's not the point."

"Then, what is? I think, Rebecca, it's terrific that you could answer the question. Let alone understand what in the world that topic is all about." Grinning broadly, Beverly couldn't resist. "Now don't you go getting egg-headed on me."

Rebecca didn't crack a smile. Rebecca didn't feel smart. Rebecca, at the moment, didn't much like her new school.

"Then what happened, Rebecca? You knew the answer. So what was the problem?"

It was all she could do to answer, what with fighting back tears she so wanted to let fly.

"When the teacher picked me, immediately I stood up next to my desk and delivered my answer. Guess old habits die hard."

"What do you mean?"

"Don't you get it, Beverly? Nobody stands up when addressed in the public school. I just stood there humiliated. I heard their snickers. It didn't matter that they had covered their mouths with their hands. I heard them just the same. It was awful. I just wanted to crawl into a hole."

And you call this a stupid mistake, Beverly thought to herself? But, she didn't let on and reacted as she knew Rebecca expected.

"You poor dear, what did the teacher say?"

"What could he say? He just said my answer was good and that next time I was called upon, it was okay if I answered from my seat. I'm telling you Beverly, I could feel my face turning dark crimson." Under her breath, she muttered. "Stupid, that's what I am, stupid, stupid, stupid."

"Stop being so hard on yourself," Beverly came to Rebecca's defense, as if it made a difference here in the Driscoll's kitchen. She banged her fist on the table, adamant in her outburst. "Respect never hurt anybody, Rebecca. Too bad your classmates don't follow your example. Now, never you mind. They don't know any better. Besides, you'll get on to the ways of your new school. It may take a little time, that's all. So until then, Rebecca, hold your head up high. Don't you let those turkeys get you down."

"Beverly, you surely have a way with words."

"I mean it. You are better than that." Rebecca wasn't quite sure what she meant and not confident enough to ask, she let the last comment go by. Maybe at a later time, she would be secure enough to bring it up. "This place is starting to feel like a tomb. You know Rebecca, I hate when things get morose." She sipped her lemonade then put the glass down on the linen covered table. Grinning from ear to ear, she said affectionately, "Now tell me something happy that happened today. There is always a little something happy in a day. Sometimes you just have to look a little harder for it." She waited for Rebecca who seemed to be struggling.

"I don't know if this counts. But it's all I can think of."

"Go ahead. Tell me. Nothing is too small if it makes you happy."

"I feel dumb. Here goes. I dropped my pencil and one of the girls picked it up for me. See, what I mean? Dumb?"

"That's okay. Think about it. Did that simple act make you feel happy?"

"Come to think of it, I did feel better."

"Good. Now, finish your meal. It's almost time to help Annie with her homework. This evening's gossip talk was the first of many. Therapeutic for one, an obsession for the other, sometime they talked late into the night. Although the next few weeks passed by relatively uneventful, they never missed their after dinner tête-à-tête. After all, Beverly was convinced, in just a matter of time this kitchen would be abuzz with Rebecca's' romances. Yes, these chitchats would uncover any and all her lovey-dovey trysts. Trysts, Beverly knew for certain would be hazardous to the young girl's health. Trysts, Beverly would never let happen. No way. Not on her watch.

At times, Beverly even amazed herself. She was good at keeping her intentions secret. Through it all, Rebecca, totally enjoying their shared friendship, remained clueless.

"And, how did it go today?" The daily ritual started out with that question.

"Okay, Beverly. But it has been two weeks. It's about time that I know the ropes, don't you think?"

"Wait a minute, young lady," Beverly moved closer for a better look. "What's that I see on your face?"

"What?" Confused, Rebecca brushed her fingers across her cheeks. "Whatever it was, it's gone now."

"I still see it." Grinning, Beverly said, "There it is. You're wearing an ear to ear smile. You can't fool me. Come on, tell me quickly. What little, or should I say not so little, happy something happened today?" Slapping her knee, Beverly chuckled aloud. "Why, Rebecca, I do believe you are blushing. Spit it out."

"Okay, okay. If you must know, my day ended on a high note."

"Uh-huh! I knew it. What's his name?"

"Who said it was a he?"

"Your star-filled eyes gave it away. Now, fill in the details."

Rebecca loved these talks with Beverly. She may have considered her as a surrogate mother but she was finding out, more and more, she was a real friend, too. The two-way teasing was fun. Pretending to give her a hard time, Rebecca put her off a little longer.

"It's not polite to talk with a mouthful."

"So, chew already. If you don't tell me about him soon, I won't be responsible for my actions" Giggling, Rebecca didn't hold out any longer and in one, long, breath provided details.

"He is tall and dark, handsome, a piece of perfect and, he is in my English class and he sits next to me in Math class, too, and did I mention that he is handsome?"

"You know you most certainly did. You little imp."

Feigning a lack of understanding, Rebecca retorted. "Why, Beverly, whatever do you mean?" Now, there was a definite tinge of pink on Rebecca's cheeks. She was more than just a little flustered and never more pleased to see little Annie run into the room.

"Are you going to help me get ready for bed now, Rebecca? Are you? Are you?"

"Of course, Annie, let's go." Taking the girl's hand, they headed toward the door where Rebecca turned and winked at Beverly. "Talk to you later when I get back to help with the dishes."

Beverly knew full well this particular conversation was tucked away for the night. Hopefully, she would hear more about it in the not too distant future. That Rebecca, she thought, sometimes it's like pulling teeth. These things have to be nipped in the bud.

To Beverly's delight, she didn't have to wait long at all. Toward the end of the week, Rebecca raced excitedly into the kitchen. Beverly took one look at her glowing face and, like a phony, pretended to be shocked. Knowing perfectly well it could be nothing else, smiling she remarked, "Oh, no, this can't be about that boy again. Sit down, Rebecca and have a chocolate chip cookie fresh from the oven."

Dying to tell the world, Rebecca held back until she poured herself a tall glass of milk. Warm chocolate chip cookies and cold milk were long ago established as her all time favorite after school snack. Today, however, she could not dawdle. Not with the important matter at hand. Even extended teasing was out of today's picture. There just wasn't time. Quickly, she devoured her treat then jumped right into her exciting news.

"Guess who was asked if she was going to the Saturday night's school dance and, guess who asked? You'll never believe it, Beverly. I don't." With each question the sound of Rebecca's voice grew more excited. Louder and louder, she shared the good news until finally she was shouting.

Hiding behind a big smile, Beverly thought dark thoughts…and now it begins. Pretending to play the game, she put up a good front.

"No, Rebecca really, who are you talking about? I haven't the foggiest." Rebecca delighted in the silliness of her friend but was pressed for time.

"You know, Beverly. It's Lance, who else?"

Rebecca sat back in her chair, closed her eyes and mentally pictured dancing round and round the floor in the arms of that hunk. Lance was holding her tight and it was all too wonderful. But suddenly, that vision was gone as she jumped up from her chair. "Oh, no, I can't go."

"What is it Rebecca? What's the trouble? What do you mean, you can't go. Of course, you can."

"You don't understand, Beverly. I just remembered I never danced with a boy before. Sure, my girlfriends and I use to dance together. Well, kind of. Mostly, we were fooling around and mostly to our own singing. Most times we didn't even have real music. It can't possibly be the same. What if I can't follow him? What if I embarrass the both of us? Oh, where's there a hole in the ground, when you need one?"

"Get hold of yourself." With raised eyebrows, Beverly jumped in. "Enough. Cease and desist. You're getting yourself worked up over nothing. You'll do fine in the dance department. You know the basics. Now, if you want something to worry about, try this one on for size. Have you asked permission from the Driscoll's yet? Will they let you go? They are, after all, your guardians."

"Great. Now I really have a problem. I didn't even think of that."

"Well, you better and you better ask this very evening. There's not a lot of time left before Saturday night."

"Maybe I won't have to ask them. Maybe I just won't go."

"Now that is a foolish conclusion, if I have ever heard one. You are not taking the easy way out. Just march yourself into that living room right now and ask the question and be extra polite about it."

With that, Rebecca felt the pressure of Beverly's hands on her back pushing her in the direction of the Driscoll's. There was no turning back. She had been seen by Mrs. Driscoll who had just put the evening paper down on the coffee table.

"Rebecca? What is it?" It was a legitimate question since Rebecca was not very often seen at this hour and never infringing on their evening time in their living room.

Rubbing her hands together nervously, she turned her head slightly toward the kitchen door. If she was expecting moral support from Beverly, she could forget it. The door was shut. She had to do this thing on her own. Beverly retreated behind closed doors. No, she didn't like the idea of Rebecca stepping out. But she knew it was only a matter of time and she was set up to carry out her plan. Rebecca could go out, but Beverly would monitor her every move.

"Mr. and Mrs. Driscoll, please excuse the interruption." Not knowing what else to do, she came right to the point. "It's just that there is a school dance this Saturday night and I would very much like your permission to attend. May I?"

There, she thought, wasn't so bad. Dead silence. What's taking them so long? Please, please, please, let the answer be yes. I just can't miss this dance.

"Ahem." Mrs. Driscoll was about to say something. Rebecca waited on pins and needles.

"You may go, but there are certain stipulations."

Whoopee. I'm going. Okay. Pay attention. Don't take a chance on goofing up a regulation. Listen. Rebecca paid close attention.

"All Saturday chores have to be completed with satisfaction. You are to be home by eleven o'clock and you will wear clothes from your closet. We do not intent to pay for a fancy outfit. Of course, it goes without saying. You must get up in time for church on Sunday."

If it goes without saying, then why did you say it? Rebecca's thought. I get the clear picture. I understood more than you think. Basically, you appreciate my work and you like me. Well, not too sure on that score. But, when the chips are down, I am still only the help. Therefore, other than your acquiescence to the request, you don't feel too much for me. Contain your enthusiasm. Don't tell me to have fun or anything. Would it kill either one of you to wish me a good time? Sticks-in-the-mud, that's what you are. Well, it's your loss. I'll save my hugs for someone who really cares. Doesn't matter because bottom line, I'm going to the dance.

And finally, the long, awaited Saturday night got here. As far as Rebecca was concerned, it took its sweet time. Up early, she rushed about keeping her end of the bargain. Finishing her chores with time to spare, she now luxuriated in a bubble bath. Looking at the foaming effervesce she thought, how novel. Immediately she was reminded of the quick, lukewarm, sometimes even cold showers she had grown up with and decided there are the haves and the have-nots. They are like night and day and the haves definitely have the easier way.

She had to admit, she liked these pleasant bubble baths tons better. So soothing, they often had a tranquilizing effect. If fact, she had been known to fall asleep amidst the fragrant, warm bubbles. But absolutely, not this time. There wasn't enough hot water or bubbles in the world to quell her excitement.

This is it. It's time to dress. The outfit carefully chosen from her closet turned out to be in vogue. She made sure of that by keeping a close eye on the current style all the popular girls were wearing. Thankful, too, for Mrs. Driscoll's good taste, she would fit in. Determined to look chic, she would never give them a chance to laugh at her again.

There was a knock on the door. "Rebecca, are you decent? May I come in?"

"The door is open, Beverly," she knew that voice anywhere. "Come in, I'm just about finished dressing."

Her mission kept secret, Beverly entered. It wasn't that she didn't want Rebecca to have fun, it was just she didn't want her to invite too much fun. Now she seemed so blasé about this whole thing. But inside, she was scrutinizing every detail. Immediately, her heart sank. It was just what she feared most. Rebecca looked much too attractive. I just know it, she said to herself. She'll be bait to those miserable, male sharks out there just waiting to prey on her naivety. Good thing I got here when I did.

With her painted smile, she began what she came in to do to make sure Rebecca passed her inspection with flying colors.

"Let's have a look at you."

"Ta Da. Well?" Rebecca twirling around asked anxiously.

"Ooh!" Folding her hands and closing her eyes, as if to savor the vision, Beverly declared, "You look absolutely scrumptious, Rebecca."

The teen-ager tingled in the flattery of the compliment.

"But, what's this on your face, a tiny smudge?" Beverly prided herself on her cleverness. Always present the positive first. Then go for the kill with the negative. Quickly, grabbing a washcloth, and before Rebecca knew what was happening, she was washing the girl's face.

"Got it, now stop scrunching up your face so. There's just a smidgeon too much blush here and the lipstick is a wee bit too heavy here."

Ah! What the heck is she doing? Rebecca wanted to shout stop, already. But, with her darn upbringing, no way was that about to happen. Instead, she said nothing, and didn't even try to stop the woman rearranging the make-up on her face. This after Rebecca had taken such pains getting it just the way she wanted.

Jeez. She better not make me change my clothes. News Flash! No I just won't. Quickly, she added, not unless she really makes me. Haunts of her background, again? Not fair.

"I love your outfit, Rebecca, especially your sweater. That color is you."

Pink is me? What's that supposed to mean? Doesn't matter, at least she likes what I'm wearing. Thank goodness because I do, too.

Stepping back admiring her work of art, Beverly was satisfied.

"There. Now you look lovely."

"Thank you Beverly," she said. All the while thinking, but isn't that what you said when you first came in? And I don't want any more changes. Still I'm not sure about the collar. Dare I ask? she did.

"You don't think this collar is too much?"

"No. It's just right. Now turn around and let me get a good last look." Obeying the woman obviously in charge, Rebecca twirled around. Catching her reflection in the mirror, Rebecca liked what she saw despite the new, soft-pedaled, almost pale facial.

She did look pretty in her light grey, flannel, poodle skirt that reached down to her calves. The big, white, sassy poodle appliquéd near the bottom of the skirt was darling. Sitting on its two hind legs, it was begging with its two front paws and sticking out its cute, pink tongue. Its collar, studded with rhinestones, sparkled.

The white crinolines she wore under her skirt were full and guaranteed the top flannel material to billow out, just as it was intended. She wore a light pink cardigan sweater tucked into the waistline of her skirt. Of course it was worn backwards with all the buttons securely buttoned down the back. That alone took some doing. But it was worth it. Wearing one's sweater backward was the in thing and she wasn't taking any chances. Dressed like this, she fit in with all the other public school girls. At her waist, she wore a wide, black cinch belt that hooked in the front. Its elastic material made her tiny waist look even smaller. The collar in question was the lace one interspersed with tiny, fake pearls. It simply hooked in the front and accented her pretty sweater. She had debated whether to wear it or a colorful scarf tied in a big, square knot. With Beverly's vote, the choice was unanimous. The collar won.

To complete her ensemble, she wore thick, white bobby socks, carefully folding the cuffs over twice to make them even thicker. On her feet, she wore black and white saddle shoes with the white parts just freshly polished. She even put a dab of cologne, a welcome gift from Mrs. Driscoll, behind each ear. Turning this way and that, she decided she was as ready as she was going to be.

"Well, do I pass inspection?" She used the term lightly never guessing the seriousness of Beverly's fine-tooth comb maneuvers.

"You most certainly do. Now I know you will have a wonderful time but be careful of what Lance may have on his mind. You know, my dear, when a boy wants a girl's favor, he is usually talking about more than just a kiss or two and he will say anything he thinks she wants to hear to get what he wants. So you be very careful."

Whoa! Where in the world did that come from? Shocked, Rebecca stopped dead in her tracks. She didn't say a word. She couldn't. But she could feel her face getting warm as she blushed with embarrassment. No adult had ever spoken to her about sex before. She learned what she needed to know from science class and, in the end it was really her close friends who set her straight. They were the ones who explained the authenticity of it all. She knew now that it was much more involved than the reproductive parts of a flower.

Inside, Rebecca fumed. Outside, it didn't show. Disillusioned, Rebecca surmised, obviously, Beverly has no confidence in me. Not only that. She's insinuating that Lance is something less than a gentleman.

My Lance! What's wrong with her? Maybe I just don't know her as well as I thought. One thing for sure, I don't like this shocking side of her. Hurt, annoyed, saddened and disappointed, Rebecca figured, the one adult here I finally come to count on the most just let me down the hardest. I thought she trusted me.

Talk about feeling betrayed. This uncalled for surge of counsel came straight out of left-field. Guess we learn some lessons the hard way. This unexpected and undeserved verbal attack did it for me and I know one thing. From this time on, my lips are sealed fairly tight. I'm not going to be as free talking about my social life anymore. I'm just afraid of the consequences. It's a shame, too, but she breached the comfort zone. Now Beverly will know only those things I feel safe sharing.

Here I am again, hit by another betrayal. First it was Mother Superior, then Father Larkin and now Beverly. This one is close to hurting the most.

But I can't think about that now. I have a dance to go to. The first of many, I hope. I feel pretty, Lance will be waiting and I intend to have a good time. I've been down before, so I'll pick myself up and push this issue behind me. I'm not letting anybody steal my thunder. It's getting late. She could see the sunlight rapidly disappearing and only a few dancing shadows remained on the edge of the window sill. "I better get going," and she headed toward the door.

"What? No hug for me?" Beverly asked with outstretched arms.

"Of course, sorry," and Rebecca returned, gave her a gentle squeeze and wondered if it was too polite. If it was, Beverly, basking in her accomplishment, never noticed.

"Don't forget your curfew."

"I won't." And with that, Rebecca was out the door.

Worn-out Beverly flopped back on the bed. Staring up at the ceiling, she uttered, "Done." Reflecting on the success of her well-executed plan, she was glad she caught her in the nick of time. "My word, all that make-up, wow, that was nothing more than a flashing neon sign inviting trouble. Thanks to my intervention, that girl looked refreshingly lovely."

Refreshing lovely was not what Rebecca had in mind. Try alluring, with the intention of sweeping Lance off his feet. Now that's the look she wanted to wear. Blind to even a hint of that possibility, pleased with her efforts, Beverly patted herself on the back. Her rationale was first-rate, to her, anyway. She thought, of course I want her to enjoy her teen years. Of course I want her to have romance. I'm not a prude. I just don't want her to wind up pregnant. To that end, I'm here for her. She'll thank me for guarding her future. She will. Holding that thought, she turned off the light and walked out of Rebecca's room. She was content, too, with the reason why her plan was working so well. Because, she thought, Rebecca always tells me everything.

Chapter 17

The school gymnasium was decorated in a manner the likes of which, Rebecca had never seen. The creative work of the art class was everywhere. Beautiful, gigantic, flowers of all colors practically covered the walls. Huge, fake palm trees sat in clusters at the four corners of the gym.

Outside of class time, the usually empty hall had now been invaded by round tables and chairs strategically arranged. Two or three tables deep, they surrounded the central area reserved for dancing. Along the wall in the back of the gym, a rectangular table held refreshments, a huge punch bowl filled with pink lemonade and trays of sugar cookies.

The lights were dimmed and a colossal, rotating, spherical ball covered with small mirrors hung from the ceiling. A red, green and blue color wheel sat on the floor in just the right spot. Focused on the ball, it allowed the mirrors to reflect its changing colors. A shimmering light glimmered high above the dance floor. Dots of color were everywhere. It was magical. Having never seen anything even remotely like this, its beauty momentarily took her breath away.

Designated as their meeting place, she headed for the palm tree in the right hand corner. So taken in with this place's ambience, she didn't even see him approach. She felt a gentle tap on her shoulder, turned and there he was. Her heart skipped a beat for sure and, maybe a dozen more.

"Hi Rebecca, you look nice." Slightly flustered, she managed a soft thank you. Holy Hannah, he's handsome. Now what? She stood there kind of awkward not knowing exactly what to do next. It's impolite to stare. So stop it. But how? She couldn't help it. No matter what she told herself, her eyes focused on his broad shoulders and big-league biceps. How weird is this? I've never looked at a guy like this before. Oh, darn, there goes my face. I swear. I'm blushing. I can feel the heat on my cheeks. Thank goodness the lights are low.

"Sit here, Rebecca," he invited pulling out her chair, "while I get us drinks."

Grateful for the direction, she did as she was told. The pause gave her time to re-group. She hadn't noticed before but behind the DJ's table hung posters of popular recording artists and movie stars. Would you look at that, she thought? The one most prominently displayed is my all time favorite, James Dean. His poster is hanging so close. It can't be more than three feet from me. Holy Hannah, he is flat out handsome. Look at his eyes. They're hypnotic. They seem to follow my every move. He was so good in 'Rebel Without a Cause.' What a movie. Resting her chin on her hands, she sat staring at the poster and enjoying her mini movie flashback until Lance returned.

"Your lemonade."

"Thanks."

He sat next to her, gulped down his drink and waited. Sipping hers slowly through a straw, impatient, he asked anyway.

"Want to dance?" Taking his outstretched hand into hers, she could feel the invasion of goose bumps. She saw the DJ and his stack of 45 RPM records and she could have sworn the music started on Lance's command. Was it her imagination or did the DJ take his cue from Lance? With a nod of his head, it appeared as if slow dance music began.

Then Lance held her. They fit together so well. Rebecca thought to herself, I worried for nothing. It doesn't matter that I never danced with a guy before. He makes it so simple. Closing her eyes and snuggling close, she thought warmly, he leads and I follow. That's all there is to it.

It was hard for Rebecca to believe she was actually in the arms of the one she considered flirting with in class. Of course, she was short on self-confidence. But as it turned out, Lance had more than enough for the both of them in that department. He didn't hesitate.

Sitting behind him in class, allowed her to look without being obvious. What a hunk! Not only that, she thought, he looks so much like James Dean, I could die. It's unbelievable. Then she went through this mental comparison exercise. The one she did in class. Both wore their thick hair in a DA. Both rolled up their short-sleeve shirts to hold their pack of cigarettes. Both wore tight-fitting jeans with deep, folded-up cuffs. Both wore penny loafers. She could go on and on and would, too, except in class there was always a teacher or bell that interrupted.

Dancing with Lance here and now, she felt lucky. Maybe leaving the orphanage wasn't such a bad idea after all. Here's Lance with his terrific personality. Absolutely, nothing square about him. Why he could be James Dean's twin. What a bonus. I have my very own movie star and, to think, he picked me. Fantasizing in the magic of the moment and feeling a little giddy, she looked toward the James Dean poster and gave the silent order. Move over, James Dean. Sorry. As much as you mean to me, he means more. Holding her close, Lance delighted in the pleasant aroma of her hair and the sweet-smelling, floral scent, of her perfume. He liked that and he liked her, too. Was it the shy way she lowered her head to laugh? Or was it the perky, little shuffle as she walked by? He wasn't sure. He just knew ever since she came to this school, he couldn't keep his eyes off of her. There were so many nice features about her. He liked all of them.

Whispering in her ear, he asked, "Do you like this song?"

"Love it." The song playing was Connie Francis' 'Who's Sorry Now'? The beat, perfect for their slow dance, was what Rebecca liked best about it. The lyrics, well they were way off. There wasn't anything for them to be sorry about and neither heart was aching. In fact, they couldn't be more ecstatic.

Hey now, she thought dreamily, it can't get any more clear-cut. I like everything about this guy and Rebecca's head spun with her best ever inventory. The way he kind of sways when he walks, the way the dimple in his chin seems to grow deeper when he smiles. Then there's the way he pulls out his small comb and runs it through the sides of his hair followed by a sweep of his hand making sure it stays in place. I can see a hint of Vaseline petroleum jelly he uses on parts of his hair to keep it nice and slick.

Absolutely, the piece de resistance! It's got to be that little curl he creates by pulling it down to sit right in the middle of his forehead. It doesn't get any niftier. Phew! No doubt about it, he is far out.

Am I falling hard for this guy or what? The very sound of his voice makes me shiver and with his touch, I tingle. Stop it girl. Snap out of it! You're getting way ahead of yourself. It's only the first date. Slow down and don't be stupid. Was that the voice from her upbringing? Or was it, in the end, Beverly's? No matter. She pushed it aside for now.

Relaxing as they grew more comfortable with each other, moving their feet and bodies to the music, they danced in perfect harmony. Not only that. Except to stop for an occasional drink of lemonade and maybe a cookie or two, they danced every dance. Holding each other in this enchanting setting, starry-eyed Rebecca found herself wondering. Is this the beginning of a beautiful friendship? She couldn't answer for him but as far as she was concerned, she hoped not. She wanted a lot more. But for now, like silhouettes, they danced in silence.

Suddenly and without invitation, who popped into her head? Sister Regina. What in the world is she doing here? I don't understand. Wait a minute. Aha! I get it. It's time for a silent thank you. If it hadn't been for Sister Regina, I wouldn't be up on tunes. That would be freaky. I wouldn't be here dancing, that's for sure and that would be a heart-breaker.

Boy, what a stroke of luck that was having Sister Regina in charge of cleaning the Community Room on Saturdays. She never batted an eye when we asked if we could play the radio. Just as long as the music wasn't too loud, and it didn't interfere with our work, it was okay with her. Better, yet, every Wednesday after school, she would let just a few of us spend a half hour or so, in the rarely used Visitor's Room. We could use it as long as there were no guests. It had a TV some organization had donated to the nuns. They never used it, or maybe they did, once or twice to watch some kind of church related program.

That Visitor's Room, that's where I really learned how to dance. I watched Dick Clark's, American Bandstand and by following the teenagers on his show doing all the latest hot dance steps, it didn't take long before I was almost as good as the TV dancers. Oh, and I remember when a new artist and song were introduced. My friends and I use to rate them on a scale of one to ten right along with those in the TV studio. It was so much fun. God bless that liberal Sister Regina. She did a lot for me. The music ended and Lance interrupted her thoughts.

"I could use another drink. How 'bout you?"

"No thanks. I'll finish the one I have."

This time, Lance drank more slowly. It gave them a chance to talk a little.

"Got a favorite song?" he asked.

"Not really. I like them all." She didn't want to sound like she was bragging but she really could name the song and the recording artist in hearing just a few notes. It was kind of a game she and her friends played back there. Who could match up the most song titles with the right artists? The winner got a few extra minutes of shower time the next day. No way would she throw out that piece of information for him to digest. As far as he was concerned, she transferred from another school in another town. The orphanage part was her secret to keep.

"Do you like all kinds of dances, too?"

"You bet."

"Listen. That's another good slow dance. Shall we?" Lance wanted to find out a little more about her interests but decided it could wait. For now, he wanted to dance a slow number. He liked holding her close. Without saying a word, she was up and in his arms. In her head, she already identified the melody as 'Where the Boys Are' song by Connie Francis. Now she had done it. Her tune-naming wheels were set in motion and she pegged everyone as the couple danced the night away. Fortunately, they pretty much just stayed in her mind. She didn't want to be guilty of singing along. Oh, I like this one. 'All I Have To Do Is Dream,' Everly Brothers. This one, too, 'Tears On My Pillow,' Little Anthony and the Imperials.

She and Lance danced the gamut of music styles ranging from rock-n-roll jitterbug through jazzed up versions of the fox trot and two-step, and in between they did the hand jive, the stroll and the bop. They made a good dance team. Rebecca's shyness dissipated as she realized all eyes seem to be on them. She felt like one of the dancers on Band Stand. What a terrific feeling. Finally, she was a somebody.

She knew all the fast dance steps, too. It was fun dancing to Bobby Darin's 'Splish Splash', the Coasters 'Yakety Yak' Then there was 'Lollipop' by The Chordettes, 'Rock Around the Clock' by Bill Haley and The Comets. The dances went on and on. Chuck Berry's, 'Johnny B. Goode,' Little Richards' 'Good Golly Miss Molly' and Bobby Freeman's 'Do You Wanna Dance?'

All the girls screamed when the King's record started. 'Heartbreak Hotel.' After Elvis, came the Platters, 'The Great Pretender.' Rebecca, unfortunately, related to this one more than any of the others. Listening to the title and lyrics, she felt a twinge of guilt. She knew how to play that part so well. She assumed the role every time there was mention of her parents. There was a side about her of which she was not proud. Yes, she was a great pretender, a hypocrite and wished the DJ had skipped playing that song. She shivered as she forced the sad fact back to the recesses of her mind.

"Are you okay, Rebecca? Are you cold?"

"Oh, no, I'm fine Lance. Guess I'm getting a little tired."

Lying seemed to be her thing. But couldn't she have picked a better one? She wasn't the least bit tired and in his arms, she could have danced all night.

"Well, I think the DJ is getting ready to wrap it up anyway. This is probably the last song for the night." The words barely out of his mouth, the overhead lights flickered on and off three times followed by the song, 'Good Night Sweetheart.' It was the Dance Committee's way of announcing the evening was drawing to a close. Drat, she thought. It's over way too soon.

Walking her home, Rebecca felt secure in the warmth of his arm wrapped around her waist. Oh, if only this feeling could last forever and wondered if he shared the same thought. They walked slowly, like eating a lollipop, savoring the long lasting flavor. Strolling most of the way in the quiet of the night, he was aware of her curfew and was glad they still had twenty minutes left.

Reaching the steps of the Driscoll's house, not quite sure what to expect, but longing to taste the sweetness of a goodnight kiss, Rebecca didn't say a word. Nervously, she stood there just shifting from one foot onto the other, not really knowing what to do. He knew. Lowering his head, Lance cupped his hand under her chin. Gently tilting her head back just far enough so her lips lined up perfectly with his. With that simple, easy and flawless maneuver, Rebecca was introduced to her long-anticipated first kiss.

It left her breathless, with a warm sensation in her heart while cold shivers ran down her spine. Giddy with delight and weak in the knees, she leaned into his strong body for support. What a perfectly, indescribable, delicious feeling, she thought. Please let it last forever. Maybe it was the promising harvest moon's shining light or maybe it was the mesmerizing gurgle of an unseen brook in the park across the street that captivated and escalated this euphoric spirit. Intoxicated with happiness, she saw it all as ensuring the brightness of her future.

Wow! It took all she had to come back down to earth. She tried to express her feelings of the evening as calmly as possible. At that, it was a stretch. "I had a nice time tonight, Lance and thanks for walking me home." All the while her insides were screaming, kiss me again, and again.

"I had a good time, too." Lance didn't say much else. He was thinking what a winsome innocence about her. *Charming and attractive in a sweet way, I've never met anyone like her. I've got to see her again.*

"Next Saturday night, would you like to go to the amusement park with me?"

Would I? Spend more time with you? You picked the perfect time to ask. Wild horses couldn't keep me away. Okay, she thought, *I have to let tonight end but knowing there's another date sure makes it easier. Calm down,* she told herself and *stop analyzing. For heaven's sake, he's waiting for an answer.*

"I would like that. Let me check at home and I'll let you know when I see you at school on Monday. Okay?"

His response came by way of his gentle kiss first to her neck, then to her chin, followed by a soft kiss to each eyelid.

"Wow." The sensation of it all heated an already warmed Rebecca as she turned and slowly ascended the stairs.

Their dance night together turned into their amusement park night together into their movie night together. In other words, every Saturday night turned into their date night and before long, she was wearing his school ring.

It was inevitable. They were in love, no ifs, ands, or buts. Sitting on the park bench after the movie one night, he took her hands into his. "Rebecca, will you go steady with me?" It wasn't something she hadn't thought about. It just came quicker than she had anticipated. *Of course she would go steady. Are you kidding?* She was thrilled.

Nodding, she softly whispered, "Yes, and while her heart was beating a mile a minute, ready or not, Lance slipped his ring onto her finger. It was a serious moment turned comical when his big ring, on her small finger, immediately turned upside down. It fit over two of her little fingers to keep it in place.

"Looks like you'll need a little yarn," he joked.

"I think a lot," she smiled. With that conclusion drawn, he leaned down and kissed her the way she so enjoyed.

She was right. It took a good bit of yarn to wrap around his big ring in order to make it fit. Didn't matter, because it was on solidly and gave out the message, loud and clear.

Everybody knew what it meant. Well, not exactly everyone. Those at school did. Those at home were not too sure. The first time she saw it, Beverly was beside herself with worry. It was at the breakfast table she confronted Rebecca.

"That's a pretty big ring you have there, Rebecca. What's that all about?" she wanted more than ever to learn of its significance. The entire time she kept a smile on her face but thought, darn, this girl doesn't talk to me like she use to. So she simply asked, "And how come you don't talk to me anymore?"

It was true. Their relationship had changed but as far as Rebecca was concerned, Beverly had absolutely nothing to fear. She and Lance both had good heads on their shoulders. Rebecca did not counter Beverly's complaint. They didn't talk much. In fact, their conversations consisted mainly of small talk. It was the best that Rebecca could do.

She had to admit, it was times like this that made her feel melancholy. How she missed her friends. They would love sharing the best thing that ever happened to her. Oh, sure she could write. But it wasn't the same. It would be nice letting someone in on her excitement right now. Goshdarn, Beverly! Why did you have to go and ruin a good thing?

"Well, Missy?"

"Oh, this?" Rubbing her hand over the ring, made her feel better. "It's a school ring. It's nice, isn't it? A lot of girls wear them," she said nonchalantly. With that, she thought, too bad that's all I can tell her. I better get out of here before I get bombarded with her questions. Glancing up at the kitchen clock, Rebecca jumped from her chair.

"For heaven's sake, Beverly, I almost forgot. It's Friday. Annie will have a fit if I miss it. I've got to run. See you later." Relieved, off she went.

Although it was on every day during the week, Friday was the only day her parents permitted her to watch it. Unlike most of their friends who had

TV, the Driscoll's considered the television set an intrusion on the way of family life. Rebecca didn't quite get it. It wasn't like they spent the rest of the time with their daughter. Oh, well, she thought, their choice.

It was Annie's special time of day. It was that time when she and Rebecca religiously parked in front of the TV set for an hour before dinner. Annie had no homework assignment on week-ends and Beverly didn't need help in the kitchen. Friday's meals were usually low keyed. Annie liked sharing her special show with her grown-up friend.

The little girl's giggles turned into robust laughter as antics of her favorite characters on the Howdy Dowdy Show kept her in stitches.

"It's time, Rebecca. Hurry! You don't want to miss the beginning."

"I surely don't want to do that." Rebecca got a real kick out of watching Annie interact, not only with the man dressed as a cowboy with fringes on his sleeve, known as Buffalo Bob Smith and the clown clad, Clarabell, but with the TV marionettes, as well.

The funny acts and shenanigans of all the wood characters especially the freckled-faced, loveable Howdy Dowdy and the intimidating Mr. Bluster who was always shooting off his mouth, were amusing.

That Clarabell didn't speak didn't seem to bother him. He just went around communicating with the use of tiny, twin bicycle horns that were mounted on a box he wore on his belt. He used the horns a lot. At times, it annoyed Rebecca. Obviously, it never bothered Annie. She laughed heartily at the silly sound each and every time the mute Clown used it, no matter its repetition.

Rebecca came running into the room, flopped onto the couch and sat next to Annie in their very own peanut gallery, and just in the nick of time. As they watched the show on the vacuum tube, black and white TV, they listened for Buffalo Bob's important question. It was the same one he asked at the beginning of every Howdy Dowdy show. Just before he did, a relieved Annie waggled a finger of caution as she chided Rebecca for almost being late.

"Boy, you made it just in time."

"I know. I surely don't want to miss it."

With that Buffalo Bob Smith's question came out in a booming voice. He addressed it to kids everywhere.

"Hey kids. What time is it?" And it was answered by children all over as they broke into singing the familiar ditty. "It's Howdy Dowdy time, it's Howdy Dowdy time, Bob Smith and Howdy, too, say howdy do to you. Let's…" Annie clapped her hands in glee as she and Rebecca finished the entire, well-known song. It was so much fun.

"Look out, Buffalo Bob. He's right behind you," squealed the excited Annie to the man in the TV set. She was trying to warn him that Clarabell was coming armed with a bottle of Seltzer water which he keep concealed inside his horn box. "Look out." She screamed again.

To Annie's delight, Buffalo Bob always turned just in time. But Clarabell was swift to chase him through the studio with his impulsive Seltzer spraying until he finally hit his target. By that time, all the kids sitting in the studio's peanut gallery were cheering and laughing just as hard as Annie was here at home.

"That was fun. Wasn't it Rebecca?"

"Sure was. Now we better eat and then get rid of all our excited energy."

Depending on the weather, sometimes they went outdoors to play games on Friday evenings. Rebecca learned how to roller skate to keep up with the little tyke. Annie never knew that skates were non-existent in the place where Rebecca had lived. Little Annie had fun pulling her around by her hand. Going faster and faster made the skate key hanging on a string around her neck bounce and Annie got a kick out of Rebecca's fear of falling. She never did fall but Rebecca's face was funny just the same. Rebecca liked playing with Annie. It felt like she was capturing a part of her lost childhood.

Sometimes they played Red Light, Green Light and Annie clapped when she successfully reached her destination without getting caught. They played Kick the Can or Mother May I or they toned it down with a simple game of catch until the porch light came on. It was their signal from Beverly that it was time to come in.

Rebecca thought to herself, now this is the way it should be. A little girl should have parents and friends and games and good times. Forget about struggles and stress and worries and hunger. She made a silent promise. When she had children of her own, they would have it all. She would see to it. With the passing of time, Rebecca enjoyed her life here with the Driscoll family and, thanks to Lance she was enjoying the public high school, too. The transition was tough at the beginning but he showed her the ropes and made it easier and easier for her to adjust.

Yes, she was content with the way her life had fallen into place. It had structure. It had purpose. It had security.

She was really glad that there was no need for any more changes. Unfortunately, Mrs. Driscoll had other plans. Her thinking, most certainly, was not on the same page as Rebecca's.

"Rebecca, after you get Annie to bed, Mrs. Driscoll would like to talk with you in the living room."

"What's this all about, Beverly, do you know?"

"I don't. But when Mrs. Driscoll asks to speak to the help, you can bet it is important." With that little bit of information, an anxious Rebecca headed upstairs and quicker than usual, tucked in her happy, but tired charge.

She entered the living room and sat on the chair that Mrs. Driscoll suggested. It was one of the two Queen Ann's wing-back chairs that graced the sofa on either side.

Sitting there waiting, not knowing what to expect, Rebecca's curiosity was tinged with a hint of fear. Despite the warmth emanating from the burning logs in the fireplace, Rebecca felt chilled. Turning her mind to the beauty of this room, she hoped it would alleviate the pressure of too much anticipation. She liked this room. Different from the rooms where she grew up, she especially liked the way the center wall featured a used red-brick fireplace complete with a large woodbin that held rough hickory logs. She prided herself on keeping the brass fireplace screen and tools polished, always in readiness for the relaxing evening fire. She inhaled to enjoy the lingering aromatic scent of hickory.

The sturdy oak mantel displayed Mr. Driscoll's treasured trophies of various size and shape. An avid golfer, his rectangular and circular trays and chalices were nice to look at but Rebecca declared hard to keep clean. In fact, she thought, they could use another dusting about now.

Arranged under the double casement windows opposite the bookshelves was the deep piled, blue crushed velvet sofa she thought was nifty. Velvety soft to the touch, the large cushions invited a leisurely visit for most. Of course, she thought, not for me since I only get in here to clean. Once a week she ran the vacuum over them and then gently fluffed them back into their comfortable shape. Sometimes she would hug the cushions to her face. Such luxury, she always concluded, more unnecessary extravagance.

The well used, oval coffee table was arranged directly in front of the sofa. It was a reminder of the many delicious refreshments Beverly had prepared and served to the Driscoll's, and their guests over the years. A single cup of hot tea sat on the corner of the table releasing the delightful fragrance of brewed mint. Rebecca was not offended. She had never been invited to share a cup of tea with the woman of the house. Why would this time be different?

The floor covered with a white, woolen carpet was so very soft. In fact, to Rebecca, who had walked mainly on concrete and bare wood floors for most of her life, walking on this carpet must be exactly what it would feel like if one could walk on a cloud of marshmallows. Well, Rebecca thought, I've pretty much surveyed the entire room and still, I'm waiting. Mrs. Driscoll picked up her tea, sipped it and seemed to be in no hurry. So Rebecca figured when the tea was gone, so would be the silence. Until then, the quiet was deafening. In self-defense, she turned again to the room. This time she focused on the beautiful, colonial brass chandelier hanging from the ceiling. On sunny days, it put on quite a show. Rebecca liked to watch the prism rainbow form on the sparkling, crystal, chimneys.

Enough! If this lady doesn't soon talk, I'm going to scream. Please say something. For heaven's sake, there isn't anything left in this room to distract me. Finally, thank goodness, the tea cup was empty. Now, quick, tell me what this is all about.

"Rebecca, while Mr. Driscoll and I are pleased with the way you handle all your chores and the time you spend with Annie, we feel that you need to do more."

More! What the heck is she talking about? Rebecca was surprised and shocked at this woman's brash suggestion. Why, with all I do around the house now and with taking care of little Annie and helping her with her school work, I barely have enough time for myself as it is.

"What do you have in mind, Mrs. Driscoll?" Puzzled, Rebecca asked, rubbing her hands nervously. "I'm afraid I'm confused."

"Then I will get right to the point. Rebecca, you need to get an outside job. I suggest you find employment where you can work on Wednesday and Friday nights after school and then, again, all day Saturday." The sound of authority in her voice left no room for debate as she continued. "I know for a fact that J.J. Newberry's has openings for several cashiers. Stop in tomorrow and fill out an application."

Oh, my nerves. Here we go again. She's rocking my boat and just when I was sailing along so smoothly with the way things were going. Why? Before she had a chance to ask, Mrs. Driscoll robbed her of her curiosity and supplied the answer.

"Rebecca, as you grow older, you need to earn your keep."

I thought I was doing that all along. She dared not voice her deduction.

"Now, the stipend we give you is not much but it does add an expense to our budget. Plus, we feed you and provide your necessities. It all adds up and now the time has come for you to help financially. You will give us half of your earned salary. With all that we do, that is only fair and equitable."

End of conversation. With that Mrs. Driscoll simply walked out of the room leaving the apprehensive Rebecca in uncertainty, yet again.

Her head spinning, into her mind popped her English Literature class and the sixteenth century clergyman and writer, Robert Burton who said, 'Fear keeps men in obedience.' Rebecca got the job.

Chapter 18

1955

First things first, Rebecca dropped her extra-curricular activities. There were only two. Each Friday night she wrote an article for the school's newspaper dealing primarily with songs in the mainstream and their celebrity artists. She had a lot of fun with it. Then every Wednesday night, she helped man the refreshment stand at the football game. That was fun, too, with a lot of interaction with her peers. But, a new job gave her no choice. There just wasn't enough time to do everything.

She was willing, well reluctantly, to make changes. Still, there was one exception. No matter how heavy her schedule and responsibilities, no matter how little leisure time was left, she adamantly refused to encroach on their date time. Saturday nights belonged to them. Case closed. If that meant she might have to work late into the night to finish chores when she got home from her date, so be it. Lance came first in her book, he was, after all, the center of her universe and she would not bend. If Mr. and Mrs. Driscoll didn't like it, then they could just lump it. If worse came to worse, she would live in the local YWCA. That's big talk for someone with such a small purse.

Fortunately, it never came to that. She managed to juggle time and tasks and, in the end, the cashier's job at the local five and dime store, actually turned out to be advantageous. Up to this point, her experience dealing with money was limited. With her earnings, she was learning a valuable lesson, one that would travel on with her in life; how to budget.

* * * * *

Graduation was rapidly approaching and the Driscoll's made it clear there would be no special celebration. Once again, Rebecca was told to meet with the Driscoll's.

She wondered, now what? At least this time, Mrs. Driscoll did not make her sit and suffer in anticipation. She jumped in and let her have it with both barrels just as soon as Rebecca was seated.

"Rebecca. As you know, you will soon be graduating from high school. Mr. Driscoll and I don't know what the hullabaloo is all about. While we know there will be some parties to honor the event, we want you to know we do not believe in that sort of nonsense. So don't expect anything from us."

Rebecca had not even entertained the thought. Why she never even had a real birthday party before. So why would she expect a party for any other occasion? She couldn't help but think, man, these people really are from left field. But she sat and listened, just the same to the explanation they felt needed to be expressed.

"Think about it, Rebecca. Why would you reward someone for doing what is expected? Rebecca, you are expected to graduate. That is, after all, the reason for your schooling, isn't it?"

If she was expecting Rebecca to answer, she didn't wait. She simply went on with her assessment. "If you have your eye set on college, forget it. College is totally out of the picture."

College? What picture? Where is she coming up with this stuff? I've had more than my share of classrooms. College never entered my mind. I can hardly wait to be over with school, once and for all. Why is she telling me this? Why didn't she just ask my opinion in the first place?

Bottom line, according to Mrs. Driscoll's account, men went to college. Women married. "Don't think for one minute, that we have plans to finance a college endeavor for you. In this household, this is how it works." With that set-up, Mrs. Driscoll outlined the drill while Mr. Driscoll nodded his agreement. "Rebecca, you will work until you meet a reliable young man. After a respectable period of time, you will marry and move out."

So that's it in a nutshell, Rebecca thought, I'm being kicked out. Why? Suddenly, it hit her. Holy Hannah, I get it. What connivers. They get a live-in maid and nanny for practically nothing. That's their angle. When I leave they can just go back to the orphanage and wangle their way into getting another younger servant for lesser wages. And I thought these were decent people.

"Now, as far as Annie is concerned," Mrs. Driscoll was still talking. Rebecca just wasn't still listening. "That is another matter. She is, after all, family." Had the Driscoll's cared just a trifle more, Rebecca said to herself, they would have noticed the male school ring on my finger. It would have assisted them in their assessment and saved them this grief. That is if they considered this to be grief.

"So, now we understand each other, correct, Rebecca?" the lady of the house asked. "There's no room for hard feelings." It sounded like an after-thought with an added smile. "We do wish you well."

"I understand. Thank you." What else could she say?

"Good. You are excused."

Rebecca went straight to her room. Stewing over this last scene, she flopped on the bed. I'll never really understand these people and their talk about college expenses. I never asked them for anything. In fact, they were the ones who requested I live with them. It wasn't the other way around. It doesn't matter. College isn't for me. I'm content with the status quo. My heart is set on marrying Lance. The only continuing schooling I want is what we will learn together as a married couple and she fell asleep under the cover of that warm thought.

The school schedule for the next week was changed as it always did for the seniors. Classes over and exams taken, students were basically just putting in time to cover the state's attendance requirement. There was nothing more to do except rehearse for the commencement ceremony. It was a lazy kind of fun time without responsibilities, never to be recaptured.

Sitting on the school's stone steps, Lance and Rebecca waited for practice to start. It was the daily routine now that graduation was just a few days away.

"Rebecca, my folks are having a small get together with family and friends to celebrate my graduation." He chuckled, "Guess they thought this day would never happen. I kind of owe both of them bragging rights. They earned it. Anyway, we would like for you to join us, that is if that doesn't interfere with any of your graduation party plans."

Rebecca had met Lance's parents. It was briefly one night, before they headed out to a football game. Lance stopped in with Rebecca draped on his arm, naturally to show her off. Rebecca liked his folks right off the bat and they liked her.

Lance knew that Rebecca lived with friends. She had told him that story some time ago. It had been during one of the times when they had stopped in at Cee's.

Cenon's Shop was the local teen hangout that served the best burgers in town. Cenon, simply known as Cee, was Greek. Proud of his heritage, he lived up to the meaning of his Greek name. Appropriately, it meant friendly. Anyone entering his shop received the same greeting. He flashed a warm smile and, in broken English, shouted out in his native tongue, 'Yasou.' Anybody even remotely acquainted with Cee, knew it meant hello and responded in kind.

In the front of his store, were several glass cases that housed homemade chocolate candies. In a small room in the back, he mastered the art of candy-making. One bite of his delicious creations was all the proof needed. They were the best in town. The middle of the store had a soda fountain and a grill where he cooked hamburgers to die for. Toward the back of the store, he had thoughtfully set up several booths and installed a jukebox which he kept up to date with the latest hits.

Having no family of his own in the United States, this proud, naturalized, American citizen hung all teenyboppers who frequented his shop, on his family tree. For them, he even had set aside a small section for dancing. Almost daily, the regulars stopped in after school or after a ball game. They would eat, dance and even do a little homework together and he loved every minute of it.

His young people came for a hamburger or a cherry coke or vanilla shake or float from the fountain and for his good humor. It was well known that money didn't grow on trees. Quite simply, there wasn't a lot of it to circulate and it was not uncommon for a couple to order one shake with two straws. He didn't mind.

Today, Rebecca and Lance sat in a booth in the back away from the rest of the action. Lance wasn't prying. The subject of parents just came up in the course of their conversation. In fact, Rebecca was the one who initiated it.

"Your folks are so nice. Your Dad, well, he is something else. Every chance he gets, he taps my nose and tells me, I'm cute as a button. He makes me blush."

"Yep, that's Dad's way. Did you hear him when you were about to leave? He said you were the prettiest thing that came down the pike."

"I did, and that really clinched it. I felt my face go beet-red."

"He is an out and out flirt, but he's harmless."

"Like father like son?"

"Hey, that's not fair. I'm not a flirt."

"Like fun you're not. But as long as it is with me, it's okay," Rebecca declared with a huge grin on her face. Then the inevitable happened.

"Rebecca, tell me about your folks. I know you live with family friends but I'd like to know about your family."

Oh, gosh, how did I not see this coming? I feel like I've just been hit with a ton of bricks. Trapped, her mind racing, she had to choose and quickly.

Should I tell him about the orphanage and risk losing him. I mean, who wants to date an orphan? Or should I bite the bullet, step up to the plate, and hit the proverbial, pretend homerun made up of my familiar deceptive facts? My head hurts. Ouch, now, I'm getting a headache. One good thing, the lights are always dim in here. Way to go Cee. Save on that electric bill. Her decision made, she took a deep breath. Here goes nothing but I've got to stick with what I know best.

"There's not much to tell, Lance," she said calmly, all the while knots were tying up in her stomach. "My parents both died when I was very young. I was raised by an aunt until she died and then I went to live with friends of my aunt's. That's how I came to live with the Driscoll's."

"Tough break." Reaching across the table, Lance gently held her hand. "Do you remember anything about your folks?"

Darn, she thought. It's hard lying to an understanding person. But, Lance was sincere. He felt badly for his Rebecca being raised without parents. Although he fooled around with his parents giving them a hard time, he loved them and they were always there for him. He couldn't imagine it any other way.

That opened the door and she was right back in the orphanage surrounded by her friends embellishing stories about their families. "I do remember some things and some things were told to me along the way." Well, she said to herself, part of that holds some truth. "Let me see, now, my father? He died in the war. He was a hero."

"A war hero, wow!" Lance was impressed and his enthusiasm reignited her imagination. Eager to hear more, he sat quietly. Rebecca took a sip of the cool, refreshing, cherry coke they were sharing in hopes that it would refresh her memory. It wasn't at all necessary. Rebecca had this part of her story engraved on her heart. It came directly from the orphanage's small library. How well she remembered copying the information and carrying it with her in her pocket. She recalled, too, as a little girl, how she had struggled with the pronunciation of some words. Tenaciously, she studied the written description of that soldier's past events and in time, was able to commit it to memory.

The encyclopedia described an account of a real live war hero which she immediately adopted. Although she had said a little prayer for him at the time, she had long since forgotten that man's name. She didn't need it. She had inserted her fabricated father's name for so long, it was to her, that which belonged. It was the only father she had ever known.

"I'm told that he served in the 82nd Airborne Unit during World War II and he was one of a select few chosen to perform a jump for General Dwight D. Eisenhower, and the Russian General Zhukov."

"Jumping for the president! How cool is that?"

"Well, he wasn't president yet. At that time, he was only Supreme Commander of the Allied Forces in Europe."

"Yeah, only," he teased, "Rebecca that was still a fantastic honor. That must have been something else. I can't imagine being brave enough to jump out of a moving airplane in the first place. Then, jeez, you have to depend fully on the rip cord to release in time. What if the giant umbrella chute didn't open? No way could you descend safely to the earth. No way could I ever do that." Shaking his head, intrigued, he continued,

"Can you imagine being on the ground looking up and seeing a sky chock-full of paratroopers dangling from those mushroom-shaped gadgets actually falling? What a sight that must have been?" Impressed with those courageous thoughts, he said, "Boy, Rebecca you have every right to be proud of your father and I bet jumping for Ike, must have been really something else for him, too."

Rebecca smiled and slipped back into her fairy tale pleased that she remembered the popular 'I Like Ike' slogan to add credence to her story. Back then, it was found everywhere. Caught up in her own story, she shared her feelings with Lance. "You know, I like to think that my father was a bit like Eisenhower. I know Ike was the only professional soldier to serve as president in this century but, my father was courageous with a lot of militant nerve. Strong, undaunted, just plain brave and I like to think had he not been killed in action that maybe he could have filled those shoes." She knew she was stretching it but it didn't matter. Right now, her imagination was racing to put her made-up dad high on the pedestal right where her real father would belong. She could just feel it and she couldn't help herself as she went on with the grandstanding.

"He had a lot of Ike's attributes." Smiling, she added, "What a president he would have made." She had always wondered what it would have been like to actually have a father. No doubt about it. She had been cheated. She definitely had earned bragging rights. She ranked this presidential speculation high above the others.

Closing her eyes, Rebecca savored the story she relayed to Lance. At this point, she wasn't trying to impress him. It just felt good to indulge in the warmth, once again, of her fabricated father's heroism. It was, after all, hers to keep and from time to time, relive.

Lance waited in anticipation. It was a short wait as Rebecca soon continued.

"Apparently, he also led the patrol behind enemy lines and knocked out a railroad and three coastal guns and for this brave action he received the French medal, the Croix de Guerre with silver gilt star." For a moment, she remembered how long it had taken her to get the pronunciation of that medal just right. But nailed it, she did.

"Wow, Rebecca I can understand how that must make you so proud."

"It does. Wait until you hear this." Now, she was really getting into the spirit of her father's bravery. How could she not? It was exciting no matter when she told it.

"He was awarded other medals, too."

"Really?"

"Yes. There was the Bronze Star Medal both the First Oak Leaf Cluster and the Second Leaf Cluster, the Good Conduct Medal and, I almost forgot, he actually participated in five theaters. Now let me think." She paused feigning her ability to gather her thoughts. It was convincing and added more credence to her story. "Oh, yes, he received the European-African-Middle Eastern Campaign Medal. And, one silver service star in lieu of five bronze service stars. That was, of course, for participation in the Southern France, Rome-Arno, Rhineland, Ardennes-Alsace and, let me think. Oh, yes, the Central Europe Theater. He also was presented the Army of Occupation Medal with Germany Clasp."

She was pleased she had that information down pat. The soldier from whom she had borrowed the accolades had earned more awards but Rebecca thought she should stop at this point. It was, after all, one thing to impress her orphan friends who lived vicariously through her story and quite another to make it sound viable to her boyfriend.

Lance sat there spellbound. She could see he was hooked. Why? Finally her curiosity prompted her to ask.

"Tell me, Lance, what is this fascination with military history and war stories that grip so many men?"

"Well, I can't speak for others but mine started with my older brother, Dan."

"Tell me about him."

"Okay. Dan was drafted into the Korean War. It was a lottery draft and I thought my brother was one of the lucky ones. Of course, my folks didn't see it that way. When he came home his stories were enough to make me wake up shivering in the middle of the night. It was the craziest thing. I wanted to hear and at the same time was afraid to listen. Somehow there was this bond, brothers, a kinship, strengthened by glamorizing the horrors of war. Maybe my brother didn't know or maybe he didn't care that the United States was in pursuit of ideological and political objectives. He never mentioned it. He just went there, like so many other young, drafted soldiers, to stop those red commies in the North from invading the people in South Korea. He told me the North Koreans were ruthless. They caused a nightmare for those in the South and, I have to tell you, Rebecca, I lost a lot of sleep over the things he said went on. Like I said, war is fascinating -hell, but fascinating."

He paused to sip on his coke. She sat waiting trying not to imagine what heartless people did to each other in true life.

"My folks viewed the war differently. They just wanted their son back in one piece. They liked Ike, but mainly because he finally brought Dan home. It was in 1953, when the fighting stopped. That's when the Korean War Armistice Agreement was signed."

Rebecca could feel the passion within him deepen but, didn't say a word.

"You know, I liked hearing about the DMZ zone set up but, funny thing. Dan never filled me in on that. My father, who faithfully followed the happenings in Korea, was the one who explained that part of history to me. He explained how the fighting stopped but it was never replaced by permanent settlement. He told me about the DMZ, standing for demilitarized zone, that was a geographic buffer zone set up between North and South Korea. Basically, Rebecca, it was designated as no man's land. The unoccupied strip of land runs across the width of Korea. Nothing is there. That is nothing except some wild life." It became apparent to Rebecca. Lance was too young to really understand all these affairs of state but, old enough to appreciate heroes like his brother Dan in one war and Rebecca's father in yet another.

"Does that answer your question about my fascination with war stories?"

"I think it does, and thanks for sharing it with me."

"Okay. Now, we covered your father and war and I think we got off track a little with my interest in the subject. Tell me about your mother."

"Not much to tell, Lance. She was kind and loving but, she got sick. It wasn't a long illness. It was just that the kind of cancer she had spread quickly and destroyed every cell in its path. I still can see her dressed in a floral housedress and apron, cooking with a large spoon in one hand and a dishtowel in the other. I'm afraid I don't remember much more, but my aunt did tell me my mother was the best cook. Apparently, she was famous for her pot roast. Sometimes, I pretend that I can smell its aroma cooking with lots of potatoes and carrots and onions." She closed her eyes and inhaled a deep breath of made-up scent memories.

Lance just sat there quietly digesting what Rebecca had told him. He didn't want to upset her but, all he could think about was how hard it must have been on her losing her parents, especially at an early age. How many times, when he was younger, did he need his parents? How many stray cats and dogs did he bring home where his mother helped him to nurse them back to health? How many math and science tests did he pass because his Dad, after a hard day's work, spent time teaching him? Even now, at his age, he still brought his problems to his parents. Excellent sounding boards, they listened. His parents were there for him and he could not imagine his life without them.

How tough her life must be going it alone. He thought it but, didn't voice it. Instead, he took the road that would least hurt her. Holding her hand, he reassured her. "Rebecca thanks for telling me about your parents. It sounds like they were great and, I'm glad you have good memories." He wanted to hear more about her mother but, this wasn't the time. He could see that Rebecca was already close to tears.

"You're welcome." The words came out almost too quickly but, then it was her story. She need never be ashamed of her background. It was such a good one. Only sometimes, but not too often, the way she got it really bothered her.

* * * * *

Needless to say, Rebecca was able to participate in Lance's graduation party.

Like a giant umbrella, the white canopy tent sheltered beautifully decorated tables filled with food, and lovely dressed guests from the warm sun. Rebecca was impressed. A record player provided festive music for the occasion. It was all so amazing. Taking her by her hand, Lance's mother happily escorted Rebecca to the head table.

"How do you like the cake?" she asked.

"Oh, Mrs. Miles, what a nice surprise." Rebecca was genuinely touched.

"What are my two favorite girls up to?" Lance asked as he approached them.

"Your Mom was showing me the graduation cake. Isn't it something, Lance?"

"Nothing but the best comes from my Mom." And he gave his mother a bear hug. Loving every minute of it, she struggled just a little. Then she urged, "Oh, Lance. Stop. Really now, let me show you and Rebecca the cake." Releasing her, she went on to describe her masterpiece. "I decorated it myself. See, first I made the cake in the shape of a graduation mortarboard. I added two tiny diplomas, one for each of you, and then I used white icing for writing the message."

"I think the cake and the message are beautiful, Mrs. Miles. Look Lance, it reads, Congratulations to Lance and Rebecca." Turning, she gave his mother a hug.

"I can't thank you enough for including me, Mrs. Miles. That was so very thoughtful of you."

"You are welcome, my dear. Can't have two graduates and only one name on the cake now, can we? Here now, you and Lance hold the knife together to cut the first piece. But wait until I get the camera." Rebecca was impressed and deeply moved. It was good, too, to hear honest-to-goodness-related people talking and laughing. Some even bombarded Lance with memorable childhood tales. Naturally, they felt it their duty to embellish just a little and Lance loved it. Of course, like a stand-up comic, he jokingly denied every word. Thanks to Lance's family, it was a happy day filled with good friends, good food and the makings of good memories. Before she knew it, the party in which she was remembered was over. Rebecca was in for another surprise. It was nice when she got home and found that Beverly had not forgotten her, either.

"Come. Sit here, Rebecca. I made a chocolate cake for you with your favorite milk chocolate icing."

"Why, thank you Beverly." Rebecca sat. Although still full, she found space for a slice of the cake made with Beverly's love. "This is for you, too." She handed Rebecca a beautifully wrapped gift. "It's not every day, we have a graduate in the house."

Speechless and with fingers shaking just a tad, Rebecca opened the unexpected gift. Beverly's thoughtfulness brought tears to this graduate's eyes. Never in her entire life had Rebecca owned a watch before, let alone a Bulova.

"Beverly, I don't know what to say. It is absolutely beautiful. Do you realize this is my very first watch, ever?" Slowly, she took the treasure from the safety of its box and gently put it on her wrist. Smiling, she held her wrist to her ear and listened. Then, stretching her arm out as far as it would go, and bringing it back in close again, she never took her eyes off the watch, giving it the admiration is deserved.

"Look how it sparkles, Beverly." Rebecca twirled around in her delight. "It's absolutely exquisite. Thank you so much." With that, she gave Beverly a big hug. "I can't believe it's mine."

Having never owned a watch, Rebecca was not familiar with its features. She just thought it was convenient to be able to look at your wrist at will and know the time. Beverly, on the other hand, having spent hours in the local jewelry shop discussing its various characteristics felt it her obligation to educate Rebecca on the design and benefits of this particular time piece.

It had cost Beverly a pretty penny but Rebecca's reaction was worth it. It was a special watch for a special, young lady.

"Let me tell you a little about what you are wearing. It's a 17 jewel, Bulova, ladies wristwatch. As you can see, it is gold with a diamond on each lug. And look at the diamonds. They're set in white gold to really make them sparkle while the rest of the Bezel is yellow gold."

"The what? Sorry Beverly, I don't know what that is."

"It's the grove that holds the watch crystal. Here, let me show you." Taking Rebecca's wrist, she pointed out the Bezel. Rebecca nodded her head in understanding so Beverly continued. "As you can see, the watch has a matching gold band and the dial has raised gold numerals and hands. I especially picked out a square dial because it is so much more readable. Of course, look here." Beverly proudly pointed to the face of the watch. "It is Bulova signed." Rebecca looked and sure enough, there it was, the word declaring its distinction. *Bulova* was printed right at the top.

She couldn't resist. Placing her hand over her forehead displaying her watch, she announced seriously, "Oh, it is so hot in here with my new Bulova watch on." The action elicited hearty laughter from both the giver and the recipient of the impressive gift.

Rebecca found herself to be the proud owner of her very own watch. It was hard to believe that it actually belonged to her. It was hard to believe that she had actually graduated. It was hard to believe, come Fall, Lance was heading off to college.

Chapter 19

1956

Changes were in the air. Summer, quickly fading, was making way for the Fall and Fall was making way for the start of college. They spent as much time together as possible because they knew, come September, separation was inevitable.

She tried not to think about it but, that in itself was a problem. She found herself walking around with a giant lump in her throat, ready to cry at the drop of a hat.

It was Saturday and this afternoon she promised to take Annie to the playground.

"Let's ride the bike. Please Rebecca," Annie begged. "I like when you tote me on the handlebars and, I promise I won't wiggle well, maybe just a little, but not much. Please, please."

"I much prefer to have you sit on the seat where you can hold onto my waist."

"Oh, please. It's more fun on the handlebars and besides the playground is just right up the street. Pleaseee."

"I don't know, Annie. Let me think." Clapping her hands excitedly, Annie was sure she had the solution.

"I know, Rebecca. I know how we can decide." With that, Annie extended her clenched fist. Rebecca, familiar with this decision-maker method, took her cue and extended hers as well. Then gently tapping each fist, one and then the other, in rhythm with the words, Annie began with the all important tie breaker...- "eeny-meeny-miney-mo, catch a tadpole by the toe, if he hollers let him go, eeny-meeny-miney-mo." The person whose fist is touched last when the ditty is over, wins. It was going in Annie's favor until Annie sneezed and lost her place.

"Do over, do over." Rebecca seized the opportunity and quickly proclaimed her right. This time, Annie delighted in her do-over victory and with Rebecca's help, excitedly climbed onto her favorite bike spot.

"Okay. Here we go. Now be careful. Keep your feet away from the spokes."

"Wheee." Annie shouted gleefully and they were off.

The two were riding Annie's bike which was still too big for her. It had been a birthday gift from her parents and was given with the idea that she would grow into it. While it was a good plan, to date, it was not yet workable. The Schwinn was a beauty with its white frame edged in hot pink, a pink chain cover and long, pink fringes that flowed out from the rubber handles on each handlebar.

Thank goodness for Lance. He was an excellent teacher and Rebecca, a good student. Rebecca felt if Annie was going to get any use from this bike, it was up to her. But first, of course, Rebecca had to learn. Lance patiently taught her and that is how Rebecca found herself in the driver's seat today.

She was glad for the bike's chain guard. At least she didn't have to use those annoying pant leg clips. The guard was enough to prevent her slacks from getting caught in the moving chain and causing a disaster. She was a quick learner and within two weeks time, Rebecca was riding everywhere. She wanted to be an expert before she would chance toting her precious cargo.

The ride to the playground was just as much fun for the big girl as it was for the little one. Once again, Rebecca was reminded of childhood fun lost for orphans.

"Push me. Push me higher, Rebecca, higher." The little girl squealed in delight as she sailed on the high-flying swing. Back and forth, back and forth she went until finally, she had enough and used her feet to help slow her down to a gentle halt.

Jumping off the swing, she headed right for the sandbox with Rebecca close behind.

"Rebecca, want to help me build a castle?"

"Just try to stop me. Wait, oh Annie, look over there." Mesmerized by a furry caterpillar, they paused in their architectural endeavor. They watched enthralled by the syncopated movement of this creature's many legs.

"Can I touch it, Rebecca? Can I?" "Of course you may," Rebecca quietly reminded Annie of the correct usage, "but very gently."

Annie moved her hand slowly and just when she was about to touch it, lost her nerve. Quickly, she drew back her hand. "Don't be afraid. Here, give me your hand. We'll touch it together. Okay?"

"Oh, it is so soft," Annie cooed proud of her bravery.

"See, Annie. Caterpillars won't hurt you. And you know what else?"

"What?"

"Fuzzy caterpillars turn into beautiful butterflies. Did you know that?"

"No," she answered amazed. "I like butterflies. I like chasing them. I never caught one. But, some day, I will."

"That would be something. So you see Annie, without these caterpillars, there would be no butterflies." While the caterpillar was still the center of Annie's fascination, Rebecca, took the moment to add to her lesson. "Remember Annie, if you love butterflies, you must at least like caterpillars."

"Hmmm." Annie thought about that for a second. "Know what? From now on, Rebecca, I'm gonna do both." Rebecca smiled as they watched their fuzzy caterpillar crawl into the grass and out of sight.

"Well, well, what have we here?" The familiar, masculine voice boomed. They turned to find Lance stepping into the sandbox to join them. Pleasantly surprised, Rebecca asked, "Hi Lance. We have a date tonight. What brings you to our neck of the woods so early? I thought you had to mow the lawn for your folks?"

"I did. Not only that. I also helped my Dad fix the screen door that was sticking. I don't fool around." Grinning ear to ear, he boasted of his accomplishments. Then slowly, the smile vanished as he turned serious. "The truth of the matter, Rebecca is that I wanted to finish quickly so I could get here to see you. You mentioned you and Annie were going to the playground. So here I am."

The expression on his face was puzzling but, she didn't say a word. She was glad to see him here. She just wondered why the early visit.

"Rebecca," he asked, "could we sit on the bench over there and talk? We can keep an eye on Annie from there."

Now she was more than a little concerned. She had no idea what to expect. Nodding, she quickly agreed. "Annie, darling, see how big you can build the castle. Lance and I will be on that bench right over there for a while, okay?"

"Sure." Not about to take a chance on messing up her building, Annie answered without even lifting her head.

The sun had gotten up hours ago and ruled the day still. Rebecca sat back and titled her head to savor the warmth of its reign. It was just for a moment before she started thinking about his strange behavior. That quickly, terrible thoughts popped into her head. Oh, no. He's sick. She sat up straight and he had her full attention.

"I just can't do it, Rebecca."

"Can't do what?"

"I can't go away to college and leave you behind for four, long, years. I can't and I won't. My mind is made up. I wanted you to be the first to know."

He wasn't going to die. Rebecca could breathe again and, of course, she was elated with his plans just shared. It was wonderful news. Still, she felt a twinge of guilt. How could I be so selfish? His parents will be devastated.

"Lance, you have to go. Your parents will be absolutely sick if you don't. They have all these grandiose plans for you. They want you to…" He didn't let her finish.

"That's just it, Rebecca. All the plans are theirs. I never really wanted college. That was always their dream, not mine. I just want to settle down with you for the rest of my life. Is that so wrong?" She watched his shoulders begin to droop. If ever he needed her support, it was now. She didn't expect this. Not now, anyway. Oh, sure, they had talked about marriage but that was for after college. Just the same, sitting here next to the man she loved, thinking about taking that big step, she couldn't help feeling all tingly with goose bumps dancing on her arms. Yes his desires would fulfill her every dream. But then, again she could not let him throw away his future. Or could she? It was, after all his choice to make, wasn't it? Isn't it odd, she thought, how rationalization always works in favor of the person doing the analyzing?

Then she knew. She wasn't being fair. She simply was justifying her cause.

"Lance, listen. Go to college. Get your degree. Then when you graduate, you can get a good job and we can get married. Four years is not all that long when you think of it in terms of then spending a lifetime together."

As logical as that plan was, the idea of separation still didn't make sense. Her smile weak, followed by an uncomfortable silence, her attempt to sway his decision wasn't working. He wasn't buying it.

Taking her hands into his, looking directly into her eyes, he made his intention very clear.

"Rebecca, I want our lifetime together to start now. Will you marry me?"

Stunned, she sat speechless. Her reluctance, taken as a need for additional convincing, moved him quickly to lay out his very sound plan.

"I don't need a college degree now. I just need you. I plan to get a job and then we can marry. I'll save money and enroll in night classes to earn my degree. Don't you see, Rebecca? We can have the best of both worlds, marriage now, college later. Please say, yes." He was not above pleading, if that's what it took. "Please?"

Rebecca still wasn't sure if they should or should not wait. What was very clear was the proposal just made by this man. This man she loved without any doubt. I'm sorry Mr. and Mrs. Miles, she thought. Forgive me. I can't help myself.

"Yes, Lance," she whispered, "the answer to your question is yes."

Releasing a sigh of relief, it was exactly the answer he wanted to hear. Still, far from being cool, calm and collected, nervously he pulled Rebecca close to him. She gulped back happy tears. Resisting the desire to smother her with passionate kisses, he simply held her gently. Had they been anywhere but in public that is precisely what he would have done. For now, his hug would have to fill the bill. Rebecca was more than happy with that arrangement. That plus knowing soon she would become Mrs. Lance Miles was enough to have her floating on cloud nine. "Holy Hannah, Lance, I'm getting married."

"I know, Rebecca, me, too," he smiled.

"Tonight, Rebecca, I'll tell my folks. Okay?"

"We're in this together. We'll tell your folks. I'll be right there at your side."

"Good, Rebecca. See you tonight." With that and a quick kiss, he went on his way.

"Let's go Annie. Beverly doesn't like us to be late for dinner. Climb aboard."

Rebecca barely touched her food. How could she? Her mind was happily devouring re-runs of Lance's proposal.

"Rebecca, you haven't eaten much. You're so quiet. Are you okay?"

"I am, Beverly. Guess I'm just not hungry." Should she or shouldn't she? Here we go again. Decisions, decisions, but she just wasn't sure. Sitting there quietly eating a roll, she came to a conclusion. "Beverly, would you like to know why I'm not hungry?"

"Of course." Immediately, Beverly sat down opposite Rebecca, folded her hands on the table and was all ears. Now, the happy candidate for marriage could contain herself no longer. Gone was her somber mode and like Mount Vesuvius, out flowed her excitement. "Lance and I are getting married."

It only took a matter of seconds for the message to register in Beverly's brain and one more second for her arms to wrap Rebecca in a tight hug. "Well, I'll be dipped."

"Beverly, you always have a way with words." Then after eagerly filling in the details Beverly was dying to hear, reluctantly she admitted her apprehension. "Meeting with his parents is not going to be a cake-walk. I don't mind telling you, Beverly, I'm nervous."

"Now, don't worry about what they think. It's your life. You live it."

Just as genuinely happy as she was for Rebecca, Beverly was for herself. After all, this was no shot-gun wedding. Aah, she thought, tonight I get a good night's sleep.

Rebecca was glad for her decision. Sharing her news with Beverly was exciting. Now she could hardly wait to surprise Theresa, Annette and Annmarie. She would write to them tomorrow. For now, first things first, it was almost time to go.

As coincidence would have it, it was date night. Only it wasn't about entertaining themselves with a trip to the movie theater or to an amusement park excursion. This date night was unique There was no fun involved, just high stakes. D-Day, they were about to launch an invasion on his parents.

"You can't mean this, Lance," his mother slumped in her chair crying softly.

"Please, Mom, don't cry." He hated to see her like this, although honestly, the possibility of her reaction was anticipated. Surely, the tears would stop just as soon as she had a chance to digest and accept their plan.

On the other hand, his father's explosive reaction caught him off guard. He was absolutely livid. Lance had seen his father's temper flare before but, always it was sudden and short-lived. Never had he witnessed this outrage. Frankly, he started to feel the jitters.

Maybe, he thought, this isn't such a good idea. Maybe there's a good chance he won't let our early marriage fly. It wasn't easy for Rebecca, either. Where was the good-natured man she knew? This stranger flipped his lid and threw her for a loop. Holy Hannah, she thought. I knew this was going to be stormy but, I never expected to run into a hurricane.

"Are you nuts?" his angry father yelled. "You're throwing your future out the window. Do you hear this, Jennie? Your son has gone crazy!"

"Tom, please, your blood pressure," his concerned wife advised.

"Look. Look at your Mother. Are you proud of yourself?"

"Dad, please listen. I'm sorry I didn't mean for Mom to cry. But I have a plan. It's a good one, Dad. Please stop screaming and listen."

"Don't you dare tell me to stop. I'll scream if I want to." His anger triggered mind games. He wasn't yelling sense; just yelling for the sake of yelling.

Frightened, Rebecca in her quiet way intervened. She had to do something. Taking him by his arm, she aimed the loud man in the direction of his recliner. "Mr. Miles, sit here, please. Try to calm down. Your face is so red. It's not good for you." She wasn't sure where this was going, but thank goodness, he was receptive to her suggestion. He went on with his interrogation shooting question after question but, at least he did it from a sitting position and actually lowered his voice.

"How in blue blazes do you expect to support yourself and a wife?" He didn't wait for answers. He just kept throwing out his arguments, one after the other. "Where do you expect to live? What are you going to do for a paycheck? How do you plan to earn a living?" Then he fired off the big gun. "What about your dreams of being a doctor?"

"That's your dream, Dad. Not mine." Lance finally jumped in. He couldn't let this one slide. "I just want to be with Rebecca. Don't worry. I'll support her. I'll support the both of us."

As promised, Rebecca stood right by his side but, unfortunately, this unexpected confrontation hurt the cause. It pulled the pins out from under her and as much as she wanted to back him up, she couldn't. It went against all that she had been taught. It wasn't about defending anyone's logic. It was plain and simple. Adults were to be respected. So she just stood there, this woman with her strict Catholic upbringing and while he defended their case, she cringed in her cowardice.

"Mom, Dad. Listen. It's obvious, this is going nowhere. But I will say this. Like it or not, I'm going to marry Rebecca sooner than you thought. Despite what you may think, I do have a plan." Before putting his cards on the table, and half expecting his father to balk, Lance paused. Then using his father's missed opportunity, Lance turned it into his advantage. Finally, he got to explain.

"Both Rebecca and I will work and I will attend night classes. I will earn a degree. Just not in your time frame and not in the field you picked. Obviously Mom, Dad, we would very much like your blessing. But, you have to know. Our minds are made up. With or without it, we are going to do this. Let's go, Rebecca. It's time to leave."

He said all that he had set out to say. Yet, his father's hard-nosed reaction threw him a curve and managed to put a twist in his confidence. It was enough to make him think the better of his mandate. Maybe it was too strict. Then, again, maybe he should just appeal to them once more. Now he was willing to give his parents another chance. Besides, he just couldn't walk out on them.

Taking Rebecca by the hand, he stopped at the front door and extended the olive branch. "Mom, Dad, we know this is all a shock. Rebecca and I apologize for rocking the boat. But, won't you please just think about it? Just think about what was said. Maybe, if it's okay with you, we can talk again?" His father didn't say a word. It was his mother who nodded in agreement.

"In a few days, that will be fine." As she watched her son walk out of her house, she shuddered to think, he might just as easily walk out of her life.

Sleep eluded those immersed in the clouded issue, except of course, for one. Beverly slept like a baby.

Jenny and Tom almost talked the night away. By morning, nothing was settled. Like a yoyo, the pros and cons of their conversation went up and down. At moments, heat entered the discussion while other times, talk was civil.

"I just don't get it, Jenny. He has the world at his fingertips and he's just flipping it away. Everything we worked for is going down the tubes. Does he even think of the extra hours I worked saving for his college education? I trusted him to do the right thing and this slap in the face is the thanks I get?" He punched his pillow. "Wish I could re-shape his half baked ideas as easy as this pillow."

"Tom, be honest. You're hurt."

"Damn right, I am. What do you expect after all I did for him? This is how he repays me?"

"Now, just wait a minute on that score. Since when did it become mandatory that our boys pay us back for raising them? They never even asked to be born. So forget that. Besides, you are not the only one who is hurting. Sure it would have been nice if Lance had become a doctor. But, let's face it. That's not what he wants. Think about it."

Jenny reached over and gently massaged his shoulders. "Relax. You know, Tom," she said softly, "the plan Lance outlined doesn't sound all that bad. After all, it's not like he is giving up college altogether. Night school works. He can get a job and Rebecca can help."

"Come on, Jenny," she may have softened his muscles but not his stance, "Admit it. That won't work. They're too young. They are making a big mistake and I just can't see it any other way." Jenny lost round one.

The next few days were no fun. Tom and Lance gave up talking to each other and it was driving Jenny mad. Finally, she lowered the boom. "Tom, turn off that TV set and listen to me." She was determined. "This silent treatment has got to stop. So his plans are not what you wanted for him. It's not the end of the world."

"Maybe not, Jenny. But, I am so mad. After all I've done for him…I wanted the best…"

"Stop. He knows. We all know what has been done for him. Let it go. Don't drive him away. Let's give them our blessing and help them get started. If we don't, who will?"

It took a lot of soul searching on his part. Still not totally convinced, Tom conceded; not with all the love in his heart, but with more than enough. The determining factor was clear. This clash of wills could escalate into a full-blown feud with disastrous results. He did not want to lose his son. Bottom line, instead of planning to send their son off to college, they found themselves working on his wedding arrangements.

Dictated by circumstances, etiquette took a backseat. For this wedding, the financial responsibility rested squarely on the shoulders of the groom's family. For this, the young couple was equally grateful.

It was to be a small wedding with guests including Lance's family, several relatives and a few of their mutual school friends. After all, everyone knew poor Rebecca's family members were deceased.

Beverly would be there. Rebecca did invite her. How could she not? As for the Driscoll's, Rebecca felt most likely they would resent the need to buy a wedding gift. Needless to say, they did not get an invitation. Should their absence be questioned, Rebecca would simply say they had been called unexpectedly out of town on an urgent personal matter. Too bad little Annie had to be left out but, as Rebecca saw it, she was part of the Driscoll package. As to her dear, old, friends Annmarie, Theresa and Annette, she sent just an announcement. She was sure they would rejoice in her happiness and Rebecca suggested they pass on the good news to their favorite nuns. The announcement, in lieu of an invitation, was intentional and sent for several reasons. First and foremost, she did not want to embarrass her friends in the event they could not afford to send a gift. Secondly, she had not yet formally introduced them to Lance and thirdly, if they could somehow manage to attend, Rebecca risked the chance of exposure. Her life as an orphan was hers to keep hidden. Not even Lance knew. She kept that closet door shut tightly with no intention of ever opening it again. It was that simple.

The weeks ahead, filled with escalating excitement were busy. What with the work involved getting ready for a small wedding, Rebecca wondered how in the world a wedding on a larger scale happened.

Lance's mother and his aunts were heaven sent. They handled the many details Rebecca didn't even know existed.

Rebecca's biggest area of responsibility rested in selecting her bridal gown. Today she planned to ask Beverly to help with this assignment. Beverly was honored.

"Good morning, Beverly. I wondered if there are scramble eggs and, by the way, I wondered if you have any free time today to help me pick out a wedding gown?" Rebecca, casual in her request, took delight in inciting Beverly's enthusiastic reaction.

"What did you say?"

"You mean about the scrambled eggs?"

"No, what did you say after that?"

"Oh, you mean about you helping me pick out my wedding gown?"

"Bingo! Rebecca, you little imp." Hardly able to contain herself, Beverly smothered Rebecca with a hug. "What time do we leave? I'm honored." Of course, she was honored. She earned it. Wasn't she, after all, the one who kept Rebecca on the right track?

Rebecca smiled, "We leave in an hour." She would forever remain unaware of Beverly's secret mission of good intentions.

"I'm ready when you are."

Both excited, they couldn't get to the bridal shop fast enough. Each gown more beautiful than the last, it was the third gown Rebecca modeled that held Beverly spellbound. "Oh, Rebecca, it's absolutely perfect. You look like a fairytale princess. Oh, gosh, I'm going to cry."

"Don't do that, Beverly. Tears are contagious," and the bride-to-be choked back hers.

"Okay, I'll be good." Dabbing at her eyes, she said, "Now turn around. Let me get the full effect."

"Your wish is my command," and Rebecca twirled around to give Beverly the benefit of the gown as seen from all angles.

"Oh, yes, this one is you, Rebecca. It's definitely you." That was all Beverly managed to get out. Like trying to talk while riding over a bumpy road, her voice came out all shaky.

This time, Rebecca let it go. She smiled from ear to ear. "I like this one best, too. It does make me feel like a princess. But there's another reason why I like it, Beverly."

"What's that?"

"Well, it's a vintage 1930's style wedding gown and I like to think that maybe that's around the time my mother would have married. I can't prove that and you probably think I'm crazy. But when I close my eyes, I like to imagine that she wore a gown just like this one."

"I don't think that at all, Rebecca. In fact, I think it is very touching."

"I'm glad Beverly," and Rebecca watched the girl in the mirror turning this way and that with a faraway look in her eye. "I can almost see her in this gown now, so beautiful." As she envisioned and fantasized that woman to be her mother, Rebecca's eyes sparkled with the fabricated apparition.

She was glad for the perk. Being an orphan gave her permission to be very selective in the choice of her parents. She deemed her mother to have been a beautiful bride in a vintage wedding gown and therefore, she was.

Time has a way of marching on and before Rebecca knew it, the special day arrived. Nerves jangled, altar flowers arranged, guests seated, groomsmen ready, two ushers pulled the crash, the long, while linen cloth, down the center of the aisle. When Rebecca first heard its word, she was thrown off guard. She couldn't help but think it was an odd term to be associated with the start of a marriage. It certainly sounded menacing. Almost like walking down on the crash surely led to a collision. She thought it inappropriate and surely it was named by some male pessimist. Well, call it what you want. That will never happen to us. Our marriage will always be right on course.

Nervously, the bride stepped onto the crash and magically, Richard Wagner's Wedding March Processional sounded from the beautiful pipe organ. As the organist played the march, familiar to the congregation as, Here Comes The Bride, the people stood as a sign of their support.

Rebecca clenched the arm of Lance's favorite uncle, took a deep breath, slowly released it and started the distinctive bride's walk up the aisle.

All eyes focused on the lovely bride. Beverly was especially proud. She thought the beautiful gown that combined white lace with chiffon was elegant. It was the perfect choice. She liked the way the lace on the upper portion of the fitted bodice hugged Rebecca's body. She liked the entire gown with all its features: the long sleeves that ended with a wide ruffle and the waistband created with a wide, horizontal band of lace. She liked how the lace continued over the top of the full skirt of flowing white chiffon. The hemline of both the gown and short train were edged with wide lace trim, as well. Oh, yes, she certainly picked out the best for her Rebecca.

Taking a deep breath, she continued patting herself on the back. The headpiece was perfect. It was the unique way the point of the teardrop-shaped headpiece fell exactly at the center of Rebecca's forehead that had caught Beverly's eye. Covered with fake pearls and iridescent sequins, it sparkled. At her suggestion, Rebecca carried the perfect touch, a single pink rose.

Beverly was basking in Rebecca's glory. She was especially pleased with the way the lining on the gown's bodice created just the illusion of a deep "V" neckline. Rebecca liked the neckline, too, but contrary to Beverly's belief, modesty was not the motivating factor.

Instead, it was, in Rebecca's eyes an absolutely perfect showcase for the introduction of her most precious piece of jewelry. Sharing its beauty for the first time, on this her wedding day, Rebecca's purple gold made its debut.

Truly the piece de resistance, it highlighted her bridal ensemble. Getting dressed her fingers trembled as she hooked the clasp of the gold chain protectively holding her heart-shaped amethyst gem. A gift from her mother, she could hardly wait to tell everyone. It was true. At one point in her life, it had, indeed, been given to her by her mother.

Putting it on, Rebecca admired its brilliance in the mirror and was immediately reminded of Sister Regina's words. 'It will bring you love and good fortune.' Smiling, she thought. Well, Sister it begins today. Echoing, too, were her mother's written words –'give this heart to my daughter and tell her I love her.' Rebecca felt her closeness.

Although both the day and the wedding were picture perfect, the wonderful celebration came to an end much too quickly. All the planning and preparations and partying were done and over-with. In fact, it seemed the entire day flew by in one gigantic whirlwind. With its end, for better or worse, began the married life of the young Mr. and Mrs. Lance Harrington Miles.

Chapter 20

~

Mr. and Mrs. Lance Harrington Miles

"Y ou be sure to visit me now, won't you, Beverly?"

"Just try to stop me," she said dabbing her misty eyes. With that last farewell, Rebecca left the Driscoll's household ending yet another chapter in her life.

Despite their disappointment in Lance's choice to marry young, his parents were there for them and provided them with a comfortable place to live. Converting the upstairs of their garage into a cozy apartment, Rebecca had a new home.

* * * * *

Captivated by love, the heat from their passion seared their hearts and nothing could ever extinguish its flame. Yes, she happily thought, our marriage will last forever. She had no reason to think otherwise. Little did she suspect in just two short months, trouble would raise its ugly head.

It is reputed that a deficiency in either the sex or money department of any given marriage is the assailant of unsuspecting couples. Rebecca and Lance had an abundance of one and a pittance of the other. It was just a matter of time before the enemy would creep into their alliance.

Lance was still unemployed. Of course, it didn't matter. They were, after all, newlyweds and he would find a job. They were both sure of it or so they said.

Sitting in bed, he wrapped his arms around her. Expecting more, she was surprised to discover his only intent, at the moment, was in talking.

"Listen, Rebecca. I know you're concerned but I'm going to get a job. Just wait and see."

"I know you will Lance." Sitting here with him, she shared his confidence. Yet there were times, when she felt a nagging she couldn't explain. Maybe it had something to do with the fact that she had heard this promise before and that it was always Lance who brought up the subject. It seemed to be bothering him a whole lot more than it did her.

Presenting his assurances affectionately, he tucked his hand under her chin, lifted her face to his, and kissed her as only he could.

"Now, don't worry. We have each other and besides," he added, "we still have wedding gift money left. Okay?"

"Okay, Lance." If he was trying to make her feel secure, this conversation missed the mark. It wasn't like him and she was concerned.

Nestled in his arms as he started to doze, she thought about her new life and how much she loved it. Keeping house, cooking and cleaning for just the two of them, she reveled in this new found freedom. The schedules and cooking were hers alone to work out. She cuddled close to her new husband. It was her turn to predict the future.

She whispered softly. "Don't worry. You'll find work and I promise to be the best wife and homemaker ever. Just wait and see." Rebecca worked on keeping her end of the bargain. Being the loving wife was easy. Housekeeping, well that was another story. Still she was learning and having fun in the process. So she burned a few meals. He didn't mind. In fact, he seemed to be enjoying his wife in her new role and, except for this money issue, he in his.

Another plus fell into their laps. His folks, not only furnished their apartment, but provided them with a television set, as well. Life was good.

＊ ＊ ＊ ＊ ＊

"Rebecca, it's time for Lucy. Here, let me help carry in the TV dinners."

"Thanks, Lance. She handed him his Swanson's dinner. She carried hers.

"Hmmm, smells delicious." Closing his eyes and inhaling he asked, "What is it?"

"Tonight, Sir," pretending to be a fancy restaurateur she said, "the entree is turkey, with corn bread dressing, gravy, peas and whipped sweet potatoes."

"That sounds great. Let's eat."

It was great. The entire recent idea of TV dinners was great. Rebecca had never seen anything like it. There was just enough food on a tray for one person and the tray fit just so on the person's lap. She never got to eat while watching TV before. For that matter, she barely got to watch TV. What a treat and she had absolutely no trouble with this kind of cooking. A whole new world was opening up to her. It was remarkable and the Monday night Lucy show was always hilarious.

Tuesday nights they followed the same procedure only with a different Swanson's dinner entrée. That, plus this night belonged to the priceless comedian, Milton Berle. Uncle Miltie's antics kept Lance and Rebecca in stitches.

The show opening with the Texaco Service Men singing the Texaco jingle was known by heart and the television audience sang right along with them. With the first note, Lance and Rebecca, their heads swaying from side to side, joined in.

"Oh, we are the men of Texaco, we work from Maine to Mexico..." Singing the opening jingle was part of the ritual. They listened, too, but did not join in Uncle Miltie's closing. That was his alone to sing and the quiet audience appreciated his sincere rendition of "Near You."

Lance turned off the TV. "You know Rebecca that was the funniest show yet. Don't you think?"

"Well, it tickled my funny bone. His jokes seem to get funnier each week."

Carrying the empty TV trays to the kitchen, Rebecca stood facing the sink. Suddenly, Lance was behind her. She could feel his strong arms wrapping around her waist. Resting his chin on her shoulder, nuzzling her ear, he whispered endearments that sent shivers up and down her spine. Tingling with goose bumps, she closed her eyes, leaned back into the contour of his body and savored its warmth.

His hands she thought, oh, the wonder of feelings he could elicit with them. Running them up and down her sides, her heart raced. She could feel every accelerated heartbeat; and every nerve flutter. Their chemistry so perfect, she could stand it no longer. Turning, she kissed this man she loved with such passion, and blushed.

In metamorphosis, this young girl transformed. Changing from that little, shy, Catholic orphan who knew very little about sex, agonizing over every moment of uncertainty into a beguiling, enticing, sexy woman knowing just what to do. Lance and nature's inherent tendencies were excellent teachers. Once again, she was grateful he had skipped college. How could they have ever waited four years? Why they could barely keep their hands off each other from day to day. Gently he lifted his companion, his lover, his wife all tied into one and carried her to their bed. Life was good for these newly-weds. Enjoying endless time together, they had it all and, like in a fairytale, Rebecca wanted it to last forever. It did not. With bills mounting and money dwindling, the realization hit her. Sooner or later all good things must come to an end. Their money surely did.

Lance's unemployed days turned into his unemployed weeks followed by a good deal of frustration mixed with anxiety. He just couldn't think of a job that measured up to his expectations. He wasn't sure what that was but knew that's what he wanted.

With a twinge of guilt, Rebecca kept her thoughts to herself. It was just that she felt any job would be okay as long as it paid the bills and if he would stop building castles in the sky, there would be a reliable paycheck.

＊ ＊ ＊ ＊ ＊

Their pleasant breakfast of warm buttered toast, raspberry Danish and steaming, hot, coffee, was rudely interrupted.

"Who can that be at this hour?" he asked.

"I'll get it." Tightening the sash on her robe, Rebecca opened the door and quickly satisfied their curiosity.

"Why, Dad, good morning. This is a pleasant surprise. Come in and join us."

"Just coffee, thanks, Rebecca." He gave his daughter-in-law a quick kiss on her cheek then immediately directed his attention to Lance. Seeing him sitting at the table just loafing away another work day, made him see red.

Lance slumped down knowing full well what was coming next. He knew the signs. The way the veins in his Dad's neck bulged and the way he drew his lips tightly across his teeth as he spoke, meant one thing. His peeved father, was about to light into him and give him a hard time. Oh, he was agitated all right and Lance knew for certain, he was his father's agitator. Here we go, again. He has a bone to pick and ten-to-one, it's about me not working yet.

Lance never let on. Despite his churning insides, defensively, he came across as nonchalant, laid back. No way was he about to add fuel to his father's fire. He didn't need any more heat.

Yeah, he knew, all right, why his father had a burr under his saddle. Worse yet, but not about to openly admit it, he felt the same torment. Man, he thought, how's that for a kick in the teeth?

"Hi Dad, how's it going?" Lance got up, pulled a chair out and motioned for his father to have a seat.

"Could be better, listen, Lance. I didn't come here to chit-chat so I'll come right to the point. The fact of the matter is neither your mother nor I are pleased with what's going on. Frankly, we're concerned about the future for both of you and Rebecca. It's high time you learn you can't live on love alone." Unfortunately for Lance, his father on a roll, didn't mince words and wasn't about to let up. Barely stopping long enough to catch his breath, he charged ahead. "Don't get me wrong. Love is terrific but, how many bills have you paid with it?" His words dripping heavily with sarcasm, even Rebecca flinched.

"You are never going to get anywhere staying home day in and day out. It doesn't work that way. You need to be practical. You need an income. For God sake, Lance, what's it going to take for you to take your responsibilities seriously?"

Jeez, here we go again. Lance wanted to shout, it's none of your business, and how many times do I have to defend my position but, he held his tongue. At least he was trying to keep his cool.

"What do you mean, Dad?" He sat up straight at attention and, spoke in a civil tone. The accusation stung. Resentful, he countered, "I'm a very responsible person, a decent husband and I take my marriage seriously." He was doing a good job controlling his anger. Even the tone of his voice didn't give him away.

"You want to know what I mean. I'll tell you. I mean you can't stay in here all day with your wife, as nice as that may be. You need to provide financially for her. Look at you. You got married on a whim. Now you need to get off your duff and get your keister out to work."

"On a whim? I got married on a whim?" Now that really rubbed him the wrong way. Rebecca watched the disappearance of Lance's mild-manner and the introduction of the crimson color creep up his neck. She knew he had reached his limit and it was up to her to nip this thing in the bud. He was, after all, talking with his elder.

Putting her finger to her lips begging his silence, she warned, "sshh, Lance, enough. Stop before words come out that you'll regret."

Refilling the coffee cups, she was hopeful both the drink and slight lull would be constructive. She figured the temporary time-out would afford both men a chance to take in, not only the coffee, but more importantly, the seriousness of the words at hand.

"Look son. I'm pleased that your marriage is good. I'm not arguing with you on that score. Believe me, that's not the point here."

"Then, what is, Dad?"

"Listen. It doesn't take much for a good marriage to sour. I just don't want that to happen to you and Rebecca."

Frowning in disbelief, Lance interrupted. "Come on, Dad. There's no chance of that happening to us."

"Why are you being so thick, Lance? Can't you see, without money, you jeopardize what you two have together. Nobody lives on love alone, not even you. The long and short of it all, Lance, is you need to get a job. The issue is not debatable. It's sheer fact. That's all I'm trying to get across."

Lance had heard enough. Disgruntled, he picked up the classified section of the newspaper that his father had placed on the table.

"I've circled some positions that sound good. Take a look at them. Lance, I'm just trying to make life a little easier. Okay?"

"Okay, Dad. I'll look them over."

All this fuss about money, Rebecca thought. It never occurred to me to question our financial status. She never needed much and for them, money just seems to always to be here. Listening to his father now, she wasn't too sure.

"Good, son," laying his hand on his son's shoulder, he continued, "I've said what I came to say and now I'll take my leave. Check the ads I circled. Some sound promising."

As he opened the door, Lance simply replied. "I will Dad."

"Wow, that's the second time I heard your father upset."

"Yeah, well, don't let it worry you. He does this kind of thing from time to time. You get used to it."

"Lance, are you really going to look in the paper?"

"I promised him, didn't I? In fact, I'll start tomorrow. So you go get dressed. When you're done, we'll take a nice walk to the park. We'll feed the squirrels the left-over toast, okay?"

She smiled. She didn't recognize the procrastination or if she did, it didn't matter. Anything he wanted to do was just fine with her. She couldn't dress fast enough thinking, I've got to hurry. I'm sure Lance needs me by his side.

Actually, Lance was glad for the alone time. It gave him a chance to regroup. He had worked at not letting his hurt and anger show. But the more he thought about it, the angrier, he got. How dare my father walk into my home, well, okay, technically it belongs to him, but that's beside the point. He still had no right to embarrass me in front of my wife. Not only that, what's the first thing he did when Rebecca was out of earshot? I knew it was coming. He started in singing that same old tune. You got married too young, you should have gone to college and then the one he likes to use best, I told you so. Man, he came loaded for bear. He carried so much ammunition I had trouble dodging the bullets.

Gulping the last of his coffee, questions swirled uneasily in his head. Why doesn't he just leave me alone? It's not like I'm not trying. What does he want from me? Reluctantly, he picked up the classified ads. As he read, his mind raced to a place he didn't want it to go. I hate to admit it. Dad was right. He was as right as rain. Heading straight for worry, he cringed. What am I going to do? The money is running out and, darn it all, it does take a lot more than love to make it.

Limping through, two weeks later, Lance was employed. Up early, showered and dressed in his gray, flannel suit, he headed out. Answering the ad, the world was now his oyster; the pearl just waiting to be plucked. Faithfully, with hopes soaring, he pounded the streets going door to door.

It didn't, however, take long, before he found himself murmuring in disappointment.

"Rebecca, no matter how much enthusiasm I have, I'm just not cutting it. As a vacuum cleaner salesman, let's face it. I stink."

"That's okay," she tried reassuring him. "It's not the only job in the world and if it doesn't suit you, then quit."

"I knew you would feel that way. I already did." There were other jobs out there. Too bad none worked. Time and time again, he just couldn't cut it and failed in the string of menial jobs that followed. Lamely fumbling for explanations, jobs just ended.

He tried his hand at delivering newspapers, at being a soda jerk, and light construction work. For a while, he was even a pin boy at the bowling alley. It wasn't that the work was hard or required the brains of rocket scientists. None of the jobs were fulfilling. None were for him so he changed, willy-nilly, from one to the other.

This road that Lance traveled was rough and his income meager. He was well aware that he had to build a bridge over this gap or drown and it had to be soon too, if his goal was to journey on a smoother road to success. But it was getting tougher. Going from high school king-pin to low-man on the working totem pole, was getting harder and harder to take and too much time was lapsing.

Unfortunately, this allowed his inner sun to turn off and his disposition went dark. Worry produced a malignant spirit in him, as he went from gloomy to downright morose.

He was caught off guard. Of course, he rationalized, none of this was his fault. How could it be? It was hard to soar like an eagle when he had to work for turkeys.

Tensions mounted. Love-making slowed down and Rebecca found the entire predicament sad and confusing. To add insult to injury, no matter what solutions she suggested, her ideas got shot down.

Certain she could get her cashier's position back, she even offered to work. He wouldn't hear of it, fussing and fuming all the while reminding her that he was the head of household and the sole bread winner.

Her argument that the bread was rapidly being reduced to crumbs didn't help matters any, either. This unresolved money issue served only to put more distance between them.

"Look around, Rebecca. How many married women do you see working? Their job is just like yours and that's to keep the home fires burning. Don't take me wrong. I appreciate your trying to help but think about it. In this day and age, what respectable man depends on his wife for income? I'd never be able to face myself in the mirror. Now do you see where I'm coming from?" he asked soberly.

"Put that way, I do." Rebecca's hurt turned to a shade of understanding mixed with regret. It troubled her that the inadequate monies coming in were simply not enough to cover household expenses and more than enough to cause marital problems. What price could be placed on self-esteem?

"Let's just go to bed, Lance. It's late."

It was obvious. The book he was supposed to be reading was nothing more than window dressing, a cover up to legitimately allow him to wallow undetected in his troubles.

I hate seeing him this way, she thought, so tense with not even a hint of a smile on his face. Poor Lance. Then in a manner both consoling and loving, she gently touched his arm while moving her body closer to his.

"Lance, come here," she invited. "Let me give you a good backrub."

"Not tonight, Rebecca," he said, gently, but firmly, removing her hands. The color on her face slowly faded. Rejection was no stranger to her. Rejection from the man she loved was. It hurt. But the time she devoted to feeling sorry for herself was cut short with his distressing admission.

"Rebecca, I lost my job today." Oh, not again. She wanted to yell, what's wrong with you? But then with pangs of empathy and a whisper of disappointment, she thought, no wonder you're so down. Quickly, dismissing his unkind rejection, she gave him her undivided attention. "What happened?"

"It wasn't my fault Rebecca." His palms were damp as he delivered his side of the story. "The boss was so demanding. He wanted me to work longer hours. I can only do so much. He flat out told me if I wasn't willing to put in more time, then I needn't put in any. I guess I got a little miffed so I agreed, and here I am. That job wasn't for me anyway."

Lance, she was starting to realize with regret, always had a way of justifying his work related failures. Still, she hated to see him so down and besides, tomorrow and a better day was really just around the corner.

"I'm sorry, Lance. Try not to be upset. There's a job out there with your name on it just waiting for you."

"Well, it better be in giant letters."

Finally, he drew her into his arms but, just as she was beginning to feel better, he lowered the boom. "Rebecca," he paused, "I have an idea."

"What is it, Lance? Tell me."

"Just as a temporary measure, understand. Just to hold us over until I find that job with my name on it, I thought, well, that is…" struggling, he couldn't express his thought.

Rebecca sat upright. "What is it, Lance? Just say it."

"Okay. Here goes. Now hear me out, okay?"

"Of course."

"Your purple gold is the ticket that will get us out of this mess but only on a temporary basis, you see."

"No, I don't see." She frowned in puzzlement. "I don't see how my purple gold could possibly help"

She didn't have to wait long for an explanation. His unbelievable answer was the farthest thought from her mind. She was grateful she was sitting down as suddenly, she felt weak.

"We could pawn your purple gold. It must be worth a lot of money. It…"

Whatever other words of rationalization came spewing from his mouth, fell on deaf ears. Shocked, all she heard associated with her precious treasure was the word *pawn* and she went ballistic.

Her heart pounded. Jumping out of bed, she stood with her arms straight and tight to her body. With clenched fists, face red with anger, she leaned toward his face as closely as possible and spit out her objection.

"Lance, you know I back you on everything you do but not this time." Shaking her head, she repeated emphatically, no, not this time. I will never give my permission to pawn my purple gold, never."

"Be reasonable, Rebecca. And for heaven's sake, stop calling it purple gold. It's a heart-shaped gem, Rebecca that happens to be purple in color."

"Obviously, it is. But I don't know how you could identify with any kind of a heart considering right now, you don't seem to have one." The barb stung but not enough to change his mind. She hurt more and told him so. "Lance, how could you have such audacity? You know what that necklace means to me. How dare you? How dare you suggest putting it in jeopardy? It's outrageous. I'm furious and I'm crushed. Really, Lance. How could you?"

"It would only be for a short time." Rebecca hit the roof. "You aren't listening. You haven't heard a single word I said. Listen. I don't care if we have to beg for food from the soup kitchen. I'll do that before I'll let you pawn my purple gold. And, yes, I said *purple gold*. If that's what I want to call it, I will." She felt strangely frightened but determined and managed to give her parting shot. "Subject closed."

So was the bedroom door she slammed shut racing out of the room in tears.

Man, I just keep getting in deeper and deeper, Lance thought. Jeez, I'm not even sure why I mentioned this idea to her. Pawning her prized necklace, what the heck was I thinking? If only I could take back my words. I love her so. But love is not a prescription to hurt. With that thought foremost in his mind, he ran after her and in a flash, had his arms around her offering heartfelt apologies.

"I'm so sorry, Rebecca. Forgive me. I made a gigantic mistake – no, it's more than that. It's monstrous on my part." He stroked her hair lovingly. "I had no right to ask you to part with your necklace, not even for a minute. I promise I will never pawn or even mention the thought of pawning your *purple gold* ever again."

He made it a point to call it by the name she had christened it. Gently, he kissed her eyelids and rocked her until her crying subsided then guided her to the bed. Her purple gold safe; he was forgiven.

It was their first major argument. As in all marriages filled with peaks and valleys, it would not be their last.

Chapter 21

1957

Just before his time limit to render him penniless ran out, Lance was rescued. Once again, his father stepped in and saved him from that danger. The phone rang.

"Hi Lance. It's Dad, I have some news."

"Good or bad?"

"Depends on your viewpoint. I think it's good. Listen. There's a spot opening up at the bank here. You know Mr. Pendy at the Market Street office? Well, he's retiring at the end of this week. Bill Fischer is moving up to fill that position. Then that leaves Fischer's job wide open. I think that's where you could fit in. It's a nine-to-five, five days a week job and the pay's good. What do you say? Want me to get you an application?"

Do I? Elated at the very idea, Lance wanted to shout his answer. Not wanting his father to know how desperate he was at this point or how terrific his father's timing and suggestion were, or one better, that his father had been absolutely right all along, he simply answered nonchalantly, "Sure."

To say he was pleased with his newly appointed job was an understatement. Finally, work that held all appealing characteristics plus he was actually good at it. He knew, in the right setting, he would be. Lance fit the bill for The Farmers and Merchants Bank and the bank fit the bill for Lance. To his advantage, he discovered the importance in business, valued its success and his ability to incorporate records and numbers in a systematic and orderly fashion.

That he was naturally friendly and trustworthy helped and to top it off, he was well liked by peers and superiors alike. His willingness to attend training programs did not go unnoticed. Starting at the bottom rung, with his qualifications, it would not take this Bank Clerk long to climb the corporate ladder.

Once again, the couple living in the tiny garage-converted apartment was truly happy. At least they had been for the past year of Lance's steady employment. But then, it was Lance who expressed his discontent, concluding their tiny home was just that; tiny. Further, he surmised a man with a reliable, respectable income with salary increases just waiting in the wings, needed space to expand. Besides, he had managed to pay his bills and still save a goodly portion of his weekly paycheck. It was time to move.

"Rebecca, that meatloaf was delicious. You've become quite the cook."

"Thanks." Beaming with the compliment, Rebecca started to clear the dishes.

Taking her by the hand, he guided her back to her seat. "That can wait. I want to discuss a serious idea I have."

"Holy Hannah Lance, not another one of your serious ideas." She pulled away laughing weakly. "Remember the last one? It almost cost me my purple gold."

"Relax. Not this time. I promise you'll like this. Listen. I've saved enough money for a down payment on, are you ready?"

"What? Lance, please. You're driving me crazy with suspense."

"Our new house."

Totally caught off guard, Rebecca sat speechless. Her tongue quiet; her mind shouted. But I'm happy where we are. It's fixed up just the way I like it. I've devoted a lot of time, I've kind of mastered the art of cooking and I've even learned how to entertain, with the aid of the Better Homes and Gardens Cook Book that Beverly gave to me. I've learned so much about keeping house. I even learned regrettably, that not one single method of table setting which was followed at the orphanage, applied. She thought how odd the mind works when it's trying to escape an unwanted ending.

My cookbook has nothing to do with moving. Who am I kidding? I can't shake this feeling. If we move, it will never be the same. Besides, I don't deserve to move up in the world, not with my humble background. I haven't told Lance the full story. No matter how it is sliced, a half truth is a whole lie. Rebecca didn't count on the realization that fear is hard on one's mind. It harbors all types of negative possibilities.

"Rebecca. Did you hear what I said? We can afford a bigger house. Isn't that exciting?"

"Um...well, yes it is. I guess, Lance, it's just that you took me by surprise."

Again, her mind filled up with quiet thoughts. Can't you see? I'm content with you and my life and with this tiny apartment. I know every nook and cranny. I don't want to leave our precious Lilliputian paradise.

"Well, think about it. Okay, Rebecca?"

"Okay."

She did give it thought. It didn't take long to recognize her main hesitation. It wasn't that she would not welcome a big, new house. It was deeper than just leaving the little apartment. Haunts of her past; she simply feared change.

Three weeks later Lance announced excitedly, "Prepare for a wonderful surprise." He barely got in the door from work when he scooped Rebecca up in his arms, kissed her and twirled her around. "We're moving."

Chapter 22

~

1957 – The Suburbs

Their new house was unbelievable. Yet she had quietly cried a little the night before their move. She would miss their tiny haven where he and she had learned to grow up together towering over the inconsequential, and some not so inconsequential, problems of newly-weds.

Now this home was an adventure in prosperity. It was 2000 square feet of good fortune. Astounded, Rebecca admitted, "Lance, we could have put our entire apartment into this kitchen. It's huge."

"Just look at the latest conveniences, Rebecca." With that, he gave her the grand kitchen tour. Like she needed convincing?

"See, it features a double built-in wall oven. Remember the apartment barely had a two burner stove and forget the oven. It was always breaking down. Not only is this oven built-in, there is a complete, separate cook top with four working burners separated by this heating tray in the middle."

Bouncing from appliance to appliance, like a kid at Christmas, excitedly, he continued his presentation. Pointing to this and that, he continued. "The woodwork is birch and the space just above the oven is the perfect spot for, are you ready, a George Nelson designer clock.

Yep. See the huge, sunburst clock? It is actually 18.5 inches in diameter and features red and walnut spokes that surround the round clock. I know because, my dear, I hold its description pamphlet right here in my hand." He laughed at his clever enthusiasm and went right on talking. "Take note, Rebecca, of the sleek electrical appliances. The refrigerator, stove, and the sink all match in their yellowish-green avocado color. Note, too, the kitchen walls are painted in a soft lemon."

"Lovely sir, it's just lovely." Following his lead, she announced, "I do believe this kitchen has the potential of becoming my favorite room in the house. May I see the rest of this palace?"

"Indeed, madam. Follow me."

The ranch-style house rambled with more rooms for her use than Rebecca had ever had in her life. There was a living room with walls painted in egg shell and a formal dining room, the walls of which were painted a light apricot. Why anyone needed a den was beyond her. But they had one, just the same, along with three bedrooms and two full bathrooms.

Outside, there was a nice front yard complete with shade trees and a small flower garden. There even was a three-sided carport to house a car which, they did not as yet, own. How silly is this, she thought?

Well, in less than two weeks time, Lance remedied that. He parked his brand new 1957 Chevrolet Impala in the empty space. Should have seen that one coming, she thought.

Commuting by foot was out of the question. No doubt about it. Living in the suburbs required the use of a car. She had to admit, it was a beauty.

"Don't you just love this car, Rebecca?" Lance excitedly questioned as he parked it for her to admire. "See here. With its two-tone blue exterior and gray cloth and vinyl interior, it looks great in the carport. Of course, it will serve its purpose, too. I plan to drive to work in style."

"It's terrific, Lance. This house and now the car are just perfect. I must say you did a wonderful job. You have a very good eye."

Delighted with her approval, he was as happy as a kid on the fourth of July. Rebecca believed in the man being the head of the house. But it was her turn now. She picked out the furnishings, while he agreed with her choices.

* * * * *

Their lives were changing as were the lives of all middle class Americans. It was a good time for all and it seemed they wanted for nothing.

What does one do with one's time after all the furniture is in place and all the housework is done? In the suburbs, the men worked. The women, left to their own devices, joined forces. Rebecca quickly learned that living in the suburbs was very different from city life. The suburban communities, actually kind of isolated, posed a problem for women. For social interaction and to defeat the loneliness of the long day, they formed an unspoken bond. There was about them an esprit de corps – camaraderie and companionship.

"Move the footstool out of the way Rebecca, then help me push the coffee table to the wall."

"Done. Anything else you want me to do, Joy?" Rebecca questioned her neighbor and today's hostess.

"I think that about does it and just in time. I'll turn the television set on and everybody get ready. Take off your shoes."

They took turns and every morning, at ten o'clock, a group of women met in the designated house for that given day. There, everybody chipped in pushing the furniture to the side of the room. They needed all the space they could get. Off came the shoes and in stocking feet, bending and twisting and stretching, they followed their television exercise leader.

She took them through an invigorating series of calisthenics. Together, doing push-ups and sit-ups, they worked on keeping trim bodies. Exercise was always followed by a koffee klatch that brought not only good conversation but delicious treats, as well. No matter the pounds just lost were immediately found. It was fun just the same. It was the opportune time to exchange recipes and decorative ideas, and, of course, gossip abounded. Ah, life in the suburbs.

How many times did Rebecca silently thank Beverly for her kitchen bible? That cookbook was just the ticket when it was her turn to host the koffee klatch.

Being a true suburbanite now, she also joined the afternoon bowling league that met once a week. She learned the game quickly and to her surprise, turned out to be a pretty good bowler. Then there were the community dances which she and the other wives saw to all the arrangements. Husbands joined their wives and enjoyed this evening event together. Indeed, life was good for the suburbanites.

For Rebecca and Lance, it was about to get even better.

Chapter 23

1958

"Lance, I'm pregnant." They had been sitting quietly while Lance worked on a bank report and Rebecca sat on the easy chair with a magazine resting on her lap. Suddenly, and without warning, she whispered her sensational news.

"What did you say?" He asked, not sure he had heard her correctly. Then there she was standing in front of him. Beaming, she nodded her head repeatedly and murmured softly, "I'm expecting."

He was beside himself. Immediately, he jumped up. "This is too good to be true." Taking Rebecca into his arms, he held her and covered her face with tender, butterfly kisses. Ecstatic, he went on breathlessly. "Wow! Rebecca, this is wonderful. This is big, really big. We're going to be parents. Imagine that, Rebecca, you and me, parents." She wasn't sure who he was trying to convince but, she let him go on. Excitedly he declared. "Let's have five kids or six kids. Maybe we could have them a year apart and we could…"

"Whoa! Slow down, Mr. Future Father of the Year. How about we just start with this one? Then who knows how many more there will be? Let's just do one at a time. Okay?" He could see the sparkle in her eyes and he was reminded all over, again, why he loved his

Rebecca so much. There she was as always, beautiful and logical. She had it all.

Like a cricket, his mind jumped all over the place. "I know. This week-end, don't make any plans with your friends. We'll use the time to get the nursery ready. See, now aren't you glad we have the extra bedrooms? And you thought this house was too big." His reaction surprised even him. He always liked kids. He just didn't realize until now, how much.

"We'll paint it blue. Okay, Rebecca? It's going to be a boy, right?"

Grinning, she declared, "We'll just have to wait and see."

"No, there's no doubt about it, Rebecca." Patting her stomach gently, he proudly announced, "It's a boy." He didn't stop to take a breath. "Hey, I've got a sensational idea. Let's take a drive over to my folks and let them in on the good news."

"Good idea."

Needless to say, the Grandparents were thrilled. With a slap on his back and a hearty handshake, Lance's Dad extended his congratulations.

"Our first grandchild, this is terrific son. Good going."

"Thanks, Dad." Proud as a peacock, Lance accepted the praise. Not as fussy as their son, they didn't discriminate. Any gender, boy or girl, was okay with them. His mother made her wishes known. "Just so the baby is healthy. Mr. Miles broke out the champagne and when everyone's glass was filled, toasted.

"This is to the health and happiness of our grandchild and to the new parents to be." In unison, everyone responded with glasses raised. "Hear, hear."

* * * * *

Several months into her pregnancy, Rebecca became concerned about Lance and his insistence that the baby would be a boy. So much so, that she decided to discuss the issue with him right after they finished eating. The last bite of dessert finished, she started. "Lance, you do know that this baby may be a girl, right? I mean you are determined that it is a boy. But, just what if it isn't? What then? You are making me nervous now."

"Rebecca, there's no need for you to worry. You know if the baby turns out to be a girl, I will love her just the same. I promise. Okay?"

"Okay."

"Feel better now?"

"I do, Lance. I really do."

"Good." Then with a twinkle in his eye, he teased "But I'm positive. It's a boy." She could do nothing more than chuckle at his insistence and boyish charm. She was anxious to share his deduction with her friend and neighbor, Joy. Living next door presented the opportunity for them to get together more often than they did with the rest of the neighborhood group. The two had a lot in common. Both had lost their parents. Both married young and both had successful husbands. To top it off, they had moved in on exactly the same day and even their house floor plans were identical.

Although Joy was more knowledgeable in the ways of the world, their personalities clicked from day one. They liked each other. That was the key. Best of all, secure with each other, they were free to share thoughts and secrets. Rebecca still missed the close female camaraderie of her school friends. Joy's friendship helped fill that void.

So many similarities and yet, there was one major difference. However, that too, was soon to be evened out. Joy and her husband George already had a baby, an eighteen-month-old, darling, little boy. Rebecca stood in the driveway saying goodbye to Lance. It was her daily ritual. She always walked Lance to the car, leaned in through the window and gave him a little send off kiss. Waving him off to work, he drove down the road. Familiar with the routine, Joy stepped outside and extended an invitation.

"Rebecca, I just put on a fresh pot of coffee. Come on over." Her house was filled with the delicious aroma of freshly baked cinnamon roll and the run on gibber-jabber of the plump, baby boy. Sitting contently in his high chair, Gary was adorable. Watching Joy's small cherub attempt to pick up and eat tiny cheerios with his round, chubby fingers gave Rebecca a warm stir. Gently, she rubbed her tummy in a protective, nurturing fashion. The mini massage, a typical trait of a mother-to-be, was carried out in an act of love. Hurry up and get here, baby. She silently instructed.

Joy lived up to her designated name. Always cheerful; she was a delight. Her effervescent and lighthearted personality was gratifying and her sunny disposition endeared her all the more to Rebecca's heart. To top it off, she was generous. She readily shared the benefit of her expertise regarding pregnancy and the pending child birth, although, Rebecca could have foregone hearing about that inevitable maneuver.

"Keep an eye on the baby for me, won't you Rebecca? I'll be right back."

"My pleasure," Although short-lived, it was. Carrying a cardboard box, as promised, Joy was back in a flash. Placing it on the chair beside her, she reached in and pulled out, what Rebecca concluded to be, the most darling maternity outfit, ever.

"I thought you might like to wear these. I have tons of maternity clothes and I don't plan to need them any time soon. What do you think?"

"Oh, Joy. You are too much." Fingering the fabrics, Rebecca was truly touched.

"This one will look great on you." With that said, Joy handed Rebecca a pretty floral print shirt blouse with a pair of toreador pants outfit. It had a matching skirt. Next she pulled out a red, flared, tunic that buttoned in the back. It came with a white blouse with push-up sleeves.

"These are lovely. I can't wait to wear them."

"Well, it won't be long until you will and then it won't be long until you'll be longing to get out of them and into your own clothes, again." They chuckled as Joy forecast that tidbit of irony. "Look at this one. It's my absolute favorite." Rebecca inspected the top of a navy blue maternity suit.

"Lovely." Then turning her attention to the skirt, she was puzzled. "What the heck is this?" Holding up the skirt, she discovered a huge, circular hole in the front of the garment. "I'm afraid there's something wrong with the skirt. Too bad, it's such a lovely outfit."

"Let me see. What do you mean?" Joy took the skirt. "It's fine." Running her fingers over the garment, it passed her inspection. "There's nothing wrong with it."

"No. Look here in the front, Joy. A piece of material is missing. See. There's a big hole." Poking her hand through the opened space, she demonstrated her point.

"Boy Rebecca, you are naïve." Joy doubled over with laughter. "Sorry. I'm not laughing at you. Well, come to think of it, yes. Yes, I am. A hole…" And she laughed all the harder. "Okay. Let me in on it. What's so funny?"

In between her outburst, Joy finally pointed out the reason why she found Rebecca's innocent simplicity so humorous. "The hole, Rebecca, is intentional. Look. I'll demonstrate." With that Joy slipped into the skirt which tied at the waist. Just below the waistline, she pointed out the necessity of the hole. "See. It's especially designed for your baby belly. It lets you grow out all you want and still manage to keep your hemline straight. Clever, isn't it?"

Aha." A little red-faced but taking the ribbing as it was pleasantly intended, Rebecca nodded in agreement and then found herself chuckling, too. She remarked, "Planned holes in your clothes. What will they think of next?"

* * * * *

As the months moved on Rebecca, grateful for the maternity clothes, wore them as a badge of honor. They told the world she was having a baby. She and Lance could hardly wait as she and her time grew, she bigger; it closer.

Nine months is not all that long except to those who waddle under the strain of the extra weight. Then is seems like an eternity. Rebecca fit the category. The waiting was tough. Struggling to get up from her chair, Rebecca sighed with a mixture of delight and despair. "Our little cherub is breaking down my resistance. Gee, Lance, I wish it would hurry up and get here. I don't think I can wait much longer. Look at me. I'm as big as an elephant. I can barely move."

"You made it this long. You're in the home stretch," Lance encouraged. "Hang in there."

Just two days later, finally, the appointed time arrived or so she thought. She was more than ready. The baby wasn't all that sure. It held out through Rebecca's dawn, daybreak, sunrise, twilight, and sunset. Still it resisted on a second go around until after twilight when, in the end, the baby decided to test the waters. Shortly after sunset on the second day into labor, Rebecca and Lance got the surprise of a lifetime as the world welcomed not one but two baby boys. Identical twins, David Lance and Dennis Lance Miles crying noisily, announced their arrival.

"Twins? Oh, my gosh Rebecca, and both boys. What a shocker! How did this happen?" Flabbergasted, and beside himself, the new father's questions were rapid fire. Overwhelmed, the new mother didn't have a clue.

"I don't know. The doctor never mentioned two babies. Maybe one heartbeat was stronger than the other? Maybe one baby was hiding? Who knows? Who cares? They are here and they are ours."

She felt a short-lived twinge of disappointment. Not because she had twins. No, never. She dearly loved the little guys but because she was unable to answer Lance's question. Again, being an orphan got in the way. Twins didn't run in Lance's family but she had no idea if they did in hers. If only she knew her background. But she didn't and that was that.

No matter, she still was the mother of these tiny miracles. Let it go at that, she told herself. Tired but excited, Rebecca looked at the tiny bundles laying one in each arm. Wrapped snuggly in soft, blue receiving blankets, only their little, pink faces could be seen.

"They are beautiful, wrinkled faces and all." Looking from one to the other, it hit her like a ton of bricks. "There are two of them. There actually are two of them."

Beaming, Lance kissed her gently on the tip of her nose. "Thank you Rebecca for the twins. I told you it was going to be a boy. But not in my wildest dreams did I think we would have two."

"*We* didn't." Rebecca smiled. Shifting into a more comfortable position, she was quick to remind him. "*I* did."

"Yes you did," he smiled. "You did it Rebecca and I'm so proud I could pop." Hardly taking time to breathe, he talked quickly filling her in on his plans. "I'm going to be the best father ever. First I'm going to teach them how to throw a ball, and then how to swing a bat and then how to ride a bike and then….."

"Whoa. Slow down. Maybe we should teach them a few other things first. You know, like talking and walking and…"

"Now don't you go getting practical on me." The happy couple laughed together and shook their heads in amazement. Twins! Unbelievable!

"Rebecca, you've made me the happiest father in the world."

"Bet all fathers say that," she teased.

"No. Just me, and guess what? Our healthy surprise bundles both weighed in at seven pounds nine ounces."

"No wonder I'm exhausted." Rebecca responded just as she drifted off to sleep. The nurse took the babies from the sleeping mother. She congratulated the obviously tickled pink new father who, in his excitement, offered her a cigar as he rushed off to tell the world.

* * * * *

It was good to get home from the hospital, and thanks to Joy, Rebecca found the house spic and span. Not only that. Between Joy, her husband George and Lance, a second crib identical to the first was assembled and in place in the baby friendly nursery. They saw to it that two of everything needed was provided.

When the dust settled, a whole new world opened up to the young couple. Known as the adventures of parenthood they learned, laughed and even cried together.

As is the case with most young fathers, Lance willingly helped with one end of the babies but, adamantly denied the other. He didn't mind feeding the boys their bottle as often as he could. But changing diapers, well he insisted he didn't know how and let it go at that. Good thing their neighbor was so helpful.

"Joy. You're such a blessing. These little guys didn't come with instructions. What would I do without you?" It was true. Rebecca listened, observed and learned and as far as she was concerned Joy knew all the ins and outs of baby rearing. Like right at this moment, Joy was in the process of solving a major problem. The boys were so identical, everyone including their mother, was having difficulty telling them apart.

"This is for you." Smiling, Joy simply handed Rebecca a bottle of red nail polish. "Now let's go identify a baby." Together, one holding the boy's thumb, the other painting his thumb nail, they marked the older boy. By all of one minute and ten seconds, David was the first born. Therefore, the twin sporting the bright red thumbnail was, without doubt, David. It was so easy. All Rebecca had to do was periodically freshen up the polish.

"Thanks, Joy. You certainly make my life easier. Don't think I don't appreciate the time you spend helping me when Lance goes off to work, I do."

Rebecca learned quickly that most chores associated with babies automatically belong to the mother, and anyone else she is lucky enough to enlist.

That there was double work didn't matter because her system worked. She and Joy handled the day shift. Lance and Rebecca the night shift, and Joy's husband filled in around the edges. They had to be doing something right. The babies thrived. As the months went on, they grew bigger, healthier, and more fun to be with each day. That is with the exception of last month.

In her mind, Rebecca tucked away that troubled month almost as if it had never happened. Still several times without warning, visions of blurred, white uniformed doctors and nurses rushing about in organized chaos blatantly shoved their way into her mind. The very thought of sticking needles and inserting tubes into her precious, little, boys, brought tears to her eyes.

Leaving the boys the first time the boys were admitted to the hospital was tough. Neither Rebecca nor Lance got much sleep. The next two stays did not get any easier. They had no choice. David's fever climbed. Dennis could not hold down food. Both boys screamed when touched. The doctor called for tests and observation, although they did not tell them much. The boys slowly improved. Relieved, Rebecca and Lance got the boys out of there. Back in their own home, they did okay. Nothing was ever found. Rebecca shushed her mind's nagging voice. As far as she was concerned, the twins were just fine. She refused to be a part of what she considered to be the medical profession's gloom and doom probability.

"Lance, come watch this." Rebecca had both boys sitting in their highchairs. It was feeding time, serious business for the little guys. Eating was one of their favorite past times. "Watch this neat trick I've discovered."

"I'm watching."

"You know how impatient David and Dennis get when it's time to eat and how they both want to eat at the same time? How when I feed one, the other cries? And how I can never move fast enough to keep them both happy? Well, check this out."

He did. He kept his eye on her the entire time she demonstrated her technique. On the tray of each highchair, she placed an opened jar of baby food. She picked up a spoon, actually two spoons, one in each hand then deftly, with a flick of her wrists she scooped up a portion of food from each jar. Synchronizing both hands, they worked in harmony. As they approached, like baby birds, the boys' tiny mouths opened wide and in she shoveled the food at the exact same time. Eureka! Equal contentment! Instant success!

"See Lance, it is true. Necessity is the mother of invention. This way nobody waits. Everybody is happy. Including me," she beamed.

"I'll be darned, Rebecca. That has to be the cleverest execution of food feeding that I've ever seen."

No doubt about it. Twins were double the work but, rewardingly, double the fun. On Sunday afternoons, they greeted the neighbors as they took their boys out for a walk. Lance pushed one baby carriage; Rebecca the other. With everyone interested in getting a glimpse of the little guys, their stroll didn't take them very far. But then, showing off their babies was part of the deal. It was intentional. They wouldn't have it any other way.

Home again, and with the twins tucked in bed, they headed for the comfortable sofa in the rec room and their nightly glass of sherry. Lance poured both drinks then sat next to Rebecca.

"To the twins." Rebecca raised her glass to the toast, "and to the end of their hospital trips"

"I'll drink to that." Gently they tapped their glasses together, and sipped the wine.

"I'll tell you Lance, last month's horrifying experience is one I don't want to repeat, ever."

"It was tough," he agreed, "how many doctors did they finally wind up seeing?"

"Too many. Let's see. First they saw Doctor Mason. Then there was Doctor Simpson and Doctor Roberts. I'm glad that's all behind us. Thank goodness the tests didn't find anything wrong. Remember all that talk about inserting a trach tube? I shudder, just thinking about that."

"It's over now, Rebecca. Whatever they had was just a fluke," and he changed the subject. "Did I mention that I'm in line for a promotion?"

"No, you didn't. I'm excited for you. Tell me all about it." He filled her in on the new responsibilities. They talked well past their bedtime. It was good for the two of them to just sit and talk.

The next few days found them back to their busy schedules. With his new position, Lance had to work late a few evenings. Rebecca was happily involved with planning the boys' first birthday party. Let's see, what would the boys like the best? Tapping the pencil on her to-do list, out of the blue, a clown came to mind. A party clown with fuzzy, red hair and a red nose wearing floppy shoes, that's the ticket.

The clown triggered her memory. Annette, she thought, I'm using your party clown. She remembered it straight from their story-telling days under the big tree at the orphanage and smiled. Later, she told Lance about her big plan. No mention was made of the idea's origin.

"A clown to entertain the boys," he chuckled, "Leave it to you Rebecca"

"Won't that be fun, Lance? Speaking of fun, after we eat what say we go for a walk? The boys haven't really been out much today. I thought maybe we could just take them around the block, interested?"

"Sure. Actually, I sat at my desk much too long today. It will do me good, too."

Their short walk didn't take long, still the exercise was good. They went around the block and then headed back home. Before long, it was time to get the boys ready for bed. "You have to admit, Rebecca, these little guys sure do keep us busy. Don't they?"

"Indeed, they do. But, you and I both know we wouldn't trade our busy life-style revolving around our two boys for all the tea in China."

"I can't imagine living without our precious David and Dennis."

"Neither can I, Lance."

But then, they didn't have to envision it. Unfortunately, suddenly and without warning, it was no longer just a concept. Sadly, the option of imagination was closed.

Out of their hands, the choice was no longer theirs. Forced to face reality so cold, complicated and difficult to understand, they learned life's cruel blows the hard way.

Two weeks before the twins' first birthday, tragedy struck. Within six hours of each other, both sons were dead. Instead of planning for the twins' first birthday celebration, now grief-stricken, they found themselves making funeral arrangements.

The tragic night started out like any other with the unsuspecting parents happily getting the boys ready for bed. Their routine was the same as always. Nothing was done differently. Yet, everything was different. In the end and in catastrophic desperation, life would never be the same.

"Come on little guy." Slinging David onto his shoulders, Lance headed for the bedroom announcing, "bed time."

Little Dennis giggled as he sat straddling Rebecca's hip. "Up to bed with you, too."

Except for taking turns carrying each boy, the bedtime ritual was always the same. Each twin happily accepted his favorite teddy bear before being safely tucked in his crib for the night. Rebecca and Lance lovingly watched over them patting them gently while reciting a silent prayer. Next, Rebecca turned the little star-shaped nightlight on as Lance turned the overhead light off. They left then, whispering in unison, "Sweet dreams."

In the middle of the night, Rebecca thought she heard a funny noise. A kind of moaning mixed with a whimpering cry. Lance did not stir. Maybe I'm mistaken, she told herself. She sat upright and listened. There it is again. Quickly, she slipped on her robe and dashed off in the direction of the weird sound. A sick feeling washed over her and set her stomach to churning. Not again. Oh, please not again. The mystifying sound definitely was coming from the boys' room.

Her knees weakened. Her motherly intuition kicked in. She knew. Something was wrong and maybe it was even worse than the last episode. Without warning, as quickly as the noise had come and awakened her, it was gone. Quiet filled the air. Was it fear? No. It was sheer panic. It penetrated to the depth of her soul as she became acutely aware of the invading eerie silence. She raced to her babies. Her throat tightened in trepidation of the unknown. Hitting the light switch, she screamed.

Blood-curdling, it went through him like a knife.

"My God, what was that? Rebecca, where are you?" he questioned the empty side of their bed.

"Lance," she screamed alarmed, "Come quick."

Out of a dead sleep, he still was at her side in a flash. Now wide awake, he threw worried questions at her.

"What's the matter Rebecca? What is it? For God's sake, tell me." He focused his concern on her and that temporarily robbed him of the complete picture. He didn't see it right off. "Tell me."

She didn't answer. Her eyes riveted on little David, Rebecca just stood paralyzed.

"Oh my God, oh my God," she repeated louder and louder. He saw then what was holding her attention captive. Over her shoulder, he saw David in trouble. It hit him like a ton of bricks. They had a crisis on their hands that demanded immediate action. The initial shock waning, he took command.

"Rebecca, listen to me." His was a quick panic. There was no time to spare. Taking her by her shoulders, abruptly with brisk movements, he shook her. Awake from her stupor, she obeyed and like a drill sergeant, he roared out instructions.

"Rebecca. Get hold of yourself. Go call for help. Call an ambulance, hurry."

At break-neck speed, Rebecca bolted to the living room where use of the phone offered encouragement. Help was on the way. Simultaneously, Lance turned his attention to his son. His throat tightened with fright at the very sight of him, justly so, for David lay too still.

His face ashen, his glazed wide-open eyes terrified Lance. Even more spine-chilling; realizing his worse fear; David was not breathing. Frantically, regretting his inattentiveness in boy scouts but, grateful for what he did remember, Lance quickly put his first-aid training into action. Frantically, he administered mouth to mouth. Please God, he silently bargained, let my son live. I'll do anything. You'll see me in church every Sunday. I'll volunteer for committees. Anything, Lord, only please, please, let him live. Yelling in between breaths, he desperately urged his son, "Breathe. David. Come on. Breathe."

Lance wasn't sure how long he had been engaged in his frenzied struggle. He just knew he could not quit. Not until David showed signs of life. Forming an unimaginable bond between father and son, he just kept up with the mouth to mouth until he felt a hand on his shoulder.

"Step aside, sir," the paramedic instructed in a kind but urgent voice.

"I can't. My son's still not breathing." Clinging to his son, working feverishly trying to fill him with life, Lance knew. In his mind, he knew the hopelessness of the situation. In his heart, he dared not give up. Deeply perceptive, he knew if he stopped there would be dire consequences. It would make it all too final. Finality carried an agonizing high price he refused to pay. Ignoring the request and in desperation, once more he commanded David, "Breathe."

"Sir, please." Another urgent directive from the kind voice, "we'll take it from here."

"No. You don't understand. My son just needs a little more help" He refused to acknowledge the real possibility. He refused to let go. He refused to let his son die.

Sobbing, Rebecca wrapped her arms around his neck.

"Lance, please stop," she pleaded. "Let these men do their job."

"But I'm his father. David depends on me," he reasoned. "I can't desert him. Why didn't I pay more attention in the first-aid class? All this is my fault." Illogical thoughts often accompany logical actions.

"Stop blaming yourself. It's not your fault. It's not anybody's fault." Rebecca, alarmed at his reaction, yelled. Shaking with fright, she thought, this isn't easy for me, either. Okay, now Lance is the one in need of encouragement and there isn't time to waste. David must get professional help. "You did all you could, Lance. Now, please let these men take over," she begged.

Exhaling a pitiful, shuddering sigh, he conceded. Quickly surveying all that was happening, he turned his post over to the anxiously awaiting paramedics. Drained, Lance stepped aside. He leaned back on the wall, slid to the floor and buried his face in his hands unable to watch the men carry his son's limp body away.

Both sobbing now, Rebecca and Lance clung to each other. Too bad the closeness was not destined to last.

Despite everybody's efforts, David was pronounced dead in the hospital emergency room. Beside themselves with grief, the distraught parents couldn't understand. He was here and then, that quickly, he was gone and with absolutely no warning. None. But what exactly had happened? What went wrong? Why was he dead? That was the haunting question and no one, not even the experts, had the answer.

"Please. Have a seat, Mr. and Mrs. Miles." The doctor's office so sterile with its white painted walls and cold, metallic, chairs did nothing to encourage compassion. Even his consoling words were of little comfort. Besides, it wasn't kind words Rebecca wanted.

"You have my deepest sympathy for your loss."

"Thank you." Rebecca spoke softly. Hating the reason for being here, despite the degree of support offered, this meeting only added credence to the unbelievable nightmare. Her bewildered mind was off and running in so many directions down so many confusing lanes. This happened a lot since they took David away. Robbed of concentration, nothing was making sense. To top it off, she found herself harboring serious trust issues. Nothing was clear. Speculations probed her foggy mind as she looked to the doctor for answers.

Skeptical, she scrutinized this man sitting opposite her hiding behind thick, horn rimmed glasses. Had he always been honest with her? She wasn't too sure. Stress ruled her day. Confusion, pain and anger conjured up weighty questions. If only her tongue was not tied then she could speak them aloud. If only Lance would help. But he just sat there in a daze.

Silently asked questions rewarded her with exactly the same, silent answers. Unfortunately, the unspoken words prolonged her captivity in agony. She was devastated.

Now, her reflective silence found her angry. Angry at God, angry at Lance, angry at this doctor, all of them were at fault. None of them saved him. All of them let David die. The room was quiet for what seemed like forever before the doctor spoke.

"May I get you anything, coffee or a glass of water?" Both refused. All this delicate posturing skirting around the issue, Rebecca thought. My son is dead. Why? The question burning deep in my heart is unasked still. Refusing to come out, the words are stuck but not my thoughts. Not moving a muscle, she aimed her quiet attack at the man wearing the white, lab coat.

I'm a good judge of character. But then, you wouldn't know that doctor. To me, you are the healer, the medical expert. You are the one with all the answers. The sentiment echoed in her ears. Her mind ramblings didn't stop as she pressed on with her soundless interrogation. Who are you, really? Why didn't you save him? A baby just doesn't die without a reason. What are you hiding from me? Her endless, unspoken, questions left her weary. Dabbing her run away tears, she tilted her head. Not much, but just enough. It was all that was needed to bring a wall full of credentials within her peripheral vision. Beautifully framed diplomas verifying this doctor's abilities and accomplishments, his manifesto qualifications hung right there in view for all to appreciate. Most especially, his incredible credentials, were right there in front of her probably to lock in her trust. Yet, their purpose missed the mark. Despite the written endorsements in English and some even in Latin, they did not catapult her over doubt.

Okay, she thought. So you are licensed to practice the healing art of pediatrics. That's what it says. But, where did you rank in your class? None of your certificates specify.

Somebody has to come in last. Was it you? She didn't have the courage nor did her long ago training allow her to openly point a finger. Doing only what she could, she remained silent. Staring him straight in his eyes, she delved into his makeup, wondering if he had been in the profession too long. She wondered, too, if he just going through the motions. Why didn't you help him?

So caught up in her sorrow, so intent on placing blame, Rebecca missed the point. He did care and very deeply. She just didn't see it. His self-controlled, stoic manner unjustly tainted him as apathetic.

The doctor traveled a rough road. This was not the first time he had to break the hearts of loving parents and each process chipped another sliver of his. He did sit quietly. But it was out of concern for them. He allowed them time to calm down and collect their thoughts. He knew it was not easy for them. To digest the bitter pill he was about to dispense was going to make it worse.

The awkward silence continued as did her mind. My son is dead. Be however you need to be, doctor. Go ahead just sit there cold as stone. I don't want your sympathy. I want answers. The knot of bitterness had taken root and was growing rapidly.

Fumbling for the right words, she voiced the question she could fend off no longer, the one to which she dreaded to hear the already known answer.

"Doctor, are you sure? Are you really sure David is dead?"

Lance winced at the very mention of finality in connection with his son's name.

Despite his grief-stricken face, Rebecca did not feel pain for him. Now, only her hurt counted. She was at a loss as to why she had asked the stupid, uncalled for question. How many times did she need the doctor to confirm the tragedy? Why does that nagging from deep within compel her to place blame? She wasn't sure but she couldn't shake it. First she held the doctor accountable. Now clearly the guilt belonged to Lance. Yes, the fault was his. He didn't work hard enough. He let David die. How quickly she had forgotten his courageous effort. His long, hard fight to restore David to life was dismissed in her inability to accept her son's death.

Unaware of her desperate verdict, still stinging from the word association, Lance turned his attention to the doctor.

"Doctor, what happened? Clearing his throat, his shaky voice came out a little stronger. "The last check-up you told us nothing was found.

You even told us to go home and enjoy the boys. You led us to believe the boys would get better and now this?" Disbelief and resentment escalated as did his voice. Finally, he erupted. "Why did our son die?"

Pensively chewing on the end of his pen, the doctor hesitated. He knew the importance of venting and waited to be sure the hurting father got rid of all that lay heavy on his heart. He was also very much aware that he did not have a concrete answer to offer. His only hope at this point rested on the autopsy report. Maybe it would provide a fragment of satisfying information even if it didn't change the sad ending.

Immunity to personal torment was not given due consideration in Medical school and the parents' pleading eyes did not make it any easier. For the doctor knew the bottom line. There is no antidote for death, and that he could not say aloud.

Returning the pen to its holder, taking a deep breath, he answered the distressed parents to the best of his ability.

"I'm sorry Mr. and Mrs. Miles." Pausing, he thought how much he detested this part of his duties. "To be perfectly honest with you, I don't know for sure why your son died. You did do all the right things. Since birth, I've watch the love you showered on both your boys. It's just that the body is very complicated and even doing your best, something can go wrong.

'Now, there is a strong possibility that it was sudden infant death syndrome, known as SIDS. Unfortunately, it happens. Again, I'm not sure. I have ordered an autopsy. I'll know better after I learn the results."

"SIDS?" Rebecca gave him a quizzical look. "I don't understand, doctor. What exactly is it?"

"Basically, Mrs. Miles, it is the unexpected sudden death of a child under age one in which an autopsy does not show an explainable cause of death. Some refer to it as crib death." Baffled by this strange condition, Lance needed details.

"But what causes it?"

"The cause, I'm sorry to report Mr. Miles is unknown. Many in the medical field believe it is not a single condition that is always caused by the same medical problems. The belief is certain factors increase its risk."

"What factors? What risks, doctor?" Soul-searching, Rebecca cringed. "Oh, dear God, did I put David at risk?"

"Please, Mrs. Miles. Don't think that for one minute. The most common risk happens when a baby sleeps on his stomach and I know for fact that did not apply to your twins. It's listed on their charts. I can show you where you completed the questionnaire with that information."

Rebecca remembered how supplying that information came about. Crying and kicking, both boys loudly protested being placed on their stomachs. Early on, it was learned that the way to keep everybody happy was easy enough. It had nothing to do with medical protocol, everything to do with comfort. Whenever the boys were tucked in, it was an automatic rule which Rebecca and Lance followed to the letter, on backs only.

"What about the other risks?"

"Mrs. Miles, I assure you, they don't apply. You did absolutely nothing wrong. This brings me to a vital point that concerns the both of you. I'm afraid there will be a period of time when guilt will enter into the picture. Fight it. David's death is no one's fault."

Having said all that he could for now, and knowing the rocky road the couple had yet to travel, he again, extended his deepest sympathies. That concluded their meeting. "Just as soon as the autopsy report is in, I will contact you. But if you need me at any time, please don't hesitate to call me. I am truly sorry for your loss."

That's it? Rebecca questioned cynically. Other than the SIDS related issue, she had not asked her many anguished questions. She didn't feel she had to since Lance had covered the most pressing. At that, the doctor's totally unacceptable answer still left them in the dark. The cause of David's death remained a mystery. But there was nothing more to be done here. They had no choice. They would wait for the autopsy. But then, what difference would that make now.

Just as Lance reached for the door, the head nurse charged into the office like a freight train. "Excuse me. This is an emergency." Conspicuously nervous, she closed the door and rushed to the doctor's side. Whatever she whispered got the doctor's immediate attention. Gut feeling told Lance they should have walked out the door when they had the chance.

"What? What did you say, nurse?" Sure her repeated message was not a mistake, the obviously shaken doctor motioned for Rebecca and Lance to be seated. Focusing on this unbelievable latest development, and in their best interest, he didn't pull any punches. Words of support and encouragement could come later. Now, they needed to know what was happening. Without dramatizing his own reaction, he told them.

"Mr. and Mrs. Miles, your son, Dennis is in the emergency room. I'll take you there."

"Dennis is here at the hospital?" she asked. "What are you talking about? He's fine. He's home with our neighbors." "Is this some sort of cruel joke, Doc? If it is, it is not the least bit funny." Lance's mind and nerves were near collapse. "Come on Rebecca, let's go."

"Wait, Mr. Miles. Listen. We are wasting time. Your neighbors drove him to the hospital. They got scared when he wasn't breathing right. Come with me." The doctor insisted as he quickly ushered them through the door and to the emergency room.

Sure enough Dennis was there already in hospital pajamas and surrounded by a medical team. Rebecca and Lance could only watch the experts' swift movements as they followed vital commands.

"Lance," Rebecca begged, "tell me I'm sleeping. Tell me this is a horrible nightmare?"

"I know, Rebecca. This is crazy. First David and now Dennis, how can this be? They said they were getting better. They said…" his voice trailed off as now they were being escorted to the waiting room where Joy and George waited anxiously.

They had been told about David and were now awaiting news about Dennis. A tight embrace was all Joy could offer. That was all right. Hugs were not exactly what Rebecca was looking for. She wanted answers.

"Joy, George, what's going on? What happened? Dennis was fine when we left him with you." Rebecca's accusatory implication hurt but was short-lived as Joy could clearly see her dear friend was terribly distraught and justly so. So was she.

Wide-eyed, Lance and Rebecca listened to Joy's explanation. "Dennis slept for most of the time you were gone. Then about an hour ago, he woke up crying. When I touched him, he screamed and was burning with fever. He was gasping for air. That's when we rushed him to the emergency room. Lance, did the doctor say anything to you yet?"

"He only told us to sit in the waiting room. But as many as they have working on him, I think that's a good sign." Lance wasn't sure who he was trying to convince. He resented missing the chance to help his Dennis as he had his David. It's funny how one's mind works. Stressed, his failed attempt was quickly forgotten. This time, given the chance, he was positive he could have successfully navigated his emergency medical maneuvers but, wisely, he kept those thoughts to himself.

The waiting was intense for the four friends. Finally, Lance jumped to his feet and anxiously announced, "He's coming." Rebecca held her breath and felt a knot forming in her stomach. Stay calm. She told herself. Stay calm. She fought to control her erratic breathing. She glanced over at Lance. If his face was an open book, she hated what she could read.

Removing his surgical mask and cap, the doctor wiped his brow and took a deep breath. "Mr. and Mrs. Miles, I'm sorry. There wasn't anything anybody could do to save your son. Dennis just stopped breathing. We did all we could. He just..." Frozen in shock, Rebecca heard no more. She just stood there shaking her head. She saw little Dennis' beautiful eyes and his curly hair and how the ringlets fell across his forehead. She saw his ear to ear smile showing his tiny, straight, teeth. She saw her son, perfect in every way except for one. And that, she refused to believe. Too much to bear, Rebecca slipped into oblivion.

She opened her eyes to soft, white-covered walls and briefly enjoyed its serenity. That is until her memory and reality set in. "Hello. Lance, are you there? Is anybody there?" The more she remembered, the more she panicked. "I had this horrible nightmare."

"You're awake, Mrs. Miles," the nurse assured her. "Your husband just went to get coffee. He'll be right back."

"Where am I?"

"You're in the hospital? You fainted. Just relax now. Would you like anything?"

"No, thank you. I just want my husband." As if on cue, Lance came into the room carrying two cups of coffee which he put on the table to cool. "I was hoping you would be awake. I brought you coffee."

Confused, Rebecca reached out.

"Lance, what am I doing here? I had this most horrific nightmare. It's almost too scary to talk about but I have to. I really thought the twins died. Is that insane?" He closed his eyes and hung his head. That's all it took. If someone had put a knife through her heart, it could not have cut deeper. Screaming hysterically, she beat on his chest. "It's not true. It's not true."

"Please Mrs. Miles, calm down," the nurse insisted as she quickly and efficiently administered the shot. "She'll be fine now, Mr. Miles. She needs to rest."

He had to be brave for her. He didn't have time to treat his shattered heart. At the doctor's insistence, Rebecca had been admitted to the hospital. This unbelievable tragedy was too much on the young mother. He knew, too, that the next few days were going to be rough on the young couple.

"She'll be sedated for the night, Mr. Miles. You may as well go home. Get some rest. She'll be ready to be discharged tomorrow morning. You can come back then."

"Thank you, nurse," he said and took her advice.

At home alone, the quiet of the empty rooms roared. Eating him alive, Lance couldn't stand it. Everything in place, yet nothing as it should be, his pain was intense. He longed for the happiness of yesteryears.

Lifting his eyes to heaven, he yelled. "How could you do this to me, God? You took both my boys and after all the promises I made." Crushed, sobbing bitter tears, he fell to his knees, and cried like never before.

Emotionally worn out, he went to bed but was denied sleep. His brain wouldn't give it a rest. Somebody was guilty. Somebody, right after God, had to be blamed. It didn't matter what the doctor claimed. It was somebody's fault. Rebecca was that somebody.

Self-pity is one of the quickest ways to irrational satisfaction. It's just wrong.

Like the cigarette smoke circles he blew into the air, his reasoning was clouded. His irrational thoughts against Rebecca were cruel...she's the mother, she should have seen how sick they were, she should have taken better care of them. She didn't. Guilty as charged. Now they were gone and she was sleeping soundly while he was wide awake.

That Rebecca was given a sedative didn't matter to Lance. That kind of thinking would let her off the hook and he wasn't ready for that.

The next morning Lance went to the hospital. They didn't have much to say to each other. Turns out, he wasn't the only one placing blame. Shackled within their minds, understanding and compassion refused to be rescued. Secretly blaming one another resentment did nothing but produce a cycle of negative consequences.

Arm in arm, more for security than comfort, the shattered parents walked out of the hospital. Except for the muffled sound of her crying, they rode home in silence. Engrossed in private thought, each silent concentration, unfortunately, was riddled with ugly accusations. Joy and George were there for them. Food was cooked, the house straightened and necessary phone calls placed. These neighbors even helped with the funeral arrangements. It was hard on their good friends. They had grown close to this family. People just don't know what to say in sad situations. Their actions showed what their voices just couldn't express. Soon it was time for them to go home.

"If you need me, I'm just next door."

"Thank you, Joy," Rebecca uttered softly and did not linger in the arms of her sympathetic friend. Misery cried out from every fiber of her being. Retreating to the solitude of her room took top priority. She couldn't get there fast enough. Yet once safe within the room's confines, away from the torment, the compelling drive to escape did not dissipate. There simply was no place to go. The unresolved problem now clearly identified, she could not run away from herself.

Flinging her body across the bed, endless tears streamed down her face. Reaching for tissues on the night stand, she caught a glimpse of the ghastly reflection in the mirror. That can't be, she gasped involuntarily. That pathetic image peering back can't be me. Mesmerized, the longer she stared, the more she realized she could not hang on to the denial. Cringing, she accepted the disagreeable truth.

She managed to wipe away the tears, but was unable to stifle her cries of despair. Arising unexpectedly straight from her agony, the relentless, uncontrollable sad sounds filled the room. Wrapping her arms around her legs, she pulled them up to her chin then gently rocked back and forth.

Torn with anguish, her mind traveled back to her orphanage days when it was the norm to frequently talk to God. She remembered, despite the years gone by, how the talks centered round questions and how promises accompanied petitions. She remembered the childish bargaining chips used in negotiations, like an A on my exam for two extra prayers.

With Rebecca's maturity came the realization that bargaining type prayers were the property of the very young. Except for perfunctory prayer, her ardent devotion had diminished. But now, in need of His attention, she closed her eyes and fell to her knees. Burning a hole in her soul, her blistering questions came blasting out.

"Why, Lord? Tell me," she begged, "They were just babies and had so much to live for. Promises cut short." She pressed on with her interrogation. "Tell me why? I'm sorry for lying most of my life. But that was never their fault. It was always mine. I'm to blame. You took the wrong ones." Full of anger and confusion, Rebecca took her recourse a step further. "Or you could have taken Lance. It's his fault, too. He let David die. He didn't try hard enough. He wasn't even there for Dennis. Now, it is too late."

Grief robbed Rebecca of logic and filled her head with irrational thinking. Why live? Convinced, the solution so obvious, she screamed it into her pillow. "I'll just end it all."

Yet even as the weight of her burden escalated, she heard the tiny voice from within shout out loudly in protest. A lesson deeply ingrained from her years in Bible Study...*But only God can take* a *life.* That cautionary message coming in loud and clear expelled the destructive scheme. Her breathing came short and quick, and suddenly, with the realization of the sheer selfishness on her part, the inner voice was free to vanish.

Lance, tired, too, had now come to bed.

"Are you okay? Rebecca." Still shaken at the foolishness of her last thought, her answer was not what he had expected.

"Lance, there's nothing I can do now. I tried to be a good parent, but I didn't get a fair shot."

"I know. Neither one of us did."

The caskets so tiny, the tears so many, the hearts so broken, the funeral was understandably a doleful blur. Looking into the side by side satin lined coffins, Rebecca's desire was to snatch both boys up and run away to safety. Crying, she reached in and lovingly brushed the once rosy, warm cheek of one and then the other twin. Now they were pallid and cold. If only she could warm them, wake them. If only...

"Here, my darlings," she said with a strained choking sound. "Here are your favorite teddy bears. You can't go without them." She seized the moment of passing solace to place the chocolate brown bear with the red bow tie in next to David. She did the same for Dennis with his cherished champagne colored bear with the blue bow tie. How many times, she thought had they fallen asleep hugging their bears? But they always woke up.

In her mind's eye, she could see them standing in their cribs chomping on an ear or chewing on a leg. Not this time. Why, she agonized, did David and Dennis have to die mere babies? They're gone. Death is so final.

Falling to her knees, she wept. Lance lifted her and held her arm for support. Poor Rebecca, he thought. At the same time, he wondered, who would hold him up? His legs were like rubber. His sons' deaths were a crushing blow almost more than he could bear. He held back tears but every fiber of his body cried.

How he grieved and, again aimed his anger toward his Creator. Children are not supposed to die before their parents. I never got a chance to play ball with them. You know I'm not much on religion. I have this love/hate entity going on. Right now, the love part is tough. Like Rebecca said, neither one of us had a fair shot at being parents.

Lance's mind and feelings were muddled and along with confusion, came fear. Certain deep-rooted teachings from his Bible Study Class of yesteryear pushed their claim of caution into his mind. The lessons reminded him that he could not chance provoking his Creator to the detriment of his boys.

Despite his anger, he quietly petitioned. Keep my sons in Your protective care. Since you took them, please welcome them, two more lambs into your fold. Help me make some sense of this ordeal, to accept what is, and to believe with the death of my two sons, comes the birth of two little angels.

His heart and head ached. He could think no more of himself. He had to focus on Rebecca. Somewhere in sorting his thoughts, he came to the realization that maybe Rebecca was not to blame. It was a confusing time.

The service over, neither grieving parent could remember all that had transpired. They could never, however, forget that with the deepest of farewells, they buried their sons. With that burial, sadly, a part of their marriage submerged, too.

The very foundation of their lives shaken, thrown into despair, never again would their marriage be filled with the fantasy dreams they had planned for and with each other.

For days following, Rebecca was out of it. It was her mind's response shielding her from even the smallest of any additional hurts. She seemed anesthetized in dealing with the shock of it all. Unfortunately, the time came when that no longer worked. The anesthesia wore off. She tried keeping busy. Never-the-less, despair became the norm.

She blamed herself and deep down, she blamed Lance for no other reason but that as head of the household, it was his duty. He should have saved her sons. Now, nothing he said or did was right. Joy tried her best, too. Some time her company was welcomed; other times, rejected. Rebecca turned within herself. Lance turned to his work. Regrettably, neither turned to the other.

Their pattern of life changed drastically. Not wanting Lance near her, yet resenting his absence, Rebecca lashed out at him. He didn't stand a chance. Engulfed with loneliness and guilt, she knew Lance was hurting and she was aware of her hostility toward him. Yet, she could not stop herself. She really didn't care. It's called depression.

Lance tried everything. He pampered, he yelled, he cried. Nothing worked. He was losing Rebecca. Still mourning the loss of his sons, now he mourned the loss of his marriage. Short of a miracle, it was destined for destruction. Then one day help and hope arrived from the least expected source. Offering guidance, advice and spiritual assistance, it came by way of a letter from Rebecca's long ago teacher and friend.

In an effort to ease the pain, Rebecca had poured out her agony in letters to her old friends. Over the years since leaving the orphanage they kept their promise. Theresa, Annette, Annmarie, and Rebecca faithfully wrote to each other. Rebecca, in heart-breaking detail, told each of them of her anguish. Although she knew there was no way to protect her heart from being hurt, somehow putting it on paper and sharing it with her dear friends was therapeutic.

It was Theresa who took the initiative. Taking it upon herself, she wrote to the one person she felt could help. Theresa cried when she read

Rebecca's sad news. For days, she was melancholy. Finally, she could stand by no longer. She never asked Rebecca's permission. She just followed her heart and penned her letter.

$$* * * * *$$

Sympathy cards were still arriving. Today was no different. The cards continued as an out-pouring of heart-felt sympathy and love. Lance off to work, Rebecca sat in her bathrobe finishing her morning coffee. Quietly reminiscing, her thoughts were interrupted by the mail carrier. It was just as well. She needed an intrusion. Something to chisel, from within her tired mind, the images of her lost babies lying in little coffins, sealed in concrete.

Picking up the mail that had been slipped thought the slot on the front door she sifted through the correspondence sorting first class from junk mail. Suddenly, she stopped cold in her tracks and rubbed the goose bumps materializing on her arms. She could not believe her eyes. The return address on the letter she held in her hand was one from out of the blue, but one she knew so well. Totally unexpected, it weakened her. Quickly she sought the aid of a kitchen chair.

"This perfect handwriting can belong to only one person," she said aloud. "But it can't be. She has never written to me." Puzzled, a scary thought popped into her head. What if Lance had gotten the mail first and questioned the return address? Now fear of exposure added to her state of depression. I've lost my twins, she thought, but I'm not about to lose my secret. I have to hang onto something. I've got to get rid of this envelope. That's all there is to it. Immediately, tearing it to shreds, she threw it in the trash.

Wiping small beads of perspiration from her brow, she shuddered to think of the threat. Haven't I suffered enough? Is my past out to get me, too? Trembling, she held the letter as steady as possible as her eyes went directly to the writer's signature. She was right. It was from none other than Sister Regina and that's all it took to open the floodgates.

Reaching for her handkerchief, she blotted her tears, took a deep breath then delved into the words of the unexpected letter.

My dear Rebecca,

Theresa wrote me of your sorrowful loss. Oh, how my heart cries for you. Surely, this tragedy hurts beyond words. You must be frightfully heartsick. If I could be there this very minute, I would cradle you in my arms in hopes of lessening the pain.

There are not enough anesthetics in this world to totally numb you of your agonizing torment but try to accept whatever comfort, no matter how small, that is offered. It is a beginning to your healing.

Surely, you must be haunted by the senselessness of all that has transpired and full of guilt ridden 'if only and what ifs'. I pray this counterproductive nagging subsides. You have suffered enough. Let it go.

Actually, there is no viable answer, at this time, as to why your precious twins had to leave after such a brief visit and, any attempt at clarification would be in vain. You are not ready. No matter what reason might be suggested, you would have every right to indignantly reject the explanation. You need time.

When I think of you, Rebecca, I remember your determination and optimism and I envision you with your beautiful smile. It saddens me to think they are gone and I truly pray they will soon return. Until such time, I can do only two things. First, I can remind you of the very core of our faith. Jesus is always with us. Sharing our pain, accepting our doubts and anger and holding us close in our grief, and this, even, when we think He has walked away.

Suffering and death strike at any time because death plays no favorites.

Secondly, I can share in your sorrow. I offer these words of Ralph Waldo Emerson in hope that they will bring you a measure of comfort.

For each thorn - there's a rosebud...
For each twilight – a dawn...
For each trial – the strength to carry on...
For each storm cloud – a rainbow...
For each shadow – the sun...
For each parting – sweet memories, when sorrow is done.

Rebecca, you have loved and have been loved not only by your sweet babies but also by your devoted husband. He loves you still. Don't turn against him. I write Rebecca, asking you to search your soul, and remember that he, too, suffers. He needs you now more than ever. His world is falling apart. Don't push him away. Give him your unwavering love and support, and know that a pain shared is diminished to half a pain.

Don't dwell on the past. It is gone. Look to the future. It is, to a large degree, what you decide to make of it. I pray you choose to make it happy again both for your sake and that of your dear husband's. Rebecca, when you forgive, you love...when you love, God shines love on you and, happiness is only real when shared.

Sometimes tragedy pulls people closer together. Sometimes, it creates a chasm of despair that destroys all hope. Don't let it sabotage your marriage. For now, Rebecca be encouraged and gather strength, remembering 'Blessed are those who mourn; for they shall be comforted.' Matthew 5:4.

I implore you. Embrace your husband before it is too late. If you need me, I am here. Until then, know that God loves you and so do I. You are ever in my prayers, my precious Rebecca."

In Christ's love,
Sister Regina

Rebecca read the letter a second time then sat staring at it for a long time before tucking it safely in her bible. Suddenly, with uncontrollable tears streaming down her cheeks, she ran to the bedroom and flung herself across the bed. With the nun's unforgettable words swirling around in her head, overcome with emotion, she cried like there was no tomorrow.

Oh, Sister Regina, she sobbed. You are so right. You put my feelings into words. I refused to admit it but you hit the nail on the head. You'll never know how much I needed your wake-up call. It's true. I don't want to lose Lance. I promise my poor behavior toward him will stop. I have shut him out for too long. I just hope it is not too late.

Washing her face and adding a touch of lipstick, she moved in hopes of reversing her neglect of Lance. Sister Regina's letter, a shot in the arm, got her thinking and moving, at last, in the right direction. Running the brush through her hair, her mind kept up with the pace. It won't be easy, she thought. There will be struggles and set-backs. But I'm determined to cry less, to spend less time on resentment and more time with Lance. Like Sister said, the past is over. Walking toward the telephone, she added. Hopefully, I can start our future now.

Good thing Lance was not holding his calls today. This particular call was well worth answering. The familiar voice on the other end simply said, "I love you." Like music to his ears, they were the very words he had been longing to hear.

"Me, too," was all he managed to respond. He took the rest of the day off and hurried home.

Greeting him at the door, she welcomed him into her arms and then into the kitchen for a home cooked meal. "It's been a long time, Lance. I hope you still like my meatloaf."

Lance would never know what changed her. He didn't care. She was changed and that's all that mattered.

"I love your meatloaf, Rebecca." Taking her into his arms, he kissed her gently and whispered, "And you, even more."

A mature Rebecca and Lance evolved from their sad experience. Successfully living through all the necessary stages of grief, they were ready now to love and be loved again.

Life presented them with a second chance; a second courtship, so to speak. It took time but, it was so very good and in the end, their love was rewarded. Rebecca was once again, pregnant.

"Are you okay in there?" he asked, knocking on the bathroom door.

"Think so," she managed to get out before the next wave hit her.

"I'm coming in, okay?"

He didn't wait for an answer. Lance found Rebecca sitting on the floor hugging the toilet bowl. Quickly, he got a wet cloth and held it to her forehead.

"What's wrong, Rebecca?"

"Must have picked up a bug."

"Feeling any better, now?"

"I am." She answered as she got up and made her way to the bedroom.

"I want you to make an appointment with Dr. Roberts today."

"I will." Still feeling a little queasy, Rebecca was not about to argue.

"Call me at work if you hear anything."

"Okay. Now don't worry. I'm fine."

He never got his call. Maybe she couldn't get in to see the doctor today, he thought. But then no news is good news. None-the-less, he was anxious to get home at the day's end.

"I'm home," he announced hanging his jacket on the clothes tree. "Where are you, Rebecca?"

"In the kitchen."

There was something different about her. He couldn't quite put his finger on it but then he saw it. Rebecca was absolutely glowing. Without fanfare, Rebecca quickly satisfied his curiosity.

"I'm pregnant."

The color on Lance's face slowly faded. He couldn't believe his ears. On one hand, it was too good to be true and on the other hand, it conjured up painful memories mixed with scary possibilities.

He need not have worried. This time, they became parents to a beautiful, eight pound girl. They named her Emily Ann.

Chapter 24

1962

As Emily's first birthday grew nearer and nearer, more than once, he woke up in a cold sweat. Nightmares of little coffins and still babies haunted him now more than ever. Rebecca, jumpy as a cat, suffered in silence and neither talked about it.

It was Saturday evening and Lance's parents, invited to dinner, were due to arrive at any minute. "Lance, do me a favor. When your parents get here, please don't argue with your father."

"Wasn't planning on it."

"Good. I swear, sometimes the smallest issue sets you two off. It's not a sport, you know and it makes me and your Mom nervous. Let's just have a relaxing time."

"Okay. But if he starts…."

"No buts. Now answer the doorbell."

So far, so good, Rebecca thought. As it turned out, Lance and his Dad actually got through dinner without a single eruption.

"Rebecca," her father-in-law announced. "You have outdone yourself. That pot roast was delicious." Patting his full stomach in appreciation, he was forced to decline dessert.

"Thanks. I'm glad you enjoyed it. How about you, Mother Miles? Are you ready for cherry cobbler with vanilla ice-cream.?"

"I shouldn't, but how can I say no? I can't resist. You make the best cherry cobbler." Wiping her lips with the linen napkin, her mother-in-law got up from her seat. "In fact, I'll help you. I'll pour the coffee."

"You know son," Lance's father said, "It's hard to believe that our little Emily here will soon be one-year-old, isn't it?"

"Yeah, Dad. Time flies by." To himself, he said, "But not swiftly enough."

I wish her birthday was here and gone already. Then I'd be sure she is safe.

As if he read his son's mind, Lance's father filled in the blanks. "Now, you listen to me. Nothing will happen to our Emily. Nothing."

"What's this about Emily?" Lance's mother asked returning from the kitchen.

"Well, Jenny, you know how I believe in coming straight to the point. Lance and I were just saying her birthday is just around the corner. Now that we are all together, I have something to say." His tone so serious, he had their complete attention.

"Listen. Let's stop beating around the bush. Being anxious about Emily's fate and thinking what happened to the boys might happen to her is illogical and a waste of precious time. Think about it. What happened to the twins was a fluke. Even some of the doctors seem to lean towards that conclusion. Odds of it happening again are astronomical, if ever."

No longer able to sit still, he got up. Without skipping a beat, he went on with his ardent tirade, walking around the table as he spoke. "You are all intelligent people." Pausing, he snickered, "Or at least I like to think so. Seriously, do any of you really believe that some Great Power sits next to a switch that controls life and death and pulls it willy-nilly? Or can't wait to hit the connection when Emily turns one? Ludicrous? You bet. But that seems to be your mind-set. Change it, people. Whatever will be, will be, just stop the useless torture." He sat down now a bit drained but at peace with himself.

He said what had to be said and felt sure they heard what needed to be heard. He was right, of course. Worrying never changed a thing and no one was out to get Emily.

Fortunately, the darling little girl continued to happily celebrate birthday after birthday.

Chapter 25

1969

"Hap-py birth-daay dear Em-i-ly," the gathered guests sang, "Hap-py birth-daay to you." Remembering her father-in-law's sage wake-up call of eight years ago, Rebecca smiled gratefully as she watched her daughter huff and puff and blow out the candles. Going on nine now, their growing, little girl was as cute as a button.

"Open this gift, Emily," her excited Grandmother encouraged. "Here let me help you. Well, how do you like it?" she asked.

"I love it, Grandma. How did you know Mickey Mouse is my very favorite?"

"A little birdie told me. Look on the back of the frame."

"There's a note, Grandma."

"That's right and it's from me and Grandpa. Here, let me read it to you, okay?"

"Okay," she said nonchalantly handing her Grandmother the note.

"It says ...Happy Birthday, Emily. You're going to Disneyland."

"Yippee!" Screaming and clapping her hands all the while jumping up and down like a jumping bean. When she learned the importance of that piece of paper, her nonchalant mood changed instantaneously.

"Wait. Emily, there's more on the note."

"I think you lost her, Mom," Lance laughed.

"Well, okay, then. I'll just tell you and Rebecca the rest. It's our treat for all three of you for a week's stay."

"Wow! Now, I'm excited, Disneyland! Thanks, Mom. Thanks, Dad. You're the best."

* * * * *

School was out for Spring break and excitement filled the Miles house mainly with the one word that had been the topic of discussion since Emily's birthday.

"I can't wait, Mommy. When are we going to Disneyland?" Emily could hardly contain herself.

"It won't be long now, Emily," her mother assured her. "We leave in the morning."

"Yippee," Emily cheered. "And guess what?"

"What, dear?"

"I get to fly on an airplane for the very first time in my whole entire life."

"Indeed, you do." It was her amused father this time that backed up her declaration.

The little magpie went on and on in anticipation. "And when we get there, I want to see Mickey Mouse and Cinderella, and Snow White and Alice in Wonderland and, mostly, I want to ride on Dumbo. I wish my ears were as big as his then I could fly all over the place."

"No, no. I like your tiny ears just the way they are. Imagine how you would look if your ears hung down to here." Laughing, Lance gently tugged on her ear lobe, let go and exaggerated its length by touching his hand down to the floor. Giggling, Emily retorted.

"But think how good I could hear you, Daddy. I would listen and go to bed the first time you told me to."

"Now, that would be something. Speaking of which, little girl, it's time for bed. We have a big day ahead of us tomorrow. Now, off you go." It was Rebecca who brought up the subject. In bed about to doze off, she mentioned it to Lance. "Wouldn't David and Dennis love to have seen all the cartoon characters, too."

"Please, Rebecca don't torture yourself. Just enjoy Emily's excitement."

"I know you are right, Lance. I usually do okay. It's just on special events that I feel so sad that they missed out."

"I know. I do, too."

The morning couldn't get here fast enough but when it did, they finally found themselves on the plane heading to California.

"Sit here, honey. Right in the middle of Mommy and me and when we get up in the air, you can switch seats for a few minutes so you can look out the window. I think you'll like what you'll see out there."

Watching Lance and Emily, Rebecca wondered with love in her heart, which of the two was more excited. Emily was such a bundle of joy; Lance, a bundle of enthusiasm.

"Are we there yet?" Emily asked in a sing-song voice.

"Not yet, Emily." Rebecca answered for the tenth time and couldn't help but wonder how many times and how many parents were asked that very question in the course of a lifetime? Giggling to herself, she figured so far on this trip alone, Emily must surely have gone over her allotted quota. Finally, Emily got the answer she had been seeking over and over again.

"We're here, Pumpkin." Lance announced as the plane came to a safe stop. Off the plane and onto a shuttle bus, caught up in this adventure, Emily didn't have much to say.

But on the shuttle ride to the hotel, seeing signs advertising Disneyland added to the excitement, she more than made up for it. Fortunately, with the time change from New Jersey to California, they arrived with plenty of day light left to explore. Barely dropping off their luggage at the hotel, they were back out the door with Rebecca thinking about that Walt Disney fellow and how he surely created a wonderful adventure.

Emily's eyes grew as big as saucers. "Mommy, look over there and, over there and, over there." Pointing out so many highlights, Emily wanted to see them all.

"I see." Holding Emily's hand, Rebecca could feel the little girl's excitement. Turning to Lance, she extended the feeling. "Lance, there's so much to see and so much to do. Gee, this whole place is too magical. I bet it's the happiest place on earth. Well, to us today, for sure."

"It is great," he answered. "I can't get over how realistic the animation is. It's fantastic. Disney was a genius."

The place so big, they walked and walked taking in all the sights. Energy abounded and like Jiminy Cricket, Emily was everywhere.

"Before we take you to the ride section, Emily, let's get something to eat. I'm hungry, okay?" It was Rebecca's way of getting Emily to slow down while affording Rebecca and Lance a much needed short respite, too.

"Aw, do we have to?" she pleaded pathetically.

"We do." Sticking to their guns, the parents walked into the restaurant. Once their food was served and Emily practically inhaled her grilled cheese sandwich. Kneeling on the booth bench to better reach her straw, right in the middle of a sip of milk, she looked up. Gulping hard, she managed to get the milk down, and then squealed. Pointing her finger, she yelled. "Look Mommy. Look Daddy. It's Mickey and Minnie."

"Well, I'll be darned," Lance said in amazement, "So it is." Sure enough the two Disney characters had quietly strolled right up to the table to visit with Emily and, Emily was thrilled beyond belief.

"Mickey and Minnie," Emily yelled then jumped down from her seat and run right into the outstretched arms, first of Mickey and then of Minnie. Lance whipped out the camera. It was a real Kodak moment and a great beginning to a wonderful, magical vacation.

Leaving the restaurant, Emily tugged on her mother's sleeve and seriously declared, "I'm so glad *I* was hungry, Mommy." Rebecca laughed and off they went to Toon Town and the Small World section with all the rides.

"There he is. There's Dumbo. Oh, hurry. Let's ride him."

Waving as she rode round and round on the happy faced, huge-eared elephant, Rebecca stated the obvious. "We'll never forget that look of sheer happiness on Emily's face."

"Nope, we sure won't." That he captured it on camera was just for extra insurance.

Each fun filled day came with new fun filled adventures. At night, they enjoyed unforgettable fireworks and the festival of lights. They liked the fantastic parade so much they went to it several times. Featuring the Disney characters marching to familiar Disney medleys, it was a potpourri patchwork of Emily's make-believe friends. When the vacation drew to an end, naturally, she did not want to leave.

"Can't we stay for just one more day?" she begged.

"I'm afraid not, Pumpkin. Our plane tickets are for today." It didn't take long. They had been on the plane for about fifteen minutes when Lance mentioned it.

"Look at her, Rebecca. She's sleeping like a log. And she wanted to stay another day. She must be exhausted."

"Well she should be. We crammed an awful lot into this vacation."

Sleeping with her head tilted to one side, Emily proudly wore her Mickey Mouse ears, her Disney souvenir; her treasure forever.

Chapter 26

1978

Marching to the quick cadence beat of a drummer, time stands still for no one. Before they could turn around, it seemed their little girl had grown into a fun-loving teenager eager to do it all.

Actively involved with the school newspaper, and the glee club, she served as vice-president of her junior class and president of her senior year. Emily even tried her hand at field hockey. As it turned out, she did okay.

Actually, she was pretty good at it. She played center and although proud of her, Rebecca could not count the many bruises, especially to the shins, that Emily earned and wore like badges. At the end of the hockey season, Emily's team won the State Champ title.

To her parents' delight, Emily possessed an artistic talent, too. The medium she liked best was watercolors. There, again, she excelled and for two years running, she took first place in the local art show. It seemed this girl was good in everything that held her interest.

She had so many favorites that Rebecca had a hard time keeping up with the program at hand. Diversified, Emily enjoyed going to the ballet just as much as she liked going to baseball games just as much as she liked going to the movies and, high on her list was, listening to all kinds of music. Gets that honestly, and Rebecca was pleased with that thought.

Her maturity level advanced. She thrived on movies with substance, with those that focused on important issues. John Steinbeck's compelling social testimony, 'Grapes of Wrath' and Margaret Mitchell's historic Civil War saga, 'Gone With The Wind' were among her favorites, as was James Hilton's tribute to his own school teacher father, 'Goodbye, Mr. Chips.'

Then there was this neat attribute about Emily; her ability to engage in intelligent discussions with friends with similar interests while maintaining friendships with those who preferred movies or books of lesser involvement. With them, she laughed loudest at movies like Mel Brooks' spoof 'The Young Frankenstein.' Indeed, Emily was popular with her peers.

Pleased, Rebecca had kept the promise made years ago. She was proud of it, too. While not being spoiled, and as far as Rebecca was concerned she wasn't, Emily wanted for nothing. Emily was living her youth to the fullest as well it should be. Needless worries would never be her haunt. Rebecca made sure of it.

Before Rebecca and Lance knew it, like an old Mickey Mouse movie where movement was produced by quickly turning frame after frame, Emily was going to the prom. Then came graduation day and then off she went to college. The flying years caught them off guard and much before they were ready, she was their little Emily Ann, planning her wedding.

Chapter 27

1973

For as long as she could remember, Emily's father seemed to be more affectionate than her mother, although, she was sure her mother loved her, too. It was just the funny way she had of showing it or maybe it was just that her mother was too overly protective. Emily didn't know. She couldn't put her finger on it. But that's why nine times out of ten, when she wanted something, she asked her father first.

Liz Ingle had been Emily's best friend every since their first day together in kindergarten. Like two peas in a pod, they talked the same, dressed the same and even shared the same likes and dislikes. Mostly, they both were adventurous. The greater the risk, the more worth-while taking it. Together, they could do anything or so that was their young, focused mind-set.

Twelve-years-old now, they were pumped up and eager to help their Scout Troop.

"Mom," Emily yelled. "Me and Liz are going to sell Girl Scout cookies, now. We'll be back in time for dinner. Okay?"

Rebecca came rushing into the den where the girls were gathering paperwork for their big sales project.

"Hold on. Why don't you just wait for your father to get home from work? He'll be here in twenty minutes and then he can take the both of you out to the streets beyond our neighborhood. You'll sell more cookies that way. Besides, it's starting to get dark out."

Frowning, Emily resisted. "Twenty minutes? Gee, Mom, we could sell a lot of cookies in twenty minutes time. Why can't we just go now?"

"Emily. You heard me. Please don't argue. You'll go when your father gets home."

Taking off their jackets, the girls sat down and waited as they were told. Disappointed, Emily muttered under her breath, "It's not fair." With her arms folded across her chest, sulking, Emily whispered to her friend.

"Liz, my mother is so mean. She never lets me do what I want."

"I know. My Mom never lets me do anything either."

"I can't wait until I grow up. Then I'll do just what I want."

"Yeah, me, too. Wanna play checkers while we wait?"

"Sure."

Lance didn't make it home in twenty minutes, not even in thirty. He got tied up at work for well over an hour.

"Daddy, finally you're home." Running to greet him as he slumped down on his chair, Emily asked, "Can you take us to sell Girl Scout cookies now?"

"I'm sorry, Pumpkin. It's late and I'm tired. Tomorrow is Saturday and we can get an early start, okay?" he asked solicitously.

Sticking out her lower lip, Emily pouted. "Gee, Daddy we really wanted to go out tonight."

"Now, now, don't go away with your nose out of join. Where's my hug?" Arms outstretched, he waited. Emily liked hugging her father and tightly wrapped her arms around him. "Ah, that's better. That's my girl. We'll go out tomorrow, okay?"

"Okay, Daddy," she agreed reluctantly, and then returned to the checker game.

"Thanks, Lance. You know I'd much rather the girls go out under the protective light of day."

Lance was very much aware of Rebecca's lingering private fear. Although it had gotten better, she still couldn't totally shake it. She just had to keep her only child safe.

"I know, Rebecca. But you have to let go sometime."

"Right, and I will, but not just yet."

"Okay, but be careful, Rebecca. Don't let your holding her so close, wind up pushing her away."

Rebecca refused to see it that way and thought clashes between mother and daughter happen. It's inevitable.

"She's just asserting her independence, Lance, that's all."

"Mom," Emily came bounding into the kitchen, "Can Liz sleep over tonight?"

"It's *may* Liz sleep over and yes, she may." Rebecca added to herself, and I, my child, am not saying yes because I feel guilty. Tomorrow is really soon enough to sell cookies.

"Liz, call your mother. Check if it's alright with her. If it is, Mr. Miles will walk you and Emily to your house for your overnight things."

What a relief, Rebecca mused. In the excitement of Liz's overnight, Emily already has forgotten all about cookie selling. She's such a good girl. Still I wished at times, she would be less contrary. Boy, it's not easy raising her. Like I told Lance, she's just learning to assert her views. At least that's what I'm going to use to pacify my rationale. She didn't have time to give more thought to the situation before the girls returned. Mission accomplished, the eager girls rushed back into the house and made a bee-line straight to Emily's room.

Hidden in Liz's bedroll right next to the flashlight and comic books were her goodies.

"Emily, here's my stash for tonight. Look, I've got pretzels, cookies and jelly beans."

"Great. And I've got two candy bars and potato chips and two bottles of pop. Isn't this exciting? Let's stay up all night."

"Oh, let's do."

Pajamas on, anxious for their sleepover to begin, the girls went to say good night.

"Goodnight, Pumpkin." Lance kissed his Emily. "I have a feeling that I won't be tucking you in tonight." He winked and she giggled. How well he knew his daughter. When she and Liz got together for an overnight, very little sleep entered the picture.

She went over to Rebecca and with all her short-term thoughts of meanness gone, lovingly kissed her mother, too.

"Night, Mom."

"Goodnight, Sweetie and goodnight Liz. Now, don't let the bedbugs bite."

"Yuk, Mom. What a terrible thing to say. Bug bites, yuk!" With crinkled up noses in protest of the bug chomping possibility, the girls ran out of the room, 'oohing' in disgust.

"Why do kids always have to run, Lance?"

"To beat the possibility of changing their minds? Or, maybe they figure it gives them a head start on doing what they want. Then, again, maybe they just want to get where they are going faster? Who knows?"

"Oh, to be that young again, full of energy and no worries in the world."

"Would be nice but then, I couldn't kiss you like this, now could I?" Wrapping his arms around her waist, and tenderly planting quick, little, nibble kisses to her neck instantly generated goose bumps. In a matter of but seconds, she felt the tingle down her spine.

"Lance, stop."

"Really?"

"Well no." And she melted in his arms. "But isn't it a bit early for us to go to sleep?"

"Sleeping is not exactly what I have in mind, my dear," he said breathlessly as he quickly checked the front door and switched off the lights.

The girls waited for what seemed like an eternity before they were willing to take the risk.

"Are you sure they're asleep, Emily?"

"Yep. Listen. That's my Dad snoring. They're asleep all right."

"Good. It's dark now. Let's go."

Tingling in anticipation, ever so quietly, they headed out in search of adventure.

With only the aid of flashlights, slowly they tiptoed past the grown-ups' room to investigate secrets only uncovered by dark of night.

"Sshh. Don't you make a sound." Emily warned her friend. "Come on. I want to show you what I found the other day. But, for heaven's sake, don't make any noise. If my Mom or Dad wake up and find out, I'll be grounded for life."

"For life? Oh, Emily, you sure do exaggerate." None-the-less, just in case, Liz offered that tidbit of information in a soft voice.

Slowly, they made their way to the den. In the center of the room was a big, green trunk serving as a coffee table. Emily had never seen its contents. Covered with magazines and knick-knacks, it was just that, a coffee table.

"So, what's the big deal, Emily? It's just a table."

"No. No, it's not. Listen, Liz. Last week, I accidentally discovered this coffee table opens. I jumped off the couch when my Mom was out of the room or she would have flipped. When I did, I bumped the latch with my feet and the thing popped open. I wiggled my fingers into this small space and the lid opened just enough for me to see something in it. I couldn't see what and then I saw my Mom in the other room so I quickly snapped the lock closed. But I've been curious about it ever since."

"Wow, Emily. What do you think is in it?"

"Don't know. Maybe it's full of candy or stuffed animals or..."

"Or," Liz jumped in, "Snakes."

"Gee, Liz, did you have to say that? Now you got me scared."

"Come on. Don't be such a scaredy-cat. Help me move the magazines."

"Be careful with my Mom's knick-knacks." Together and very slowly, just in case snakes should happen to live in there, the girls carefully lifted the lid. Cautiously they peered into the big box and immediately, in sync, they crinkled their noses in disappointment. It was a case of the anticipation being greater than the event. Turned out it certainly was true this time and rapidly the excitement wrapped up in their risky venture headed down the tubes.

"Why, there are just photo albums, Emily." Liz sounded frustrated. "We've been tricked."

Crestfallen, Emily tried to cover up her let-down. "Yes, but look how old they are. Maybe we have royalty in our family or something." Her eyes widened. "Maybe I'm a princess."

"Oh, sure," Liz said sarcastically, "And maybe, Emily these are just pictures of old people like your Grandparents. You know like King Grandpa and Queen Grandma."

"Oh, what do you know?" Emily sassed and rolled her eyes. "Now shine your flashlight over here so I can see better."

Gently removing the first album and after turning page after page, Emily had to confess. She didn't recognize all the people in the photos. Her parents and grandparents were a given but who were these darling little boys dressed in cute outfits?

Oohing and ahhing all over the place, Emily shared the photos. "Look, Liz. Here they are wearing sailor suits and baseball outfits and dungarees. Here they are standing in cribs playing with teddy bears and here they are riding little rocking horses. Gee, the entire album is filled with these boys." Her smile faded at her disappointing discovery. "There's not a single picture of me." Out came her lower lip as she uttered in a pout, "Not even a tiny-winy one. Wonder how come?"

"Who are they, Emily?"

"I haven't a clue, Liz but I can't stand it. I got to find out who they are. Know what?"

"What?"

"I've got an idea. Let's play detective and solve this mystery."

"Yeah. We can be girl detectives just like Nancy Drew. Oh, this is going to be so much fun and know what else?"

"What Liz?"

"Playing with only flashlights will make it scary, too."

"Totally. Now, you keep shining the light on each picture and help look for clues. I'll turn the pages. Okay?"

"Okay. Let's go."

Looking at picture after picture, lost in their mysterious challenge, neither girl heard nor noticed them enter the room. But there they were. Suddenly, the overhead light came on. Latching onto each other, scared out of their wits, the girls screamed out in unison.

"Ahhhh."

"Hush! Stop screaming girls. Listen. Dare I ask? What in the world are you two doing?" Her face flushed with anger, her tone harsh, there was no denying it. Emily's mother was fit to be tied. The more the chiding and third degree, the more Emily turned pale with apprehension. Not only that. Now, her father joined in, and on her mother's side, too. Waggling her finger, Rebecca's tongue-lashing continued. "This trunk is not a toy, young lady."

"Your mother is right," Lance more than a bit perturbed backed Rebecca, "Who gave you permission to open this?" he asked.

"Nobody." Blinking back tears, Emily's shaky voice offered her little girl apologies. "I'm sorry, Daddy. I'm sorry, Mommy." Then in her defense, she confessed, "I just wanted to know what was in here. I didn't mean to hurt it or anything."

"You didn't. But that's not the point." he spoke sternly. To Emily, his voice now matched that of her Mom's. I don't remember, Emily thought to herself, ever hearing Mommy or Daddy talk so mean. But I'm not a crybaby. Even as her eyes welled up, she fought off tears. But it was getting harder and harder to be brave. "It is just that this is not your property to open." He continued giving her the dickens. "Not only that, Emily you were supposed to be in bed not sneaking around in the darkness."

Emily was a tough, little cookie, but this sudden, unexpected, and seemingly unending abuse was too much for her to endure. To top it off, they were scolding her right in front of her best friend. How embarrassing. She was on the hot-seat a tad too long. "I said I am sorry." She all but yelled it out this time. Then hiding her eyes with her hands, trying desperately to hold back the waterworks, she lost it. The floodgates broke loose and her sobbing became downright pitiful. As disturbed as Rebecca was with this unexpected photo album turn of events, she found herself now agonizing over Emily's frenzied behavior. Saturated with a mixture of emotions, ebbing and flowing from anger to compassion Rebecca's thoughts were muddled until tenderness emerged. I knew this time was coming, she told herself, but I wasn't ready for it to be today.

Look at her. She's crying her eyes out. So sad. So worked up. So vulnerable. Oh, my goodness Emily, you're breaking my heart. This isn't fair. You think all this commotion is because you opened some run-of-the-mill photo albums. No. Opening the albums isn't the culprit in all this fuss. It is the inadvertently opened can of worms. Therein lies the blame. But what else could you think? We never told you, poor Emily. It is not your fault. It's ours. You had no way of knowing our plan to keep the can tightly closed for all time. Too late now. The lid is off.

Possessing typical traits of a mother, Rebecca's protective and nurturing qualities kicked in. These highlights, simply the nature of the beast, tugged at the very strings of her heart. She grieved at the delicate, unfortunate situation this had become and the hurt it caused her dear daughter.

Gently, pulling Emily into her arms and rocking her in a tender hug, she encouraged, "Sshh, don't cry." Kissing Emily's forehead, and wiping away her tears, she assured her of their understanding. "We know you didn't mean any harm, don't we, Daddy?"

"Of course, we do Pumpkin." Lance responded to Rebecca's lead. The truth be known, he hated to see his Emily in tears. She was, after all, Daddy's little girl.

It was just lousy circumstances and now, caught in the middle, poor Emily was forced to suffer the consequences. He struggled with his position. His soft heart leaned toward total absolution, yet Emily, in her failed dead-of-night maneuver, was guilty as charged. As head of household, the role of disciplinarian automatically fell to him. His main objective now was to be fair. So far, he realized with regret, that the punishment did not fit the offense. Too much yelling had already bounced off the walls. This, all due to a little girl's unsanctioned adventure. More importantly, all this commotion was as a direct result of the decision her parents had made years ago surrounding the well-guarded secret buried within the found albums.

Lowering his voice and gently stroking her hair, Lance spoke in soft tones. "Emily, we don't like to shout at you. You know that, don't you?"

Sniffling, she nodded and assured him, "Yes, Daddy."

"But you must understand that there are certain rules that we all must follow. And that includes respecting each other's property, right?" He was trying to help her understand their disappointment in her unacceptable conduct and in doing so, justify their reaction.

"Right," she whispered.

"Now, what you did tonight was wrong. But Emily, just because your Mother and I don't like what you did, does not mean we don't like you. Understand?"

"Yes, Daddy."

"Emily," he wanted to be sure she followed what he was saying. "We both love you very much and don't you ever forget that." Smiling, he asked, "How much do you love me?"

"I love you to the moon and back, Daddy." That was always her answer ever since she was a tot. He gave her a hug.

"Now kiss us good-night and get into bed. Tomorrow we will all talk about these photo albums. Okay?"

"Okay, Daddy." Emily was feeling much better now even though she didn't exactly know what there was to talk about. Just knowing that both her parents still loved her was all that mattered. Neither she nor Liz needed a curtain call. In a flash, both girls scurried off and jumped into bed. Pulling the covers up over their heads, they dared not to stir for the rest of the night. Poor Emily. She had no way of knowing the importance of the cache she had stumbled upon hidden away in that trunk coffee table.

"Sit with me a few minutes, Lance, won't you?" Rebecca asked pulling her crocheted throw over her lap. "I'm too keyed up to sleep and we really need to talk." Despite making her request in quiet tones, its urgency came through loud and clear.

"Okay, Rebecca." Agreeing, he sat next to her. "I'm pretty sure what's on your mind is about Emily and what happened tonight. So go ahead."

"Well, yes, my mind is filled with thoughts about Emile but, to be honest it's about our sons, too. It kind of all works together."

"How so?"

"It's just that tonight, I think we used poor judgment. I mean poor Emily. Think about it. Have you ever seen her so upset? And why? What did she really do, Lance, that was so bad? So she found the albums. Big deal."

"Actually, Rebecca," he interrupted, "It is a big deal. I'm sure you haven't forgotten that agreement we made long ago?"

"You mean, Lance, the one when we decided to lock out the heartache of losing the boys by just erasing its very existence? Of course I remember. How could I not?" Pulling the throw a little higher for warmth did not chase away the chill that suddenly invaded Rebecca's space. Trembling, she recalled that difficult time of long ago. That agonizing episode, in which long hours of discussion and dissension were spent trying to determine how best to deal with the disaster they could never change; and, then, too, how to protect themselves against future hurt. The very thought of the possibilities aimed at re-opening their wound was inconceivable. Fearful, they both wanted a guarantee of some measure; neither knew how to bring about its success. At first poles apart, it took a lot of work on both sides to close the gap. At that it was with a somewhat viable understanding.

"You know, Lance, back then we were young and so very lost. We had to do something. We just didn't know what. Now, I'm not sure that we made the right choice." Inhaling deeply, she offered her seasoned viewpoint. "To be honest, I think we made an immature decision. I mean we both knew the depth of such heartache could not simply be dismissed by a decree. Yet, we had to try to make our lives worth living. Reliving that tragic memory day in and day out for what seemed like forever, took its toll. I don't know how you survived. I know I made it because you were there for me. I wasn't that generous. You were my sole support until Emily came along. Then with each passing day as Emily became more and more a part of me, yesterday's pain became less and less. I could better stand on my own two feet. Now, I can even talk about our sad time and I'm okay with it." Lance put his arms around her drawing her close to him as much for her sake, as it was for his.

"Rebecca, I'm sorry you suffered so. It was hard on the both of us. Maybe our agreement held hints of immaturity. But facing the facts we had to deal with at the time, I still feel the decision we made was the right one. Think about it. The bottom line, we were hurting. We weren't really living. We just went through the motions. Maybe our solution was a little off the wall. I just know we needed a way out to forget and to move on."

Rebecca snuggled closer into the protection of his strong arms. "I know, Lance. It was awful. But maybe we took our promise to extremes. I mean not only did we vow to lock the heartache out forever but, we also pledged to keep the boys a secret from any other children we might ever have. Doesn't that sound strange now?" she questioned with sincerity.

"Maybe, Rebecca but, again, we convinced ourselves that it was for their protection as well as ours. I'm not sure how we figured out that one but, somehow, our minds let us believe it. You have to admit, until tonight, our plan worked. Very rarely did we mention our sons. We even hid their pictures and all the other baby keepsakes and for that, we hurt less. Listen, Rebecca. At the time, we did what was best to save our sanity."

"I'm still not totally convinced, Lance. Maybe it was a stupid road to take. Maybe we were just selfish and couldn't see it that way."

"Wait. I think we are forgetting an important stipulation."

"What's that? Lance," she asked somewhat perplexed. "I thought we covered all of it."

"No. At the last minute, remember? We agreed to change one condition. Instead of never telling any of our future children, we decided to tell them if, and when, the time seemed right."

"Holy Hannah, how in the world did I forget that? Besides what we did, right or wrong doesn't matter now. Tomorrow Lance, the secrecy ends. Agreed?"

"Agreed. We're on the right path. Emily is entitled to know about her family. We know about ours."

No. I don't. Oh, Lance darling, you are so wrong. Rebecca's heart sank as she screamed her answer in silence. I don't know my family. Not one single member.

"Rebecca, where are you? I'm talking to you and you seem to be far away."

"Sorry. What did you say?"

"I said, yes. All this ends tomorrow"

"Okay Lance. It's been a tough day. Tomorrow will be better. But I'm afraid it won't be easy."

The maturity of the relationship contributed to their mutual respect and they went to bed where one slept so much better than the other.

The next morning, breakfast over and Liz out the door, it began.

"Emily," Lance spoke quietly. "Come with us into the den. We'll pull out the albums and answer any questions you may have. Okay?" He was trying to be as gentle as possible and regretted his harsh words that so frightened his little girl the night before.

"Sit here right between Mom and me." Wanting to quickly put this to rest, he got straight to the point. "Emily, those little boys you saw in the photo album are your twin brothers. They were born years before you and sadly, they got sick and died."

Pausing, to let it sink in, he could see tears quietly streaming down Rebecca's cheeks. Handing her the box of tissues, he thought, she was right. This isn't easy.

"I had twin brothers?" Emily asked in amazement. "What are their names?"

"Yes, Emily, you did," he said. "They were named David and Dennis. Here, let us show you." Opening the velvet covered album, he placed it on Emily's lap.

Rebecca was as ready as she was going to be. It had been a long time and still her stomach clenched just seeing the darling little boys again. No doubt. This photographic journey of her precious lost sons would be bitter-sweet.

"Ooh, they are sooo cute." Emily leaned closer to the pictures. Not having the heart to pop her enthusiasm, Rebecca kept the correction of tense to herself. *Were* so cute, Emily, she thought sadly, not *are*.

Again the album excited Emily's curiosity. Off the hook now, with last night's reprimand all but forgotten, she delved into the cool task at hand.

"Look. Here's one of Grandma holding them and look at Grandpa." Laughing, she was quick to point out. "He looks like he can hardly hang onto two at once. Look at this one, and this one…" Having gone through two albums, it was only a matter of time when Emily would drop the bomb. She did. "How come there's no pictures of me? I'm not in a single one. Not one."

"You weren't born yet." Lance answered to his satisfaction; not to hers.

"But there are empty pages in the back of this album. Why didn't you just put some of me in there with my brothers after I was born?" Out of the mouths of babes, he thought.

Bewildered, neither parent was able to answer. It never occurred to them. What they viewed as necessary to keep reminders hidden away, Emily saw as an opportunity to be with her brothers. Never mind that it was in photo form only. Didn't matter. They would be together. Never in a hundred years would they have guessed Emily's way of thinking. Now, of course, they could see where, to a child, it would make sense.

Emily set her heart on learning the whole inside story. Looking at pictures of the tiny tombstones, she wanted to know. "Where are they buried?"

Lance could tell the question threw Rebecca for a loop. Keeping it simple, he quickly answered. "In the church's cemetery."

Emily's next question; another surprise. "Can you take me to visit them, there?"

Quietly, Rebecca left the room. It hurt too much. How in the world are we going to carry out her request? Emily's ambitious plan means traveling back to a time of tremendous sadness. I don't think Lance will go for it. Yet, as she was leaving, she heard him give his stamp of approval. "Of course, we'll visit tomorrow."

"But, Daddy, why can't we go today? Why can't we go now? Please, please, please, she begged."

"What about selling cookies?"

"I'll do that when we come back, please Daddy."

"You know what, Pumpkin?"

"What?"

Pausing, immersed in thinking, he rubbed his forehead and answered. "You have a point. It's Saturday and it's still early. Let's check with your mother. If it's okay with her, then we'll do it. Now, just in case, let's put these albums away and get ready."

The task finished, Emily made a beeline to the door. Lance went to Rebecca.

"We can do this." He assured her. "Why put it off? Let's just go today for everybody's sake." The ride didn't take long. The quiet cemetery looked nice with flowers here and there. For the most part they rode in silence. Each wrapped up in their own thoughts, the conversation proved to be sparse. Lance parked the car and Emily followed her parents.

Stopping along the walk, she picked a pretty bouquet of violets. She wanted her brothers' place to look just as nice as those that were decorated with flowers.

"Here we are, Pumpkin." Lance announced in a strong voice. He so wanted to make this event seem as natural as possible. Especially since up to now, most of all that involved the twins had been far from it.

Kneeling down, Emily carried out her flower mission. "Now, it looks pretty here, too." Pleased with herself she stepped back admiring her handiwork. In doing so, her eye caught another neat object. "Look, Mom and Dad. Look at the little, stone lambs sitting on top. Ooh, aren't they just too darling?" In her excitement, she didn't allow them to answer. In her anxiousness, she shared her next conclusion. "My brothers have baby lambs to keep them company. How neat is that?"

"Pretty neat, Emily." Lance answered and thought about that time when they chose the carved lambs. Back then, they just stood as symbols of innocence. He liked Emily's interpretation a whole lot better and was moved by her compassionate feelings.

"Look here, Emily." She knelt down next to her father. Pointing to one photo encased in a glass bubble and then to the other, he introduced the brothers and sister. "This little boy is David and this one, Dennis. And boys, this is your sister, Emily."

"Do you think they can hear us, Daddy?"

"I like to think they can, Pumpkin."

"Look at her, Rebecca, talking to her brothers. How amazing, huh?"

"Amazing," Rebecca answered and felt a pleasure she seldom allowed herself to feel, as far as her lost babies were concerned.

"Funny," he said, "this visit is turning out to be therapeutic and I'd say the little therapist is smart beyond her years. I think, at long last, healing is really taking place."

Giving Lance's hand a gentle, squeeze and nodding her head in understanding, Rebecca answered, "Me too."

Emily was doing some grown-up thinking on her own. Sitting on the grass with her legs crossed Indian style, she talked in a whisper so her parents couldn't hear. Her conversation was directed to her baby brothers. "I'm so glad I came here today and since you haven't been around Mom, I want to tell you something very important, okay?

Listen. Mom is not mean. I know now why she never lets me do anything and why she always says no to me. Well, not always, but mostly. It's because she lost you guys. Now, I bet she's afraid I might die on her, too. Yep, that's it. So remember. Mom is the best Mom in the whole wide world. Okay?"

Healing was indeed taking place on this day in more ways than Lance even imaged.

"It's time to go, Pumpkin."

"Okay. Daddy. Bye David. Bye Dennis and, don't forget what I told you."

Rebecca and Lance exchanged smiles. They were pleased that Emily had not yet mastered the art of whispering softly.

On the ride home Emily made another request which had never occurred to her parents. "Mom, can I have a picture of my brothers?"

"Of course you may. Tell you what. When we get home, you pick out the picture you want from the albums and I'll have it framed for you."

"Great. And I know just where I'm putting it. It goes on my dresser right next to my favorite picture of Mickey Mouse. Boy. Wait until Liz hears about this."

Chapter 28

1978

As far as her parents were concerned, Emily's elementary and junior high school years had wings. It was hard to believe, but Emily was now in the eleventh grade.

"Come on Liz. Hurry up. We can't be late for this game. It's the big one."

"I can't go any faster and how come I'm always stuck carrying my helmet and both hockey sticks?"

"Oh, stop grumbling. I'm carrying my shin guards. That evens it out. Besides, you like being goalkeeper. Now move it."

The game over, the girls went to Emily's.

"From the looks on your faces, I'd say your team won right?" Rebecca asked with genuine interest as both girls got drinks from the refrigerator.

"You bet, we did. And next week we get to play for the championship. You and Dad coming?"

"Try keeping us away. Now, let's take a look at all those bruises." On closer examination, Rebecca chided. "Wow. You're going to be one black and blue cookie tomorrow."

"Don't worry, Mom. They just show everybody they can't intimidate this Center."

"For heaven sake, Emily, you wear your bruises like badges. Can't you at least try to stay out of the way of a wild, deadly stick once in awhile?"

"Nope, can't do that, Mom. Field Hockey is not a game for sissies."

"You can say that again." Liz added her two cents as she sat drinking her cool lemonade. "Seventy minutes dodging sticks and fighting for the ball is mighty demanding for both teams. Got to admit, they were a pretty tough opponent."

"Yeah, they were, Liz. But you know what?" Emily questioned.

"What?" Liz shouted.

"We were tougher," Emily proudly answered. "In the end, we walked away the winner."

"Three cheers for us. They chimed in together and yelled a happy and loud praise.

"Hip, hip hooray! Hip, hip hooray! Hip, hip hooray!"

According to Emily and Liz, all the aches and pains were well worth it. The following week, with Rebecca and Lance cheering them on, their school team captured the State Championship title.

"Talk about being on a high, Lance, did you ever see two happier girls?" Rebecca asked, as the elated girls proudly joined the team on the field in the acceptance of the trophy ceremony.

"Well, they certainly earned it. That game was tough. Could have gone either way. In fact, if Liz hadn't been such a good goalkeeper, especially on that last save, they would have lost."

"All the same, I'm glad the season is over. Maybe Emily can concentrate on her watercolor painting now. You know she's planning to enter the Art Show next month. At least then any black and blue marks that show up will be only on canvas."

"She's a pretty good artist, Rebecca. Not that I'm prejudice or anything. Don't know where she gets it. Nobody in my family has any artistic talent. It must come from your side."

There it is again, Rebecca thought, my darn, troubling, unknown family tree. I wish Lance would stop saying things like that. It rips me apart every time. But then how could he know? It's not his fault his words inadvertently hurt me so.

"Mom, Dad, okay if I go with Liz and a bunch of girls from the team to celebrate? Marsha's folks are throwing us a victory party."

"Sure. Have fun. Just don't come home late." Lance gave his conditional permission.

"I won't, bye." Excitedly, they were off.

"Wow, Liz, this party is rocking. The place is jammed."

"Yeah and get a glimpse of that cute guy standing by the refreshment table, Emily. Who is he?"

"Don't know, Liz. I didn't even know boys were invited. Did you?"

"Are you kidding? Get real. A party at Marsha's without boys would be like the fourth of July without fireworks. Of course I knew. Come on. Let's mingle and remember I saw that cute guy first."

"Don't worry. He's yours. I've got my eye on that Sam Preston. He's in my math class and he has the dreamiest blue eyes."

"Well, don't just stand here gaping at him. Go for it, Emily. See you later."

Following Liz's lead, Emily mingled her way over to where Sam was standing.

"Hi Sam. How did you like the game?"

"Hi. I liked it a lot especially when the score was tied. It was darn exciting. Had me worried for a little bit and then it was that last goal that did it. You played one heck of a game, Emily."

"Thanks."

"Want a drink?"

"Sure."

Emily, waiting for Sam's return, checked out the place. The joint was jumping. Music blaring, kids dancing, there certainly were a lot more here than just the hockey team, that's for sure. There were no adults in sight. Probably upstairs, she thought. But it didn't take Emily long to figure it out. There simply were no chaperones. Had her parents known, this party definitely would have been off limits.

"Here you go, Emily," Sam said, handing her a paper cup and then joining a few of his other friends.

"Thanks," she yelled over the music and took a big gulp. Stunned, her eyeballs bulged, her throat burned and it was all she could do to swallow. Too late, she realized it was beer. Yikes! Mom and Dad will have a fit. Waving she got Liz's attention.

"What's up?"

"Liz, this stuff is beer."

"Yeah! What a way to celebrate, huh?"

"Liz, you can't mean that."

"Emily, come on. Don't be such a prude. Let your hair down. You got to drink to our victory. It doesn't taste half bad once you get used to it. Besides, one beer can't hurt you. I've already had two and I kind of like the buzz. Keep drinking, you'll see what I mean."

"What if my folks find out?"

"How will they? Marsha's folks don't even know. In fact, they haven't come down to the rec room since we got here."

"Yeah, Liz, don't you find that a little odd? I mean, come on. Face it. There is no adult supervision at this place."

"Well, that's more reason for you not to worry about getting caught, and anyway, some guys slipped the drinks in under cover. So relax and have fun. Nobody is going to tell your folks. Come with me out to the porch. There's a lot of action going on out there."

"But Liz, what happened to your dreamboat?"

"He's already on the porch. Come on and meet him." Standing with a few other people, Liz found Mark and pulled him aside. "Come on, Mark. I want you to meet my friend."

"Emily, this is Mark. Mark, Emily."

"Hi. This one is yours," he said, handing Emily a lighted cigarette.

Dumbfounded, her face gave her away as the crowd round her snickered.

"Got to start sometime," he said, "Here is yours Liz. I was holding it for you."

Glancing at each other, the girls nodded the go ahead and leaning over, Liz whispered in Emily's ear. "What the heck?" Why not? It's a party, right?"

"Here goes nothing," Emily said taking a drag. Surprising herself, other than a hint of sputtering, she did okay. But, she had to admit, she was relieved when Sam invited her back into the house to dance. That was definitely more fun and she managed to stay indoors for the rest of the evening. She noticed Liz finagled it, too.

Before they knew it, the fast paced party was over and both girls headed for home. Emily, holding Liz by the arm to keep her steady, was feeling almost as giddy.

"You know, Liz, we didn't drink all that much. This is all in our heads."

"Yours, maybe, Emily, mine went straight to my legs." I drank a lot more than you did. Can you believe it? Not only did we celebrate our championship victory, and meet swell guys, we got to experience our first cigarette and first beer? Man," she said smiling ear to ear, "what a night!"

"Yeah Liz, and my Mom and Dad would flip if they knew."

"Hey," Liz said with a sly grin, "I won't tell, if you don't tell. And they won't ever know."

Emily's eyes sparkled. "When you're right, you're right and wahoo," she shouted. "That party was a blast! The dancing was fantastic and to top it off, I actually got a date with Sam Preston for tomorrow night. Can you imagine, Liz? Me and Sam Preston?" Crinkling her nose, Emily admitted, "the beer and cigarette, well, to tell you the truth, I could have done without, but a date, and with Sam Preston."

"Way to go, girl."

"Here we are Liz. Now promise me Liz you won't make any noise. Just go in your house quietly and go right up to bed. Promise?"

"Sshh," Liz whispered putting a finger to her lips. "Mums the word."

Emily managed to make it home and hurried up to bed without much contact with her parents who were still watching TV. Tonight was fun but I can't wait until tomorrow night's date. When she got up the day seemed to drag until the doorbell rang. After quick introductions, her parents told them to have fun. Out the door they went.

"This baseball game is fun, Sam."

"Well, being with you is more. Want a drink?"

"What do you have?" This time Emily asked.

"Could get you a coke but look what I have in this small cooler?"

"That is coke," she said.

"Okay, so have one."

Again with the big gulp, came a big discovery.

"It's beer."

"Sshh. Don't let the world know, Emily. Just drink it and enjoy the ball game."

The game had reached the seventh inning stretch when he asked her.

"Time to take a break. Want to walk to the park across the street?"

"Sure."

The lights from the ball park cast shadows all around but it was nice and dark at the bench where Sam led her. Perfect for what he had in mind. He didn't waste time.

Almost immediately, he wrapped his arms around her and kissed her in a way that was brand new to Emily. He didn't mind her inexperience. He kind of liked the challenge and eagerly provided her with instructions.

"Don't hold your lips so tight. Open your mouth just a little. I'll do the rest. Relax. You'll like this."

With that promise, Emily was introduced to what she had heard some of the other girls rave about, French kissing. Well, his promise didn't hold water and it wasn't all it was cracked up to be, either. Not only that, before she knew it, Sam was all over her.

"Stop it, Sam."

"Emily, don't be like that. Come on."

"No, stop. I mean it." Pushing him away, Emily was dead serious.

"Okay. Okay. I'm stopping," he said angrily, "just so you know.

There are a lot of other girls who can't wait for me to date them. So, I'll take you home and then you can forget about ever going out with me again. You had your chance. You blew it."

At home, Emily got into bed shaking with confusion and anger. "Guess what, Mr. Preston," she whispered into her pillow, "I don't care. You aren't worth dating, anyway. Boy, wish I had told him that to his face, him and his beer…Losers." Burying her head in the pillow, she cried herself to sleep, all the while thinking, darn you, Sam Preston for being such a jerk. And me, for being a bigger one. I really thought you liked me. Well, you can go jump in the lake for all I care. There's plenty of other fish out there, then anxiously added, I hope.

For now though, the sting left her resentful and willing to put boys on the back burner. Some of her friends, pretty much in the same boat, decided to stick together. There were, after all, a lot of fun girl-only activities. Boys were not totally ruled out, mind you. It was just that Emily, in learning a valuable lesson, made an important discovery. When it came to dating, she simply would exercise her right to discriminate. That she was called stuck-up by some didn't bother her. That she was liked by the majority of her peers, now that's what counted.

* * * * *

Sitting in the living room, Rebecca interrupted Lance's reading. Putting down his magazine, he turned to listen.

"What is it? Rebecca?"

"I'm just sitting here thinking about Emily. Wasn't it terrific that she won first place in the Art Show?"

"You bet. Her seascape looked professional as all get out. I liked the way she captured that lighthouse, too. It's so real. It's almost like you were standing right there. I swear she has the Midas touch in everything she tries."

"Lance, we are truly lucky. Since Emily has been with us, life's been one happy unexpected whirlwind after another. She's such a good daughter. She gets good grades, enjoys her social life and she has a good head on her shoulders."

"Well, she keeps us on our toes. That's for sure. With Emily's unpredictable change of direction, you never know what's coming next."

"And that's what keeps us young, Lance."

"I believe it is, Rebecca," he sat grinning, "Now, her latest venture, she's running for President of her class. I don't know where she finds the time or energy."

"Well, she does. But I think she's starting to grow up a tad too fast, Lance. Before we know it, our little girl will be in college." He pondered the inevitable thought of Emily's life flashing by and didn't like it. No, not one bit and let his feelings be known.

"Whoa! Don't rush it. She still has another year of high school left." Rebecca honored his request, but could not resist reminding him of tonight's prom. In a way it was to help prepare him for when he would see his little girl all dressed up and looking very grown-up in the beautiful prom dress she had chosen.

In school, that day, the air was a-buzz with excitement for most, in anticipation of tonight's prom. For Emily, her enthusiasm was two-fold. Not only was she looking forward to attending the prom, but during Assembly, she had just learned of her victory. Elected President of her junior class, she welcomed the challenge and was sincerely appreciative of her supporters.

Her acceptance speech included her intentions of carrying out her platform policies and ended on a personal note "Thanks gang, all of you for your vote of confidence in me. Without your help campaigning and your votes, I would never have won."

"You are welcome," came back in sing-song unison from a few of the more vocal in the class. Of course, after the program, walking back to homeroom, Liz couldn't resist adding her two-cents. "Now, don't go getting uppity with us just because you have Presidential powers," she teased and those in ear-shot chuckled.

"But that's the fun of it," Emily retorted.

Emily, all kidding aside, kept her promises. As the year went on, she worked hard with the other class officers establishing committees to set up new hall monitoring regulations, fund-raisers for the band, and a no-homework on week-ends policy, among other procedures that gave more leeway to the students. Everybody was glad for Emily's accomplishments. In fact, so much so, although unaware of their future approval, in her senior year, she was a shoo-in for class President.

* * * * *

But before the end of this exciting day, in preparation of tonight's prom, Emily and Liz spent time checking last minute details scrutinizing the gym.

"Look at this place, Liz. What do you think"?

"It's cool. I'd say somebody did an excellent job on the prom decorations."

"Wasn't me. It was the Decorating Committee."

"You really have a thing for committees, don't you Emily?"

"Don't knock it. They get the job done, right? Besides, Liz, you were on that committee, weren't you?"

"I know. I headed it. Just like getting a rise from you."

"You would. Come on, let's get home. Our work here is done. Now, we have to get ready for tonight. I can hardly wait."

"Me, either, and wait until you see my gown. It's really something, if I must say so myself, and I do."

"You know, Liz, that's what I like about you. Your modesty." Both girls chuckled and hurried home to get ready for the big event. The hours passed quickly. Before long their handsome escorts, totally decked-out in stylish tuxedo duds, arrived.

"Gee, Emily, you look terrific."

"Thanks, Jim and thanks for the lovely corsage."

"Wait. Wait," Rebecca instructed. "Let your father get a picture of Jim putting it on your wrist."

"Sorry, Jim," Emily smiled and rolling her eyes offered an apology of sorts. "Don't worry. My parents are the same way. I think they have the camera sitting out just waiting to embarrass me."

"Listen, young man," Rebecca teased, "it can't be as bad as all that and besides, we parents earn the right to pictures."

Changing the subject, Lance came to the rescue. "Emily, are you two going with Liz and her date?"

"We are Dad. And we really have to get going. See you later, Mom, Dad."

"Okay. Have a good time."

"We will."

At the dance, their dates took the girls wraps to be checked. The coat room and checker had been another of Emily's ideas. Adding a touch of grown-up sophistication, the system worked well.

Waiting, Liz leaned over, "Emily, I have to tell you. You have outdone yourself, girl."

"Thanks, and you were right, Liz. Your gown is something. Oh, and most of all, thanks for setting me up with Jim. He really seems nice and he was so relaxed with my folks. I think they liked him. That's always a plus, you know and Liz, I'm glad Joe's your date and not Mark. I think finally breaking off with him was the best thing you ever did."

"You got that right. And ditto with you and that Sam Preston."

"Oh, that loser. I wrote him off long ago. He was such a creep."

"Okay, ladies, shall we find our table?" asked Jim returning from the coat check station.

"Here it is," he said pulling out Emily's chair. Cute and a gentleman, too, she thought pleased as punch. Happy in her observation, Liz winked her approval at Emily.

"Emily," Jim said, "I'm glad I'm in Liz's French class or chances are I would never have met you. Your French class meets in the morning, right?"

"Right. Guess that means I have Liz to thank for our date tonight, too."

"You sure do Kiddo," Liz piped up, "and don't you forget it, Emily my friend."

"Okay, then, Liz, Mercy beaucoup."

"de rien," Liz responded. "That better mean you are welcome," she joked. "Anyway, I think that's how you say it," and laughed at the uncertainty of her pronunciation.

The entire evening went like that. Teasing, laughing, and dancing like the four had known each other forever. As far as Emily and Liz were concerned, with one exception, it was absolutely heavenly. The one regret? It ended all too soon.

On the drive home, Emily snuggled as close as she could to Jim without interfering with his driving. Joe sat with his arm around Liz in the back seat until they arrived at Liz's house. Hers was the first stop along the way.

"See you at school, Liz," Joe said as he kissed her goodnight at her front door. Next Joe was dropped off at his house and that left Emily and Jim. Parked out front, Jim walked Emily to the door.

"Jim, I really had a terrific time. Thanks."

"So did I Emily. It was a blast."

Boy, she thought how different he is from that disgusting Sam Preston. He's not in any hurry to leave and yet he's not all over me. He really is nifty.

"Can we talk a little, Emily or do you have to go right in?"

"Well, for a little while."

"Tonight was fun, Emily and I wonder if we could go out again?"

"Sure. I would like that."

Not really having too much to say but not wanting to leave, Jim stood there enjoying the closeness of the girl he took to the prom trying to come up with something clever to impress her. He knew what he came up with was pretty lame but it was all he had at the moment.

"I have to tell you, Emily, you made quite a hit with my Dad."

"I did? How so? He doesn't really know me."

"Well, when he heard I was going to the prom with the newly elected class President, he gave me a pat on the back and said he was glad to see I was getting up in the world. In fact, I hadn't given it much thought until he made such a fuss. Then I got nervous. I didn't know what I was getting into. Turns out, you are not the least bit high and mighty. I like you, Emily, a lot."

"Well, I'm not sure what your Dad was thinking, but now you know, I'm just ordinary me, who happens to like you, too." The silent pause begged for conversation. But the best Emily could come up with was letting him know it was time to leave. "I better go in now, Jim. It's getting late." He didn't ask and he didn't push. He simply and gently kissed his beautiful date goodnight. No more, no less; for which Emily was delighted. "So it's the movies, next Saturday?"

"That would be fun."

"I'll pick you up around eight." With that, he simply kissed her on her cheek, made sure she was safely in the house, and left.

"I'm home."

"Well, how was it?" Rebecca asked, "come into the rec. room, she invited. Tell us all about it. Here, sit right next to me on the couch. Did you have a good time?"

"Don't grill her, Rebecca," Lance said laughingly and then turning his easy chair to face Emily asked, "Well did you?"

"You folks are too funny. Yes, Mom. Yes, Dad. I had a great time. The prom was fun. My date was cool and, guess that's about it. And now I'm off to bed." Taking off her heels, she made a beeline to her room. As her hand turned the doorknob, she stopped and yelled, "Oh, yeah. By the way, I have a date with him on Saturday. Goodnight." Then she disappeared into her room.

"She's an imp, Lance."

"Well, she's your daughter."

Laughing, Lance turned out the lights. "Guess we may as well head up to bed, too. She's done telling us all she wants us to hear and, Lord knows, we'll need all the rest we can get. Who knows what she'll come up with tomorrow?"

Poor Lance, definitely not an advocate of his little Emily maturing at this fast pace, knew there was not a thing he could do to stop the process. Emily was fast approaching adulthood. Not only was she old enough to go to this Junior/Senior prom, but when, all too soon, the following year, she attended the last of her high school proms, he was again caught off guard and reminded how out of sync his timing was with Emily's plans of leaving the nest. Rebecca and Lance discussed the very issue of Emily's growing up that inevitably meant they were growing older, too.

"Boy, trying to keep up, don't you sometimes feel like we are getting old and decrepit, Lance?" Rebecca teased. "Even your hair is turning gray."

"You're not helping matters, Rebecca," he chuckled. "Besides, you were the one, if I'm not mistaken, who said her diversified actions keeps us young."

"But that was before I got so caught up in trying to make sense out her fast paced activities."

"Well, at least we can be glad that our sense of humor hasn't grown old, right?"

"Okay, that's better. But I just wish time would slow down a little. I know fat chance of that happening."

Emily as a senior, again had her fingers in many pies. The time just swooped by and before he knew it, his little girl was looking into colleges for grown-ups.

Emily and Liz sat in the rec. room enjoying homemade chocolate chip cookies and cold milk as they poured over their college acceptance letters.

"Here's one from Trenton University. Did you get one, Emily?" Liz asked with a mouthful of cookies.

"Yup. Now that makes three from the same places so far that we both received. Making our decision is going to be tough. I like all of them."

"Me, too, Emily but to tell you the truth, I'm leaning toward Montclair University. It has a terrific program for a Bachelor's Degree in Elementary Ed. You know I've wanted to teach elementary school since forever."

"I know, Liz. Me too, only I want to specialize in Social Studies and the Arts."

"Okay. Listen to this description. I think it is right up your alley. 'These studies allow you to focus on the diversity of communities by weaving together history, geography, social studies, and the performing arts.' I think that covers it all, Emily. Don't you?"

"The more I think about it, you're right Liz. I really think we are both bound for Montclair University, and like the brochures states, that's the college of education and human services. That's what we both want, so there. That wasn't so hard after all, was it?"

"Considering, Emily, it took us two months to finally decide, I wouldn't classify our decision as a piece of cake, either. But we made it. That's what counts."

The graduation ceremony came and went. Emily gave the Valedictorian speech. Rebecca and Lance, so filled with pride, just about popped a gasket.

Then before they knew it, the last, lazy days of summer took their final bow for the season. Just as quickly, the scent of the crisp autumn breeze filled the air. With its arrival, Emily, with mixed emotions, left her parents and headed for college and a new chapter in her life.

Chapter 29

1980

Compatible on the college personality questionnaire and the fact that Emily and Liz made mutual requests on their applications, the two were designated roommates.

"Don't you just love this, Emily? It's like a perpetual sleepover only this time, we get to call the shots."

Enjoying their first taste of independence, the roomies did just that. Some nights, snacking and talking into the wee hours, there was no lights out. It was fun but eventually, even they realized freedom carries a price. Some classes had to be attended while nursing a headache caused by self-inflicted sleep deprivation.

College life suddenly dropped a new set of responsibilities on Emily. For the first time in her life, she could come and go as she pleased. If she decided to skip class, she did. No one was there to chastise her or to remind her of an upcoming project deadline. It was all up to her and just as long as her grades were good, so was life.

When her boyfriend Jim headed out to a college in Pennsylvania, both agreed to remain friends but to also make new friends, as well. Emily soon found herself frequently being asked out on dates. It was a whole new ballgame. There was no mention of going steady. That wasn't the hot item in college as it had been in high school.

Being Emily, it didn't take long before she became actively involved in various undertakings. Student Council, the Campus Christians Organization, the History Society and the Debating Club, benefited from her loyalty and know how. Before long, she was, once again in the grove, well-liked and pretty much queen-pin on campus.

The joy and hard work of college life helped the two nervous kids straight out of high school better appreciate the opportunity of education and all that it offered. Time didn't stand still. No way. In fact and before their very eyes, and maybe a little too quickly even for them, ready or not, they matured.

Sitting in the cafeteria with Emily and Liz were several members of the debating team. One freshman, in between munching on a salad, lamented how fast the year was coming to an end. "Seems," she said, "we just started and here it is final exam time. I can't believe it. Jeez, even worse, in just two weeks, we'll be home for summer vacation. Now that's plain impossible."

"You're such a skeptic," Emily chuckled. "You better believe summer vacation is just around the corner and just to boggle your brain power a tad further, try this one on for size." Emily enjoyed challenging the troops. Keeping their interest piqued sharpened their minds; good exercise for debaters. "It's only going to take repeating our schedules a few more times. You know like now it is summer vacation, then back to class and, again, before you know it, summer vacation, back to class and repeat that routine a few times. Before you can blink an eye, we'll be saying adios to this place."

"Bite your tongue girl," Liz instructed in protest, "I'm in no hurry. I like what we have going on here."

In the end, of course, Emily's prediction won out. She was right. Time showed no mercy. Marching right over their sophomore year, journeying through their junior year, it progressed well into their senior year. Emily and Liz found themselves in the middle of their final year with Spring break sitting in the wings. No turning back now. They had no choice and never mind that it was scary. It was almost time to face the world.

"It's such a pretty day, Liz," Emily reported her plans. "I'm going to the Student Union to finish reading the hometown paper my Mom sent. So I'll see you later."

"Okay. Fill me in on the juicy stuff when you get back."

"From our home town? You have got to be kidding." Walking in the direction of the Student Union, Emily chuckled to herself, juicy stuff, right. That will be the day. Liz's laughter sounded in the background, along with her repeated instruction. "Don't forget now, Emily. Vivid details"

Sitting with newspaper in hand, nursing a large coke, Emily did not notice the young man approach from behind. Gently covering her eyes with his hands, he questioned, "Guess who?"

Placing her fingers over his, recognizing the huge protective hands, not to mention his deep reassuring voice, she smiled and gleefully answered. "Hmmm. Let me think." Playing the game to the hilt, she speculated. "Are you my very own Santa Claus? No, no. Wait. I have a sneaking suspicion. Could you be my Superman?"

Laughing appreciatively, the mystery man better liked the idea of being equated to Superman.

"Well, since I'm not rich enough to be Santa, I'm opting for Superman."

Game over, removing his hands, she tilted her head back just far enough for him to reach down and kiss her.

"Mmmm, so this is what it's like to be kissed by a man with super powers, is it?"

"You bet," he boasted, smiling from ear to ear. "Well, my Lois Lane seems newspapers are in your blood. May I join you?"

"Of course. Here sit in this chair next to me."

Michael Brian Wendell, a senior majoring in Political Science, had become the love of her life. They met at the Home Coming Dance and in the last six months, had rapidly become more than fast friends. So much so that finally, a pact was made.

"I think we should do it," he suggested to her at the time.

"I think we should, too," she answered in absolute agreement. From that moment on, totally cutting out dates with others, they became exclusive.

"Anything good in the newspaper today?" he asked scanning the headlines of the spread out publication."

"Not really. It's my hometown paper. Need I say more?"

"Nope. But I have something to say," and went on nonchalantly to declare, "I love you, Emily Miles. Not only that. Have I told you lately why I love you, Emily Miles?"

"Only about a dozen times," she grinned.

"Well, get ready for number thirteen. You may as well just sit back and enjoy this because it's going to happen. It can't be helped."

Rolling her eyes in feigned protest, Emily sat back and readied herself to hear all the delightful reasons, yet again.

"Emily, I like everything about you, your vitality, your grace, your sense of humor, your lovely looks and your girlish laugh."

"Okay, Michael. I got it," she said holding up her hand as a signal for him to stop. "Your message is loud and clear. You can stop any time, now."

"Now, you just wait, young lady. You know there's more." Ignoring the interruption, he continued. "I like you because you are comfortable with quiet time and respect my occasional need for solitude."

"Okay, Michael."

"No Emily, here comes the best part, well almost. I like the fact that while you have the capacity for liberated joy, you are also very good at discussing politics."

"Is that it?"

"Just the best part is left."

"And that is?"

"No holds barred, I love you Emily Miles, for being you."

She melted. She always did at this ending and whispered. "I love you for you, too, Michael Brian Wendell." Smiling, she offered him her coke. Taking a big gulp, Michael pleased with the events of the day so far took her hand into his. Together they sat back and basked in the warmth of the sun and, most especially, in their shared feelings.

"Michael," she said, caught up in the moment. "This is wonderful. Right now I feel we are captivated by our passionate, emotionally-moving, love."

"Whoa. Big guns, Emily!" Scratching his head mocking disbelief, he said, "I totally agree with what you said but can't believe you actually said it. Boy, Emily, when you get serious, you get serious. Well done! On the flip side," he snickered, "Sounds like something right out of a Victorian novel. Don't get me wrong. You just invented reason number fourteen for my loving you."

She couldn't help herself. Meant to be sincere, it sounded anything but. Just thinking about her melodramatic words cracked her up. He caught her contagious laughter. Taking advantage of the silly situation, she was quick to point out her observation.

"You know this is your fault. I mean, you and your way with words and all those reasons you keep reciting, why I'm just doing what you do so well. Only I do it very poorly." Pausing, she looked him squarely in the eye, trying to be serious. Her sparkling eyes gave her away. She couldn't keep a straight face if her life depended on it. Finally, she spit it out. "Guess I really should rephrase my sentiments."

"Too late," he protested, "the cat's out of the bag and anyway, you'll never top that gem. Not in a hundred years."

"Okay, okay, stop." Her hand flew up in feigned objection. But can we at least keep it our secret? Can you imagine if this got out, the field day the debating team would have?"

"Better yet," he egged her on, "think how fast they would demote their eloquent leader. You, dear silver-tongued Captain, would have to kiss your term goodbye."

"Michael Brian Wendell, you are enjoying this, aren't you?"

"Nah. Well maybe. Yeah, guess I am at that," he chuckled.

"Please. Don't tell anybody, okay? I'm begging, Michael."

Locking his lips with his pretend finger key, he agreed, "mums, the word."

All she could do now was embellish the comedy. Giggling, she pointed out. "And to think, all this intimate, romantic exchange is set right here in the middle of the crowded Student Union, for God and everybody to hear."

Pretending to be shocked, Michael shot back. "You're lucky, young lady, that I'm such a good sport. Just for that, I'll have more of your coke and a kiss and I'll take the kiss first, if you don't mind." He was having fun with his best girl. He kissed her gently. Then reaching for her drink, he continued. "Just for your information, I'm also changing the subject."

"And well, you should. Rescue me, my Superman, before I die of embarrassment."

He couldn't resist teasing just a tad longer especially, with her unintentional lead-in. Sounding off, he sang, "Here I come to save the day."

"You Silly," Emily chuckled, "that's Mighty Mouse's theme song."

"So it is. Anyway, to the rescue Emily. All kidding aside, wasn't last night's show terrific?"

"Sensational. I never thought any show could have such a profound effect on me but I'm telling you, Michael 'The Phantom of the Opera' took my breath away."

"Now, aren't you glad you didn't drop membership in the Campus Activities Committee when your workload got heavier and heavier? A lot of other people appreciated what you and the Committee did. I know it wasn't easy. Blood, sweat and tears went into its making and it wasn't exactly good for your nerves, either. As I recall, and if I remember correctly, didn't you say it took close to a year just to book the cast?"

"You have a good memory, Michael. Yes, it did. Remember, too, the reason for the long wait. We wanted only the best. I still can't believe we actually pulled it off. Imagine, Michael Crawford and Sarah Brightman, big time celebrities agreeing to honor little us, not only with their presence, but by performing right here on our small campus."

Emily stopped talking and momentarily, they shared a reflective silence. Then sipping the coke, she offered, "Would you like the last of this drink?"

"Thanks." Finishing off the refreshment, he went back to discussing the show. "Emily, when Crawford came out wearing his Phantom, half mask and Sarah as the naïve Christine walked on stage, the audience was spellbound. The entire performance was electrifying. For sure that spectacular entertainment will be the sensation and talk of this college for years to come."

"You're right. Both of them were outstanding. The music, oh gosh, Michael, I keep hearing the haunting melody of the 'Music of the Night.' It just lingers and plays over and over in my mind. I can hear it now and I love it all over again."

"I know, Emily. Andrew Lloyd Webber's songs, wow. You know, I'm glad we went to the Old Silent Film Festival a few months ago. Remember how different that showing of 'The Phantom of the Opera' was?"

"Indeed, I do. That was, after all, the original 1925 version starring Lon Chaney. The marvel of that production was that except for its musical score, it was silent. You have to wonder how in the world they made that film turn out so well without benefit of Webber's unforgettable music."

"Yeah. And you want to know the real shocker, Emily? I don't even like opera."

"I know, Michael. Getting you to go the first time around was like pulling teeth."

"Got to admit, I was just so-so with the original version but that last show we went to, changed my way of thinking."

Reaching for his hand and holding it tenderly, she smiled. How she loved this gentle side of him just as much as his pretend macho side.

"Listen, Michael. I want to discuss some plans for Spring Break, okay?"

"Wow! You hop from one subject to another. But I like the cricket in you, too."

"Don't start that again Michael," she said wagging her finger. "Anyway, Spring Break is right around the corner. Are you planning on going home?"

"Not necessarily. My folks will still be out of the country celebrating their twenty-fifth wedding anniversary touring England, Scotland and Wales. So if I go home, I'll pretty much be home alone. Why?"

"I would very much like for you to meet my parents."

Chapter 30

1982

Vacation time, be it for a week-end or a summer, whenever Emily returned, was an opportunity to rejuvenate relationships at home. Anticipation of her visit was in the air. Rebecca made sure all menus revolved around Emily's favorites and she cleaned the house from top to bottom. Not that Emily would notice, or for that matter, care. To her it wasn't the degree of cleanliness that counted. No, to her, it was the incredible sensation of security and happiness experienced each time she came through the front door. Surely the roof of this house was held up by love. This time, even the guest room for Emily's friend benefited from Rebecca's domestic energy. No matter the viewpoints differed; the excitement never changed. This visit, however, did.

The element of another person, most especially the possible seriousness of this friendship between Emily and said person gave her mother cause for anxiety.

Finishing dinner, the night before Emily's arrival, Lance and Rebecca sat back enjoying their coffee. "It won't be long now until we get to meet this special friend of Emily's. Boy, did you hear the excitement in her voice when she called? She's really anxious for us to meet this Malcolm guy, isn't she, Rebecca?"

"It's Michael and, take it with a grain of salt Lance. You know Emily. She tends to wear her enthusiasm on her sleeve."

"Yes, but in all her past excitements, she never invited any other male friend home before."

"What's that supposed to mean, Lance?"

"Well, maybe Malcolm..."

"Michael," she corrected patiently.

"Okay, Michael. Well maybe Michael is more than just her friend. Who knows, Rebecca? Maybe he's the one. I got to tell you, I think it would be nice to have Emily married and settled. Understand, nobody is ever going to be good enough for our little girl, but if this guy is her knight in shining armor, then we don't have any choice. We have to give it our best shot, make the guy feel welcome and all. What do you think?"

"Whoa," Rebecca snapped, "No one made mention of marriage. Aren't you putting the cart before the horse? I mean, really, Lance, inviting a friend home for a week-end visit is not a precursor to a lifetime commitment, now is it?"

"You never know these days. It could happen like that. Besides, Rebecca, I don't understand why you're being negative about the possibility. You know it's only a matter of time."

"You really don't know why I'm concerned, do you?"

"No. I'm afraid I don't. We're not going to be here forever, you know Rebecca and, frankly, I see marriage as Emily's security for the future. So what's bugging you?"

"The twins, Lance, the twins. Don't you see?" she asked holding her head in her hands. "What happens when Emily has children? If she has to go through that same agony, the loss would kill her. Now do you understand?" Time seemed to stand still, as he sat motionless mulling over the horrible possibility just presented. Taking a deep breath, he snapped his body straight and, spoke in a soft tone.

"Listen. That likelihood never occurred to me. But I have to tell you, since you brought it to my attention, the jolt aged me. Now, here's my thinking. We have to be logical. The odds of that happening again are probably nil. We didn't lose Emily and the doctor never led us to believe history would repeat itself, now, did he?"

"No, he didn't. We never asked either, did we?"

"No. I guess there was no need for the question back then."

"Or maybe it was just easier to bury our heads in the sand."

"I still don't think there is anything to worry about but obviously, Rebecca this has you upset. Okay. Your point is well taken." Pausing, he lowered his head and added, "I know Emily is strong but still, I would never forgive myself if she suffered because of my ignorance." That disturbing moment past, he pulled himself together, and continued.

"I have a suggestion."

"What is it?"

"Right after this week-end, we'll focus all our energies into a full investigation. We'll concentrate on learning all we can about the backgrounds of our relatives and any health issues involved. We'll start with the histories of our immediate family members. Hopefully, in an all out effort, we'll be lucky enough to uncover clues. Now, let's not say a word to Emily just yet. We don't know her plans for sure, anyway. So by the time she is ready to marry, we'll be ready with answers, too. Whatever we do, there's no reason to alarm her. When we get all our ducks in a row, we'll sit down with her and share our findings. Agreed?"

Nodding, Rebecca only managed to mutter, "Yes." Stung by her conscience, her mind racing, her heart pounding, fear invaded her very being. Oh, Lance, she silently lamented, how right you are. Yet, she thought, the more you talk, the more I suffocate. It finally happened. My past has caught up with me and my world is closing in on me. There's so much at stake. Just thinking about it scares me. But this is about Emily now and for her sake, I must take my chances. I only pray strong love will bind us together when all is said and done. What a pyramid of lies I've built over the years. I'm to blame for this self inflicted heartache and now I feel like a hostage. If only I had been honest with Lance long ago. Well, I wasn't and now this is it. It's time to level with him. Her courage waning she concluded, I'll tell him. Only not just yet, but before we start researching, I'll fill him in on every detail. Most especially since he has no idea how complicated this research may become. I don't know what he will do when he learns the truth. But I have no choice. I....

"Rebecca, Rebecca, earth calling Rebecca. Come in. Do you hear me?"

"What? What did you say?" Called back to reality, finally Lance had her attention.

"I said since we're both in agreement with the plan in place, there's not much more we can do tonight so let's catch the news on television."

"Sorry, Lance. Guess I got caught up in my thoughts. I'll turn on the TV. Let's see what's going on in the world. Then, I think I'm going to head up to bed. I'm almost finished my book and I'm anxious to find out how it ends."

"I think I'll join you, Rebecca. I could use some quiet reading time myself considering it's probably the last I'll get for the week-end. I swear when you and your daughter get together, Rebecca, you'll like two magpies." Her face held a smile; her heart, an ache.

The night worked its magic and provided a comfortable night of sleep almost immediately for Lance. For Rebecca, it took a little longer. Her mind finally convinced of the good idea, welcomed the rest. The next day arrived without fanfare and was filled with final preparations needed to make the visit for Emily and her friend special. Before they knew it, it was time.

"There's the doorbell, Lance."

"Remember, Rebecca, don't jump to conclusions."

"Okay, I won't," she answered, nervously rubbing her hands together. "But what if this is really it?"

"We'll cross that bridge when we come to it. Come on now. Ready?"

"Ready."

Opening the door, Lance immediately was smothered with hugs and kisses."

"Save some for me," Rebecca instructed teasingly.

"There's enough for everybody, I promise," Emily cheerfully announced giving her mother a tight squeeze.

"Come in. Come in. Let me take your jackets," Lance invited.

Emily's eyes sparkled with excitement as she proudly made the introductions.

"Mom, Dad, this is Michael Brian Wendell. Michael, I would like you to meet my parents."

Hiding his anxious state well, Michael immediately extended his hand. "How do you do Mr. Miles? Mrs. Miles?" There, he thought. The obligatory handshakes are over and it wasn't so bad.

Lance shared the thought but voiced it, as well.

"Now that the introductions are out of the way, let's sit down and get acquainted. Tell us a little about yourself Michael."

"Dad," Emily chided in Michael's defense, "Don't grill."

"Me? Grill? Never."

"Oh, no. Not you Dad," Emily's teased, "But we do have a whole week-end to get to know each other. Okay?"

"Fair enough. So Malc..ah, Michael." He caught himself. "What part of the country do you hail from? By the way, what's your major? Oh, and yeah, just wondering what your plans are for after graduation?"

"Dad!" Emily rolled her eyes and protested loudly.

"What?" he asked hiding behind his innocent grin. "You said we have a whole week-end. That's what you said and I'm only taking a fraction of it now. I'm saving more for later, don't worry."

A tad exasperated, Rebecca shook her head. "Let it go, Emily. You know your father. You can't win."

Michael liked her parents right off the bat and didn't think twice before answering Lance's questions. As the conversation progressed so did his ability to relax. It didn't take long until everybody was enjoying this get together. Well, almost everybody.

Rebecca, sitting attentively, gave the impression of listening, all the while engaged in a skirmish pitted against herself. She was trying to reach a conclusion. Thinking it through, it was a no-brainer. Would Emily marry this guy? In a heartbeat. But wait a minute, maybe not. Okay. But then, again, what about the way she looks at him? Like a tennis ball, her thoughts bounced back and forth. Now, I'm being ridiculous. I mean can't Emily bring a male friend home for a visit without having a hidden agenda? Of course. But, Holy Hannah, I doubt it. The pros and cons tied, at the moment, her mind game was at 'love.'

For now, Rebecca put her thoughts on hold. There were hungry people to feed. Gathered around the table, she was hopeful they would enjoy the meal she had spent hours preparing. The delicious dinner served was a hit followed by an evening devoted to conversation and board games. Good people, good food, good fun in that order; laughter and entertainment lasted late into the night. Lance even lived up to his end of the bargain. His third-degree tactics were almost nil.

"Mom, if it's okay with you and Dad, tomorrow afternoon I'd like to take Michael around to all my old haunts. Then we'll hook up with Liz for dinner."

"We can handle that," Lance said casually, "right Rebecca?"

"That's fine, dear. It's your vacation. Spend it however you would like." Rebecca agreed aloud. Silently, it was another matter. Never mind that I have everything planned for your favorite vegetable lasagna. Never mind that you're cutting into our short visiting time. Never mind that you see more of Michael than of your parents. Never mind. You just go. All the while wearing a painted smile, not even Lance detected Rebecca's discontent.

A short visit it was. Long before Rebecca and Lance were ready to say goodbye, it was time for the young people to leave. While Lance helped Michael load the car, the opportunity presented itself. Rebecca and Emily, packing a travel snack bag, had a chance to be alone.

"Mom, what do you think of Michael?"

"He seems like a fine young man, Emily. You're lucky to have him for a friend."

"Oh, Mom, he's much more than that." Taking a deep breath, Emily emphatically reported the inevitable. "He's the man I plan to marry."

She kind of expected it. Still, being aware of its possibility and hearing its confirmation spoken aloud are two different things. Catching Rebecca off guard, she was flabbergasted and the announcement cost her a jar of mayonnaise as it dropped from her hands. Crashing to the floor, both women hurried to clean the mess. Engaged in their task, neither said a word. Rebecca was glad for the down time providing her the chance to get her head together.

As far as she was concerned, cleaning up the mayonnaise eyesore was a breeze in comparison to putting up with the chaos of the weekend. Now, to top it off, Emily's jolting prediction. The kitchen back in order, the interruption over and done, they returned to the subject at hand. Reaching for Emily, Rebecca's response came by way of a huge hug mixed with good wishes.

"I'm so happy for you." Despite the joy of the moment, Rebecca struggled with an inner nagging; her obligation as a mother. It simply could not be ignored. Still embracing her excited daughter, she had to ask. "Are you sure this is what you want. Emily? Marriage is a forever commitment."

"Yes, Mom, I know and I'm certain Michael is the one and only for me."

"What about your teaching career? What about his plans? There's so much to consider. Have you given this enough thought?" Grasping for straws, at this point, Rebecca felt silly and scared. Silly because she asked the obvious; scared because she harbored a deep secret.

Of course, she finally reasoned, the intelligent couple would have thought it through. Both are quite capable of making sound decisions. As if Emily had read her mother's mind, she gave her word.

"Mom, I promise. Michael and I have spent hours discussing our future. After we graduate, we plan to get teaching positions, save our money and then settle down. We won't get married for at least a year or so."

Exhilarated, no longer able to contain herself, Emily took hold of her mother and feeling so wonderfully foolish, twirled with her round and round on the now clean kitchen floor.

"Yahoo! Married? Mom, can you believe it? Me?" Emily had that lovesick look on her face and her eyes sparkled as she delighted in anticipation of her set course of action.

Giggling, Rebecca begged, "Stop Emily. I'm getting dizzy. Let me catch my breath." All the while shouting out her request, Rebecca couldn't hold her thoughts in check. Oh, how I love the whimsical side of my grown-up little girl. I wonder what her father will think of her plans. Guess that doesn't much matter. Her mind is made up. What am I going to do? She really means it. I've got to make matters right and there isn't all that much time. Okay. Just simmer down. Take a deep breath and talk to Emily. That's your first step.

"What about your father, Emily? When do you plan to tell him?"

"In about five minutes. Then on our next visit, we'll all sit and plan this thing together. Doesn't that sound terrific? Oh, and just between you and me, Mom, as far as children are concerned, don't worry. I want you to know, we gave an awful lot of thought and discussion to that responsibility, too, and we both agree."

At the very mention of that guarded subject, uninvited flashbacks chiseled at Rebecca's protective armor. It earned Emily her mother's undivided attention.

Rebecca's stomach tied in knots still gave no indication of nervousness. Instead, she fooled Emily with her quiet composure. She asked nonchalantly, "what, exactly, did you and Michael agree upon?"

Smiling from ear to ear and without batting an eyelash, she let her mother in on their future plans.

"Mom, just wait until you hear this. We want a passel of kids. Just think. You will be grandmother to at least a half dozen little munchkins. I think the name Mom-Mom suits you. Don't you? Gee, Mom, I'm getting off track here. I can't help it. Michael and I both love children. It all sounds too marvelous. So what do you think, Mom?"

With that declaration, Rebecca keenly felt the awareness of an impenetrable curtain that seemed to hang between them. Her old haunt back, she stood on shaky legs. Time was closing in on her. Her head started to ache. If I want this worrisome burden to end, it is inevitably up to me, she thought. More importantly, given the circumstances, Emily has a right to know. Oh, dear Emily, she pleaded in silence. Don't hate me.

Saved by the bell. How could she have answered? There was so much to tell. This was not the time, nor place. No wonder she was extremely grateful for Lance's interruption. His perfect timing not only granted her a reprieve but also conveniently suspended the mother daughter conversation. More importantly, arriving when he did, Emily's question was left open-ended.

"Come on, you two. Michael is in the car waiting."

Holding the door open, Lance hugged Emily and got a good, warm hug in return.

"Safe trip now," Lance gave fatherly instructions. "Call and let us know when you get there, hear?"

"We will, Dad." Anxious to let her father in on their intentions, Emily was quick to answer. Still flying on cloud nine about ready to pop, Emily shared their news flash.

"Dad, Michael asked me to marry him and I've said yes."

"Well, what do you know? Congratulations to the both of you." He kissed Emily on her forehead and gave Michael a firm handshake.

"I kind of sensed that was going to happen. Well, darling you arrived as my little girl and you leave as a grown woman." Shaking his head, he muttered, "How did you manage that?"

"Don't worry, Daddy. I may be Michael's wife but I'll always be your little girl, I promise."

The door closed, the house straightened, the lights out, it was time for bed. Contrasting Rebecca's pensive mood, Lance was talking up a blue streak.

"Rebecca, look. I understand there are obstacles to overcome and I know you are worried about them but I have to tell you, this Michael fellow is okay. He's intelligent, knows what he wants out of life and his plans indicate that he doesn't seem to be afraid to go after it."

Feeling good with the direction of his summation, there was more to say and there was no stopping him. He even went right on mumbling his point through a mouthful of toothpaste. "Obvisly, zay ub e ofver, Becca. You av ti mit. E trees er lak a ween."

Rebecca chuckled. "You know what's funny, Lance. I actually understood what you said. We have been together too long, you think?"

Smirking, he flashed his clean teeth and with feigned sarcasm, tested her. "Okay, Miss Smarty Pants, what did I say?"

Rolling her eyes, she reiterated most of his words, only this time, clearly. "You said, and this is close quoting...Obviously, they love each other. You have to admit he treats her like a queen."

"Not bad," he admitted, "but seriously, you saw how much they love each other. That's more than half the battle, isn't it?"

"It is. But remember, half is the key word here. You know what happened to us Lance and we dearly loved each other. We just didn't have the strength to fight the whole battle." Shaking her head in defeat, she said flatly, "There's no denying it. Totally unexpected, our insufferable heartache almost destroyed our marriage."

"But in the end, we didn't let it. Rebecca, listen to me," he said in a kind voice. Gently, taking her hands into his, he needed to impress upon her the importance of his counsel, and to stress her right to exercise the power of choice. "I want you to give serious consideration to what I'm about to say, okay?"

"Okay, Lance."

"It's precisely this. The past can only affect the present, if you let it. Think about it and don't look back. That's over, Rebecca. Let it go."

"Oh, Lance, that makes so much sense. If only I could let my past go. But, you know I just can't." Frustration sounded in her voice and could be seen on her face. "Honestly, Lance," she went on to explain the reason for her decision. "It's just that I'm afraid. It's Emily's future we're talking about here and there's a lot at stake. She shared their plans for children, Lance. They both love them and want six. Six, Lance! What if that destroys her marriage? What if it turns out that she can't save …"

"Stop Rebecca, don't go there." Lance interrupted abruptly. "You don't have a crystal ball."

"I know. But I'm afraid for her. Can you understand where I'm coming from?"

"Of course I can, for now, Rebecca. That's why I want you to keep in mind what I said. We both know fear is ruling you. All I ask is that you don't let it ruin you. Rebecca, it's true, you are captain of your own ship. Steer it in the right direction and work on taking complete charge, okay?"

"I know you are right, Lance. I promise to make a sincere effort." "Now that's my Rebecca. I've seen your courage. You can do it. I promise you will not have to do it alone. We'll work together in our efforts to do all in our power to keep Emily and Michael, too, from getting hurt. We'll get to the bottom of all this and we will find out what happened to the twins. We'll make it our mission. We'll turn every stone. Okay?" Pulling her closer, he held her tightly in his protective arms. "For now, let's be happy for them in reaching their decision. Our little girl is getting married."

Resting her head on his chest, hearing his strong heartbeat, Rebecca felt encouraged. Of course you're right, she thought. Trouble is you don't know there is another issue and that only part of the problem stems from losing the boys. You are right. I do have to take a stand. Mulling it over, I know procrastination is no longer an option. It's now or never.

I hear it, Rebecca said to herself. It never really stops. I hear the haunting little voice in my head nag, nag, nagging. Over all those years I've listen to it and then never took action to make it go away. Taking a deep breath she commanded. This is it. If I open this door, there's no closing it until we walk through together. Only the Lord knows what

Lance's reaction will be and only the Lord alone knows where we will go from there. All I can do is start at the beginning. I'll not stop until the entire story is told.

Her ambitious plan in place left her shaking and it didn't take long to lose her battle to tears. Down her cheeks they streamed as she squared her shoulders, and left the security of his arms. Now she advised herself, I begin my story and only heaven knows its ending.

Her throat tightened. "Lance, this isn't going to be easy. I've something to tell you."

Perplexed with Rebecca's unexpected reaction, Lance felt uneasy. Both her tone and choice of words put him on edge. Watching the color drain from her face clenched it.

"It's okay. Rebecca, I'm listening. You know you can tell me anything."

"I know Lance. It's just that…" hesitating, Lance put his arm around her.

"Rebecca, you're shaking. Relax. What is it? Come on now," he coaxed. "It can't be all that bad."

"Forgive me, Lance. What I am about to tell you is cruel but please believe me. It was never intended to hurt you."

That did it. Anxiety and tension took over and Lance could not stop the convincing thoughts running rampant in his head. Without warning, suddenly, his stomach bunched up in knots. In desperation, he turned to silent prayer. Oh God, no. Not that. I couldn't live without her. Thinking the worst, he voiced his fear. Sober concentration spurred by heartache of the past, he dared to ask.

"Are you sick Rebecca? Do you have some incurable disease? Please tell me."

"No," she whispered. "I'm not sick. Don't worry. Physically, I'm fine."

Taking her hands into his, he looked lovingly into her eyes. Quietly, with a mixture of delight and relief, he sighed, "Thank God."

That quickly his anxiety level lessened. Too bad, it brought only temporary relief. For just as quickly, the pending uncertainty only increased confusion; and in a flash, his fear of the unknown, once again, soared. He could not help himself. His thoughts were taking him into dangerous territory. Still, the treacherous ramblings insisted on full steam ahead.

No. Not that, he thought. She wouldn't. Not my Rebecca. We've been together for too long. No way. He shook his head to rid it of his despicable premise. Logic chased the mocking voice in his head and still he couldn't help himself. His thoughts muddled, sweat beaded his forehead. Shaking his head in disbelief, it was too late. His mind had already condemned her. He was convinced. She was having an affair.

Squaring his shoulders, he resolved not to raise his voice. It didn't work for long. . Shouting, he almost blew a gasket. "Rebecca, whatever it is, spit it out. My patience and nerves can't stand this suspense." He had planned to listen, to give her a chance to explain. But before he knew it, his tongue lost control and out lashed the hurtful accusation. Angry, sad and bruised, he shouted out in outrage, "You're having an affair. Aren't you?"

"An affair? An affair?" Rebecca glared at him. "No I am not having an affair. How could you even think such a thing?"

"How could I not?" he challenged. "You're acting so strangely, weird. You're scaring me, Rebecca. Whatever it is, tell me. Tell me, now," he demanded.

With shades of sadness evident in her eyes and the pained expression on her face, there was no need for Rebecca to confirm or deny it. He believed her now, as he realized with regret how cruel the accusation and wished he could take back his words. Of course, he could not. Too bad it just doesn't work that way. He knew that look of hurt would haunt him for a long time. He knew he deserved it. He knew he must repent. He whispered, "I'm sorry." Consoled, she lingered in his remorse trying desperately to shake the shock of his cruel charge. Apology accepted, she wondered how she didn't see that one coming. Why she thought, we have been together for so long. I really thought I knew every chink in his armor; obviously, not.

So this is it. No turning back. Struggling still, Rebecca thought, my moment of truth. I really believed my secret was forever safe within me. How naïve! She took a step back from his closeness and with this unpredicted change of direction, began.

"Lance, listen. I'm not sick and I'm not unfaithful. I'm a fraud." With those few words, the floodgates opened and an onslaught of non-ending words poured out attacking her very origin and core of credibility.

"What the heck are you talking about? A fraud?"

"I lied to you, Lance from the very beginning. I'm not who you think I am. I don't know if my father was a war hero and I don't know if my mother died from cancer. The truth is I don't even know who my parents were or are, if they are dead or alive. You see, I was left at an orphanage and raised by nuns." Almost in a whisper now, as if to avoid detection, she added, "I was an orphan."

Her situation explained at last, the shocking realization hit her like a ton of bricks. All those many years of living a lie, died in a matter of just a very few minutes. Terminated just like that, without so much as a hint of a how-do-you-do. Logically, why should there be? The burden lifted, she was relieved. But by the same token, some how the intensity and longevity of the consuming conflict, challenging her savvy talent, now forever over, left her feeling a tad perplexed. Glad she was no longer forced to hide in the shadow of a contrived past, at the same time, the speed at which she was vindicated left her feeling almost victimized.

Speechless, Lance found himself trying not only to comprehend, but to digest the baffling information his wife had just divulged. An orphan? Is that what has Rebecca so upset? Why? Why the attempt to shatter our firm foundation? Why wait to tell me now? Why not before we married? Why the mystery? She's an orphan. So what? I don't get it. So many questions invaded his unsettled mind.

"Say something Lance," she pleaded, "Please."

"I don't know quite what to say. I'm confused Rebecca. You caught me off guard." Turning, he faced her and finally managed to ask a few of his unspoken questions. "What about the medals you said your father earned and what about that necklace? You said your mother gave that to you before she died. What's that all about?"

Grabbing a box of tissues from the dresser, Rebecca attempted to fill in the gaps.

"Those medals belonged to some soldier. I just read about them in the library and stole the idea. The necklace did come from my mother but it came through a nun who found it and a note in my file directing it be given to me when I turned twelve. With each word, her voice grew louder and louder and shakier and shakier.

"Calm down, Rebecca."

"I can't. This is so painful. On one side of the coin, I stand to lose my perceived heritage which got me through most of my life; on the other side, I stand to lose you. Right now, I know it sounds crazy but I so desperately want to hang onto both." It had been too long in coming. Depression and panic arrived in waves and all she could do was sob uncontrollably.

The initial shock over, her words slowly sinking in, he took her into his strong arms and rocked her. "Stop crying," he gently asked and held her close. "This isn't the end of the world. How about we try to look at this as a beginning? Come on now. Think about it. Compared to what we've been through, this is nothing. You're still the same woman I married, aren't you?"

Nodding, she cried all the harder for his miraculous understanding.

"So what's the big deal? You were an orphan. There are a lot of adopted people in this world. Why would it matter?"

"Oh, Lance. That's just it. There are a lot of adopted people but I'm not one of them. I was never chosen. "Shuddering, she said, "adoption day was awful."

"Adoption day?" puzzled, Lance asked, "what was that all about?"

"On the first Monday of every month, come hell or high water, everybody had to be on their best behavior and wear a smile all day long.

Want to or not. We were paraded past several couples who checked us over like so much cattle. They thought nothing of talking about us right in front of us like we weren't even there."

"Like what, Rebecca?" He couldn't imagine.

"They would say things, oh I don't know, like that girl's teeth are too crooked or that boy's ears are much too big. Hurtful things like that. To top it off, the older kids never were picked, only the cute little ones. It was sheer torture, hoping yet knowing, deep down, you didn't stand a chance. I was always rejected. The hurt and humiliation was horrible."

"I'm sorry, Rebecca."

"Me, too. Many hearts and dreams were shattered on each and every first Monday of every month for many years. You have to remember, Lance, all this happened years ago. You are right. It's nothing being an orphan today but back then it was different. Being an orphan carried its own stigma. Marked for life, it was simple. Orphans just weren't good enough for parents, or people for that matter, to love. Being youngsters, not knowing any better, we blamed only ourselves for our predicament. It became ingrained. As we grew older, the less people knew about us, the better chance of surviving. Being an orphan was best kept a secret. I still don't want people to know. It hurts just telling you."

"Jeez, Rebecca, that's tough. But you did nothing wrong. So what if you created fictional parents? It's not a sin wanting to belong to a family. None of that bothers me. Did you honestly think I would love you less because you don't happen to know your roots? You were the one cheated. Not me. Oh, Rebecca. I love you for you; not for whoever is hanging on your family tree. I could not care less about your lineage." They both knew he meant just that. Pulling her even more tightly into the contour of his body, Rebecca felt safe. That's where she fit best.

"Poor Rebecca," he whispered into her ear. "I'm so sorry you had to grow up feeling unwanted. How hard it must have been on you protecting your secret for all those years. I'm proud of you, Rebecca. It took enormous courage just now." Kissing her tenderly, he added. "You know what? You were too chosen. You were chosen by me. Don't ever forget that Mrs. Lance Miles. Tomorrow, I promise, we'll start learning what we can about the twins. We'll get to the bottom of the problem. We won't let Emily down. Okay?"

"Okay, Lance." Funny how that worked, Rebecca thought. Until that burden was lifted, I didn't realize how much it weighed me down. Relieved and emotionally drained, she fell asleep in the security of his love and protective arms.

Chapter 31

1982

The rain came down early in the morning and gave no indication of letting up.

"What a crummy inconvenience. I wish you didn't have to go in this miserable weather. Are you sure, Rebecca, you don't want me to drive you?"

"No thanks, Lance. This is something I must do myself. Besides, the best way to get started is for me to go back to the beginning. Let me find out about my biological parents and we'll go from there."

"I agree. The fact-finding mission starts at the orphanage. I'm all for your going. It's just that I don't want you driving in this mess. You have enough on your mind. You don't need the added stress of nasty weather to add jeopardy."

"Tell you what. If it will make you feel better, I'll take a cab."

"I'd appreciate that and keep me posted every step of the way. Let me know just as soon as you learn anything."

"I promise," she said sealing it with a gentle kiss. "I didn't hurt your feelings just now, did I, Lance?"

"No. Of course not. In fact I'm touched by your passionate pursuit and I'm convinced, if anyone can get to the bottom of this, it will be you. Now, let me call you a cab."

* * * * *

There was no need to stay overnight. It had taken less time than predicted, mainly because not a lot was accomplished. In fact, she had spent more time touring her old haunts and reminiscing about old times and the course her life had taken. Now, much sooner than anticipated, she found herself in the cab heading for home with the promise of only better things to come. Reverend Mother would see her again in three weeks at which time, hopefully, she would provide necessary papers for Rebecca to officially begin her quest with Lance at her side. No more secrets.

It wasn't raining as hard now. She could better see out the window. Still her mind, reflecting on her bizarre visit, wasn't all that clear. Mostly, it was hard to grasp how all her life she had been without parents and now, in three short weeks, she would know who was responsible for her very being. Shivering that staggering concept, not the dampness of the day, gave her a chill.

Lance was sitting in his easy chair reading the paper when she walked in and dropped her overnight bag on the floor next to him. In a flash, he was up on his feet greeting her.

"You're home," he said. "I'm surprised. I thought you were staying. You didn't call. So how did it go?" Anxious and full of questions, he aimed them at her one by one.

Walking into his out-stretched arms, she snuggled close enjoying the warmth of his welcome.

"There wasn't any point in calling. There was nothing to report and there wasn't a need to stay, either. The Reverend Mother didn't have immediate answers. So she is arranging for me to see her again." Surrendering a long, trembling sigh, with regret she added, "In three weeks, Lance. Hopefully, she'll get me some information by then. But how in the world can I wait three more weeks? Three weeks? She may as well have said three years."

"Whoa. That would be a remarkable stretch, Rebecca," he said in an effort to lift her spirits. "Seriously, listen," he lovingly assured her, "You waited forty-four years, what's three more weeks? Think about it. That will be here before you know it. Now, tell me, have you eaten yet?" She shook her head no.

"Come on. I'm taking you out to dinner."

"How do you do that, Lance?"

"Do what?"

"Always know just exactly what to do."

"Because I'm me," he teased, helping her with her coat, "and because I'm hungry, too. Let's go."

That night Rebecca slipped into her delicate, pink, satin nightgown. She loved the way the soft material felt next to her skin. So did he. She loved the way his huge hands gently touched her. So did he. She loved when they made love together. So did he.

Asleep now, Rebecca covered him affectionately pulling the warm covers up to his shoulders. Turning, she tried to do the same but sleep eluded her. Her body tired; her mind, unfortunately wide awake, dominated the quiet of the night.

She sat up, switched on the lamp and turned the radio dial to her favorite soft music station knowing neither would bother Lance. Reaching for her cigarettes on the night stand, she lit one then watched the cloudy smoke's unintentional artistry. Leaning her head back on the Irish-laced pillow case, she sighed, if only I could give my mind a break. If only I could sleep. Then somewhere in the recesses of her mind a philosophic deduction popped out... It's the darkness of night that justifies the ruthless invasion of one's thoughts which robs the pleasure of rest... Oh, brother. I'm losing it. With that Rebecca jumped out of bed and repeatedly, in staccato fashion, pounded her cigarette's lighted tip into the ashtray. The ashes were dead but somehow the merciless kneading released frustration, at least temporarily.

Briskly, with her arms held tight to her body and clinched fists, she paced the length of the bedroom. Confusion and anger, directed at her unknown parents, surged through her body. I'm so mixed up. Darn parents. Why couldn't you have been just like the ones I was forced to make up? No, you couldn't be that nice. You had to abandon me and now, look at all the trouble you are causing. If anything happens to Emily, I'll, I'll, curse you. Yes, that's what I'll do. I'll curse you forever. From her Catholic background, that was a mighty strong threat.

Calm down, she told herself and walked over to her most favorite spot in the room, the window bench. She welcomed the softness of the velvet covered cushion as she sat leaning against the inside panel with her legs outstretched.

Strange, the night sky seems darker than usual. I don't see even a hint of starlight. Hope that's not a bad omen. This waiting will kill me. In the end, what if I find out too much? What if I can't handle the truth? Worse yet, what if Lance can't? Now, I wish I had learned about my parents long before we were married or at least filled him in with the truth. But no, I didn't take the time. I was too busy lying.

Distressed, Rebecca buried her face in her hands. Crying, she pitifully mourned the loss of her babies and the misfortune of never knowing her parents. How ironic, she cried. They will never know theirs, either.

"Rebecca." Gently touching her shoulder, Lance was by her side.

"Oh Lance, don't tell me I woke you. I mean you can sleep through a thunderstorm and, yet, here you are answering my soft cry. What would I do without you?"

Now was not the time for talking. It wasn't time to tell her that her cries were anything but quiet. He just held her in his arms and rocked her gently.

"Sshh, sshh," he encouraged. "It will be okay."

* * * * *

Nervous with anticipation, Rebecca said. "It's time to get going."

"I suppose you still would rather do this on your own?"

"Yes, I would and I'll be fine. But wherever this takes me after this trip, I would like you to be with me."

"Try and stop me. I plan to be right there by your side every step of the way. Now, I'll call the cab so you can get started."

Adjusting her scarf, the face in the hall mirror looked weary. Boy, have I aged but I can't worry about that now. The three weeks are up. It's time to face the uncertainty. It's time to face the facts. It's time to keep the appointment.

"Cab's here."

"Okay, Lance. I'm ready," she said as she kissed him goodbye. "Wish me luck."

Somehow, the trip this time seemed to take no time at all. Maybe it was the disposition of the sun, bright and sunny. No matter, she was there before she knew it.

Smiling to herself, she thought about her old sparring partner and how this time she was ready to duel. Holy Hannah, I can't help it. I'm feeling a bit smug. Wait until old, prune-face Donata tries to head me off at the pass. Boy is she in for a surprise. This time I have an appointment. That will show her. Well, it didn't and Rebecca felt cheated. The clever feeling of satisfaction didn't last, as it was Mother Superior herself who happened to open the door.

"Rebecca, how good to see you again."

"It's good seeing you again, Mother Superior."

"Come in and please have a seat. I've been waiting for you."

Rebecca, remembering the ropes, sat in the proper seat while Mother Superior took her place at her desk. Quietly waiting for the nun to speak, Rebecca's nerves screamed loudly as she trembled in anticipation.

Almost as if she could read her thoughts, and to say nothing of her toe tapping, Mother Superior interjected.

"My dear, there is no need for your nervousness. Your foot hasn't been still since you sat down."

Rebecca looked at her foot and smiled, "Guilty as charged."

"Well, calm down. I can assure you that it took some doing but, I was able to retrieve your records and this is what I was able to uncover." With the file folder spread open on the nun's desk, it quickly become apparent that she was in no hurry to hand it over; at least not until she made her point.

"I think this information will prove to be useful in your quest to locate your biological parents. Like I mentioned before, Rebecca, every orphan sooner or later wants to find out who the parents are." She just can't let go of her perceived purpose for the fact-finding mission. She just has to be right. Okay, already. You win. Just give me the file.

"That would be wonderful," Rebecca, of course, responded respectfully. The entire time thinking, would you just get on with it? Stop making it such a monumentally slow process. Just give me the darn file so I can do what I have to do.

"Just look at the size of this, Rebecca," she said waving her hand over the papers on her desk. "Our Bishop was kind enough to have this entire dossier retrieved from the archives."

Intrigued, Rebecca nodded the recognition, took a deep breath and about to pop, boldly posed the question.

"When may I see the contents? Have you read it?"

"Briefly, I did, Rebecca. I think you will appreciate what it has to offer. But this file is totally yours to, not only read, but to keep. Make good use of all that you learn."

With that instruction, the meeting was deemed over as Mother Superior got up, handed the sought-after portfolio to Rebecca, bid her farewell and escorted her to the door.

Clutching her bona fide pedigree under her arm at last, Rebecca hailed a cab and headed straight for home to delve into her past, whatever it held; and all within the confines of an old manila folder.

She made it to the kitchen table where Lance was waiting for her. Except for the gurgle of the freshly brewed coffee, the house was still. Waiting patiently, he said not a word. He let it up to Rebecca to decide when the time was right to jump into the inescapable.

Releasing a long, shuddering sigh, she announced, "Well Lance, here it is," as she gently placed the folder on the kitchen table. Her sober concentration spurred by an odd impulse, brought about the question, "Can you believe, a part of me is afraid to read it and a part of me is dying to find out?"

"Sure, I can. Maybe a cup of hot coffee would help. Want some?"

"Please." Sipping the calming brew, she felt a little better. "Umm, that's good." Tilting her head to one side, then to the other, she tried working the crick out of her neck.

"Here, let me." Immediately massaging her neck, he helped relieve her of the painful muscle spasm. "Better?"

"Much. Thanks. Well, guess this is it. No more stalling." Picking up the manila folder darkened with age, Lance could see her hands tremble. Just before she took the final step, she stopped and asked in a barely audible voice. "What if I find out something ghastly?"

In a manner both consoling and kind, he took her shaky hands and steadied them in his. "Rebecca, whatever you find, we'll deal with it together. But if you aren't ready to do this, then don't. You waited a long time. A little longer won't hurt. What's important here is that you have the file at your fingertips. All systems are go, but you call the shots. Just remember, what happened, happened. You can't change the past. You may not like it but you have to accept it. Remember, too, you may be on the road to helping Emily, okay?"

She nodded.

"Now, do you want me to stay or would you rather be alone?"

Boy, how selfish I've been she realized with regret.

"Stay, please." Closing her eyes for a second, she inhaled deeply, exhaled, opened her eyes and let her hands take over. She opened the file and gingerly sifted through the information page by page.

"So far, this isn't telling me much, Lance, mainly the date this baby girl was dropped off at the orphanage and what the weather was like and such. Now what?"

"Hang in there. There has got to be something of value or why would anyone bother to keep the records? Besides, you haven't gotten very far. Keep reading."

Not five minutes later, she let out an ecstatic yell. "Eureka, I found it, Lance. I found it. Look," she said excitedly. "Look at this official looking document. Holy Hannah, Lance, it's a copy of my birth certificate. This is it!"

"Fantastic," he said caught up in her enthusiasm. "Let's see."

"Lance, do you realize that in essence, this is the first time ever that I will have met my parents? Holy Hannah," she bubbled. "You read it for me, I can't."

"Tell you what, Rebecca. You hold it and I'll read it. How's that?"

"Perfect. Now, please hurry and read it before I pop."

"Okay, okay. I'm excited for you. So are you ready to find out who you really are?"

"I'm ready." She held her breath, "I think."

"Good. Here goes," and he read Rebecca's birth certificate information in a loud and clear voice.

State of New Jersey – Department of Health Vital Records
CERTIFICATE OF BIRTH

Date of Birth 02-05-38   File N. 06331880-38
County of Birth Somerset   Date Filed 02-24-38
                                          Date Issued 02-15-39

Subject Rebecca Harden
Sex Female
Father's name   D. Harden
Mother's maiden name   Lydia Wright

This is to certify that this is the copy of the original record which is on file in the New Jersey Department of Health, in accordance with Act 67, P.L. 303, approved by the General Assembly, February 15, 1939.

Charles Thompson   William Macon
State Registrar   Commissioner of Health   4017818

The full record of this birth has been carefully filed and is preserved
in the archives of the
State of New Jersey
Every Mother Is Entitled To A Birth Certificate For Her Child

"There you are, Rebecca," he whispered, almost afraid talking too
loudly would somehow take away from this precious, long-awaited
moment. "This document, in silent eloquence, has presented you with
valid parents. How does it feel to meet them at last?"

Hugging the copy of her birth certificate to her heart, she closed her
eyes and let the tears of joy flow.

"I know it's only on paper. I can't help it. I'm thrilled. I can't believe
it. Mother Superior really was right. After all these years, I have finally
met my newly acquired authors of my life. Oh Lance, you just can't
imagine my feelings. Funny, I'm happy to know their names and yet,
I don't know anything else about them. Lydia. Isn't Lydia the prettiest
name? I've got to learn more."

Her adrenaline pumping, with nowhere to go, crystallized into a
whirlwind of images and ideas and questions in her mind meant for her
parents. Curious, she wondered, which one of you do I look like? Or
maybe a little of both? Which of you was more warm and tender or for
that matter, indulgent? How did you meet and when did you marry? If
only there was a way of learning the answers. There's so much I want to
know. I guess, most especially, I want to know why you chose to inflict
such pain on me, your daughter. What did I do that was so bad that it
caused you to abandon me?

"Rebecca," he interrupted her silent speculations. "Wonder why
your father's first name is listed as only an initial. Notice that? Seems
odd, doesn't it?"

"Don't ask me. This whole giving up your baby thing seems odd
to me."

"Look further in the file, Rebecca. Is there any indication as to
where your parents were at the time of your birth? That would be terrific

information. Then, I think we could trace them or maybe someone who knew them and find out any helpful medical information they may have."

Obviously, she thought, he's happy for me and he's thinking of Emily while I almost forgot. What a dear man. Let me go through more papers. Maybe in this mess, there will be some clue. "Look what I found," she chuckled, "report cards. There must be at least twenty of them. Know what? According to these, I wasn't all that dumb. I wonder why the nuns saved them."

"I don't know Rebecca. It does seem like they went through a lot of trouble keeping this stuff together. What else is there?"

"Here, this looks like my first attempt to write in cursive and this looks like a drawing of a Christmas tree. This folder has a ton of artwork. No wonder the file is so thick. I don't get it why were they saved? Do you think they were saving them for my mother? That maybe she promised to come back and they wanted her to see my progress?"

Lance didn't want to pop her bubble. If that was the case, her mother would have come back to the orphanage years ago. Let her have her elusive daydream.

"Well, now this is interesting. I've learned something else about myself. Here are my First Communion and my Confirmation Certificates. I never told you that I just guessed at the dates when we had that form to fill at when we got married. Now this I didn't know either. When I was seven-years-old, I got the chickenpox. Then the following year I came down with the measles and the German measles. It doesn't say that I ever got the mumps. Remember when I got pregnant with Emily and the doctor asked me if I ever had the German measles, well, I just didn't know. Oh, and when Emily got the chickenpox and wanted to know if you or I ever had them. You told her yes right off the bat. I quickly changed the subject. Maybe this is pertinent information for Emily's kids in the future."

"This folder is letting you in on a lot Rebecca. Some of your artwork is really good. I told you that's where Emily got her talent, didn't I?"

"You did. Let's see what else I can find?" It took a few more minutes but she did it. "Lance, here," pleased with herself, she pulled out a handwritten sheet. "I think I may have found another hot lead."

"Let's see. Jackpot! You know what, Rebecca? You're absolutely right. Look this may be the last known address of your mother. We can go to the courthouse and find out. Now, don't get your hopes too high. It has been a long time. But this address, if confirmed, will be our first port of call. Too bad your father's neck of the woods is not listed."

"But my mother's address is excellent for starters."

"You bet. Now, let me make vacation arrangements with work. I don't want to take a chance and miss being with you on your extraordinary mission. Your enthusiasm is contagious. I'm almost as anxious as you and besides, who could be a better partner?"

"She gave him a smile and a hug, "Thanks for your help and I want you to know that I'm grateful for your understanding. It's good knowing you have your feet solidly on the ground."

"No need for thanks, Rebecca. We're a team in this together for the long haul. Now, you stay working with the file while I call my boss. Keep looking in the file."

Rebecca stayed the course and sifted through the smallest of notes, some of which were even written in the margins but didn't make much sense.

"It is set," he said with satisfaction "I've negotiated my vacation time. I figure it will take me about two days to clear my desk and prepare instructions for a temp to cover until my return. How did you make out?"

"Not that great. Let's face it, Lance, I'm just another orphan statistic. I'm almost at the end and still, nothing. Well, nothing of great consequence. Guess we found out all that we are going to."

"Like they say, Rebecca, it ain't over til the fat lady sings. Look around. Do you see a fat lady?"

"Can't say that I do," she joked. "I don't hear any singing, either."

"Well then," he teased, "don't give up until you do."

"I'll keep looking for clues but I don't know." No sooner those words were out of her mouth, when she stopped in her tracks. "I don't believe it. Look here. You were right. I just found my mother's handwritten note. The one she wrote with my purple gold. Of course, it's the very last item in the folder. Wouldn't you know? It's exactly what I remember Sister Regina, the nun who gave me the necklace, telling me." Nervously, she repeated the message aloud. *"Please give this heart to my daughter, Rebecca on her twelfth birthday and tell her I love her."*

"Oh, Lance." She practically flew into his out-stretched arms and he held her as she filled the room with silent determination. "Her words still put a lump in my throat. I've got to learn why. Why if she loved me, did she leave me?"

"She must have had her reasons, Rebecca. Don't worry. It's not like we haven't faced enormous challenges before. Mysteries are meant to be solved. We will find out why. Wait and see." Determination, occupying the tone of his voice, instilled confidence and shed a shining light into the shadowy corners of her mind, for now, anyway.

A few days later, armed with her mother's last known address, they capitalized on its importance. It was the starting point where they got their feet wet. Rebecca prayed they would not drown in their endeavor.

Chapter 32

~

The drive to the courthouse took a little longer than anticipated. At a rest stop, Lance pulled out the map to check on his plotted course. Opening it, he laid it out over the steering wheel to get his navigational bearings.

"See, Rebecca. We are here." His finger traced their intended route to their current location. He continued, probably more so for his benefit than for hers. "We want to take Route 22 to the end. That will take us into Harrison County and on to Washington Avenue and then to the courthouse. By my estimation, we should be there in about another hour or so. Want me to find a restaurant for a snack or anything?"

"No, Lance. I'm okay. I'm just anxious to get there as soon as we can. This is risky business, like finding a needle in a haystack. Suppose the records aren't there and this turns out to be a wild goose chase. What then?"

"We'll cross that bridge when we come to it," he answered folding the map back into its original creases. For the rest of the drive they rode in silence.

"There, Lance on the left up a few buildings, I can see the courthouse."

"Okay and, we're in luck. There's a parking space right out front. Now that's got to be a good omen."

Inside the building, they followed the sign directing them to the County Clerk.

"You okay Rebecca?" he asked noticing how quickly the color faded from her face.

"Um hmm. Just a little shaky."

"Okay. Relax. Sit here while I check in. It shouldn't take me too long."

Nodding in agreement, Rebecca took a seat in the crowded room. The diversion in her surroundings caught her off guard and the busyness of the place took her mind off her problem. It was a temporary relief. None-the-less, she was grateful for its intrusion. She could only speculate as to the enormity and scope of problems gathered here. There were people coming and going in all directions. All hopeful for resolutions to whatever issues dictated their presence here today.

Smack dab in the middle of her surveillance Rebecca stopped short and pulled her feet back just in the nick of time. "Whoa," she charged. "Slow down."

"Sorry lady." Not stopping, the man with obviously no time to lose tossed his apology over his shoulder. "I'm late for an appointment."

Annoyed, she thought, well you should have allowed more time. Then with the safety of her toes insured, she went back to filling the gap with people watching. Before she knew it, and interrupting her musings, Lance was back

"Okay, Rebecca, our name is on the check-in list." Theirs was not a long wait and presently they were called.

"Next."

"That's us, Rebecca."

"How may I help you?" The smartly dressed woman sitting behind her desk asked.

"We are trying to locate a woman, named Lydia Wright. Her last known address is listed as 214 Walnut Street, Oaks, New Jersey."

"Your name and relationship?"

"I'm Rebecca Miles and she's my mother." That revelation spoken out loud intimidated Rebecca and she could feel the tension grab her spine and hold it tightly preparing her for an expected jolting let down.

On cue, Lance produced Rebecca's birth certificate for proof and assistance. The woman studied the document all the while drumming the desktop with her fingers. Add to the drama, why don't you, Rebecca silently challenged.

"Hmmm, is she alive?" Her question directed to Lance was answered in his most pleasant winsome spirit.

"We're not sure." Pausing, giving her time to digest his input, he continued. "Is it possible she could be traced through tax payments if she is alive or, if not, through the recording of a death certificate?" He knew it was a stretch but he had to give it his best shot. He had to make this seemingly unapproachable woman who was just doing her job, feel like he had a handle on the subject. As in the past when the chips were down, it was Lance who handled important matters in the household. Once again, this job of top priority had his name on it. Like a savvy one man band, he satisfied the woman's many questions.

His patient demeanor and intelligent presentation impressed Rebecca. She was so proud of him. Indeed, he always knew just what to do. Yet, Rebecca felt a twinge of guilt. From deep inside, she knew he was fighting for her. From deep inside, she knew it was her battle. And in this case, her personal discovery inevitable, she realized she should have been the one fielding the barrage of questions tossed out begging results.

Checking book after book; page after page, the clerk's snail pace put them on edge. Aw, come on, Rebecca thought. At this rate, you're driving the both of us crazy. And just like that, her frustrations were quenched when the quiet, seemingly inattentive clerk jumped to her feet pouring out a valid discovery.

"Bingo, here it is. I think this is what you are looking for. Yes, I'm sure of it."

She spoke with absolute conviction. "According to the records, Lydia Wright of 214 Walnut Street paid her last tax bill on November

30 of this year. She is now residing at 1410 Hanover Street in Oaks and her last name is now Clark."

Pleased her tenacity paid off, Rebecca could almost see egotism sneak through the clerk's smile. "I'm sure this information will be helpful," the self-assured woman announced as she wrote down the Hanover Street address and handed it to the gentleman for whom it seemed to hold the most interest.

Grateful, Lance accepted the fruit of the woman's labor. Encouraged, both he and Rebecca could not adequately express their sincere appreciation. As often is the case, the best they could muster up was, "Thank you."

It was a jubilant couple who walked out of the courthouse hand in hand. Smiling, Lance announced, "Next stop, 1410 Hanover Street."

Filled with an undeniable amount of excitement and an equal amount of apprehension, Rebecca grinned broadly. "She's alive, Lance. Holy Hannah, I can't believe it. My mother is alive."

"I know. And you know what else I can't believe? I can't believe how this whole courthouse affair turned out to be so easy? It was time-consuming, but relatively easy."

"Your charm did it, Lance. Obviously, the clerk liked impressing you with her expertise. She barely tossed a glance my way. You were her total audience."

"Hey, it worked, didn't it?" he asked with a sly grin. "Besides, you're the one who always claims you can catch more flies with honey than vinegar. Not sure why anyone would want flies, but, anyway I got to tell you. I feel a lot better now than when we started."

In the car and ready for action, Rebecca suggested a slight change in their course of direction. "Let's get something to eat first. I'm starved."

"Okay. There's a restaurant just a few buildings away. I can see it from here."

Sitting in the booth, Rebecca ate her grilled cheese served with a side order of guilt. They should have gone on their way but she had to stop, even if it was under the pretext of a hunger attack. Truth be known, the closer they came to piecing the mystery together, the more she became unglued.

"Are you about done Rebecca? We have an interesting schedule ahead of us."

"I know," she said sipping on the last of her coke, "but can I tell you something first, Lance?"

"Anything. You know you can." Seeing her suddenly so serious brought him concern. Leaning across the table, he gave her his undivided attention. "I know this has got to be tough on you. But you can do this. Now what is it you want to tell me?"

"It's just that well. Um, it's just that you know I'm clinging to the business at hand. You know I dearly want to clear the road for Emily's sake."

A tad confused, he paused momentarily. Then anxious to find out what exactly was this monkey on her back, he pressed on with assurances. "Of course, Rebecca, your love for Emily has never been in question. So what is bothering you?"

Gnawing on her lower lip, she whimpered, "I'm being selfish. There, that's it in a nutshell."

"What's that supposed to mean?"

Taking a deep breath, Rebecca nervously voiced her preoccupation.

"The closer we get, the more chicken I become. When I think that I'm finally going to meet the woman who brought me into this world, I panic. It's scary and it's almost too huge for me to comprehend. I'm almost afraid of my unpredictable reaction."

"I certainly can understand, Rebecca, but that doesn't make you selfish."

"It does when asking questions relating to family health issues winds up taking a back seat," she snapped.

"To what?"

"To my wanting answers about me. I have this insatiable desire to scream at this woman and shake her until her answers fall into the blanks. I want to shout at her. I want her to squirm when I ask why she brought me into this world and, as if that isn't cruel enough, I want her to tell me face to face why she didn't keep me after I got here. I want her conscience to punish her, to saturate her with guilt."

Resentment evident in her every word, her face flushed with anger, she continued to sound off. "I can't help myself. This is my mother I'm attacking, Lance. How much more self-centered can I get? I want revenge." Then lowering her head, she whispered. "How Christian is that?"

"Jeez, Rebecca, no wonder your stomach is in knots. You have to stop being so hard on yourself. You made yourself judge and jury and even condemned yourself. Stop being your own worst enemy. Now listen to me. You had to travel on the journey to adulthood pretty much by yourself and darn it, you earned the right to your feelings and to answers. That doesn't make you selfish. For the years of heartache she caused you, she owes you at least that much. You'll see. When the air is clear and your mind satisfied, the health issues will pop back up on your priority list. Come on, give me a smile. That's more like it. Now let's go see the woman with the answers."

With anticipation running high, not soon enough, yet all too soon, they reached their destination.

The two-story, colonial house located on the tree-lined street was attractive and the front yard, with a multitude of colorful flowers; picturesque. The setting, Rebecca thought, held a hint of money and she could not keep her mind from speculating.

Reading between the lines, maybe, the money wasn't always here. Maybe that's why she gave me away. Maybe she just could not afford to raise a child. Maybe…maybe…maybe…

"Yes?" peering through the slightly opened door, the bespectacled woman softly inquired. Again, Rebecca let the better of the two take the lead. Grateful for his support, she just stood quietly at his side.

"Hello. We are Mr. and Mrs. Miles. Are you Mrs. Wright Clark?"

"I am. What is it you want?"

"It's just that my wife is Rebecca Harden Miles and she…" The very mention of Rebecca's name brought an unmistakable look of shock to the older woman's face. Visibly shaken, she attempted to shut the door. Only Lance's quick reaction prevented her success.

"Please, Mrs. Clark. We are not here to cause you any trouble. I promise. Ours is an urgent health issue that we need to address and only you can help. Please. Give us five minutes, please? Five minutes. That's all we're asking."

Regaining her composure, the unnerved woman cast her eyes directly on Rebecca. Making no attempt to hide her intentions, she scrutinized the female standing there, checking her out from head to toe. Rebecca returned the stare. She seems old and fragile; not at all what I expected. I almost feel sorry for her. I hope I don't lose my nerve and what are you looking at? Why don't you just let us in?

As quickly as the silent third degree began, it ended. Nodding; curiosity satisfied, no longer in denial, she stepped aside. At first she had opened the door cautiously just a crack. Now, she opened it all the way. In a shaky voice, she instructed, "Five minutes, only,"

I can't believe it. Rebecca thought cynically. She's fighting back tears. Does this mean she is or isn't my mother? She is or she isn't pleased to see me? Oh, for a crystal ball.

They were led into a lovely furnished living room all the while a pleasant, distinctively chocolate aroma filled the air. Neither the mystery freshly baked treat nor a simple cup of coffee, for that matter, was offered. Rebecca shrugged. She must be serious. Wouldn't want to waste time being hospitable, now would we? Heaven forbid we should go over the allotted whole five minutes. Sarcastically, resentful feelings crowded her mind.

There was so much to be said. Yet nobody talked. Contagious, the loud silence put each one of them on edge. They just sat there enduring the predicament until finally as the self-appointed spokesman, Lance broke the ice. "Rebecca, don't you have something you want to ask Mrs. Clark? Considering she is gracious enough to see us, and considering our time restraint, why don't you start?" Couldn't resist getting in the dig, could you, Lance? Good. Rebecca thought with satisfaction. Five minutes, huh? Five minutes to squeeze in a lifetime of questions. How generous of you, old woman, she thought irritably. No matter. I promise you these are going to be the best spent five minutes of my life. Wait and see. This is it. My moment of truth and I can't believe it. I've waited so long for its arrival. Here goes. Sink or swim.

With nervous determination, hesitating no longer, she took the plunge and jumped in with both feet.

"Mrs. Clark. I will come straight to the point." Rebecca could feel her anger mounting. Flip flops churning in her stomach; face flushed with apprehension, spitting out the long-awaited question that begged the long-awaited answer; she asked, no, she demanded to know. "Are you my mother?" No answer. Only more quiet maddening, waiting. Closing her eyes, Rebecca felt weak-kneed. "Are you?" She repeated a notch louder. Still, this old woman with the deadpan expression just sat there frozen in time.

"Mrs. Clark, please. Answer me."

Nervously rubbing her arthritic twisted fingers together, her poker face slowly turned into a painful grimace, and still she was mute. Rebecca had no way of knowing what was robbing the old woman of speech. The old woman knew. It was over-whelming guilt.

At long last barely audible, she whispered, "I am."

Two words that was all it took. All pandemonium broke loose. There was no controlling the righteous anger held captive for so many years. The submerged resentment came rushing into the open. Her steam-roller outburst startled Rebecca herself. But that didn't stop her. She just had not realized the depth of her unresolved issues. She really had planned on listening to this woman's story first. She really had planned to remain calm. She really had thought she could remain civil. How wrong she was.

Shocked, her true feelings hit her like a ton of bricks. Harbored resentment all those years left deep, ugly scars. Now, she knew what she wanted. Vindication, hatred, anger, lies, confusion, she wanted all of them removed from her life, forever.

The woman's admission put her right in front of the big guns. Rebecca fired off her next question and the next and the next....

"You own up to being my mother."

"Yes." The shaken woman repeatedly nodded in agreement.

"Then why did you abandon me?" The floodgates opened and Rebecca could not hold back the painful accusations that gushed out. "You were my mother. You were supposed to protect me. But what did you do? You turned your back on me. Why didn't you protect me? Did you kiss me when you left me? Did you even bother to say goodbye?" Shaking her head, she answered her own questions. "I think not. I was nothing more than a burden to you, wasn't I? How could you just cast me aside and walk away? I can't imagine what was more important to you than your own baby. Yet, you washed your hands of me. Tossed me aside and for what? Tell me. What in the world possibly possessed you to be so cold-hearted?"

Fists clenched tightly together, Rebecca's questions came flying out. She wanted answers, yet, she couldn't fully understand her callous reaction. All the years of longing for her absentee mother over, why couldn't she appreciate this amazing opportunity? Why couldn't she just reach out and wrap her arms around her mother present and accounted for? But, there was no stopping her. She didn't even pause long enough to give the distressed woman a chance to respond. Nor did the old woman attempt to interrupt. No. She knew her time would come. But for now, she really had no choice. She just sat there knee deep in accusations, enduring the bombardment of Rebecca's verbal abuse.

"All those years I longed for you. All those years I filled with fantasies. No, they were more than that. They were out and out lies. That's what they were and I created them to protect you. Can you believe that? Yes, to protect you. Why, I gave life to the most, loving, wonderful mother ever. I kept her with me all my life. She was just imaginary. But you? You were the real thing and you never even once came to visit me."

Emphatically, with a defiant lift of her shoulders, she pointed a finger of accusation. "Not once. Did you ever try to find out whether I lived or died. Did you ever even wonder what happened to me? Or how I turned out?"

Abruptly, Rebecca's words came to a screeching halt. I've made my point, she thought. I don't even know if this woman is listening, but I'm about to find out. It's her turn. "Look at me, Mrs. Clark. I'm done talking but you better start. I want, no, I demand, answers. I'm waiting." Unable to resist, one more time, she pressed into the most haunting question of all. "Why? Why did you abandon me?" Overcome with emotion, Rebecca covered her mouth for fear of what she might yet say. Almost it slipped out. Almost, she said, I hate you.

Like a shot, Lance went to Rebecca's rescue. He needed to calm her for her own sake. Holding her close, feeling her body shake, he reassured her. "It's okay, Rebecca. It's okay." Turning, he faced the distraught old woman sitting there dabbing her tears away.

"You'll get no sympathy from me, Mrs. Clark. You owe your daughter an explanation. It's overdue and she has waited far too long." Pained, Mrs. Clark cleared her throat and took a deep breath. The significance of this conversation so hurtful, breathing was difficult. In an effort to explain her defense, she realized with regret how pathetically lame what she was about to say would sound. Cringing, she pressed ahead in her attempt.

"Rebecca, it was not as brutal as you have described." Trying to make amends, her disclaimer was uttered in a trembling voice. "I did not abandon you. You must understand. I put you with people who would give you a better life than I could have at the time. Understand?"

"Absolutely not," Rebecca snapped back. "Call it like it is. In my book, putting me with strangers and then leaving me, constitutes abandonment." Shaken by the intensity of this woman's illogical reasoning, Rebecca adamantly informed her, "Abandonment hurts."

In her mind, Rebecca warned her repeatedly. Stop calling me by my first name. How dare you take such liberty? I resent it. Do you Rebecca? Her inner voice questioned, really? Holy Hannah, I'm losing it. I'm talking to myself. But the threat didn't stop the duel dialog. In her head, the awkward transitions went back and forth. Trying to convince her, one side poured it on. But she named you, didn't she? Doesn't matter, the other side defended. She gave up her rights long ago. Of course, I resent it. Oh, sure you do. Cross-examined and egged on, she was forced to face the debatable issue at hand. Then why don't you tell her to stop? You want to know why? I'll tell you Rebecca, because you like it. That's why. It's as simple as that. Admit it. You like hearing your real mother say your name.

Stop sowing seeds of discontent, she warned her mixed up conscience and shook her head to clear the conflict. If I don't wind up a basket case after this is over, it will be a miracle.

"Listen," Rebecca faced the old woman, "What exactly is it you expect me to understand? What kind of better life did you think nuns could provide me? I wish we could have exchanged shoes for a week, a day tops. Then you would have learned first- hand what it felt like to be punished for minor infractions. To have your hair pulled for talking in the halls or to get your bottom spanked for being late for class or to be forced to eat food you disliked or worse still, to go hungry because the food was sparse. Or to have to share your bed space, that's what I said, bed space because bedrooms were non-existent. At that, you had to share the space with a floor full of girls. Or to live with mandatory lights out or shiver in the cold when you lost your one yearly allotted wool hat or mittens or to spend Christmas getting charitable gifts from the local townspeople. A wish list for a kid, didn't exist, either. Or to never own a pair of roller skates, a bike or even a stuffed animal, or, or...forget it." Angry tears stung her eyes as she rapidly blinked them away.

Lance held his head in his hands as he rapidly shook it in disbelief. I can't believe what I'm hearing. I'm not going to say what I'm thinking. Not yet, anyway. It's Rebecca's turn. But Rebecca, how could you keep that mess locked up inside you for all those years? Why didn't you just tell me? As for you her mother, it takes a lot more than giving birth to earn that title. You short changed your own daughter. You thief, you robbed her of her childhood. Something good better come out of this. Rebecca has more than paid her dues. Look at you, Rebecca, he thought with admiration, when did you turn into a tiger? Get it out. Get it all out.

You better duck, old lady. She's not finished with you yet. Not by any means. My Rebecca is not a quitter. Maybe that's in thanks to you. In a blink of an eye, jumping into the fray, Rebecca was back. Ready for round two.

"Never in a million years will I accept, or understand as you say I must, that you gave me away for a better life. All those years, not knowing if you were dead or alive, waiting and hoping that maybe just once you would visit me. How cruel. How very cruel and this from my own mother? You don't even deserve the title."

"Rebecca, I didn't know. You have to believe me. You have to let me tell you the whole story. I had no choice. Times were different back then."

"I don't have to do any such thing. After all these years, I don't think I care. Nothing you can say now will change the past. It's gone."

"Please, Rebecca," her mother pleaded, "It's important."

"Rebecca," Lance interjected, "Listen. You do care. You wanted answers. Here's your chance to get them. Let her explain."

Nodding, she whispered. "Okay, Lance. But because you have asked me to." Turning to her mother, in a determined voice, she championed her cause. "I'll let you explain but before I do, I want it to be perfectly clear on several counts. I'm not here to make you feel better. Don't think for a minute that you can relieve yourself of any guilt feelings you may have. Confession is good for one's soul and frankly, right now, I don't care about your salvation. The main reason my husband and I are here today is for our daughter's sake. We have to find out my family's medical background on both my mother's and father's side. You do know who my father is?" she asked sarcastically, verbally twisting the knife deeper with each word of the implication.

Not skipping a beat, Rebecca delivered her point. "We lost two babies without explanation and now our only daughter is about to marry, no doubt with a family in her future. We need to find out if there is a possible genetic flaw on my side of the family. So you see, we are here to spare our daughter possible heartache."

She couldn't help herself. Without hesitation, the hurtful words just slid right out like so much melted butter. "You see, we happen to love our daughter very much."

Bull's eye! Lance gloated, right through the heart.

Yet, something was off target. Rebecca could not understand what was happening. After verbally assassinating her mother, satisfaction was waning. Why? All the hurt, the mental anguish, suffered for years and years. This was her long-awaited chance. Face to face, she got to tell her mother exactly what she thought of her. It should have felt better for longer than it did. It didn't. Like smoke, the gratification just kept evaporating. What a painful dichotomy, like seeing a neon sign flashing the words love, than, hate.

Absolutely at sixes and sevens, she had been thrown off balance and like Mount Vesuvius, she had erupted. Then like that eruption, when the air was cleared, there was a ton of rebuilding left to be done.

It was not by accident that the woman chose to sit opposite Rebecca. How else could she drink in all that she had thirsted for over the dry course of so many years? Her eyes, her nose, her face, even the slight tilt of her head when she talked, this Rebecca was so much like her father. Oh, what a family life we could have shared. If only...but it wasn't meant to be.

Yet, here she is a carbon copy of the man I loved, with one major difference. This copy is filled with deep-seated anger. If I could have foreseen Rebecca's suffering, would my decision have been different? I don't know. Shaking the unresolved speculation from her tormented soul, she muddled on. It is, after all, water over the dam. That part of Rebecca's life and mine is over. It can't be changed. Now, I have another decision to make. Maybe, this time I will get it right. Maybe this time I will spare her from another heartache. It's now or never because this time, is all I have left.

Releasing a long, shuddering sigh, she began. "Let me tell you how all this came about and hopefully, somewhere along the line, what I have to say will not only answer your questions, but help your daughter, as well." My Granddaughter, she thought, but dared not voice that connection.

Rebecca and Lance settled back, grateful the chairs were comfortable and coffee was eventually served, for the story Rebecca's mother was about to unfold spilled way over the original five minute allotment time deadline.

Chapter 33

~

Lydia 1914

As recipient of Rebecca's outpouring of venom, clearly, her mother was shaken. Trying to remain calm, in readiness for the long venture on which she was about to embark, she sipped her coffee and cleared her throat.

"Ahem. As I begin this chronological account it seems reasonable to start with my birth."

This chronological account? Rebecca winched and slouched down a little in her seat. Oh, brother. Who is she trying to impress? I hope she doesn't turn out to be a snob, among other things. I mean really, this chronological account?

Rebecca's flinch, if she even noticed, did not give her reason for concern. She pressed ahead now intent on her mission.

"This event took place on June 2, 1914, in a small apartment on Pine Street in Marshall, New Jersey. My mother, Mary Louise Brown, was fifteen-years-old and my father, Arthur Lewis Wright, twenty-five. My mother was a shy, sheltered, girl who fell in love with my father and married him when she was very young. Unfortunately, it was an ill fated match. My father was really unsuited for marriage or for any responsibility or disciplined life and from the beginning, the path was a stormy one for my mother. He totally lacked motivation and seldom had steady work. My mother's life was not easy. To add to her burden, a year after I was born, she gave birth to my sister, Mary Elizabeth.

'Mother did nothing else but work. She never had time to read to me but then we didn't have a book for her to read, either and I don't ever remember her smiling. Seemed she always had tears in her eyes and many a night, I could hear her softly crying herself to sleep."

Lydia had quite a story to tell and, indeed something to hide. Circumstances dictated she reveal only that which would be beneficial to Rebecca. Portions deemed detrimental would be best left to memory. Beginning her tailor-made story, she chose her words carefully.

"Sometimes, food was sparse for us. She worked much too hard, my mother did. She gathered wood from the street or driftwood from the river to keep the coal range burning so she could cook and keep us warm. My father added to my mother's stress. He wasn't home much but when he was, he was demanding. She waited on him hand and foot and his sporadic, meager, earnings were spent mostly on himself. He had a penchant for playing cards and drinking. Both of which ate up whatever little monies should have been used toward household expenses. Since I was too young to recall my mother's experience, it was my grandmother, my father's mother, who sat me down when she thought I was old enough to learn the truth and enlightened me with descriptions of past events. In a way, I wish she hadn't.

'Apparently, my father was a handsome man, charming and very likeable. Unfortunately, he also had a roving eye. His voice deep, his laughter contagious, women were attracted to him like moths to a flame. He delighted in their company while mother struggled with just keeping the home fires lit. Too many times, mother was forced to look the other way, until finally she could take it no more. Too many times the ill-omened relationship forced them to separate, at least in the beginning on a temporary basis.

'On these numerous occasions, I don't know why, mother always took my sister with her and went back home to her parents. Again, I don't know why, but on these times, I was sent to my father's mother, Grandmother Marie Jessica Miller. For years, my sister and I were shuttled back and forth, neither of us knowing how we were chosen or why we couldn't go together to one set of grandparents. We never figured that out. Not even when we grew older.

'As you can imagine, the inevitable happened. When I was four-years-old and Mary Elizabeth three, my father deserted my mother. I do remember that fateful day. The scene is branded in my memory; the quarrel, the shouting, the sound of my own cries and the image of my father disappearing down the stairway. Needless to say, this time, it was not a temporary separation. He simply left town. This time, when my sister went with my mother to her parents, it was for good. When my Grandmother Miller came for me, she took me in permanently, too. Grandmother Miller was affectionate and easygoing with me, despite running a business with a strong arm. Being with her gave me such a feeling of security; the likes of which I had never known before. I lived with her until she died. I was only seventeen-years-old at that time. It was a sad day.

'The home Grandmother Miller provided was quite pleasant. We lived in a lovely, old, three-story brick building covered with English Ivy and sparrows. It was situated on a quiet residential street. It was accented by huge, oak tree canopies providing shade in the summer cool enough to make the sun mad and, a wind barrier in winter strong enough to cheat Old Man Bluster of the North. It was a fantastic place to live. 'At the time my Grandmother took on the job of raising me, she was forty-five-years-old. That had to be hard on her but she never complained, not once. She did the job alone, too. I don't remember her ever talking about my grandfather. In any event, if he was alive, he did not live with us. Ma, that's what I came to call her, was strong and independent and self-supporting. As a talented dressmaker, there was nothing in the clothing line that she could not create. Needless to say, I was a benefactor of her talent. My clothes were top-notch. I was the envy of all the other girls. Her business did well. She had a number of seamstresses working for her right there on the second floor of our house. I remember they made dresses, lingerie, men's shirts, coats. You name it. They made it. The place was as busy as a bee hive. Activity always in a flurry, it was fun just being in the middle of the exciting hustle bustle. From a life of dire poverty, I was transported into a world of plenty. Good food, beautiful handmade clothes, our house furnished with fine antiques, indeed, I had a good life.

'Ma adored me and I am sure I was spoiled and pampered considerably. I was fairly bright and learned to read before I went to school. I had books by the dozen and loved to read and to recite poetry. We had a wonderful old, square piano, an Empire piece, I believe, on which I had lessons. We had a marvelous collection of Victor Red Seal Records and a wonderful phonograph, known as a Victrola. It had a huge wooden tulip shape horn which was its speaker.

'At an early age, I was introduced to the sounds of opera and classical music. I knew by heart the names of the opera greats of the time, Enrico Caruso, Mary Garden, Geraldine Farrar, John McCormack, Madame Homer, Madame Melba and others and Ma even took me to the opera in New York City.

'There was a fine place of entertainment in New York known as the Hippodrome. All manner of performances took place there including circus acts complete with elephants. And whenever we went to New York, we always ate in good restaurants.

'I was taken to every museum in Manhattan. Of course, we took public transportation. First, we rode the tube and then double deck buses. Sometimes, after visiting a museum, Ma would take me with her to shop for sewing materials on Hester Street. Hester Street was a trip within itself. It was filled with wonderful wares of all kinds. A very interesting street characterized by its vast variety of commodities offered for sale. It was an immigrant section and the merchants not only had small shops but push carts piled high with all manner of things for sale. Live chickens, shoes, men's suits, laces, velvets, vegetables and other sundries were lined curbside throughout that area. There is a movie called Hester Street. I have seen it several times and, not only that, it has been on television. It always brings back many fond memories.

'Mother's hobby was collectibles. There was an exquisite Whatnot cabinet of black wood trimmed with gold in our parlor. On it were shelves for all manner of pretty collectibles. I remember a Dresden shepherd and shepherdess and a lovely porcelain rose jar filled with petals. There was also a fireplace that took up the entire back wall. On the mantel was a black clock.

'Summer nights in the city could be unbearable. Sometimes, we went for rides on the Staten Island Ferry on hot nights just to seek relief from the city heat. Sometimes, Ma and I put on our nighties and sat in cool water in the bathtub.

"As a little girl, my toys were wonderful. I had a wicker carriage with a parasol cover and real china-headed dolls. My favorite toy was a small nickel replica of an iron cook stove. I had paper dolls of cardboard with jointed arms and legs and lovely paper clothes trimmed with paper lace. They came in books inside big, white envelopes.

'We had block parties sometimes with the street closed off and each house had a different attraction on its sidewalk. There were Japanese paper lanterns strung on wires with candles inside. The street lights were gas lamps and the Lamplighter came around each evening with his ladder and taper and set each flame aglow. There would be a German Band and dancing in the street and a lot of edible goodies and carnival wheels. Some of my happiest party times took place at our annual block party.

'Of course, I would be remiss if I did not tell you about the Christmas trees. They were most unusual. Full, always and if they were sparse on one side, a hole was bored in the trunk and another limb was added. Every single branch ending was decorated with either pink or white popcorn held on with a straight pin. That, alone, took hours of work. But I remember helping and not minding the time put in, at all. To me, it was all fun. There were paper chains and lovely hand blown glass ornaments from Germany. Tinsel in long strands, too. And, wonder of wonders, candles. Yes, candles in little snap on holders, lovely, twisted colored candles, were actually lit. No wonder there was so much activity at the fire department during the Yule season. The fire engines were horse drawn. On our nearby main street, we also had street cars. Closed in the winter but opened in the summer, they were equipped with a running board down each side, mostly for the use of volunteer firemen, if needed.

'Forgive my rambling but I must not forget my books. I was surrounded by them, books of all description. Ma provided me with all the children's classics of the times. I had the Chatterbox Series. The Goops who were strange looking children who managed to commit all the unmentionable naughty deeds that good children would never do. But the general idea was for the reader to learn not to act like a 'Goop.'

'I read and was read to. Ma taught me early on the beauty and purpose of words. We spoke well at our house. Poor grammar and incorrect table behavior were not tolerated. Even though Ma was not born to the upper class of society, she had class. She loved the good life which she had labored hard to earn. To me, Ma was a remarkable woman. The most remarkable I have ever met. She gave me my start in life and taught me to hunger for learning and experience and bettering myself. She was beautiful, strong as steel, well read, self-educated, willful and independent. I inherited marvelous traits. I owe a great debt to her which I hope I can acknowledge when we meet in the next world.

'In 1918, when I was four-years-old, the terrible flu epidemic sped around the world. This type of influenza was often fatal. Ma contracted it, along with pneumonia. I can't tell you how scared I was. Petrified! In those days, the disease was exceedingly serious because there were no wonder drugs. Mostly, it was up to our Maker. Either you made it or you didn't. It was His choice. To avoid my getting the flu, I was sent to live with a friend of Ma's in Newark. Fortunately, I never got the flu but I did develop pleurisy and that made me pretty darn sick, in its own right. Anyway, while I was at Miss Sally's, life was so different. I dearly missed Ma and all she meant to me but I knew Miss Sally was doing all she could for me.

'Newark, back then, was not exactly a place where you would run to build a house. There were so many refineries with enough of a horrible odor to kill a horse. I have a vivid recollection of sitting at a window one night and watching the glowing sky as one of the storage oil tanks in that oil industrial city caught on fire. More than ever, I longed for the serenity of our ivy covered house and pleasant smelling flower gardens.

'I recall, while living with Miss Sally, I began school. Although I treasured learning, I was never comfortable in that school. I never made friends as quickly as I would have liked. It was difficult getting me there and initially, Miss Sally had to walk me to and from that place. I was sad and I remember her telling me if I didn't soon smile, I would trip on my lower lip and fall. She tried, in her way. But she wasn't Ma and I was never so happy as the day it was clear for me to return to my roots.

'Enrolled in school, now was another story. My confidence returned and with Ma there to help me, I thrived. Too bad things were not destined to stay that way. In less than a year since my return, Ma's youngest son, Willard came home to live with his mother. He had been mustered out of the army. But being discharged didn't matter. He never took off his sergeant stripes. He scared me barking orders all the time. Indeed, he was a domineering, miserable, unhappy person. My Uncle definitely was a negative influence in our lives and robbed our peaceful home of its serenity. To top it off, when he left the army camp, he brought home Scarlet Fever. I came down with Scarletina which is a mild form of that dreadful disease. At this time in my life, it seemed I was always subject to any and all germs that came down the pike. I was very tall and leggy like a young colt and I guess, not too strong stemming from my poor nutritional start when my mother had to forge for food.

'Then one morning, Uncle Willard got up and took his leave. When he announced he was going to California neither Ma nor I mourned his decision. Good riddance to a bad penny, I said under my breath and a less stressful life style returned.

'Several years later, I'm not sure why, but Ma decided to move to Willow Hill, a community near Philadelphia, Pennsylvania, where I lived until I ran away at the age of seventeen. Seventeen is too young to be all grown up but I had no choice. I had to adapt.

'Whatever her reason for moving, it was a mistake. Ma was homesick for her Jersey home and the friends she had left behind. She missed, too, her dressmaking profession. Hers was not an easy life in her new surroundings. Why she did not turn to dress making is beyond me. I didn't ask and she didn't offer. Circumstances must not have allowed it. Our house was large and to help with finances, she rented out several rooms. What a monumental mistake. Those boarders turned out to be out-and out troublesome. Dissension was daily fare at that address and harmony; a foreign language.

'I helped as much as I could but I also attended school. I went by trolley to the local high school for a year. I did fairly well but an unhappy home life was taking its toll on me emotionally and so I dropped out. I decided to get a job to help Ma and my first job was in a little sandwich shop. I was doing okay but then, unfortunately, the depression came and I was laid off. No one had work. It was a bad time for everybody. Money was not flush at our house. To say the least, it was exceedingly scarce and life was not easy.

'When I was seventeen, following a week's illness, Ma died. A part of me did, too. Her death was from a kidney ailment known as Bright's disease. With all that heartache and sorrow going on, believe it or not, those scheming boarders deceitfully maneuvered a take-over of the house. To this day, I don't have any idea how they managed to pull it off. They did. Somehow, it was theirs and that left me pretty much nothing more than the privilege of working for them. They made it very clear. An ultimatum; work and continue to live under their roof or, get out. What could I do? I had very little money. No cooperation. No consideration and was, in truth, coolie labor for those oppressive, monstrous intruders. Initially, I had no choice so I worked under these conditions for as long as I could. Then, the time came when I could take it no longer.

'I packed a small suitcase with my very few belongings and I ran away from home. I went to stay with the family of my girl friend. How many times have I thanked my lucky stars for the friendship Candice and I struck up working together in that sandwich shop. Her family was so kind to me. I lived there for about three months at which time I met the man of my dreams. It was 1932.

Chapter 34

"Candice, I can't thank you and your folks enough for taking me in. I don't know what I would have done if I had to stay at that boarding house with those crude men another minute. I think I would have jumped in front of a trolley."

"Oh, stop, Lydia, don't talk like that even in jest."

"Well, I think it's almost true. Anyway, thank you for rescuing me."

"Listen, there's a dance at the Friendship Hall tomorrow night. I thought you and I might go. Interested?"

"You bet. Sounds like fun and to tell you the truth, I can't remember the last time I had fun. How much does it cost? I'm a little low on funds, as usual."

"Don't worry about it. It's ten cents to get in and my father already has given me twenty-five cents for running his errands this week. We're set to go."

"I'll pay you back, Candice, just as soon as I get paid. I promise."

"um…"

"What exactly does um mean, Candice? And what's that silly grin on your face all about? Come on. I know you. You're up to something. Fess up."

"Well, it's like this. I kind of knew you would be interested and so I've arranged for you and me to go on a double date."

"You did what? I don't believe you, Candice. You wouldn't."

"Oh yes I would and I did. Your date's name is Phillip Wilson and mine is Jeffrey Donavan."

"You do realize, Candice that I've never had a date, right?"

"Figured as much and it's about time. Don't you think?"

"I just hope I can sleep tonight."

"Have no fear. You will and you'll have fantastic dreams of you and Phillip dancing together."

"For heaven's sake, Candice, how can I visualize somebody I haven't even seen yet? Sometimes, I wonder about you girl." Hugging Candice, she added, "my dear, wonderful friend."

* * * * *

"You look absolutely lovely. Blue is your color, Lydia, and I like the way you rolled your hair under. It looks terrific."

"I like your outfit, too, Candice. Look at us. We're a couple of high-stepping, dance girls."

"Whoa. I don't like the sounds of that."

"No," she giggled, "I didn't mean what you're thinking. You are so bad."

Peering into the dresser mirror, both girls liked what they saw. Passing their own inspection, out the door they went arm in arm.

"There he is standing in the corner. Mine is the red head." Waving her handkerchief, Candice got Jeffrey's attention and that of the man standing beside him.

Leaning over, she whispered in Lydia's ear, "That one must be yours. You hit the jackpot."

"Stop it. Candice, you're making me blush, but have to admit I think you are right. Gosh, he's tall and dark and handsome and hopefully, he can dance. I need to kick up my heels."

Jeffrey, not the least bit shy, came over and kissed Candice on the cheek.

"How you doing, darling?" he asked, as if she was his lifelong sweetheart. "This is my friend Phillip."

"Phillip, hello, I'd like you to meet Lydia. Lydia; Phillip."

"How do you do?" Their eyes meet and Phillip smiled. He liked what he was drinking in. Indeed, this Lydia, was absolutely the most gorgeous creature he had every encountered. Not only that, she had a body that wouldn't quit.

Lydia looked at him with admiration. Now, if he knows how to dance as good as he looks, I will declare myself a winner. No sooner was the thought fading into her mind then he had offered his hand.

"Dance?"

Jackpot, she thought to herself, as he took her hand and led her to the dance floor. Following demurely, she silently commanded her happy heart to be still.

"Do you like Paul Whiteman's music?" he asked, knowing full well talking about music was always a good ice-breaker.

"Oh, yes. Doesn't everybody? I just love this melody. It's um ...darn, can't put my finger on it."

"It's 'Whispering.'"

"Yeah, that's it." Laughing, she followed his every lead as they moved their feet and bodies around the floor dancing the Fox Trot in perfect sync. That dance over, they went immediately into the next and this time she proudly announced the name of the song.

"It's 'All of Me.' Right?"

"Right. Now who wrote it?" He liked the funny way she wrinkled her nose when she was thinking. Shrugging, she answered, "Don't know."

"Irving Berlin." He grinned from ear to ear and they were off and dancing.

"Uh oh. Better hold onto your hat, Lydia. Listen. The band is starting to play the Lindy. Shall we give it a try?"

"I'm game, if you are? But, be forewarned. I'm not too good at it" Naturally, she thought, the Lindy is all quick movements so there goes my opportunity to show off my musical expertise. No one could possibly converse above all that. Well, maybe later I'll impress him. That is if he doesn't know how the Lindy got its name. I'll tell him first chance I get and the unspoken explanation danced in her head. With all the twists, jumps, and turns involved, dancers look like they are flying so it was only natural to name the Lindy after their American Aviation hero, Charles Lindbergh.

Laughing and jumping about, kicking legs were everywhere. Just keeping from getting bruised was a feat in itself. It was exhilarating and Lydia and Phillip handled the dance like a couple of pros.

"Whew." Wiping her brow with the back of her hand, Lydia said, "That was a blast! But I have to admit, I'm glad it's over. My legs feel like rubber."

Laughing, Phillip suggested cool drinks for which she was ever so appreciative.

"Let's sit the next few out, Lydia. Give us a chance to talk. Tell me about yourself."

Sipping her drink, she nodded. "There's not really much to tell." Filling him in on the parts she deemed to be important, she took him up to the present. "And now, I'm living with Candice and her family and that about sums it up. See. Told you, it wasn't going to be interesting. Aren't you sorry you asked? You're a glutton for punishment."

"No I'm not. Now, what does the next chapter in your book of life hold, as you see it?

"Good question. Well, I would like to get a better paying job, or for that matter, at least a better job and I'd love to be able to move out on my own. Guess beyond that, I haven't given it much thought. Who knows what's in store?" Chuckling, she added, " Oh, of course, and to live happily ever after? Now, tell me about yourself."

Phillip sat quietly, almost too pensive, Lydia thought. But when he spoke, it was clear the he had much to say.

Look at him, she thought, with his blue eyes and strong chin. Everything about him rings of kindness and consideration. Best of all, he is soft and quiet and yet, he carries a look of determination. I love his demeanor. What a drastic change from those boisterous, male boarders I left behind. Ugh! Shuddering, she pushed their ugly images far from her mind and focused on this wonderful man, Phillip. She was a good judge of character.

"I don't have much to tell, either." He too, filled her in on what he considered to be pretty much a mundane life. He grew up in the coal mines of Pennsylvania and worked the mines just as his father and grandfather before him did until he could stand it no longer. His biggest complaint was lack of sunshine. He entered the mines at dawn and returned home way after sundown. The dirt, the smell, the grime, the fear of getting black lung, these were the depressive culprits that forced him to move away in search of a better and brighter life. "Now, I am a fireman at the No. 5 Hose Company and live there at the station located on Long Street."

"Isn't being a fireman dangerous?" she asked, intrigued by his choice of profession.

"Believe me, it's a lot safer than working in the coal mines. It's not all work. Parades are fun. That's when I get to don a crisp uniform and ride the runners of a newly–waxed fire truck. It's a respectable job. People applaud their appreciation as we drive by. The pay is decent and to top it off, I have a warm bed and the cook we have makes delicious meals. Food is plentiful. I never leave the table hungry. All in all, I'm glad I made the transition." Pausing, he went silent for a minute and then decided he had talked long enough. "That's it about me. Come on, let's dance. Unfortunately, it's almost time for the band to quit for the night."

The four of them walked together. At the steps of their home, Jeffrey kissed Candice goodnight. Lydia waited but had no such luck from Phillip who politely tipped his hat.

"Goodnight, Lydia. I had a great time. Will I see you at next week's dance?"

"I hope so. Goodnight, Phillip."

Twirling round and round the room, finally Lydia flopped down on the bed.

"Oh, Candice, I'm dizzy."

"And well you should be, twirling around like a kid. No wonder."

"No, no. That's not why I'm dizzy. I'm dizzy with the thoughts of Phillip. He is absolutely the cat's meow. Did you see how well he dances? Oh, he makes my head spin."

"Not exactly, I was kind of busy dancing with Jeffrey. But if you say he was a good dancer, I'll take your word for it. Gosh, Lydia, you seem to have fallen hard for this guy. Are you rushing it just a little? I mean…"

"Don't know. Don't care. I just want to spend all my time with him. Oh goodness, Candice. I just had a terrible thought. What if he doesn't like me? He didn't kiss me goodnight. Oh no. Not seeing him again would be a fate worse than death."

"Worse than death? Girl, you do have it bad. But, I wouldn't worry about him not coming round again. Jeffrey whispered that Phillip told him he really thought the world of you, too. So, there you are. Now, I'm tired. Do you think we could get some sleep?"

Candice slept. Lydia dozed off and on, and in between all her thoughts turned to Phillip.

Two days later there was knock on the front door and an unexpected visitor.

"Lydia, there's a gentleman caller." Candice's mother made the announcement. "He says his name is Phillip."

Wings on her feet, Lydia flew down the steps. Landing on the last one, she decelerated, patted her skirt and walked slowly into the front parlor.

Immediately, the gentleman stood up. "I hope you don't mind my calling tonight, Lydia. I'm off work and thought you might like to go to the Soda Shoppe with me for an ice-cream. Interested?"

"I'd like that very much. Tell you what, let me get my sweater and I'll be right with you." Lydia basked in his beaming eyes she knew were following her as she dashed up the steps to her room.

Walking out to the shop arm in arm, Lydia looked up at the star-covered sky just as a shooting star blazed its path across the vault of heaven. "Look Phillip," she said pointing toward the star. "Make a wish."

"Okay." Closing his eyes, he reported, "Mission accomplished. Want to know what I wished for?"

"No. It won't come true if you tell."

"Aw shucks. It is such a good one, too. Sure you don't want to hear it?" he asked teasing. "It's hard keeping it to myself."

"Exactly! But keeping it secret is the trick that makes it happen."

"You, Lydia, are the most fascinating woman I've met." He could feel his uncontrollable smile stretching across his face. She made him light up like a Christmas tree. Was it her beautiful eyes or maybe her delectable perfume? He didn't know. But whatever it was surely did intoxicate him and he pulled her tighter to his side as they reached the door to the shop.

Pistachio ice-cream and the man of my dreams, it can't get any better than this, she fantasized savoring the cold creamy treat.

"Lydia, um..." struggling with his words, she could see he obviously was nervous about something. But what, she wondered as she waited patiently for him to get a grip.

"Gosh," he sighed with a mixture of delight and embarrassment. Happy to be with Lydia but, he was flustered with his inability to keep the ice-cream in its place. "See what happens when you don't pay attention to what you're doing? I've dripped chocolate ice-cream right down the front of my vest."

"No problem," she said, "I'll wipe it clean for you with my napkin." She did, ever so tenderly.

"I was saying, or trying to," he went on. "I know we haven't known each other for very long but somehow our being together just feels right. It's like it is meant to be." Wiping his brow with his handkerchief, he nervously rambled on. Taking a moment to catch his breath, he tried again. "I'm not sure how to go about this, Lydia. So I'm just going to say it like it is. I love you and want to marry you. You don't have to give me your answer now. I just ask you to think about it." Having said his piece, he sat quietly. It was the least he could do for his screaming nerves. Besides, now, it was up to her.

Faintheartedly, he was convinced that it went well and except for one minor detail, it did. It was just that in his anxiousness, he simply forgot to pop the question.

Her eyes sparkling with delight looked into his and it didn't matter. She knew. That precious oversight endeared him even more to her heart. She came to his aid confirming the deal. Making his intent perfectly clear, and flashing him a dazzling smile, she questioned, "Why, Phillip, if this is a proposal? I accept."

Like the cherry trees in spring, their romance had burst into blossom and at the end of a three month courtship Lydia joyfully became Mrs. Phillip Wilson.

"You look lovely." Candice told Lydia arranging the ribbon on the bride's-to-be wrist corsage. "Smile and let's go. Can't keep the groom waiting any longer," Candice chuckled. "He's probably pacing the floor by now worrying that you may have changed your mind. You were supposed to be at the Justice of the Peace's office ten minutes ago, you know."

"Can I help it if getting dressed took longer than anticipated? Are you sure this suit is okay? How about the felt hat? Oh, and the gloves? Okay?"

Candice, unable to resist temptation, gave the nervous woman an annoying glance then broke out in hilarious laughter. That stopped Lydia in her tracks.

"What's so funny? What's wrong?"

"Relax. I'm teasing. Lydia, listen to me. Your powder blue suit with the matching felt hat is perfect as are your gloves and shoes and make-up, and need I really go on? You get the picture? You make a beautiful bride."

Blushing, Lydia managed a soft, "Thank you," as she scurried off to say I do. The ten minute civil ceremony took far less time than it took the bride to get ready for this memorable event. No matter. As far as she was concerned, the wedding was all she dreamed it should be. The time it took to exchange vows wasn't important; that they exchanged them, now that was what counted. The knot tied, she delighted in knowing, from this moment on, she would live happily ever after, just as she had predicted.

Chapter 35

"I hate this part, Phillip. I really do and I wish it didn't have to be like this."

"Me, too. Come on now, Lydia. You promised." Pulling her closer to him, he added, "No tears."

"Easier said than done," she whispered wiping away the ones escaping down her cheek. "It's just that I feel so secure here in your arms. It's horrible sleeping alone. Do you have to go already?"

"Afraid so, it's time." Slowly removing his arms from around her soft body, he tried gentle persuasion almost as much for his sake as for hers. "It won't be for much longer; another month at most."

"That long?" she lamented. "This topsy-turvy world of ours keeps getting harder and harder to take."

"I know," he answered acutely aware of the hardship, "but it will soon change. It is plain bureaucracy and you know how inflexible their routine. At least, I was able to talk with the Captain last week and got the ball rolling. It's a good start."

"This is so unfair, Phillip. I feel like an out-and-out sneak, like I'm an accessory to some crime."

"Just toss that guilt out the window. We're married." Solicitous for her welfare, he hid his own seething frustration. "Don't forget that. We just have to play the game. It's the price we pay for not waiting for official approval."

"I know, but that doesn't make living apart any easier."

"It doesn't. But until I am granted permission to marry from my superior, we have no choice. No one at work can know the truth, not if we want to eat. If the Captain finds out we married without getting authorization, I'm out. We can kiss my job and my pension goodbye. That rule is firmly entrenched in the original by-laws. It's just the way it is."

"I know, Phillip. I know. Just the same, I think it's a stupid rule. Besides," she smiled with a twinkle in her eye, "I can't sleep without a warm body next to me."

"That better not mean just any warm body," he warned, and smothered her in a tight, bear hug he knew she relished. "I better get started. So what are your plans for this week?"

"Well, first I'm going to go job-hunting and then cheap furniture-hunting, and then I'm going to work on fixing this place up. Good thing it's only a one bedroom apartment."

"There, you see," he said grinning, "the Lord works in strange ways. You won't have time to miss me. Sounds like you have more than enough to keep you busy until I get back on the week-end and don't forget to eat," he advised handing her twenty-five dollars as he was getting ready to leave. "I know it's not much but use what's left after you pay this month's rent, for food. See, that's another bonus that goes with my living at the station during the week."

"Bonus? Now what, dear sir, may that be?"

"I still get to eat at the station so you only have to buy enough food for one. That counts for something. See, Lydia, there's always a bright side."

"And a dark one, too, like now," she pointed out. Sharing one last goodbye kiss, he left for work.

Well, here I go again, the start of another week without him. It's the pits. That Captain better not turn down his request. What a horrible thought. Just stop it, girl, she scolded. Stop it and do something constructive. Get moving. The more you do, the faster time will pass and the sooner Phillip will be home. Inspired by that happy reminder, she showered, dressed and was on her way.

I'm going to check on those two applications I put in last week. Bet they didn't pan out. It's been too long. Surely, I would have heard by now. But I'm also going to put in an application for that waitress job on Tenth Street. Who knows? Maybe the gods will smile on me today.

"Miss Wilson," the store manager Mrs. Mayer inquired, "Are you available to work five days a week and do you have any experience in this line of work?"

Lydia wanted to correct her. She wanted to shout it out. My name is *Mrs.* Wilson, *Mrs.* Philip Wilson. She had no choice. The stakes so high, she held her tongue. Not only that. Adding insult to injury, considering she was forced to leave her treasured wedding band behind, her ring finger was painfully naked. Darn secret. I hate this. Aggressive thoughts invaded her mind. I'm married, lady, she silently yelled. Just wait. Soon you'll see. The whole world will.

"The hours are from 8:00 a.m. to 4:00 p.m., Monday through Friday. Breakfast and lunch are a part of the package. And, be forewarned, we abide strictly by the rule that the customer is always right."

Have no fear, she thought. For free breakfast and lunch, they'll never be wrong. Free food, now that's what I call frosting on the cake. Lydia answered the woman's questions in a steady voice. "I have done multi tasks in a sandwich shop and I'm able to work the days needed."

"Are you reliable? Why did you leave your former position?"

"Oh, yes, very. I only left because work ran out and the shop eventually closed.

"I see. Well, your application looks fine. I think you are an excellent candidate for the position. Understand that being a waitress encompasses a lot more work than just fixing sandwiches. Do you think you could handle it?"

"Definitely," she answered assertively.

"Fine. I have one more person to interview today but I think I can tell you now that, from all that I've seen so far, you are my first choice. Stop by tomorrow and I'll give you my final decision."

Almost leaping out of the office of the small restaurant, the positive interaction put Lydia in a fantastic mood. Her spirits raised, she headed out to blitz her errands. Parting with the twenty dollar rent money was not quite as painful now as she handed the month's payment to the landlord.

Next, she dashed off to the market. Checking her resources, Lydia was pleased. She had five whole dollars left to spend on food. Wonderful! That will get me tons of food. Well, pounds anyway, and giggled at her quip.

With her shopping basket draped over her arm, Lydia walked up and down the aisles shopping judiciously. "Let's see," she muttered to herself, "what foods last longest? Ah, of course, a supply of corn meal, potatoes, carrots, onions, coffee and a chicken. Better get more toothpowder and a few toiletries, too." There, she thought smiling contently. Even Ebenezer Scrooge would applaud this thrifty shopper. With a spring in her step, she hurried to the apartment. Just as she finished putting everything in the cardboards, there was a knock on the door. "Who is it?" she yelled.

"It's me, Candice. I come bearing gifts. Open the door. They're getting heavy."

"What in the world," Lydia was taken aback, "are all these things?"

"Hello to you, too," Candice joked. "My mother thought you might like to have these. They are her cast off dishes, utensils and the like. They still have plenty of miles left in them. Here, take the bags. I carried them to this point and now what you do with them is up to you."

"Oh, my goodness," Lydia said truly touched. "Your mother is a gem. Come in. Come in. Do you mind if I check out the goodies?"

"Of course not, silly, but can you get some coffee going first? Lugging those packages just about wore me out."

"Done."

"And I want to see your new home, all of it."

Lydia stifled a snicker. "You ninny, this is all of it. See, this is our Murphy Kitchen, no chairs and no table."

"How do you eat, standing up?" Candice asked flippantly.

"As a matter of fact, we do. See, we stand up and use this pull out breadboard." Lydia demonstrated.

"Ingenious! Will wonders ever cease?" Impressed, Candice pushed and pulled the breadboard in and out several times to her own satisfaction.

"And to your right is the bedroom. Complete, I'll have you know, with a new bedroom set which, I might add, will be ours in about six months. Amazing what a few dollars deposit and monthly payments get you, and as for the living room, well you're standing in it."

"Do you have a thing against furniture or what? We have got to do something about this room." Candice stood shaking her head in disbelief.

"And," Lydia continued, "Down the hall is the bathroom that we are lucky enough to share with just one other family. There. You had the grand tour. What do you think?"

"I think I am in desperate need of coffee. Hurry up and take a look at what's in the bags. Then, I suggest we go out together and see what we can find to um...shall we say enhance your humble abode?"

"Look, Candice, potholders and towels and sheets." Digging into the packages was like Christmas. "Gosh, even a pot and there are some dishes and..."

"Hate to interrupt but, you are taking too long. Check out the rest later. Let's finish our coffee and go."

"Candice," Lydia said with love in her heart, "you are a special piece of work."

Pouring the coffee caused another fit of laughter. "Lydia, you are unbelievable. Don't' get me wrong, I'm glad that we are close friends, I mean really, but, I draw the line at sharing the same cup."

"Don't be a party-pooper. There's plenty enough coffee in that single cup for the both of us, Candice. Now drink your share, silly."

"Don't have to. Just remembered, in one of these bags, there should be four cups minus broken saucers, but who cares? I never quite understood the need for them anyway."

Rummaging through a bag, she was successful. "Eureka. Here, now, pour me a cup of coffee please in my own cup, if you don't mind?" The coffee break over, out they went.

Locking the door behind them, like silly schoolgirls, both women skipped down the sidewalk.

"First stop, Mr. Chan's Produce Stand."

"Candice, I don't' need any produce and what's more I only have one dollar and twenty-two cents to my name."

"And I have," counting the change in her purse Candice declared, "four dollars and three cents. Between the two of us, we're rich. Well, at least, we should be able to get starters."

"I repeat, Candice, what are we doing at the produce shop?"

"Watch and learn." Her voice dripping like sugary syrup, Candice approached the owner. "Mr. Chan you have the loveliest fruit and vegetable stand." Walking from vegetable bin to vegetable bin, Candice cleverly spread the compliments that generated the growing ear to ear smile on Mr. Chan's face.

"Tell me, what do you do with these empty apple crates just sitting here?"

"I use. I no throw way."

"Aha, I see. Mr. Chan my friend and I need boxes just like these and I can see you are a very good business man. Would you consider selling them to us for two cents each?"

Loaded down with empty crates, the two headed back to the apartment.

"I swear Candice. You could charm the rattles off a snake."

"Poor Mr. Chan," she giggled, "if only he had known I was willing to pay ten cents each. Did you see the look of satisfaction on his face when we haggled and he figured he won when he decided to accept no less than three cents each?"

"I did. But you still haven't told me why we need empty apple crates."

"Furniture, silly." Apple crates make great end tables and seats and, look here." Placing one in the center of the living room, she announced, "instant coffee table. Now, let's hunt down the janitor. Janitors are always good for odds and ends."

Candice was right. The janitor found an old table lamp, two chairs and a small sofa in the basement. Not only did he give them to Lydia outright but he also helped carry them to her apartment.

"Candice, this place is shaping up nicely. How can I ever repay you?"

"Have me over for dinner when you finally get settled. And, it goes without saying, I want my very own cup."

"You got it."

"By the way, Lydia, did I tell you I admire your icebox."

"What icebox? I don't have one."

"I know, silly. I'm talking about your clever way of using a galvanized tin flower box outside the kitchen window."

"Well, it works. That's what counts."

"I got to get home. Oh, I almost forgot. My mom wanted me to ask you if you would like her to make you window curtains and bureau scarves? While she's at it, I'll ask her to make covers for our handsome apple crate seats, too. What do you say?"

"That would be wonderful. Tell your mom I think she is a genuine gem."

"I will."

"Candice, would you and Jeffrey like to come to dinner on Saturday night? Phillip would love the company and I promise you will have a cup of your very own."

"That sounds great but can you afford it?'

"I'm only planning on making potato soup and a big batch of cornbread biscuits."

"Well, I'll get my mom to bake a cake."

"Wonderful. See you then."

* * * * *

"Happy Anniversary, darling," Phillip wished Lydia as they raised their glasses of champagne. "A toast to us and to, at least, fifty more wonderful years together."

To the sound of glass gently clinking, Lydia agreed, "To us." And they savored the moment. "Isn't it hard to believe Phillip that we've been married three years already. Seems like only yesterday your Captain finally approved of our marriage. Look how far we have come. With the raises Mrs. Mayer has given to me on my waitress job and the money you bring home, our apartment actually has honest-to-goodness furniture."

"Smiling, he said, "Please don't tell me you miss the rickety boxes. Lydia, I held my breath every time I sat down. You never had to worry about breaking them, but I did."

"Phillip, she teased, "Take another look. I'm not exactly what you would call petite."

"You are beautiful." Then taking her into his arms, he kissed her passionately and carried her to the bedroom. Ecstatic, Lydia thought nothing could ever mar their happiness, nothing. Sitting in bed savoring their special moment, Lydia was the first to speak. "You know, Phillip, we aren't rolling in money, still we have all that we need. Guess that's because we don't expect a lot from life and we've learned to accept circumstances the way they are. Most importantly, we have each other."

"If happiness counts, that makes us millionaires. Money isn't everything. Lydia, I'm rich just being with you. Now snuggle closer," he invited, "We have an anniversary to celebrate." Basking in the joy of his prediction, she melted in his arms. Fifty years for starters, not bad. She just knew their happiness would last forever.

* * * * *

"Oh, Phillip, how could you leave me?" she cried into her pillow. "How could you break your promise of just a few months ago? What happened to our long and happy life together? I don't know who to blame, the doctors, the pneumonia, you, me? Who? We stuck it out through thick and thin only to have it all end like this? It makes no sense. We were supposed to live happily ever after. At least for fifty more years, remember? Death was never part of the deal. It wasn't supposed to end this way."

Drowning in her sorrow, tears of anguish rolled down her cheek. The pillow absorbed the moisture but, nothing took care of the pain from her bleeding heart. We shared only three short years of marriage. Oh, Phillip, with your death, that short-lived happy phase of my life, has come to an abrupt end. I never expected it to end like this. To think you fought all those blazing fires and won, only to lose the battle to a horrible illness. It's not fair."

Chapter 36

1936

"A re you sure you want to move?" Candice asked with concern. "I'm not sure your leaving is a good idea."

"My friend, I have two choices. I can stay and drown mourning Phillip's loss in every reminder of him in this place, or leave and start over. Neither, as you can imagine, is going to be easy."

"But where will you go? Won't you consider staying close by so at least we can get together from time to time?"

"We can still do that, no matter the distance. Maybe not as frequently, but we can visit each other, just the same. But, here, without Phillip, I'm dead."

"What do you mean?"

"It's just that without Phillip, I'm no one. But, if I start over, maybe, I can become someone again. Oh, Candice, it's hard to explain."

"It's okay, Lydia. I think I understand. You go. Get settled and then call me. Now, when do you intend to move and how can I help you with it? Do you need money?"

"Most likely by the end of the month and, no, bless your heart. Phillip's life insurance policy is more than ample. I'll be just fine. I'm moving to the country and I do plan on getting a job once I get settled.

I'm entertaining the idea of perhaps opening a shop of some sort. I don't know but I think for now, I just have to get away and rest. You, Candice, my precious friend, I will dearly miss and I'll treasure your friendship forever."

"You better and it works two ways." Hugging, both in tears, they departed.

* * * * *

The sign read: 'Floral Shop For Rent. Apply Within'

Flowers! That's it. She got out of her car to look around thinking, over the years since Ma taught me the importance and pleasure gained from taking care of all the flowers we had around our house, I've developed quite a green thumb. Granted, I don't know everything but I'll get books and learn. Come to think of it, even all the plants and flowers I grew in the apartment thrived. I'm so glad Candice was able to take them. I couldn't bear to throw them away. I just know she will derive pleasure from them and I'm sure they will be a nice reminder of our close friendship.

I'm not positive, but I think taking care of nature's beauties is the right direction for me. I would like to give it a shot and if it doesn't pan out, then I'll have to go another way. For now, I'll check on the rent for this floral shop. If it's too high, then it wasn't meant to be. I think Phillip would approve of the idea, too.

"Good morning, Miss, may I help you?"

"Yes. I'd like to inquire about renting the floral shop. May I speak to the person in charge?"

"You're talking to him, Miss. I'm Peter Jones. Please come in and let me show you round the shop. It's a good money-maker. It is. And as you can see, the flowers are very pretty. I kind of hate to leave them but, I'm afraid, the time has come. These old, creaky, bones of mine have a mind of their own. They revolt. I tell you, Miss, there's a mutiny a-going on. They get out of line and fight me." Shaking his head in disgust, he felt it important to make his point. "Just can't do what I used to do. So finally, I'm forced to give in. I have to retire just as soon as I rent this place to the right person. Tell me, Miss, what is your name?"

"Lydia Wright Wilson."

"You're new in town. Will you be running this shop alone? Now understand, Miss, I don't mean to pry. It's just that if it is for you alone, or even one other person, you may be interested in the small, furnished cottage that sits right behind the shop. That is, if you need a place to stay."

"I will be doing this venture solo and yes, I would very much like to see the cottage, if that's not too much trouble." Lydia was thinking to herself, maybe my luck is changing. Who knows? Maybe I'll wind up with both a business and a place to call home in one location.

"Tell me, Mr. Jones, is the cottage vacant now?"

"Indeed, Miss. Me and the Mrs. recently moved into a small place in town closer to the hospital and drug stores and the like. Pity, but one has to think of these things when one gets up in years. Ah, the Golden Years. That's what they call 'um. Me thinks they are a tad tarnished." Shaking his head in the disappointment of it all, he went on. "Come, let me show you the shop and then we'll go to the cottage."

Curious Lydia asked, "Now, I don't mean to pry but Mr. Jones, since you moved, how can you afford to pay for a new place and hold onto this shop and the cottage until you find a buyer? From what you told me, the rent is not all that much but I'm sure you still have to pay taxes and maintenance and the like."

"Oh, I don't own either of these places, Miss. I rent them from the gentleman farmer who owns most of the land in these parts. I work for him. Oh, no, I'm not the owner. I'm the manager for Mr. Sam Manning. Mr. Manning, now, he owns this entire estate. Here, come with me." Walking out to the porch, he arched his arm as he explained. "All this, as far as the eye can see belongs to Mr. Manning." Lydia could hear pride in the man's voice, as though the man somehow had a hand in its magnificence.

"It's absolutely breath-taking," Lydia said sincerely, "It's so vast. It seems to go on forever. Mr. Manning, hmmm, now, where did I hear that name?" she wondered aloud.

"Horses, Miss. Horses. He's known for them. Why, he's a legend in his own time. You probably remember Mr. Sam Manning as the owner of the famous race horse, Hot Fudge Preacher. He took the Triple Crown, he did. That horse, now, he was something else. Mr. Manning, now, he owns many other thoroughbred racing steeds, but Hot Fudge, he was a once-in-a-lifetime champion." There was a moment of silence as if the man was paying quiet tribute. "If you decide to take this place Miss, you will be invited to visit the stables and walk the trails. That, in itself I assure you Miss, is very pleasant and therapeutic. Mighty good for the soul, it is. That is if you need the likes. Here, watch your step, the cottage is vintage," he chuckled, "That's just a fancy way of saying old and believe me, Miss, that it is. Dates back to the 1800's."

"It's charming, simply charming." Lydia was beside herself with the warm vibes she was feeling. Her guide took her on a room to room tour. It didn't take long. "This is the kitchen. Mind now Miss, it's a mite small but it does the job and the living room has a nice fireplace in it and, of course, there is just one bedroom, neither too big nor too small. Me and me wife always said it was just right. Of course, there's the privy. Again, a mite bit small but, located inside. Come winter that's a blessing in itself."

Not too big, not too small; but just right. Rebecca thought his words sounded like they came straight from the story of Goldilocks and The Three Bears. Guess I can relate to that golden-haired intruder, both of us looking for everything to be just right. Interrupting her thoughts, he asked, "Well, what do you think, Miss?"

"Where is the dotted line? I'm ready to sign. I think this place is lovely and it's more than I dared hope to find."

"Ah, it does my heart good to hear that. I have the feeling you are the kind of person that will look after this old place and love it just as much as me and the Misses."

Pausing, he looked around like soaking in memories and then suggested they take care of business.

"Let's be off back to the flower shop. I have the papers there listing the rental. Mr. Manning is a good man. He never charges too high a rent. Me and me wife never had to struggle. It will be the same for you and so I think you will be pleased about that. See, here is the monthly amount."

Holding her signed copy, Lydia asked, "When can I move in?"

"Tomorrow, Miss. Oh, and one more thing I forgot to mention. If you are so inclined, there is a garden patch in the backyard. Potatoes, beans, peppers, tomatoes and squash are planted and should be ready for pickin' soon. You are welcome to that harvest and if you want to use the garden sometime down the road to plant what you want, it's yours to do so."

Lydia could see the pride nearly bursting from the elderly man's chest and thought he must have put a lot of love into the raising of those crops. Yes, indeed, she would enjoy them.

"Thank you. Mr. Jones. I would be delighted to do just that." She couldn't tell who was wearing the broader smile.

Up early the following morning, Lydia was anxious to get started. Darn, she thought, I forgot to ask Mr. Jones the library's address. Well, I'll just have to take a drive into town and find it. Getting into the vehicle, Lydia was reminded of Phillip. What do you think, dear? Proud of me? You always wanted me to drive and not only did I finally get my license but, I bought this used car that's in pretty good shape. I got a good deal, too. Oh, Phillip, it has been a year, and I miss you still. I hurt something awful.

So this is the grand metropolis of Hawk's Point she thought intoxicated with its long-established charm. Glancing from side to side as she drove down Main Street, she took in a general store, post office, bank, library, town hall, diner and church, and said happily, "I couldn't ask for more."

Loaded down with all manner of flower books, Lydia headed back to her small shop determined to study and become as knowledgeable a horticulturist as these books would permit. Day after day, elbow deep in potting soil, donning protective garden gloves, Lydia felt a sense of contentment. Re-potting this flower and pruning that; nurturing some in need more than others, Lydia's heavy heart was gradually lightened. The floral shop business was blooming. Indeed, it was just what the doctor ordered.

Turning the key at the end of the day, Lydia closed up shop and headed to her small palace. Showered, she changed into a casual pair of white slacks and a patterned blue blouse. Grateful for the flourishing vegetable garden, she made herself a tasty supper of a mixed greens and fresh vegetable salad, and steak. Washing the dishes, she looked out the kitchen window and just like that, she felt the urge to go for a walk. Why not, she thought, it's lovely out and still plenty of daylight left. I think I'll venture on that walk Mr. Jones suggested months ago. It's about time I change my routine. Besides, I have to stop going to bed with the chickens.

Walking down the flower bordered pathway butterflies fluttering about, birds singing and splashing in the strategically placed birdbaths along the way, Lydia was captivated with the serenity of it all. Following the meandering path the view of acres and acres of green pastures opened leaving her breathless and leading her to yet another walking trail that took her directly to the pristine stables at the base of the hill. It also took her directly to a most charming stableman.

"Hello there. It's getting chilly, isn't it?"

"Indeed." Pulling her cardigan around her shoulders she was aware that the air held a bit of a chill. She was also very much aware, that he did not.

"I've seen you around. Do you ride? I do mean English not Western, of course."

"Laughing weakly, Lydia frowned and answered. "I'm afraid I'm horse-back riding illiterate. I don't know the difference in the styles. Actually, this is the closest I've been to any horse."

"Well, then I guess I don't recognize you from the horse shows. By the way, I'm Darius and you are?" He didn't let his talking interfere with his work at hand. Vigorously brushing his charge, the horse's coat glistened.

"I'm Lydia, Lydia Wright and I live in the third cottage up on the hill. That's probably where you have seen me. There or in town."

"You mean the one with all those flowers in the yard?"

"One and the same. I like the colorful blossoms." Stepping back, she allowed herself the opportunity to observe her new acquaintance more closely wondering what was happening. I haven't thought of a man in this way since Phillip died. He certainly caught me off guard. What am I doing? She asked herself flushed with embarrassment as she eyed this man as if he was some paragon of male beauty. Maybe that's because he is. Stop it. Lydia. Stop this foolishness this very minute, she chastised. Carrying on a silent two-way conversation with herself, she came to her own defense. Just look at him. How could you not admire him? His bulging muscles stretch his shirt and there's a bronze glow to his skin. Then there's that infectious twist to his smile.

Act you age, girl, her conscience was yelling, to which she shouted back, I am. She stood there taking inventory of this man and she shivered in her scrutiny. I should be ashamed for being so attracted to this handsome man. This is our first meeting. But I wouldn't mind getting to know him better to learn what makes him tick.

All I can think of is Roman Ovid's quotation… 'To be loved, be lovable.' With that, nonchalantly as was possible, she tested the waters.

"Would you like to see my flower garden and my floral shop sometime?" I don't believe I just did that. What in blue blazes was I thinking? I just invited this mega-macho man if he would be interested in seeing a mixed bunch of pansies? He must think I'm not all here.

So much for flirting, I'm so out of touch. It probably didn't work. Surely, she hadn't heard him correctly. "What did you say," she asked.

"I said, yes. Yes, I would like to see the flowers and the sooner the better."

Surprised, Lydia's smile was genuine. Thus began the relationship of the man whose first love was horses and the woman whose love for flowers was secondary.

"Is tomorrow afternoon okay with you?" she could hardly believe her boldness nor, for that matter, contain her enthusiasm.

"Tomorrow afternoon, it is." With that, he went about the business of grooming the horse almost as though Lydia wasn't even there.

Pure unadulterated giddiness filled her very being as she practically flew home. Feeling like a school girl, she raced up the hill hoping to hurry the day away.

Logically, the sooner this day ends, she thought, the sooner tomorrow begins. Begin it did, complete with perfect weather as the sun rose and ruled the day.

Prisms filled the small living room in every nook and cranny where the sun visited the glass shelves and clear knick-knacks. A rainbow of color, just like my garden, it's all too grand. I never would have guessed. He likes flowers. Yet, there was a slight nagging.

If ever the timing was right, it was now. Her inner thoughts screamed out the warning sign. She was being naïve. Even so, as clear as it was, it served no use as she refused to heed the alarm.

The bold knock on the door hammered into her mind and she shivered with the very thought of his strength. Applying the final touch of lipstick, she walked past the hall mirror. Pausing just long enough for a last minute check, she smiled at the results. Then she opened the front door.

"Come in, Darius, come in," she invited, "have a seat. Before I show you the flower beds, would you care for a drink?"

"Thank you. A scotch on the rocks would be nice, if that's not too much trouble."

"None at all," she answered although, it was a soft drink or coffee that she had in mind. Handing him his mixed drink, she sipped her coke. She was unaccustomed to hard drinks so early in the day. Phillip never did. But then that was Phillip and this is Darius and it isn't fair to compare. Besides, what good does it serve? I'm in a different time and a different place now.

Sitting on the couch exchanging small talk, Lydia only half-listened to her new friend go on and on about his favorite subject. Obviously, horses dominate his world. Wish I wasn't having such a tough time trying to be interested. Truthfully, it's really the sound of his assertive, yet gentle, voice that gets me. Look at him. His blue eyes so dreamy and his hair begging for attention, I want to run my fingers through it. …"and that, Lydia, about wraps it up. Anyway, I've bored you long enough with all this talk about horses. Forgive me. Once I get stared I just can't help it." Shaking his head in the error of his ways, he declared, "I get carried away. It's just that it's my passion."

"Good for you. I'm open to learning and I have to admit, when it comes to horses, my knowledge is very limited." Her ear to ear smile was not lost on him. He placed his empty glass on the coffee table and turned to face her. Lydia savored the pleasant aroma of his aftershave. Enjoying the very essence of anticipation, she weakly instructed her heart. Be still.

He said not a word but simply put his arms around her and drew her close. Lydia could not believe her reaction as she silently wished, please don't stop.

It was an eye-opener and she marveled at her readiness. Like the thunder following the lightning, she anticipated the shocking excitement and potential danger. He kissed her long and hard, and she responded in kind. Cold for so long, the furnace within her was stoked, once again.

She knew this was insane. She barely knew the man. She wanted more. It had been a long time of abstinence. He was absolutely wonderful and they made love filled with waves of pleasure for most of the afternoon. Yet, Lydia's mind alerted her to the irony of it all. In the course of one afternoon, we went from being brand new acquaintances to the full measure of knowing each other to our hearts' content. Watch yourself. Darn nagging alarm, go away. After all, she rationalized, what's the harm? It isn't like I intend to marry the guy, now is it? He certainly isn't Phillip. I wonder about that, too.

How I miss him, she lamented. Then for just an instant, and without warning, Lydia entertained the sad but possible true fact she had held secretly in her heart. Although, she loved Phillip and he was a good husband, maybe he had been more of a convenience. Wasn't he there when she had no one to turn to and no place to go? And wasn't he the one who came valiantly to her rescue? Indeed. Now stop it, she chastised herself pushing that traitorous thought from her mind. This is hardly the time or place…

"Penny?" he asked putting a temporary end to her confused thoughts.

"Oh, I'm not thinking of anything special," she lied, "just of our time together" which was, to an exaggerated extent, the truth.

Lying here in the arms of this man, she felt the need to regard her first marriage squarely and without prejudice. Phillip was a wonderful man. Darius is a wonderful lover. I have to let it go at that.

"Lydia, you are beautiful," he said brushing aside a wisp of hair from her forehead. "I wish I could stay longer but I'm afraid, duty calls." He headed for the shower. "I have hungry horses waiting for me."

Wait a minute, she wanted to scream. What about me? What kind of love me and leave me let down, is this? Wake up, Lydia. Recognize it for what it is. As foreign as it may be, the truth of the matter is simply this. Either we just had a one night stand or, the beginning of an affair. I suppose time will tell. Another thought popped into her head, and she mentioned it to him as he dressed.

"You know what Darius? You haven't seen my flowers yet" He stood in the middle of the bedroom listening to her while he combed his hair. "You are absolutely right. But now, do you know what?"

"What?"

"They will be my excuse to return." Smiling, he lit cigarettes; one for her and one for him. Then he kissed her gently and left. Watching him walk in the direction of the stables, and out of sight, Lydia ran the gamut of emotions. They were all there; fulfillment, excitement, happiness, sadness, confusion, loneliness and fear. Like a complex mathematical computation, it didn't add up. This had been a first for her, and she wasn't sure how it all happened? More accurately, how did she let it happen?

She asked herself questions without answers. What am I getting into? My poor brain is beat. I think too much. One thing for sure, I'm tired, emotionally and physically. Maybe a shower would help.

After her shower, still without an acceptable answer, she flung herself across the bed near to tears. Sleep rescued her from her quandary as she drifted into the uncaring state.

To her surprise, she woke up refreshed and energized. She made herself a cup of hot tea and placed it on her nightstand to enjoy while she dressed. The aromatic aroma of mint pleasantly filled the air. Nagging, again her mind was questioning. This is so unlike me. What am I doing? For the first time in ages, I feel alive. The answer was pleasing and, from here on, she decided to toss caution to the wind. After all, it's time I start living my life. Holding that thought close, gave consent and birth to their strange relationship.

* * * * *

Working only four mornings a week at the floral shop, her afternoons were free. It was an excellent arrangement. It gave her an opportunity to run errands on her mornings when she didn't work and afternoons seemed to fit him just right.

Except for the sex which was always exciting, the routine was the same. Darius visited, had a drink, made love to her for as long as time permitted then headed back to work. Lydia marveled how Darius never seemed to get into trouble for taking so much time off. She thought his boss to be quite liberal.

It was her morning off. She was there now, standing at the stables, watching him prepare to bath his horse. The sun was warm despite the coolness in the air. "Hi."

"Howdy. You're just in time, Lydia. This horse-bathing is quite the procedure. Ever see it done?"

"Never. Still not a horse person. But it's probably fun to observe." Lydia was very much aware of this man's close connection to horses and his disciplined work ethic. Wonder why he keeps referring to this magnificent animal as his? Guess, in a sense, ownership kind of belongs to the stableman, too.

"Here, come close, Lydia. He won't hurt you."

"But he's huge."

"Still won't intentionally hurt you. Now, if by mistake he should step on your foot, don't panic. All you have to do to alleviate any discomfort from his bulk, you just …well, watch. I'll show you." Demonstrating, he placed one foot close to the horse's hoof pretending it was covered by the hoof. Holding it steady and using the rest of his body, he gently leaned into the horse's hind quarter. Like magic, the horse stepped aside and by all rights, had a foot been actually trapped under his hoof, it would have been easily freed.

"See," he announced pleased with his lesson, "Just push into his hind quarter."

"Well, I'm impressed," she said and meant it.

"Another detail worth knowing is when you are walking near the horse, always run your hand on him so he knows where you are. Then he won't be startled. Now, come up front with me."

"I'm not too sure about this, Darius," she said as she followed his instructions and for her efforts, she found herself practically face to face with this large animal.

"Just rub his nose right here. He loves it."

"Again, Darius, I'm not too sure about this." Gingerly, following his instruction, she approached and gently massaged the horse's nose. Immediately, she was rewarded with such velvety softness. She lingered and the horse did not move.

"Darius, I never felt such softness."

"See. The horse isn't moving. He likes it too. Now, if you get yourself seated on that stool over there near the corner, I'll start with his bath. It will take a little time so if you get bored, feel free to walk over to the other stalls and check out the rest of the horses in this stable or go look at the ones already grazing in the pastures."

Lydia watched Darius, armed with a bucket chock-full of apparent grooming gadgets, approach the securely tethered horse. He really is getting a kick out of this she told herself as she watched him delve into the task at hand sporting a huge smile.

Caught up in his energy, she found the process interesting which made the time wiz by. Before she knew it, he stepped back admiring his work.

"I'm finished. Now, isn't he a beauty?"

"That, he is. I have to agree, Darius. His seems to sparkle."

"Sparkle? Interesting description. I never heard it put quite that way before." Chuckling, he walked over to the horse, patted him lovingly and rewarded him with a carrot. "Here, my sparkling friend," he couldn't resist, "for your patience." The horse whinnied as if in appreciation.

"Won't he get dirty before tomorrow's show you talked about?" "No. That's why we'll stable him all night. No pasture roaming for him. After all, I plan to win best of show."

"Don't you mean Mr. Manning's rider?"

"I do, and I am."

Dumfounded, Lydia's mouth dropped open. Hitting her like a ton of bricks, the realization of his identity made her feel rather stupid. How could she have not known?

"But I thought your last name was Mackey."

"What made you think that?"

"On the main bulletin board in the tack room listing the names and work schedules of all the stablemen, I saw the name D. Mackey. It was the only one that had a D. for the first name so I just assumed it was yours."

"No. That's not for me. It belongs to David Mackey. You probably have seen him. He's that tall man who wears his hair in a ponytail.

Guess you haven't met him yet. But I thought you knew, Lydia. I'm
Sam Manning's son. Dad is in charge of the thoroughbred race horses
and I'm responsible for all the show horses." Taking her hands into his
for reassurance, and feeling just a little sheepish, he continued. "I'm too
tall to ride race horses and, the truth of the matter is, I love show horses
and all that is involved with them, so much better. I'm sorry if I upset
you. I just assumed you knew. But my name doesn't matter. I'm still the
same person who thinks you are fantastic." Teasing, he added, "and who
loves your flowers sight unseen. Oh, and just in case I forgot to tell you,
the name of this horse is Run-Away-Gold. He's my favorite."

A tad dazed, she finally connected the dots and the picture created
left her feeling somewhat insecure. I'm falling in love with a very rich
man. This can't be. I don't belong in his circle of life. I'm frightened.
Where will it go from here?

Suddenly, a gush of warm air embraced her face or was she hot from
blushing with her haunted thought? Somewhere in the crevices of her
mind, a tiny voice screamed its opinion. Get hold of yourself. You're
his equal. Well, in most ways. But what does money have to do with it,
anyway? Think about it. So what if he's rich? It doesn't change the man.
It just goes to prove that it's just as easy to fall in love with a rich man as
it is with a poor man. Now accept the fact and follow your heart.

She remembered reading somewhere, 'in my garden, love grows.' She
added, perhaps in his stable, too? It's still hard to believe. Have I really
struck it rich first with love and then with money? All the struggles
of my past life, can I really put them behind me? The revelation of
possibilities is almost incomprehensible. Yet, if it is so, it would be the
most extraordinary, fantastic happening for me, ever.

His uncomplicated explanation revolving around his name, now
over, Darius moved on and while her mind was still trying to think
sharply, his words cut right into her thoughts.

"Will you be able to come to the show tomorrow?"

"What? What did you say?"

"The horse show tomorrow, I'd love for you to be there. It's asking a lot. You need to be here at the stable at 5:00 a.m. I know that's early but that's when we trailer Run-Away-Gold and head out to the Serendipity Farms about ten miles from here. Do you think you could make it?"

"Just try and stop me."

"Dress in layers. It's cool in the morning but warms up as the day goes on. We should be back around 7:00 p.m. depending on the time and course of the events I'll be entering."

She went home then with almost too many challenging thoughts whirling about in her mind. Trying to sort them out, she thought. He's a famous rider. He's rich. He's my man. There you go again jumping the gun. So you love him. Who says he loves you? What do you really have together? Good sex? That's not enough. But, on the other hand, he just asked me out on our first official date. Surely that counts for something. Okay. So, now you are justifying circumstances? Shush up! It doesn't matter. Tomorrow, I'm spending the day with him outside the bedroom. I'll take it a step further. I'd wager that he loves me, too. With that, she didn't wait for her inner voice to retaliate. She simply thanked her lucky stars and felt sure the compass that had set the course for her to follow, was one of direct happiness.

Tossing and turning, sleep was evasive and it wasn't until somewhere in the wee hours that she found it. By then, it was almost time for the alarm to go off. Dragging herself from the comfort of her bed, moving slowly, she headed for her first hot cup of coffee. The caffeine's stimulating effects worked wonders pushing in the right directions. Her head cleared of cobwebs she dressed and got ready to face the adventure of the day and, hopefully, turning point of her life.

"Good morning, Darius." She found him in the stable busy braiding the horse's long mane.

"Morning," he answered not even bothering to look up.

Gee, she thought, this is a switch. Yesterday he couldn't say enough and today, well, so far, he hasn't said two words. Why, he hasn't even offered an explanation as to the need of this braiding exercise. So not like him. Maybe it's done simply to provide an aesthetically appealing look for the occasion. At least that makes sense to me. Don't know why I even care. Guess I just always have to satisfy the side of me filled with curiosity.

Is there a real chill in here or is that emanating from him? Look at him. He's all businesslike, quite a contrast from yesterday's congeniality.

Lydia walked over to one of the stable workers she knew.

"Good morning, Thomas."

"Good morning, Miss Lydia."

"Tell me Thomas, why is it so quiet? Feels like I'm in the morgue. What's with everybody's somber mood? Now," leaning close she added, "even I'm whispering."

"Let me guess," he smiled, "this will be your first horseshow?"

"You guessed right."

"Well, that explains it. You see you are dealing with a breed of intense people who take what they do very seriously. Kind of like an obsession. It's their livelihood, really. There's a lot at stake and everything has to go just right. No room for errors. Each show day has its own unique way of working on every contestant's nerves. The stable hands are not exempt, either. What I'm trying to say, Miss Lydia, is that right now what you are witnessing is everybody's anxiousness. Like stage fright. But as the day goes on, it wears off. So I suggest you just observe and enjoy the beauty of the sport."

"Thanks, Thomas, I will try to do just that."

"Oh, one more thing, Miss Lydia."

"What's that?"

"Do it quietly," he smiled generously, and so did she. Tipping his hat courteously, he said, "Time to load him up, now Miss Lydia" and he left her to her own thoughts. Loading the horse was tricky. Watching, even she could tell the horse bucking his objection to being led up the trailer ramp, was not cooperating. With a lump in her throat, she quietly observed this risky business. Why the sheer mass of that animal, she thought, could unintentionally crush one of the workers against the trailer's side. I can't watch this, she decided. Ready to turn away, the commotion stopped. Now what? Turning back, she could tell nerves were a little more settled. Apparently, Thomas came up with the idea. He simply blindfolded the animal. Then he and another worker, each holding an end of a broom stick turned horizontally, placed the broom stick under the horse's tail. Pressing it against its hind quarters, they gently nudged the animal along until it was safely on board. Relieved, Lydia laughed weakly thinking now I am beginning to understand why the jangled nerves.

"Lydia, are you ready to go?" Darius asked without fanfare.

"Ready." And he helped her onto the front seat of the truck. As the day light began to invade the darkness, she was better able to see him and how handsome he looked now dressed in his riding garb.

She sat back, relaxed and let her eyes feast. He looks so distinguished in his dark green, wool riding jacket and, crisp white shirt. Even his green silk tie matches. Look at the elegance of the gold stick pin. Why it's created in the shape of a bugle. He mentioned that it symbolizes fox hunting prowess. I like the way his beige riding breeches hug his body and how neatly he has tucked them into his boots. His equestrian leather boots, they're in a category of their own. Wonder how many hours it took to get the polish to glisten like that? There's his riding helmet on the seat next to him. Wow, how nicely its sable brown color compliments his green jacket. My staring must be conspicuous but I can't help it. This is all so new to me. I like this world of equestrians. I like the way he looks. I like him.

At their destination, now Darius was checking the course map. She stood next to him overwhelmed at the designated twists and turns and mandatory patterns. Intrigued, she wondered how anyone could, not only remember them, but execute them, as well.

"If you sit there on the right, you'll have the best vantage point."

"Good idea. But, Darius, I still don't know what to look for. This seems complicated to me. I see here it says each rider is timed. Good grief, I'm getting nervous."

Chuckling, he assured her. "No need for both of us to suffer. You just try to relax and enjoy the show and I'll try to make it a show you won't forget."

"Okay," she answered heading toward the suggested seat, "But I got to tell you. I don't know what I'm looking for."

"That's okay," he laughed, "the judges do."

Round after round, she watched them. In perfect harmony, man and horse jumped as one. Beautifully, not knocking over a single fence rail, each and every round was totally clean. The judges ruled no faults, again and again, and, in the end, the perfection earned him the coveted blue ribbon. The huge, monetary award was considered a bonus. As for Run-Away-Gold, he delighted in the carrot reward offered him in the winner's circle.

"Talk about excitement!" Lydia squealed hugging Darius tightly, "That was intense and you were sensational. I didn't know I could love horseshows so much."

On a high, once again, he was talkative. Obviously, his mood swings were in direct correlation with the outcome of his riding events. At the successful conclusion of the final competition of the day, Darius popped the cork on the champagne bottle and filled the glasses of his entire crew. With the bubbly refreshment running everywhere, his prior somber mood had, indeed, become a mere memory.

Champagne, she thought, and yet another symbol of luxurious living. Then she lifted her glass along with the others toasting the day's victorious results. Chuckling, the effervescent bubbles tickled her nose.

"Wow! Lydia, what do you think? Exciting?" he asked above the celebratory noise.

"Beyond my wildest expectations. Now tell me. When's the next show?"

"Soon," he answered beaming. "Sounds like you caught the bug."

"I hope so. Now, I understand the reason for the daily hard work. Exhilarating, Darius, that's what it is, and oh, all, so worth it."

Lifting Run-Away-Gold's hooves one at a time, the man of the hour made sure the horse was free of any foreign objects. Confident his horse was sound, he passed on the task of wrapping the horse's legs for transport to his assistants.

Popping the cork on their second champagne bottle, Lydia and Darius basked in the bubbles seemingly everywhere, and consumed several more glasses of the sparkling delight before heading home. Arm in arm, he escorted her to the truck.

"A girl could get used to this pace and style of life." Lydia's words came out in jest, mixed with, perhaps, a smidgen of truth.

"Great. Just wait for the fun we'll have at the victory party."

"Victory party? What victory party, Darius?"

"Oh, no. Don't tell me I forgot to mention tonight's party?" Slapping his forehead as a sign of forgetfulness mixed with a tad of stupidity, he felt badly.

"How could I have been so absentminded? I'm so sorry, Lydia. I was so caught up in the show I simply forgot to invite you to the big event."

"Big event?"

"Well, yes. Is it too late to ask you to accompany me now? The celebration doesn't start until 9:00 tonight."

"Okay, 9 o'clock will give me enough time to change."

"Here I go again. Did I mention that it's formal?"

"Darius, you didn't mention anything. Formal? Gosh, I don't know."

"Please," he begged. "You must have a nice gown in your closet. It doesn't have to be new. Listen, I really feel badly about this. But more than ever, Lydia, I want the most beautiful woman in the place to walk into that party draped on my arm. Please say you'll come."

"Darius, how could I say no to that? Guess everyone has the right to forget once in awhile. You're forgiven," hesitating she added, "this time."

"Terrific. I'll pick you up 8:30ish." Smiling, he opened the door and she dashed off to her cottage.

"Thanks Candice," she yelled out to the empty room, "for letting me be matron of honor at your wedding last year. The gown is in style. Now let's hope it still fits. Where is it?" Frantically pushing the clothes in her closet from one side to the other, she finally met success. "Aha. Here it is." Then all the while spent showering she begged, "Please, please fit." It was the moment of truth.

Holding her breath, she let the towel drop to the floor then slipped into the ankle length gown with absolutely no trouble. "Fits like a glove," she squealed in delight. Turning this way and that, in front of the mirror, smoothing out the skin-hugging material, she liked what looked back at her.

"What time is it? Yikes, it's getting late. Better hurry," she told herself pulling her hair away from her face. She fashioned it in a bun resting high on the back of her head.

Applying the finishing touches, she added a hint of Vaseline to her eyelashes to better separate them and to her lips for a subtle gloss. That has to do it, she thought, I'm out of time. I hear a car.

He arrived at 8:45. Quickly, she slipped into black patent leather pumps and grabbed the matching evening bag with the lovely gold clasp. Taking a deep breath, quietly announcing ready or not, she opened the door.

Just as quickly, she stopped dead in her tracks. Goodness, that can't be a limo? Is it? I thought maybe his sedan, but a limo?

Parked outside her tiny cottage on the hill, sure enough, was this sleek, black limousine complete with chauffer.

"I'll be darned," she muttered as both men assisted her.

"Wow! Lydia, you look absolutely stunning." "Thank you, Darius." Running her hands over the soft leather seat, she went on. "I have to say I never expected to be picked up in such a lavish style. This is luxurious."

Smiling contently, he whispered, "All this pales in comparison to your beauty."

"Now, you're making fun of me."

"No. I am not." She was pleased for his sincerity.

Arriving at his parents' mansion held yet another surprise. It came complete with doormen, butlers and servants. Lydia thought silently of her Ma and thought, if only you could see me now. This is all too grand and Ma, you were right. I'm so grateful that you taught me proper etiquette. It does hold the key, and I do feel comfortable in these lavish surroundings.

Even with a modest glance, it was obvious. His parents, the heads of this manor, and this place itself reeked of money. Proof of prosperity abounded. Opulence filled every nook and cranny. Guests dressed in tuxedos and gowns were served champagne and fancy hors d'oeuvres on elegant silver trays. From what she could see of the ballroom, Lydia caught a glimpse of high-spirited couples whirling about the dance floor.

"Mom, Dad. I'd like you to meet my friend, Lydia Wright; Lydia, my parents, Mr. and Mrs. Samuel Manning." Pleasantries exchanged, Lydia liked his mother's friendly charm. She thought there was a certain air of serenity about her. His father now, she thought, conveyed quite another story; a horse of another color. That's pretty funny considering his line of work. It is obvious, opposites attract. Right off the bat, I can tell he is a take charge person in full command. It's his way or no way. Yet, Lydia thought, there is a certain charisma about him drawing me near like a moth to a flame. She felt a slight shiver. What made me think of that stupid comparison? A moth doesn't have a chance.

"Come, you lovely person. Join me in a dance. I'm pretty good at the waltz, if I must say so myself. And I do. You don't mind, old boy, do you?"

"Of course not Dad." Turning his attention to his Mother he asked, "Would you do me the honor?"

Actually, it turned out all four were light on their feet. Swirling round and round gracefully, they dominated the floor with their charming and magical movements of this smooth rhythmic dance.

"Lydia," he asked, "You look so familiar. Have we met?"

"As a matter of fact, Mr. Manning, we have. You happened to be at the cottage on the hill when the caretaker brought me the rental papers to sign. I'm your new tenant."

"Aha, now I remember. So you live on the property, do you?" Immediately, he was aghast at the thought of the situation that crossed his mind. How could this woman possibly be of any noteworthy society? Okay, granted, she's beautiful but that doesn't cut it. Not for my son. What is he thinking? I'll speak to Darius the first chance I get. I'll get to the bottom of this. By God, their relationship had better be confined to a good roll in the hay. Nothing more.

Lydia, delighting in the dance for what it was, didn't have a clue as the gentleman never missed a step, nor gave any indication that something was amiss. She had no way of knowing that because of the detrimental thoughts lodged in the back of his head, she would be dancing to the tune of disaster in the not too distant future.

Gosh, Lydia thought, I hate to think that this magical evening is rapidly coming to a close. I'm having the time of my life. Darius has so many nice friends. I'll never remember their names. I think I danced with just about all of them and my feet still aren't protesting. That's a very good sign. Darius even managed to squeeze in a dance or two with me and I can certainly see why the ladies created such a hubbub over him. I can't blame them. He's too handsome for his own good, but no matter. I'm the one he escorted and I'm the one he declared the most beautiful woman at the party. Now that I look around, I have to say, I'm in total agreement. Shame on me and I'm not even blushing. Oh, it's ending. People are beginning to take their leave. Too soon, the bewitching hour has arrived. This gala affair is over.

"Darius, the party was wonderful. Your parents are a delight. And your father, well, he's, he's…"

"Cyclonic?"

"Kind of, but…"

"Headstrong?"

"Not exactly what I had in mind."

"Impetuous?"

"Bingo," But I like him and, best part; I think he likes me, too."

"Good. I'm glad that's settled and, I'm glad you had a nice time."

"I'd say it was more like memorable, Darius, just grand." The distance short, the limo came to a stop. "Here we are, Lydia." The chauffer opened the door and Darius walked her up the short distance to her cottage. At her front door, he bent down and gently kissed her.

"Aren't you coming in?" she asked, the evening is still young."

"Not tonight, darling. It's been a long day and tomorrow I need to be up early again. I'm bushed." Holding her, he added, "but you were a hit at the party and we'll do that again. My sights are set to include a lot more victory parties, okay?"

Disappointed, she answered softly, "Of course, we will. Thank you for a lovely day and a lovely party. It was a delight."

"Believe me, the pleasure was all mine." With that fond ado, she disappeared into the cottage and he, into the limo.

Well, she thought, maybe his leaving is just as well. With all the unexpected excitement, I hate to admit it but I am suddenly exhausted. The day was longer than I thought. Quickly taking off her gown and her make-up, and despite persistent sugarplums still dancing in her head, her bone weariness was soon able to tune them out. She fell into bed and into a deep, much needed sleep.

Darius returned home in no time but his course of action to just crawl into bed didn't quite work out that way. Little did he know an altogether different game plan awaited him. The minute he arrived, there he was. Sitting by the front door so as not to miss his entrance, his father ambushed him.

"Dad," he said, "What are you doing still awake?"

"We need to talk, son," he said in a somber tone, "Come into the den. I'm sure Albert would whip us up some eggs, if you would like?"

"No thanks. I'm not hungry just dog tired, Dad. You know how long show days run and add the victory party to the mix and you get the formula for total exhaustion. All I want now is to get some sleep. Can't this wait until tomorrow?"

The color on his face turned crimson as he angrily decreed, "No it cannot. Sit down. This is of utmost importance."

Darius immediately loosened his tie, kicked off his shoes and sat as he had been told. He knew darn well that his father was not one for mincing words. For that he was glad, because he felt certain he was in for a long siege. Here we go again, he thought, I must have mishandled something in today's horse events to displease the old man. Fortunately, his father got right to the heart of the matter. It came as a total shock.

"This date of yours, this Lydia Wright, how serious is this relationship?"

"Well, we don't have plans to marry, if that's what you mean. But I do like her a lot, Dad."

"How does she feel about you?"

"To tell you the truth, I think she really likes me, maybe even more than I do her. We have mutual respect for each other. We enjoy each other's company. We have fun together."

Nuts, Darius chastised himself. I've said too much already. Darn, he threw me a curve ball. I wasn't expecting this line of interrogation. I don't need this pressure from him now. He put his weary head into his hands and rested his elbows on his knees bracing himself for what he knew was coming. It was inevitable and, he hated each and every rung awaiting him on that darn social ladder.

"As long as you understand son, she is not marrying material for you. Got it?"

He should have defended her and their position. But he justified his silence by accusing his mind and body of being too tired to fight. Besides, above all, he knew any attempt would be futile. What would be the point? His father was traveling down that same old road again, only this time at break neck speed. He wasn't about to let up.

"You know damn well, Darius, that we have ironclad plans. Are you crazy? What were you thinking? You are not going to spend the rest of your life showing horses nor are you going to marry a useless chippie. You are going to marry a socialite who will enhance your career."

"She's not promiscuous, Dad." At least he said that much in her favor.

"Maybe not, but I bet she's good in bed." That did it. The totally uncalled for remark raised his dander and Darius fought back on this one.

"How dare you talk about Lydia in such a foul manner? How dare you?" His adrenalin pumping, no longer tired, he stood up and faced his father. Noses close to touching, Darius let him know his resentment. He did not, however, deny the accusation. How could he? Maybe there had been others. She was a fantastic lover.

Completely out of character, his unexpected thunder took his father by surprise. In fact, his father had to admit to some pride in the outburst of his usual complaisant son. At least, he figured he's showing a little backbone and tempered his tone. "Look son, I don't want to hurt you or her. I just want to remind you of your social obligation and your future plans. We worked so hard. You haven't forgotten them, have you?"

"No, Dad. I have not." Again, he knew when he was whipped. Slowly he supplied his father with the words he knew his father wanted to hear; more like what his father commanded to hear.

"Don't worry, Dad. This relationship is going nowhere. Lydia won't get in the way of our plans." Your plans, not mine, he concluded but couldn't bring himself to voice it. Too bad Darius was so strong in so many areas and so weak in all areas when it came to dealing with his father. He needed to be in his father's favor. He just had to be. It was as simple as that.

"Good. I'm glad we had this chance to talk. I know you have a good head on your shoulders. Now son, get your rest. We both know where we stand, right?"

Darius nodded. The father patted the son on his back in a pleased gesture, and then together they walked out of the room. One headed up the stairs to bed; the other to the den's bar and a needed drink or two or three.

Darius never mentioned the conversation to Lydia. He just took up where they had left off. Each and every day she was falling more and more in love with him. More and more each day, he liked her. But, that was all there was in his cards. He could allow nothing more. It was simple enough. He refused to fall out of his father's graces.

The whirlwind romance went on and, indeed, she was happy. She especially enjoyed the fun times spent at the Manning Mansion. So much at ease there, time and again, she thanked her Ma for training her for life's challenges including proper social graces.

Lydia was so pleased with Darius's parents. They were so good to her, especially his father. What a nice gentleman he is. She had no reason to think differently.

The subject of a long-term relationship never came up and the few times when she kind of hinted about it, Darius casually changed the subject. This was well and good until it happened.

They had just finished enjoying a picnic lunch she had packed. The red-checkered cloth held the picnic hamper filled with leftovers. He sat comfortably leaning his back against a large oak. She sat contentedly between his legs with her back resting on his chest. The sun was especially generous with its warmth. The sky sported puffy, white clouds. Indeed, except for what she now had to face, it would have been a wonderfully, fantastic day.

"Penny for your thoughts, Lydia?" he asked of her unusual quiet manner.

The timing was right. It was now or never. Mustering up her courage, she sat up and faced him.

"Darius, we love each other, don't' we?" But before he could answer, she blurted it out.

"I'm pregnant."

"What do you mean? How did that happen"? He sounded like this incredulous proclamation held some kind of mystery. It certainly was a cliffhanger.

"I mean," Lydia reiterated, "you and I are going to have a baby. You and I are going to be parents."

Dead silence reigned. Confused, Lydia sadly was unprepared for his icy reaction. Totally devoid of joy, he just sat there grimacing looking every bit like he had just been kicked in the stomach. Drained of its color, his face was the clincher. It said it all. He was painstakingly stunned by the inevitable. Shaking his head in disbelief, he question again, "how did this happen?"

"It happened in the usual way," she answered sarcastically. "What did you expect? We make love just about every day. Didn't you think it was bound to happen sooner or later?"

"Sarcasm doesn't become you, Lydia. And don't treat me like I'm some kind of idiot. I know how it happens. I just thought we had been careful, that's all. Now what are we going to do?"

"The solutions is quite simple, Darius. We'll get married."

"But Lydia, you don't understand. I'm not ready to be a father."

Shivering, she felt there was more behind his reluctance but, even so, his next few words took her by total surprise and betrayal.

"I can't marry you."

Stunned, she thought, this is incredible. His outrageous reaction is so unlike him. He's like a complete stranger. Boldly, fighting back tears, she asked, "You can't or you won't? Which is it and why?"

"My father..."

"Your father? What in blue blazes does he have to do with this? He's not the one who got me pregnant. Remember?" Her biting words were intentional. She wanted them to sting. If she was hurting, why shouldn't he? Still, she wasn't sure her words hit the mark that is, until he made an attempt at clarification.

"Well, he has these plans." As if to justify them, he went on. "He had them for years."

"And they don't include me, right?" she asked adamantly.

He lowered his head in shame. There was nothing he could do. Why didn't she see that? He simply answered, "Right."

"Well, mister, if you think I'm taking this lying down, you have another think coming." Turning on her heel, she started to rapidly pick up the picnic hamper. Stuffing the tablecloth under her arm, she practically threw the readied basket at him.

"You carry this," she demanded, "and we, both of us, are going to pay your father a visit, right now."

If he thought he was stunned before, she just topped it. This was a side of her he had never seen before. She was determined. She was fighting mad. She absolutely planned a rendezvous with his father.

They got into his truck. Starting the engine, she could see he was heading in the wrong direction. Outraged, she yelled, "don't you dare take me home. We are going to pay your father a visit he won't soon forget."

Feeling defeated, he saw no way out of this mess. He simply obeyed her and aimed the truck in the direction of the mansion. He dreaded the forthcoming clash he could already hear in his head. She had absolutely no idea who she was about to deal with and wished he could change her mind. If only he could convince her. With his father, there was no winning. Ever. "At least let me go in first and announce you," he advised.

"Why? So you can give him a heads-up? We go in united. You don't dare tell him I'm pregnant without me. I'm dying to see the expression on his face. And I plan to stay the entire time he tries explaining all this rubbish about your future without me."

She sat there then silently cursing his father, cursing her baby's father and cursing this whole rotten mess. When the three of them finally got together, she saw one man was obviously scared; the other, obviously arrogant.

"Hello Lydia. To what do I owe this honor?"

"I have something to tell you. No, correction. Your son and I have something to tell you. I suggest we sit while we give you the news." He did not appreciate the stern tone of her voice but compiled to her wishes and sat just the same.

"Sounds like you have a problem. Now, what is this front-page news," he asked in a condescending manner, "that has you obviously so riled up?"

Clenching her fists tightly at her side, she could feel the pain of her nails digging into her palms thinking this is going to be tougher than I imagined. Mister, you don't realize how close I am to telling you off but I don't think that would get us anywhere. Besides, there is such a thing as dignity. So I'm just going to tell it like it is. Inhaling deeply, releasing a trembling sigh, she flat-out told him.

"I'm pregnant with your son's child." Out in the open, it produced dead silence. Well, she thought, is this front-page news enough for you? Say something. Oh, what a poker-face. You are good. No telling what you're thinking. Okay, I'll play your game. I'll wait.

"Go on," he finally spoke cool as a cucumber. "What do you plan to do about this delicate situation? Surely, you don't expect Darius to marry?" He didn't end it by saying *you*, but then he didn't have to. His defiant tone communicated that fact loud and clear.

"You see, Lydia, we Mannings' come from a long line of shall we say, blue-bloods?"

"I see. Bottom line, you are saying that I'm not good enough for your family?"

Your rich, sick, phony, social climbing family, she added to herself.

"Good. Then we understand one another. There now, this matter can be settled in other ways, I'm sure."

"Hold on. To answer your question, do I expect Darius to marry me? The answer is yes. Yes, I do expect Darius to marry me. Why wouldn't I? We love each other. He is the father of our child and we want to get married."

While she was fighting for their cause she could not help but hear the loud silence emanating from her lover. Darius said not a word. He just sat with his head down.

I don't believe this. He doesn't even have the guts to look me in the eye. Oh, Darius, what happened to the macho man I love?

"You see, my dear," the man just could not stop antagonizing her, "don't take this personally, it's just destiny."

Like hell it is, she muttered under her breath, as he droned on. "My son's fate is determined and he is not in the position to marry anyone. A wife doesn't fit into the big picture just yet and a baby, well, a baby is totally out."

This is not a good sign. I'm getting nowhere. With that, an absurd notion popped into her head. *Was this confrontation really happening? Or, had she, maybe, seen this scenario played out in a picture show? In which case, right about now in the story line, the screen-players would make their exit.* Panic creeping in, Lydia figured, *I'm out of here* and rose from her chair. Just as quickly, with a mind change, she sat back down. *Darn it. Ma taught me better than this. I'm not a coward. Just like her, I'm a fighter for my rights. This doesn't end here.*

"What you mean, Mr. Manning, is that *I don't fit* into your big picture. *I'm* not good enough."

"If you insist on putting it that way, so be it. Frankly, my dear, no, you are not."

With that hurtful admission, she had to ask just one more question. "If a family is not in line for your precious son, Mr. Manning, just what picture have you painted for him?" She heard the arrogance in her voice and it didn't bother her in the least. *Ma would be proud.*

"Ahem," clearing his throat, Lydia knew she was in for a long dissertation. *No matter. She wasn't going anywhere.* Besides, she had the feeling his next attack would be a dilly and she wasn't about to miss the opportunity to retaliate.

"Ever since Darius was a young man, we knew he was destined for greatness. He is an excellent horseman but that is just a hobby. We did not frivolously pick the name Darius for him. Oh, no. It goes much deeper than that. You see, there is not another Darius in the family tree. No, he is the first and only, because he is the greatest."

"What?" she muttered. *He can't really believe this boloney. What the heck is he talking about, the greatest? The greatest what? Coward?*

"If you know your history, my dear, you will know that it certainly was not by chance that Darius was the chosen name."

Another put down. I'm sure he knows ancient history is not my forte.

Grandstanding, his words came spilling out. "Darius was a celebrated King of Ancient Persia. Courageous, intelligent, he was a great financier and a master at the art of ruling. Why he was king par excellence."

"Really," Lydia countered sarcastically? "And wasn't this the same first-rate king who had Daniel thrown to the lions?"

"Indeed. But, Daniel's disobedience brought that on himself. The king had no choice. He refused to distort the law of the land. He also counted heavily on Daniel's God to save him. If you remember, recorded events reveal just that. God sent angels to fend off the lions. So you see, there again, this was a prime example of a masterful ruler."

When he announced this bit of incredible logic, Lydia could hear the pride in his voice. Thinking about Daniel's cruel fear at the hands of this horrible monster named King Darius, she cringed. But this set the stage. Mr. Manning's determined mindset was sinking in, and she felt herself slipping away to the resigned fact that she could never change or overrule it.

Names, she wondered? Is there truth to their substance? Do they really hold messages dictating future actions? If they do, then I'm glad Lydia is Greek for refined one. The gall of him to say I'm not good enough. If he puts so much stock into names, he should know better.

Still talking, his sharp words suddenly cut deeply into her thoughts and brought her back to the agonizing situation at hand. Like that ruthless king, he, too, went for the kill. Emphasizing his authority, the shrewd man stood up. Intentionally, towering over his seated son, he bluntly asked the imperative, life-changing question.

"All this talk about love, tell me, Darius," He demanded, "do you love Lydia enough to marry her?"

Please, please, please, Darius. Sitting on pins and needles with her fingers crossed, she silently begged. I know you love me but considering the circumstances, I'm almost afraid to hear your reply. Why do you kowtow to him? Don't sit there cowering. Look at me, Darius. Look at me. At least extend me that courtesy.

Finally, he spoke and his quiet answer roared loudly in her ears. Never lifting his head, he simply whispered, "No."

Had he the gumption to look, he would have seen the hurt in her tear-filled eyes. He felt miserable. She felt worse. Crushed, humiliated, browbeaten, Lydia sat there with a broken heart and an unborn child. With one single word, he had disposed of her. Wiped her out of his life; once and for all.

"There you have it." His father, with a sly, sickening smirk, wasted no time. He pounced upon the expected and only acceptable answer. Then for Lydia's sake, he added what he felt were necessary pearls of wisdom in his attempt to smooth over her defeat in this devastating event. He threw her a bone.

"Perhaps it would be helpful for you if you understand why Darius doesn't love you." If looks could kill, Lydia's would have sent him directly to the morgue. Too upset to talk, she sat there listening and thinking about this confusing mess. You selfish, miserable old man, you just had to throw up again the fact that Darius doesn't love me. I heard him say it. That was enough. I'm not deaf. And when do you plan to stop all this, you pompous ass? Obviously, not yet.

Resting his thumbs on the inside of his vest, proudly, he rambled on. "You see, Darius didn't graduate from Yale to..." the rest of his sentence was lost on her. He graduated from Yale? This man who had dirt under his nails and cleaned out stables? He never mentioned it. Oh, Darius, was Yale your choice or your father's? When I fell in love with you, you were one of the stablemen. Oh, how, I wish that had been your only credential. Her heavy heart ached and suddenly, without warning, Ma and all her teachings, popped into her mind again. Lydia felt like such a loser. Right now, Ma, this smart cookie feels terribly dumb. Forgive me. I'll make it better. Now that the die is cast, I know what I have to do, and I won't let you down. This time I rule by my brains; forget about my heart. Don't worry. I'm not letting anybody off the hook. I'm ready for the battle. With that thought, she took a deep breath and laid into the two, cold-bloodied, excuse for men.

"Mr. Manning," she began. "Whether or not you or your son can face the fact, there is no denying it. Children are life's way of celebrating love and Darius and I conceived this child in love. Granted, it was unplanned but the fact remains I am going to have a baby. A baby, by the way, who did not ask to be born." Taking charge, she commanded. "Now here's the deal."

She looked at Darius and all she could see was a spineless, jellyfish of a son who still did not have the guts to look at her. She looked at his father, who on the other hand, was impatient, irritated and chafing at the bit; eager to learn her demands. She let him squirm for a few minutes before lowering the boom.

"The forfeiture for not wanting me or my baby in the Manning family carries a high price. I assure you. It will cost you."

Why you little wench, the father thought. You're in it for the money. I might have known. Okay, girlie, play your hand. You can't hurt us. We are the Manning family, and I have more than enough money to meet any of your unscrupulous demands.

Lydia kept a straight face, masking her true feelings that were simply torn in so many broken directions. "We need to be practical. For obvious reasons, I cannot raise this child alone and Darius has chosen to wash his hands of its very existence. Therefore, we will agree that when I have this child, I must place it in an orphanage. Of course, the entire procedure will be kept under cover. No one will ever know."

You cowards. You rotten cowards, she thought bitterly. Neither of you have voiced an objection to this heartless way out. You make me sick. She returned to her defense. "This arrangement will require money. I will, too. I will need enough to get me through the pregnancy since I will be forced to quit my job before I start showing." Continuing in a business manner, her voice steady and cold, she went on, "additionally, since I am forced to give up my child, then I must be paid handsomely for such a heartbreaking endeavor."

Her eyes cold, she stared at the two men defiantly, daring their disagreement as she emphatically questioned, "Understood?"

Oh, cry me a river girl, Mr. Manning cursed under his breath. Don't celebrate a pity party just yet, you witch. You don't have a heart to encounter your so-called heartbreaking endeavor. It never occurred to him. He was the one calling the pot black. Suck it up, buttercup, he thought harshly while sporting an understanding fake smile.

"Yes. Yes, I understand," he said attempting to calculate just what his son's romp in the hay would cost him, "Go on."

"It goes without saying, I must go away. Therefore," she resumed her business like stature, "I am giving up a lot. I'm forced to give up my job, my home, my way of life and, most importantly, my child. I will have to start anew in another part of the country and all this will take money." Stopping momentarily for the proper effect, she added, "A lot of money."

"Agreed." Mr. Manning voiced aloud, but the words screaming in his head raked her over the coals. Why you miserable, money-sucking leech. Whatever did my son see in you?

She let the knowledge of needing a large sum of money sink in. Then thought, oh, no mister you aren't off the hook yet. I'm not done. Not by a long shot.

"Furthermore," she continued, "in defense of the unborn child, there is another important factor to address." Keeping her wits about her, Lydia gave no indication of her nervousness. No matter her insides were shaking like jello. She spoke out in a clear and steady voice. "This child, being born out of wedlock, will have more than enough adversity to face in life. God forgive us," she said pitifully. "We have already branded this innocent, unfortunate baby." Folding her hands demurely on her lap, her heart pounding loudly, she presented the most meaningful of all her demands. "I must insist that Darius give this baby his name."

"Whoa, wait a minute, young lady." Fuming, the old man could hold his tongue not a second longer and snarled at her in contempt. "You were no saint when this went down and now you think you're Joan of Arc? You Jezebel!" Veins in his forehead bulged and his face went red with rage as he adamantly opposed.

"Money is one thing, but this? This? Never! There is no way a Manning name can be linked to this child. Don't you know there are wolves in sheep's clothing just waiting in hiding to denounce our good name? These vicious people will stop at nothing. If this gets out, Darius will be ruined. I tell you. He won't have a chance."

"He won't have a chance? He won't have a chance?" she questioned loudly in disgust. "What about his baby's chances?"

"Lydia, I appeal to you." Thinking perhaps a sympathetic approach would better manipulate her, he softened his tone. "Don't do this. You don't understand. You see, my son has been groomed for the political world. Someday, he will be governor of this fine state. Then senator and then," Lydia could see the light in his eye actually brighten as he announced, almost with reverence in his voice, "President of these United States."

"Talk about pie-in-the-sky aspirations," she shot him down shouting angrily and rolling her eyes. "What's wrong with you? You are denying this man the status of fatherhood and yourself the joys of being a grandfather for the slim chance that Darius *may* someday accomplish all that *you* want him to." Shaking her head, she added, "how sad and misguided."

Her courage waning, Lydia sat down thinking, no more. I can't fight this any longer. Gently touching her stomach, she whispered, "Sorry, baby. I really tried." Deciding, up against the pigheaded father and the puppet son, she had no choice in the matter. It was too much for her. Resigned, she was about to admit defeat. But words of surrender held captive on the tip of her tongue never escaped. It was his almost inaudible voice that rushed to the rescue.

"Wait Dad, I have an idea."

The mouse speaks. Finally, she thought. Better late than never, okay, let's hear your eleventh-hour offering.

"Let the child have my middle name. Only the three of us will know and the baby doesn't have to carry an extra burden."

He wasn't very convincing. His tone didn't match that of his father's authoritative command but it held a hint, she thought, a slight hint of moxie.

"Absolutely not," Mr. Manning thundered. "Are you crazy? I won't stand for it."

"Now, you listen to me, Dad." Practically jumping to his feet, standing eye to eye to his father, he stood firm in his determination. Not about to back down, his voice louder now, he made himself quite clear.

"I have never bucked you on any decision or direction you made or suggested for me. Never." Spitting out words through clenched teeth, his voice was strong as he told his father, in no uncertain terms, of his decision. "I am giving my middle name to this baby. It's the least I can do."

"But, Darius, be reasonable," he argued. "Think of your future."

"Dad," his tone began to soften as did his courage, "I'm sorry. But it has to be this way."

Tension mounted. Awaiting the outcome, Lydia silently cheering Darius on, felt pangs of anguish for him.

Thrown off guard by his son's unexpected compelling action, Mr. Manning breathed deeply and, with perhaps, just a smidgen of admiration for his son's unwavering stance. Hmmm, he thought, a sign of a good politician. With no true recourse left to him, reluctantly, he acquiesced.

"Agreed." That was all he had to say. But, no, he just couldn't let it be. His had to be the last words. Dumb like a fox, this cunning monster smiled and expounded his shrewd calculation. "At least a middle name would be hard to trace."

You just couldn't resist, could you? Lydia silently accused. You manipulative demon; you make me sick.

Before there could be any chance for a change of mind, Lydia jumped on the stamp of approval announcing clearly, "The baby's last name will be Harden."

Momentarily, the room filled with an eerie silence. Devoid of joy and full of resentment, Lydia's heart was breaking. What a horrible beginning for a baby to come into the world. Forgive me, baby.

Her sorrow would have to wait. Mr. Manning was, once again, in command. Ignoring his son, he simply addressed Lydia. "Okay, Lydia you have my permission to use my son's middle name for your child."

How magnanimous of you, she wanted to scream out. Stealing your own son's thunder, but, she dare not rock the boat. Her eyes focused directly on Darius, she almost voiced it. She almost told him. I feel sorry for you.

Hold your tongue girl, a small voice warned. Wait until you get his check in your hands. Think what you want but, don't say anything to jeopardize your chances.

Realizing Mr. Manning was still talking she turned and caught the tail end of his babbling. It was worth hearing. "Now, let's get down to the business at hand."

Whipping out his leather-bound checkbook and gold pen, he sat down and began writing. He never even looked up at her. Just asked, "How does fifty thousand sound?"

"One hundred and fifty thousand sounds much better."

"Whoa. That's a little steep. Any chance we could compromise, Lydia? I am your friend, you now."

I need your friendship like I need a dose of poison ivy she thought, and answered in a firm tone. "None. None whatsoever."

What could he do? No sense trying to dicker any further. It would be pointless. He was well aware, despite all his grandstanding Lydia had him over a barrel. That's all there was to it.

Lydia, waiting for the check, knew the sum would be enough to get the baby settled and to point her in the direction of whatever the future held. Life, after all, she thought, is a journey not a destination. The sound of the check being ripped from his checkbook was loud. His final act of flaunting his affluence, it was torn out in arrogance with his warning. "We will never speak of this again."

Lydia took the check and headed for the front door ready to walk out of their lives forever. With that, the polite but sheepish, Darius started to stand.

"Don't bother. You don't need to drive me home. It's a nice day and I'd rather walk where the air is fresh." Her darts hit her target.

The day almost over, the business transaction finished, the once wonderful relationship was dissolved as well. Lydia picked up her gait. She needed to reach the comfort of her small home as soon as she could. She so needed to cry. When she got home, cry she did, all night long.

The next morning, bright and early, she headed to the bank. Trusting the man as far as she could throw him and taking no chances, when the bank doors opened, she was the first in line. She made sure the monies were, indeed, credited to her account.

Besides crying, being awake the entire night had provided her with a course of action. First, she put a 'Going Out Of Business' sign on her floral shop. Next, she filled in her regular customers. Very soon, she told them, she had to leave to tend her aging aunt. The time frame would afford her the opportunity to find a small apartment and a doctor. All her ducks in a row, she was ready. She knew thanks to the woman who raised her, she could face whatever was yet to come.

Growing closer to her departure time, Lydia's life became routine. She got up and went to work, tied loose ends at the shop; came home and went to bed. No longer did she walk to the stables. No longer did she enjoy the horses. No longer did she want him near her again. All depressing, only the beauty of her flowers was therapeutic.

Home now, just out of her shower getting ready for bed, she heard it. There it is again. A knock but I'm not expecting anyone. Wonder who… Her curiosity was satisfied within seconds. She answered the door and there he stood.

"Lydia, may I come in? Please?" He sounded pitifully pathetic like a whipped pup. Looking at him standing there, Lydia wasn't ready for her reaction. Gee, how can I feel so angry and yet so pleased to see him at the same time. He still has his father. I still have no one. I'm alone. How dare he show up? But then again, how dare he not?

"Come in," she invited in a monotone. "Have a seat." No warmth just a formality, she made no more attempts at politeness. Not even offering him a drink, she came right to the point. "What do you want, Darius? Why are you here?"

"Lydia, I'm so sorry." His voice quivering, she thought he was about to cry. "Please forgive me for hurting you. I wish I could stand up to my father." His plea so genuine, her heart felt an unexpected twinge. "But I can't. It will never happen. It's hopeless."

"I'm sorry to hear that, Darius. There's no need for forgiveness. I'm grateful you're giving the baby your middle name. As to the rest of it, you did what you felt you had to do. Let's let it go at that, shall we?"

He didn't. He couldn't. "I haven't slept for days thinking about the pain I inflicted on you. That look on your face, so sad, haunts me. Lydia, you know you mean the world to me. I'm truly sorry."

He tried reaching for her hand but she quickly withdrew. No. I won't let this happen, she screamed silently. I dare not let him touch me. I dare not let him know. Despite the heartbreak, darn it, I love him still.

Rejected, he stepped back then reached into his pocket. Handing her a small, red velvet box, he spoke softly with the deepest of feelings.

"Lydia, I can't change what happened. I wish to God I could. You know I have strong feelings for you."

Oh, Darius, she thought, and just when you almost had me convinced. Why? Why did you have to go and ruin it? Strong feelings? You have strong feelings for me? That's the best you can do? It's over, Darius, totally over.

"Open the box, Lydia. I want you to at least have a reminder of me and the wonderful times we shared."

Complying with his wish, she gasped at the sight. The necklace housed in the box was absolutely exquisite. Lydia was speechless.

"May I put it on for you?" Nodding, she turned her back to him to accomplish the deed. "There. Do you like it? I'm so saddened I can't give you my heart. Won't you please accept this amethyst one? Won't you please let it be a reminder of what we had?"

Darn it. The last thing I want to do is cry. But the uninvited tears invaded her eyes and softened her heart as she realized how much she was touched by his thoughtfulness and how much she would miss him. Oh, Darius, she thought, we could have been so happy together. It's not meant to be. But I will carry your heart with me, always.

Admiring the gift, she smiled at him; the first one since he got there.

"Thank you, Darius. It's beautiful and when I wear it, I will think of the love that goes with it and remember our good times together." He hugged her now. Not a heated hug just a loving, warm one and, she returned the same.

"Are you going to be okay?" his concern was genuine.

"I am."

"Will you notify me when the baby is born?"

"No. I can't do that. I promised your father that both my baby and I would be out of your life forever and I never break a promise."

Getting ready to leave, she saw him this broken man and thought, how sorry I am for you and the sad life you are destined to follow. Then quickly pulling herself together, she thought. Let it go, Lydia. What happens; happens.

The visit was over, as was their relationship, forever. She walked him to the door. He kissed her ever so gently on her cheek. So choked up holding back tears, they barely managed to say goodbye.

Chapter 37

1938

It's an old but true cliché. Time does have a way of healing. With each passing day, settled in her new apartment, Lydia found herself thinking more and more about her baby and less and less about her baby's father.

She had thought of everything. Her wedding band from Phillip was back on her ring finger to squelch curiosity and avoid stares and for those bold enough to ask, her husband had recently suffered a fatal heart attack. Yes, she had covered all the bases.

Except for one. Straight out from left field, she hadn't figured on this happening. She was falling in love with this baby, sight unseen. This tiny baby she had to give away. It was early in the morning and Lydia sat in bed reading, or trying to finish the last chapter of her mystery novel. She was interrupted. "Whoa, what was that?" Holding her stomach, she blew out a mouthful of air. "Yikes! There is goes again. For heaven's sake," she delighted in recognition, "You're kicking me." She laughed with a heart filled with love for her active unborn child.

Excited, now, she sat up straighter, and waited in pleasurable anticipation. It was a short wait. She saw it. There right through her nightgown, she could see movement racing from one end to the other.

She watched as the little bump on her stomach traveled in waves across the whole of her stomach. "Why you little imp," she giggled. Then begged, "Do it again." She wondered how the sporadic movement could fill her heart with love. "Come on. Do it again." She waited. Nothing. "Tuckered out, are you? That's okay. If you stay still, maybe, now we both can get a little rest." Picking up her book, her mind no longer on the story, wondered all over the place. "Gee, I wonder, are you a boy or a girl? Is your hair light or dark? I wonder if…? Stop it, Lydia. Stop getting in deeper with someone you know you can't keep. You are going to get hurt in a mighty big way." She thought about that possibility for just a minute and then simply said, "So what else is new?"

Try as she may, each time she pushed out baby thoughts of one kind, others slipped right into their place. Going to the departments store was the worst. No way could she bypass the baby department. Bassinets, cribs, playpens, highchairs, they had it all.

And the dear, little outfits in pinks, blues, yellows and greens. She couldn't resist running her fingers through the softness of the dear garments. Lydia wanted the baby to have some belongings. Each trip to the store resulted in acquiring just one more outfit. Before long, this little one already had a small-scale baby ensemble.

With each and every day, Lydia found herself more and more preoccupied with her Little Dumpling. It was the only name she had used to date. Stumbling upon it, quite by accident, after eating chicken and dumplings that didn't sit well, she tossed and turned all night. The little dough lumps robbing her of rest somehow became associated with her baby. From then on, that was it. Her baby became known as her Little Dumpling. Silly, she knew. But it was fun and endearing, too.

"Okay, Little Dumpling," she rocked on her rocking chair, "this is it." Lydia delved into the book of names she just bought. "Now, don't you worry, you'll always be my Little Dumpling and you forever have a last name. That's for sure. But I've got to give you a conventional name. No Baby X for you. No sir. That's what I heard they call babies who first come in at the orphanage without a name. Baby X, Y or Z. But not you, my Little Dumpling, so help me out. One kick, if you approve. None, if you don't."

Rummaging silently through the hundreds of names, Lydia finally narrowed it down to three names for each gender. "Okay. Here goes. If you are a boy, how do you like the name, Christopher? I'm waiting. No kick. How about Charles? Waiting. Okay, here's your last chance, Thomas? Good grief, Little Dumpling, you don't like any of those? Hmmm. Well, I think I'm going to settle for Thomas. You had your chance. Hope you get use to it."

Giggling, she liked this little game and moved on. "Girls names, now I like these three. Cynthia? I'm waiting. Esther? Still nothing. Here's your last chance. Rebecca? Whoa, back up. Was that a kick? Yes, I do believe I felt you kick. Ever so slightly, but you did kick, just the same, at the mention of the name, Rebecca. So, Little Dumpling, if you turn out to be a girl, Rebecca it is."

* * * * *

The months passed quickly. Lydia was and wasn't ready. While wanting to get the birth over with, at the same time, she did not want the precious time spent with her Little Dumpling to come to an end. She had no choice in the matter. Her nine months were up and, that's all nature allows. In the wee hours of a cold February night, Lydia gave birth to a tiny, pink faced, baby girl.

"Oh, let me see her. Let me see my little girl."

"Here you are, Mrs. Wilson," the nurse handed the blanket-wrapped baby to her mother. "But considering your plans, I don't think this is the least bit wise."

The nurse's words caught Lydia off guard. In all the excitement, she had forgotten that her doctor and the nurse on duty knew the baby was destined for the orphanage.

What do you know Lady? Lydia wanted to scream at her. Instead, she took the small bundle of joy into her arms and welcomed her.

"Hello, Rebecca. Oh, you are even more beautiful than I could ever have imagined. Let me see you." Lydia opened the blanket ever so gently and lovingly touched the dear, little fingers. "One, two, three, four, five. You have them all. And your toes? Let me see. One, two, three, four, five. You have a complete set there, too. Why Rebecca, you have the biggest eyes I've ever seen."

Lydia covered the baby again. "Can't catch a cold, now, can we? Look at you making funny faces. You make me laugh." But she wasn't laughing at her next thought. She's absolutely adorable, funny faces and all, and I have to give her up. I can't. I can't do it.

Her mother instincts were invading her private, practical thoughts. I so love you, precious baby. Now you know that is exactly why I cannot keep you. You will have a much better life without me. Too soon the nurse returned. "I'll take her now, Mrs. Wilson."

"But I just got her. Can't she stay just a little longer?"

"We must do what's best for the child and for you. It's time to let her go, Mrs. Wilson. The papers have all been signed. She will be safe at the Holy Comforter Orphanage. Arrangements are complete. You need only say goodbye."

"But I can't." Lydia cried into her pillow then, and every day thereafter, until she was released from the hospital.

Straight from the hospital, Lydia headed for the orphanage. She had to see for herself before she could finally let go. Her mind raced and filled with what ifs? How saddened and full of regret, she was. Oh, if only he had loved me half as much as his desire to please his father. Well, she told herself, he had not. So the little family, the mother, father and perfect baby girl is never to be. Under the circumstances, giving up Rebecca is best for the child and certainly for the man, I hate to admit, I still love.

At the orphanage, she talked with the kindest of nuns who reassured her of baby Rebecca's comfort.

"Take good care of her, Sister, please."

"I will. All the nuns here will. I promise." This caring woman's voice so gentle, Lydia could not help but feel a close connection with her, a motherly protective bond, of sorts. Relieved, Lydia shared her feelings with the compassionate nun. "I just had to see for myself that Rebecca had arrived and is safe."

"I understand and you can see for yourself. She is safe and, if you ever want to check on her progress, I'll let you in on a secret. We will keep your daughter's school records. You could telephone the main office about your little girl. The records will always be in her file but, we will only be allowed to pass on the information to you for one year. Still, be assured, she will safe and sound." Lydia nodded. Then the kind nun holding Rebecca asked, "Would you like to hold her?"

"Oh, I would. But I better not. Thank you, Sister." Crying, she walked toward the door and just before she let herself out, Lydia turned around. Reaching up, she undid the clasp on her beautiful necklace which she had worn daily since the time he gave it to her. "May I trouble you for a small envelop, Sister, a piece of paper and a pen?"

"Why of course." Opening her desk drawer, she pulled out the requested items. "Will these do?"

"Perfectly." Lydia put the cherished necklace in the envelope. She didn't speak but saved her silent thoughts for her Little Dumpling. This is my way of telling you Rebecca, how much I love you and your father loves you, too. I have no way of letting him know of this act of love but if he should ever find out, I'm sure he would be pleased.

Taking the pen, Lydia wrote what she felt in her heart. Handing the sealed envelope to the nun, she simply asked the nun to kindly follow her instructions.

"Please make sure my daughter gets this on her twelfth birthday."

"I will."

With that, her business here was finished. Kissing the top of dear, little Rebecca's head, Lydia smiled at the nun whose face held deep empathy; opened the door and walked out of her daughter's life.

Chapter 38

1982

She sat quietly, this old woman, Rebecca's mother, with tears in her eyes. What must she have been thinking about for so long a time? Feeling almost like intruders, neither Rebecca nor Lance stirred. They sat there, these three people, each with their own thoughts in untold silence.

Finally, after what seemed like a respectable length of time to him, Lance cleared his throat. "Ahem." It was enough to gain the woman's attention.

In an almost desperate tone, calling her by name, she immediately addressed her daughter. "Rebecca. Your mother and father dearly loved you. You must never, never think otherwise." She said no more.

How can I not, Rebecca wondered after hearing that out of the blue puzzling statement, and turned a deaf ear to the hard to believe comment. Still angry and hurt, Rebecca questioned her mother further. "Didn't you say your Grandmother raised you? Didn't you say when she died you suffered deeply from that separation" The woman nodded in agreement and Rebecca pressed ahead making her point. "Yet, there was no mention of pain when your own parents up and left you and I think I can tell you why. You still had your Grandmother.

You still had family. Well, I wasn't as fortunate. I had no one. I was truly abandoned."

Rebecca saw how her hurtful words were cutting and yet, she couldn't stop, not even if you had wanted to. There were just too many years of pent up words begging to be freed. "You expect me to accept that my parents gave me away in the name of love? And not to any family members, mind you, but to total strangers? Oh, what an odd way of showing me you loved me, all right. You want me to be fine with all this malarkey? It's propaganda! How dare you try to indoctrinate me?"

"Rebecca, calm down. It's okay." Tapping her hand gently, Lance reassured her. "Just tell it like it is but, try not to get so upset. Here, take a sip of coffee."

"Thanks, Lance. I'll try. But it isn't easy." He figured drinking slowly, would help. He was wrong and it didn't take long before Rebecca jumped right back into the fray.

"Well, tell me, *mother*," the sarcasm was not lost on the woman. "Tell me something I don't know. I came here to learn about my parents and their health issues. So far, you told me zilch. I still don't even know my father's name. What is it? It's my right and I demand to know."

Oh, Rebecca, the tired woman thought. You will never know how hard I fought for you. Without me, your last name would have been non-existent. Yes, despite your misguided belief, it was all done out of love. Oh, too many years and, too much water over the dam.

"Rebecca, I cannot tell you very much about your father."

"What? You can't or you won't? Unbelievable?"

"I can't. Please try to understand. You see, it's just that, years ago I made a promise to your father's father that I would never divulge his son's name in connection with his baby to anyone."

"You have got to be kidding." Glaring at the woman, Rebecca couldn't believe her ears. "You could name him in a heartbeat. But you mean to tell me you won't because of some promise you made years ago to a man who was not even my father? This is crazy. Then am I to understand your saying your promise was made to my Grandfather?"

"Yes," Lydia whispered.

"So you're saying that my own Grandfather wanted nothing to do with me either. Wow. What a family. Apparently, all of you are alike; miserable and selfish."

Rebecca's was more upset. "Listen to me. I have every right to know who my father is and as far as promises are concerned, don't worry. You seem to break them willy-nilly. I mean once pregnant, a woman promises to love, protect and raise that child. Obviously, that promise didn't mean a thing to you. So break another. It shouldn't bother you. Frankly, I don't care about your promise. I demand to know. Don't waste any more of our time. Tell me. Who is my father?"

Both women, visually shaken, gave Lance just cause for concern. "Calm down, the both of you please. The interruption and suggestion was just enough to help settle nerves for a short time. "Mrs. Clark, if I may intercede? This information we seek is vital. We really need it. Is there any way at all you could see your way clear to provide it?"

"Well," she nodded, "perhaps, come to think of it maybe there just may be one at that."

"Terrific. That would be how?"

"You understand I'm still not at liberty to give you the name outright. However; since the man to whom I made the promise is dead, I think if I provide you with clues from which you can fill in the gaps, my word would not be broken."

That sounds like stretching it to me, Lance thought, but kept his interpretation to himself. Why take chances? "Whatever it takes, Mrs. Clark," he said, "Rebecca and I would appreciate anything you can share with us, right Rebecca?"

She nodded. She was getting tired and they needed the information. Ironic, she thought. Sure she breaks her daughter's heart and that's okay. But heaven forbid she breaks her word on a promise made to a dead man.

"Well, then," Mrs. Clark offered, "You will be able to surmise much from what I am within my bounds to tell you." Without hesitation, she fed them pertinent pieces of the puzzle. "The man is alive still and is in politics. Actually, this should provide the biggest of clues, he is a well-known Senator."

Hearing that valuable piece of information was all it took. Rejuvenating her sapped energy, Rebecca sat up straight in her chair and immediately asked leading questions, while Lance was all ears.

"A senator? My father is a senator? Really?" Amazement mixed with a touch of skepticism, she repeated the question. "Tell me. Is my father truly a senator?"

"He is. I assure you." The woman answered without hesitation and delighted in the bonus of her daughter's reaction.

"Not in my wildest dreams would I have imagined that." Taking a deep breath, impressed and inspired, Rebecca predicted, "Now we are on the right track," and proceeded to the challenge of filling in the blanks.

"Tell me. Is he from the State of New Jersey?"

"He is."

"He would have to be an older gentleman, right?"

"He would." Again, the woman was quick to answer.

Suddenly, the room grew very quiet. By the look on Rebecca's face, Lance could tell she was onto something big. She lit up like a light bulb when she turned to him to share in her profound conclusion.

"Holy Hannah, Lance, I know who he is."

"Well, no more keeping secrets? Who is he?" Lance was excited and anxious to know, too.

"Think about it. Since one of the senators is only in his mid-forties, it has to be the older one. I think it is safe to say that I even voted for him several times. Don't you see, Lance? My father is the esteemed Senator Darius Harden Manning. There it is. The pieces fit. His name and mine, Harden, are one and the same. Mystery solved. Holy Hannah, can you believe it?"

"Wow! Rebecca. You, the daughter of a senator, well I'll be darned."

"She is. Right?" he quickly double-checked with Mrs. Clark.

Nodding her head in affirmation, she answered, "Indeed, she is."

The woman let the dust settle and never did tell Rebecca the details of her love affair. Some memories are not meant to be shared. From that point on, she simply told her what she deemed important for Rebecca to hear.

"So now, Rebecca, maybe you can understand the reason why your father was forced to agree letting you go to the orphanage. It wasn't that he didn't love you. It was political ambition that stood in the way and mostly, that ambition belonged to his father. You see, he was a dedicated son who just could not let his father down, no matter what. The price he paid for this never-ending allegiance was exceedingly high. I believe, to this day, he pays for it still." Once again, tears filled her eyes as she cleared her throat. It was imperative that what she had to say was absolutely and clearly heard by her daughter.

"Rebecca, you must know that it was he who demanded that you be given his name. Against his father's will and outrage, he stood up for you. His father was a tyrant. You just can't know how hard this was for your father. I truly believe this was the only time he did not let his father browbeat him into submission. He did it for you. Now, granted, he gave you only his middle name, but believe me, considering the circumstances at the time, it was the very best he could do. As I said before, Rebecca, he loved you, too."

Seeing the compassionate look on her mother's face, Rebecca was close to tears. "There is another matter of significant importance you must know about. That, Rebecca, is the lovely necklace I see you are wearing."

Rebecca instinctively reached up and held the heart close. "What about my necklace. It came from you, right?"

"It did. But by way of your father." She told how it came about that Rebecca was now in possession of such a cherished treasure.

The room went silent again only this time it was Lance who interrupted the quiet.

"Mrs. Clark, can you tell us anything about the Senator's health? Does he have other children? Did they all live?"

"How sad a question to ask, but I'm afraid I can't answer. I'm sorry. I stopped following his career when he first was elected Senator. I wanted to remember him as the fine man he was to me and to you, Rebecca, not by his climb up the political ladder backed by his father."

Sitting there piecing the puzzle parts together, Rebecca came to a startling deduction. The unspoken implication was very clear. Her father had never married her mother. She had been born out of wedlock. She didn't have much time to dwell on the subject as Lance was asking more questions. Unfortunately, there was, however, enough time for her to feel the painful sting.

"Your name is Clark now. Tell us," Lance suggested, "How did that come into play?"

"Several years after Rebecca's birth, I met this man by the name of Shawn Clark. Without going into unnecessary details, I will tell you that he was so very kind to me and we married. We never had children and he never knew about Rebecca. No one, other than Rebecca's father, her grandfather and myself, did. It is a well kept secret. Anyway, Shawn had money and I had acquired some of my own by this time. Hopefully, this adequately explains the wealth you see in this house."

Once again, she intentionally, left out a part of the story. She refused to tell Rebecca about the handsome sum she had received on the night of that awful arrangement she had made with Darius's father. It was the night when the destination of the unborn baby was agreed upon. Left to interpretation, what good could Rebecca gain from that knowledge? None. So it went unspoken.

Now, Rebecca thought to herself, our visit comes to an end. As she and Lance slowly gathered up the cups getting ready to take their leave, they were in for one more surprise. The woman stopped them in their tracks.

"Oh, wait a minute. I just remembered. About the health issue, there is one thing that may be helpful." Back in their seats in a flash, she had their undivided attention.

"I don't know why I didn't think of it before. A long time ago in a lost conversation, I recall now, your father mentioning that his Grandparents were lucky in love but not in marriage. When I asked him to explain, he said that his Grandfather dearly wanted a baby boy and his Grandmother did all in her power to accommodate his wishes. So much so, that the poor woman gave birth to thirteen baby boys. I remember now, he said they were all named Harold and that they all died before their first birthday."

Sitting on the edge of her seat, the loud beating of Rebecca's heart almost blocked out the rest of her mother's words.

"There was one healthy baby girl, for which your father was thankful. She, being of course, his mother and that made her your Grandmother on your father's side."

"Bingo." Rebecca almost shouted in her excitement, "Lance, this is it."

"Whoa, whoa, whoa, whoa," Lance put his hand up to halt the bizarre conversation. "Rebecca, before you get too caught up in this revelation, let's give this eye opener a bit of closer scrutiny. I mean, come on, Mrs. Clark." Turning, he looked directly at the woman, "thirteen boys? All dying so young? Tell me. Don't you think this story is a tad far-fetched? Three? Maybe. Even four, I could believe. But thirteen? I have a hard time buying it. How could you possibly not tell us immediately when the question of health issues came up?"

"I think it was shock. Perhaps, you can understand that seeing Rebecca, after all these years was, to say the least, a major jolt. That probably accounts for my not remembering about the boys right off the bat. I was consumed with so many memories that just seeing her brought back to me. Can you understand that?"

"To a degree. But I'm still having trouble believing about the boys."

"What will it take to convince you, young man?" she asked annoyed at having her credibility questioned.

"What have you got?"

"Would it help if I told you that Mrs. Manning, the sole survivor of the fourteen children herself, was the one who filled me in on the details?"

"I'm listening. Go on."

"I don't remember how the subject came up, but it was at a dinner party and I think some of the guests were complimenting the woman on her son's accomplishments. This much I do recall. She was a little flustered as she thanked those at the table. Then proudly, she announced how grateful she was to be alive and to be the mother of such a fine man. That struck me as being odd and confusing. But it was then that she leaned over and briefly told me the background. In fact, I remember her saying that the entire time she carried her child, she prayed and prayed for a healthy baby because she didn't want a repeat of what had happened to her own mother. Valid enough for you, Mr. Miles?"

Stroking his chin, still not totally convinced, Lance had to admit the authenticity of this incredible story was now closer to gaining his green light. It definitely gave him hope. Slowly, he nodded his approval.

"Mrs. Clark, that helps. We need all the pieces of the puzzle we can get. Thanks for sharing the information."

Rebecca sat quietly thinking about the progress that had been made. Grateful for the hope they had been given, she still had a question. Please Lord, let her know the answer to this one and help me to believe in miracles. "One last question, if I may? It's the sixty-four-thousand dollar question?"

"Certainly. What may that be?"

"Did anyone ever discover why all the boys died?"

There was not an immediate answer. Still Rebecca hoped she just needed more time to think. Yes, she thought, that's it. But before she had a chance to relish in the possibility of finding the elusive answer, her hopes were dashed.

Frowning, the woman said, "I don't think so. I'm just not sure. It happened so long ago and your father didn't have all the facts. I'm sorry. I just don't know. But, remember, back in those days it didn't take much for a child to get sick and die."

Rebecca held back and didn't voice the thoughts screaming loudly in her head. Really? All just got sick and died? All thirteen boys?

All dead before their first birthday? Ludicrous, I tell you and totally unacceptable. Sick doesn't cut it! Something killed them, lady. Mark my words. I intend to find out what.

By the look on Rebecca's face, Lance knew it was time to break in. He knew she was about to explode again and this wasn't the time for that indulgence.

"Mrs. Clark, can you remember anything else about Rebecca's father? Anything at all?" he asked, "no matter how insignificant it may seem to you?"

"Let me think." It was becoming clear to Lance that this woman was running out of steam. Yet, she sat there thinking. For her valiant effort, Lance and Rebecca gleaned another piece of fairly substantial information.

"Yes. I don't know if this is helpful or not but he was an excellent horseman and took first place in many shows. Tapping her finger to her forehead, she challenged her brain. "Let me think. Let me think, what else? Oh, yes. I recall that his favorite horse was named Run-Away-Gold. Oh, I don't know if this has any bearing and, you are too young to remember, but his father was the proud owner of the famous Triple Crown winner, Hot Fudge Preacher."

"That's an unusual name. I'm curious. Do you know how that came about?

"I do. Because I asked that same question at the time and I was told the horse's coat was a dark, chocolate brown, except for a ring of white around his neck reminiscent of a preacher's collar."

"Interesting. Any other memories?" Ever hopeful, Lance gave it his last, best shot. Maybe there might be just one more tidbit rattling around in the old woman's mind.

"No," wrinkling her brow she answered honestly, "none that I can share."

The visit was rapidly coming to a close. No doubt about it. They all sensed it. There simply was no more to tell and, at this point, no more to ask.

So, it has come to this, Rebecca thought in sober concentration. My yearning to meet my mother satisfied; my heart is restless still, and I'm kind of back where I started. Even after hearing her life's story, I don't really know this woman, my mother, now, do I?

Mrs. Clark, said goodbye to Lance and then Rebecca. "Rebecca, I'm so glad we finally got together. Now that you know where I live, I hope you won't be a stranger."

Rebecca didn't answer but thought resentfully, how could I not be? That was your choice when you left me so long ago. Too many fences to mend. As to our getting together again, a snowball stands a better chance in hell. Now, it is my turn. My turn to leave you. You'll soon know how that feels. After a cordial farewell, Rebecca did just that. She left.

Chapter 39

~

"Next stop. The Senator's office," Lance announced. Armed with needed ammunition, the couple came away from their informative visit in a state of euphoria. Elated with the positive direction their quest was taking, they felt sure help for Emily was just around the corner.

Their work cut out for them felt less burdensome. They had a concrete route to follow. They could solve this mystery. They could help their precious daughter.

In the car, Lance was the first to talk. "Wow! Rebecca, that was some visit, wasn't it?"

"Sure was."

"You don't sound too convincing. Don't you think we learned a lot?"

"We did. Sorry, Lance, guess the emotion of meeting my mother was more than I figured on. I'm mixed up. Happy that I finally found her and happy for learning as much as we did about her life and happy we now know our next step but I've got to admit, I'm sad, too. No, not exactly sad. Guess it's more that I'm disappointed."

"In what way?"

"Hard to explain. Maybe I just expected too much. I don't know. I mean she wasn't exactly the warm, loving type mother I always believed I had. Forget it, Lance. I'm just feeling sorry for myself. Like I said, my expectations were too high. The main point is, with her help, we are getting closer to our goal."

"I see your point. She certainly didn't come across as warmhearted or exciting. Far from it, in fact, at times, to tell you the truth, she was boring. But, give her the benefit of the doubt. Maybe she was overwhelmed with it all. I mean, think about it. How would you feel if your best-kept secret, suddenly popped up on your doorstep? That's a huge piece of your past returning, not only to haunt you, but threatening to expose you."

"I already know exactly how that feels, Lance, remember? You are right. Still I can't seem to shake it. I'm disappointed. You know, Lance, she never once asked me anything about me. A simple how are you doing would have been nice. Was that too much to ask?"

"No. But maybe, considering the circumstances, it just slipped her mind. It's okay, Rebecca. Maybe the next time she'll be able to get to know you better. At least you know where she is, if you decide you need to talk again."

"That will be the day."

"You never know, Rebecca. Close the door but don't lock it, okay?"

"Okay."

"Now, what say we head home for the night? We'll plan how we go about meeting your father; then head out first thing in the morning. Senator Manning, Rebecca. Can you believe it?" He smiled warmly, "A statesman and a well-loved one at that."

Glad for the change of discussion, Rebecca volunteered her two cents.

"Well, got to admit, he works hard for his constituents. He has to be doing something right. I mean, he serves his six year term and bingo, he gets re-elected. He's been in Congress forever and I even voted for him. Now that's weird. Talk about irony. In all these years not knowing, while I was voting for my Senator; my father was as close as the ballot."

"Yeah, that does take the cake. I voted for him, too. Let's face it, the guy is good." Smirking, Lance teased, "But then look who his daughter is."

"Don't be smart-alecky. Just for that, I'm just going to take your remark as a compliment"

"And well you should," he smiled.

"All kidding aside, Lance, I'm getting excited. I'm about to usher in another new chapter in my life. I can't wait to meet him. How do you think he'll handle my letting the cat out of the bag?"

"Oh, I'm sure it will be a shocker. But he'll be okay with it. We'll find out soon enough." He left her with that up-beat impression and hid his true feelings of concern. Being such an important man, he thought, what if he refuses to acknowledge her at all?

Tired, both welcomed the comfort of their bed. Secure in the knowledge of their plans for tomorrow, both slept rather well, considering.

"He isn't in. Wouldn't you just know it?" Rebecca hung up the phone and delivered both the unwanted message and a wanted cup of coffee to Lance at the breakfast table.

"What do you mean, Rebecca? He's not in his office yet because it's too early or he's not coming in today, period?"

"According to his secretary, the Senator has taken a short respite at his horse farm in Virginia and won't be back for another week or so."

"Good timing, Senator. Darn it all." Lance was more than a bit annoyed. "If we wait for him to return, then my vacation time will be used up."

"Well, maybe I could visit him myself, Lance. What do you think of that idea?"

"Not much. Rebecca, I promised you I'd be by your side every step of the way and I intend to do just that. Besides, I think he holds the key to our problem and I'm as anxious to meet your father as you are now. There's no way that I'm going to be left out of this last leg of the journey. No way. Somewhere along the line, this mission turned into an adventure and I'm not about to miss it. You know me better than that."

"Okay, but how then? You can't get more time off, can you?"

"No, I'm afraid not. I pushed it as it is." Gulping down the last of his coffee, he sat thinking. Within a few minutes, he excitedly announced his solution. "I've got it. If you can't get Mohammad to go to the mountain; bring the mountain to Mohammad. Or something like that, Right?"

"You're talking in riddles, Lance. What on earth are you proposing?"

"Just this, if we can't see the Senator in his DC office, then we'll go see him in his other office. We'll go to his farm in Virginia."

"Can we do that?" Rebecca asked quizzically.

"We can and we will." Pleased with his ingenious idea, Lance spouted out orders to Rebecca in between details of his plan.

"Rebecca, listen. Call his secretary again. Ask if she can arrange a meeting for us with the Senator at his farm. Guaranteed, she'll say no."

"Then why bother, Lance?"

"No, don't despair. Not yet, anyway. You see, Rebecca, that's when you get the big guns out. You let him have it with both barrels. Tell the secretary to give the Senator your very important message."

"And that would be exactly what, Lance?"

"That you must meet with him to talk about a mutual friend, by the name of Lydia."

"Oh, no, Lance. I couldn't do that. He's a Senator and that's hitting below the belt. Besides, after all these years, suppose he has forgotten her. What then?"

"I would be willing to wager a thousand bucks that he remembers Lydia. For God's sake, Rebecca, he got her pregnant. There is no way he could ever forget."

"Okay Lance, we'll try it your way, but I'm still not sure about all this. Wish me luck."

"You got it." Picking up the phone, she exclaimed, "Here goes nothing."

Chapter 40

~

Senator Darius Harden Miles

Off to Virginia. Depending on what part of the state you intend to visit, it's a good seven hour drive from New Jersey to the Old Dominion State. Not taking any chances of being late for their scheduled appointment, they were already on their way.

"Lance, you are a genius."

"No. Well, maybe I am at that," he said flashing Rebecca his biggest of smiles. "Got to admit, I'm pretty pleased with myself. Won't Mr. Senator be surprised when he meets with us? Let me rephrase that. Won't Mr. Hotshot Senator Darius Harden Manning be surprised when he meets daughter Rebecca Harden Miles?"

"More like shocked, Lance and I still can't believe we pulled it off. I mean. Normally, there's a long wait. You really do have a better shot at getting to see your congressman than you do your senator."

"I know. But your call put you at the front of the line. Bet he's never had a call like that before. Let's face it, Rebecca. You dropped a bomb on him."

"I'll say and how right you were, Lance, he didn't forget Lydia. Will we get there in time?" Rebecca asked looking at her watch. "His secretary mentioned that we should be there promptly at 10:00 a.m."

"Yeah, but that's tomorrow morning. We'll be there in plenty of time. In fact, we'll stay at a Ma and Pa motel tonight, get a good night's rest and be ready bright and early. I've checked the map and know exactly where we need to go. Oh, yeah, we'll be there in plenty of time."

"Up and at 'um, sleepy head," Lance leaned down and gently tapped her shoulder and was pleasantly reminded of her softness. "Big day ahead of us."

"Hmmm. Just five minutes more, Lance?" she petitioned in the middle of a big yawn.

Looking at his wife lying there so pretty in her delicate negligee, he whispered, "On second thought, I think you may have something there." For the moment, his thinking changed. He couldn't wrap his mind around the possibilities of today's findings. Right now, he just wanted to wrap himself around her. Gently, he kissed her ear lobe. She stirred. He kissed it again. This time, rolling over in his direction, she responded to his every move. It was a nice way to start the day. Nicer, even, than five extra minutes of sleep.

The morning progressed, as did they and before they knew it, they reached their destination.

"There it is, Lance. Up ahead. See the sign?" Rebecca asked excitedly.

"Yeah, I see it. *The Winner's Circle Farm.* Talk about an interesting choice of names."

"I know. But you have to admit, Lance, it is appropriate, what with the Senator's and his famous father's love for horses, and all."

"Pretty much, except I think they missed the mark on the last word."

"You mean farm, how so?"

"It's a little misleading, I'd say. I mean Rebecca, look at this place. Who would ever pinpoint it to a farm? It's immense. As far as the eye can see, there are acres and acres of pasture land and almost as many horses grazing. That sign would better read, *The Winner's Circle Estate.* What do you think?"

"Explained like that, guess I have to agree. Holy Hannah Lance, he lived on an estate while I grew up in an orphanage?"

"Don't go there, Rebecca. Don't do that to yourself. It's water over the dam."

Pulling up to the entrance gate, Lance gave their names to the gateman who dutifully checked his records. "Go right ahead, Mr. and Mrs. Miles. I see the Senator is expecting you. Just drive up this lane until you come to the main house. Park in the designated guest spaces located in the lot adjacent to the left wing."

Tipping his hat, the courteous gateman wished them both a good day and pressed the button that slowly opened the huge, wrought iron gates. They were in.

"That was a tad bit intimidating, wouldn't you say, Lance?"

"Nah, not for me," he teased. "Haven't you heard? My wife is the Senator's daughter."

Smiling, Rebecca snuggled up next to Lance and laid her head on his shoulder.

"Come on, now. Don't be nervous," he encouraged. "You'll do just fine. Remember, unless you tell me otherwise, I'll be at your side every step of the way. I have no intention of leaving you alone not at any stage of this encounter. Okay?"

"Okay," she said, thinking how glad she was for Lance's reliability. What would I do without him? He has given me his shoulder to lean on, since...forever. She whispered softly, "I love you."

"Me, too. Look over there, Rebecca," Trying to lessen her tension, he pointed, "Aren't those gardens lovely?"

"They are." It only took a minute before she was wrapped up in the beauty of their surroundings. "Lance, there's an arbor of purple wisteria and trumpet creeper vines. Look at all the azaleas. There are so many. I couldn't begin to count them."

"To me they're pretty flowers. But, Rebecca I don't have a clue as to their names. How do you know what they are?"

"My old tried-and-true companion, the library deserves the credit."

Breathlessly, she pointed out the next horticultural wonder. "Oh, over there, look. See all the pink and white dogwoods cleverly dotting the periphery?"

"Sure is terrific landscaping. Look there, Rebecca, old fashioned shrubs."

"That's honeysuckle and I love its heavenly scent." Quickly rolling down her window, Rebecca poked her head out and inhaling deeply savored the sweet aroma. "Hmmm, that's delicious. I just can't get over all these beautiful gardens. There are even lilacs, and verbena, and forsythia. Holy Hannah, the forsythia is everywhere."

"I take it that's the yellow stuff I see growing all over creation?" Lance questioned curiously.

"Right. All the flowerbeds are so colorful. Just like rainbows. What a neat greeting each time you drive in and out. Bet, too, there's an herb garden nearby. It's probably in the back by a vegetable garden. That's where they are usually planted, at least according to my old reliable source."

They parked in the designated lot and walked toward the impressive mansion. It was exactly that; impressive.

"Gee, Rebecca the Senator's place is no more a country farm than is the Taj Mahal. Look, it stands there so stately. It's an old Southern Plantation. That's exactly what this place is. What do you think?"

"I'm with you on that one, and over there, Lance, look at that spectacular view of the mountains."

"Like to take your breath away," he said as together they climbed the many steps leading to the massive oak doors.

Dressed in her black uniform with crisp, white apron, the maid answered the door and invited them in. "Mr. and Mrs. Miles?"

"Yes." Lance confirmed.

"The Senator is expecting you. Come in please. It's this way."

Just walking through the huge lobby on its marble covered floor and down the long, cherry-paneled hall, screamed out wealth. Unbelievable, Rebecca thought. He spends his cushy life surrounded with opulence while I grew up besieged by stark walls and concrete floors. Isn't justice just too grand?

As is so often the case, sarcasm whether spoken or just thought, holds a thimble full or even more, of truth. Wish I could stop this silly rationalization. It's getting me nowhere. Yet, I can't help it. Seeds of resentment spilled into her fruitless way of thinking.

With Lance right by her side, Rebecca entered the Senator's office and her eyes flashed it a quick once over. More grandeur. Well, forget that for now. You have more important fish to fry. For heaven's sake, you are about to meet the man responsible for your existence.

This is it. The moment of truth and now I'm as nervous as a cat. I'm not sure if that's because I'm about to meet my Senator or if it's because I'm about to meet my father. I wonder the odds? Either way, it's nerve-racking.

He stood up, then, this important man in her life and shook Lance's hand.

"Mr. Miles."

"How do you do, Senator Manning?" Turning to Rebecca, he acknowledged her presence with the mention of her name and a nod of his head. She responded in kind, her eyes never leaving his face. No, it's not there. Searching as much as possible, short of downright staring, Rebecca conceded. Darn. It just isn't there. Why, in blue-blazes, am I feeling let down? So I can't find even the slightest of resemblance, so what? Does it matter?

Rebecca's heart raced with awareness. Who am I kidding? It matters a lot. Taking in the bigger picture, suddenly, it hit her like a ton of bricks. I don't recognize this man. Imposter! Who is this fake? Who, indeed, is mocking all those years spent in my mind conjured up as a perfect tall, dark and handsome father? What have you done with my impeccably dressed fashion plate, looking like he just stepped out of Barney's New York? That's the father I've always envisioned. That's the father I told my friends about. Not you. Thief. You look nothing like that man. Give him back. Even allowing for age, I couldn't have been more wrong. Talk about misguided fantasy. Okay. You got me. Am I disappointed? You bet I am. But now what choice do I have? None. I'm forced to accept reality for what it is. Only look at you. You make it so hard. You're even much shorter than I imagined. So much for that thick, blonde, wavy hair you are supposed to sport. For heaven's sake, except for that thin, white, hairline crown growing around your head like Father Juniper's, you are totally bald. That's okay for a monk, but for you? What happened to your model image? Short and dumpy doesn't quite cut it.

Holy Hannah Rebecca, just rip the man's heart out, why don't you? Stop being so cruel. He's still your father. Okay. Now that I've torn him to shreds, let me think if there is anything nice I can say. Like the good nuns always said, look for at least one good quality in a person. Okay. This is the best I can do. He still carries an air of distinction. That should count for something. Oh, yeah. Guess being my father does, too.

"Mrs. Miles," frowning, the Senator spoke up. "You look familiar. Have we met?" That did it. That ended Rebecca's silent character assassination and brought her back to the happenings of the moment. Seems Rebecca wasn't the only one staring.

"Not that I can remember."

"Funny. I could have sworn." Shaking his head, he muttered, "No matter. Now, would you kindly elaborate on your phone message?" Rebecca noting he was all business came straight to the point.

"Senator, our daughter is getting married by year's end and there is a health issue that must be addressed. You see, we lost two baby boys mysteriously without warning or substantial diagnoses. We are in dire need of family health history."

He interrupted her. "Just what does that have to do with me?"

"Everything! You see senator," Rebecca charged, "You are my father."

Totally baffled, surely he had not heard correctly, he questioned. "I'm your what? What did you say?"

"My father. I said you are my father. It's true." Placing her birth certificate on his desk in full view, she insisted, "and here is the proof."

He didn't read it. He didn't even look at it. He stood up outraged. Challenging her declaration, his face went beet red with anger as he loudly voiced his objection.

"You people will go to no ends when it comes to money. You find a rich victim, see dollar signs, and immediately figure out a way to cash in on the wealth. Just last week, in my DC office, a woman came to me with the same claim. I didn't buy into her scam nor do I intend to buy into yours. I am not your father. Please leave before I have you escorted out."

Defending Rebecca and true to his promise, Lance was on his feet and by her side in a flash. "Now just wait a minute, Senator. My wife is telling the truth and I resent your accusation. She is not a fraud. If you would come off your high-and-mighty horse and just read the birth certificate, you will see she is not lying."

Way to go, Lance. Wide-eyed in surprise of Lance's justified outburst, Rebecca cheered silently. You tell that bald-headed, old stuff-shirt.

Lance was hot. Without giving thought as to the office of this man, he quickly yanked the certificate off the senator's desk and practically shoved it into the stunned man's face.

"See, right here," he pointed. "It is written clearly. I assure you this certificate is authentic. The name, Lydia," tapping his finger on the key word, "is right here. Lydia Wright ring a bell?"

Put that way, the senator had no choice but to concede. Picking up the paper and reading the testimonial, Rebecca swore it brought tears to his eyes. Trembling, his shaky hand could barely hold it. Now he knew why this woman sitting in his office looked so familiar. He saw in her the very features of his love of years ago; his Lydia.

Just before he lowered his head, Rebecca caught a glimpse of his doleful eyes. Defeated, the man in his defense muttered, "I never knew of your birth."

Maybe not, Rebecca thought, but then again, ignorance is a difficult defense. I can't feel sorry for you now. You had your chance and turned your back on it. Well, there's no denying this, dear father. Remember this? She unhooked the clasp of the necklace she was wearing and presented it to him; the piece de resistance. Until she called it to his attention, it just had not been noticed.

With a flick of her wrist, she placed her purple gold right smack on the middle of his desk just inches away from his face.

Squinting at the lovely necklace, he could hardly believe his eyes. This mature man of distinguished prominence simply cried. Trembling, he whispered softly, "I gave this to your mother many years ago"

"I know," Rebecca answered, "she told me, and when I turned twelve, she made sure it was given to me."

Appealing to her, he quietly pleaded. "Forgive me?"

"Forgiveness is a gift from God not from me." I have to let it go at that, she thought. There's no other way. Not right now. I'm not ready. Years of harbored anger, resentment and outrage, in just a few minutes time were released, as she lashed out and whipped him with cruel words.

I can't believe the depth of my anger against this man. I didn't attack Mrs. Clark to this degree. But then, my mother at least provided a roof over my head. Granted it belonged to an orphanage, none-the-less, it was a roof. My father, on the other hand simply washed his hands of the whole situation.

Once rationalization kicked in, there was no stopping her condemnation of this man. Like Mount Vesuvius, that catastrophic eruption of centuries ago that buried Pompeii, Rebecca spewed forth her long harbored feelings. With the deep-seated desire of burying her father under the rubble of her destroyed childhood, she hit below the belt. Determined, she was going for the whole nine yards and, in no uncertain terms, she blasted him with a mega piece of her mind.

"Parents are supposed to be the ultimate teachers setting standards for children. Where were you when I needed a model? When you were feasting on delicious and plentiful foods served on silver platters, I was eating leftovers. Yes, the unfinished foods from an earlier meal. They were served on paper plates while I sat on hard, wood benches in an orphanage. You didn't care."

She could feel hot tears welling up in her eyes, all the more reason to keep firing her ammunition. She was very well aware of the reason for her deeply ingrained resentment against this man. In all these years, it had not changed, nor did the pain go away. It was simply his cold logic supporting his ability to just walk away. He misunderstood two essential elements; love and fear, and in his confusion caused Rebecca more heartache than he could have ever imagined.

"You abandoned me and I despise its very meaning. Abandonment hurts beyond words and at this moment, I detest you, too, dear biological father of mine."

That, in essence, her mother was guilty of the same charge, did not, at this moment, enter into the picture. Right now her battle was with him. Her long-awaited verbal assault continued.

"You never even tried to find me. If you think, for one minute, that I owe you thanks for your so-called magnanimous generosity in giving me the use of your middle name, don't hold your breath. You owed me that and so much more." Like syrup running from a maple tree, her criticism was thick and like the claws of a tiger, her attack sharp. "You never married my mother. You know what that makes me with or without the use of your middle name?"

She was yelling now. In a flash, Lance was at her side. "Rebecca, calm down. Come on now, stop." But, the knots of bitterness had taken root. Deeply hurt, resentments grew and there was no turning back.

"No, Lance. I won't. I've waited forty-four years to have my say. I'll not wait a minute more." The unnerved Senator just sat there trying desperately to dodge the bullets. "How could you just walk away?" Rebecca shot at her target. "Why didn't you live up to your responsibility? The truth of the matter, dear father," she said sarcastically, "is that you never cared for Lydia and, certainly, you cared even less for me. Do you know how unloved I felt for years? Think about this gem, dear father. While you stood on your self-serving principles, I stood on concrete floors longing for affection. Unfortunately, some nuns, like you, shoved me aside, too. Hugs were at a premium." Still crying, tears came down like rain and she let them. "You made me feel like I was nobody, and even worse, you made me feel like I didn't deserve to be loved. Funny thing, I could never figure out what I had done wrong?"

Almost, she was finished. Almost her tirade was coming to an end. Just one more jab. "Why didn't you marry my mother?"

Battered from her unexpected verbal assault, the crushed man made a feeble attempt to defend himself. If nothing else, he was compelled to address her questions. It was important that he make her understand. He wanted her to know that all his wealth and his life were not as they appeared. They were not a godsend. No. He had paid dearly and the price was staggering.

He knew now the credibility of her words. Hadn't the necklace alone proved her credentials? Without doubt, this forthright woman, calling a spade a spade, was his daughter. He was guilty as charged. He knew he had, in every sense of the word, abandoned her. Weak-kneed, he slumped down in his chair submerged in emptiness. It was as if she had scooped out his very soul.

His actions had to be explained but he was having trouble finding the right words. He encountered problems with other parts of his body as well. His head and his heart; both ached.

"Mrs. Miles, please try to understand." He almost called her Rebecca but lost his nerve. At least he had the presence of mind to lead off by divulging the most critical of facts pertaining to her existence. "You were conceived in love. Lydia and I loved each other. The problem rested with society. You see," he paused and took a deep breath, "I came from a very wealthy and prestigious family. My father was regarded as a very influential and powerful man." Contempt, not pride, could be heard in his voice. That theirs was a love/hate relationship was not mentioned. "He never let anything or anyone stand in his way. It was always his way or no way and he had monumental plans for me. Unfortunately, Lydia was never a part of them and they were never open to debate."

His explanation was a long time coming and Rebecca sat hanging on his every word.

"I tried to tell my father of our love and desire to marry but he wouldn't hear of it. Finally, he enforced his solution." Hesitating, and from the look on his face, it was plain to see her father was struggling. Rebecca had no idea it was out of concern for her.

Hadn't she suffered enough? How do you tell this person that her own grandfather financed her mother's silence? Bought her out like so much cattle? Yet, he knew she had the right to know. Cautiously in a calm voice, he revealed the pathetic secret he had kept hidden all these years. "When Lydia told him of her pregnancy, he simply bought her off."

That he sat in that same room during the excruciating ordeal for Lydia, and that he denied his love for her to be strong enough to marry were never mentioned. Nor did he elaborate on the fact that he agreed it was in everyone's best interest, if she moved away and put the unborn child in an orphanage. The truth of the matter; he did nothing to buck his father. "My father always aimed high and he wasn't above pulling necessary strings or calling in favors to get me recognition in the world of politics. For as long as I can remember, he told me he wanted to be the father of the President of the United States. He was, without doubt, an aggressive, determined, power-hunger man. I can't really explain it and I don't expect you to fully understand it. Believe me. I had no choice but to be successful for him."

Rebecca blinked away tears. The Senator felt the chill of her cold stare. If eye-daggers could kill, surely, he would be dead on the spot. He hesitated momentarily. It was his mistake. That small window of opportunity let Rebecca come back at him with venom on new charges of wrongdoing. In a matter of seconds, an onslaught of resentful words came charging out.

"First you give me concrete assurance by telling me I was conceived in love. Just as quickly, you pull the plug. Now, would you have me believe that you left my mother and never acknowledged my birth because of your father's ambition for you?"

Guilty on both counts, he could do nothing but nod in affirmation.

"Unbelievable," she said shaking her head, "It boggles my mind. What kind of man are you? Ever hear of a backbone? Even now, you're placing the blame on your father."

"I resent that implication. For years, I have stood up for the good of the people in New Jersey when situations were destined to fail. I came through and fought for them. I have the courage to do whatever it takes."

"For your constituents sure, you're right there Johnny-on-the-spot, but what about for your own daughter? Grasping for straws, are you, Senator? You deceived my mother and you more than cheated me. Look at your clothes, for instance, beautifully tailored and bet they always have been. Want to know what I wore? I'll tell you, anyway. I was a fashion plate in my scruffy, bedraggled, threadbare uniforms. I never even had a new dress until I turned sixteen. Okay, you say you took good care of the people in your district. Commendable, you are a regular crusader rabbit," she just couldn't resist the barb. "But, again I ask, what about me, your daughter? Why didn't I count? I'll tell you why. It's because I stood in the way of your political climb. You heard me right and I deliberately made no mention of your father for sound reason. You were the one, not him, doing the climbing. You know what I think? It's a biggie. I think, while your father liked riding on your coat-tails, you loved sporting the entire outfit."

"Now just a minute. Listen," he tried again, "I will admit that my father was not totally alone in his aspirations for me. His goals were my goals. Only his drive was more ambitious than mine and a scandal would have blown the both of us out of the water. Only my father's ambition and sound head on his shoulders kept it from happening."

"No ambition in the world," she delivered slowly and sarcastically, "justifies breaking another person's heart." Looking him square in the eye, she continued. "God gave you free will. You didn't have to go the route of your father."

"But, but..." he stumbled for words before he found them. "Yes, God gave us free will. But with that free will, comes the burden of making choices. I made the one I thought was best at that time."

"You mean best for you, don't you?" Like I said," repeating to make sure he had gotten it straight, "ambition does not justify breaking hearts. As far as my mother was concerned, I feel sorry for you. Never seeing her for the woman she was and for the wife she could have become. You were climbing up the wrong ladder of success."

Rebecca's mouth went dry. She wished she had at least some water. But refreshments were the last thing on his mind. He never offered. Parched as she was, she wasn't about to stop. Cotton-mouth and all, a barrage of cutting words gushed out.

"You sacrificed the opportunity of having a happy family life and for what?"

Grimacing, as her words hit home, he managed to affirm, "I had to think of my career." Then, rigid in his ways, added, "I still do."

"So by your own admission, that's it in a nut-shell. In other words, you were in a pickle back then with my mother and, now you're in a predicament with me. Face it. You were afraid of Lydia ruining your political life and now you're afraid of me. God forbid we should be the cause of your political demise. But fear not. You're not worth it. Don't worry," she said sarcastically, "your secret is safe with me. Can't risk someone finding out now, can we? Oh, no. No one can know the existence of the illegitimate daughter of this honorable, principled statesman."

He felt lousy. This woman was not about blackmail. No. She was about finding out who her father was, what kind of a man he was, and why he never laid claim to her. She was sincere. She would never expose him. His career was safe and more than ever, he genuinely felt the need to remedy the hurt. He was fully aware it was too late to totally bury the hatchet, but if he could just somehow help her. If he could just take her under his wing; he had to find a way.

"If you need money..." She slashed the air with her hand in three quick movements and advised him to cut it out.

"Don't even think of going there."

"Sorry. Is there anything else I can do?" Ah, Rebecca thought, finally real opportunity knocks and it's about time.

"Yes, there is. Grant us access to your family's medical records."

"Medical records," he asked in puzzlement, "but why?"

"Because we think they hold the key to unlocking the mystery surrounding the death of our sons. Listen. Lydia told us about your grandparents and the account of their losing thirteen sons before their first birthday. Our boys had not yet reached their first birthday, either. So, after much soul-searching, we concluded the problem has to deal with heredity. Of course we don't pretend for one minute to understand very much about genetics. But, as we see it, our only hope is to present records from both sides of the family to the experts in the field."

"Hmmm. I have to admit, other than knowing it is complicated, I'm pretty much genetic illiterate myself. Do you really think this is the route to take?"

"We've exhausted all others. Oh, and there is something else you could do for us."

"And what might that be?"

"We would like you to tell us anything that you may remember about your grandparents' incredible story. It's important that we find out, barring embellishment over the years, its validity. The more pieces of the puzzle we can give the experts, the better."

"I'll do what I can on both scores." The Senator tired from his unexpected and unusual experience, gave them his assurance.

"Thank you, senator," Lance said, "we appreciate any help you can give us."

He stood up now, this distinguished man, an indication of this meeting's end. He looks older than when we first came in, Rebecca thought. It's almost like he actually aged during the course of our visit. That's not possible, is it? I wonder?

"I'll get those records to you just as soon as I can," he assured them. "Oh, and in trying to gather my thoughts, as to the thirteen baby scenario, an idea just occurred to me. A starting point if you will?

Would you like to visit the cemetery in New Jersey where all my young uncles are laid to rest?"

Shocked but pleased with his peace offering of sorts, Rebecca looked at Lance and they answered in one voice.

The senator looked at his calendar to make sure there was an opening. This busy man planned to take them to the cemetery himself. It was agreed. Rebecca and Lance would meet him at the front entrance tomorrow at seven o'clock in the morning.

Driving back down the lane, Rebecca was beside herself. "I can't explain it, Lance. I've got this sudden surge of energy." Clutching her heart she exclaimed, "I feel so alive. Isn't it too wonderful, Lance? I mean the way things are shaping up."

"We really are making progress Rebecca, and no wonder you're excited. Not only did you find both of your parents, you got to talk with them and you set the wheels in motion. I mean, you got this thing moving in the right direction. We're getting closer to answers. Think about it, and tomorrow, the cemetery. Yup, you've come a long way, baby." He reached for her hand and held it tightly. Thoughts of tomorrow's plans left them somewhat unsettled as they headed for the motel, dinner and much needed rest.

As is so often the case, it seems a visit to the cemetery is accompanied by rain. Today was no exception. A slight drizzle fell. It was just enough to be annoying but not enough to stop them. Actually, at this point, not even a monsoon could prevent them from keeping today's appointment.

They rode in style, the senator quite at ease with its familiarity, Rebecca and Lance, on the other hand, less so, but still impressed. It was, after all, their first limo ride. Not only that. They were riding with a dignitary.

As they traveled to Jersey in the comfort of the limo, it was reassuring to know that their, not as comfortable, car was being driven back for them. The Senator provided a driver for that convenience. He wanted, no, he needed this time for them to be together. Yes, he used it to fill in gaps about his dead uncles as best that he could. More importantly to him, he used the time to get better acquainted with his daughter.

The man was far from being a fool. He couldn't let this be a missed opportunity. No. Ever the politician, he could not let it slip through his fingers. Although, except for the very beginning stages of Lydia's pregnancy, he gave little thought to his child. Guilt caught up with him and now tugged pretty darn hard at his heartstrings.

She had hit more than a few chords with her outburst delivered in his office. She was right. He knew it. He had lived the life he wanted for which he paid a terrible price. The cost of his career had been almost too high for even him to pay. He had to do whatever he could now. Most likely, he would never get time like this to spend with her again. He felt the certainty in his aging bones.

She was a beauty so much like his Lydia. He wanted to hear about her struggles. Sure they hurt but, by the same token, reminded him of yesteryear's selfishness. He thought of it as a punishment of sorts, in his quest for much needed forgiveness.

His attaché case was opened and most of its contents were spread out on the limo's built-in working table. It served him well, this office on wheels, especially when the conversation got too close for comfort. Then he could move papers about searching for anything in which he could hide his apprehension.

There among his important documents, Rebecca saw the old treasure almost exactly at the same time the Senator picked it up for her to examine.

"Lance, look," she said patting her husband's knee to share the find, "the family bible. Isn't this exciting?"

"It sure is," and whistled in amazement.

"I thought," the senator allowed nervously, "we could go through the record of family births, deaths, and marriages together. There are some old tin-type photos, too. Granted, these old pieces may not hold all the answers. But maybe they might help clear up or at least shed light on the controversial affliction of those babies." Holding the bible, lovingly fingering the words on its cover, Rebecca thanked this man, her father.

"Senator, you have our deepest appreciation. I can't believe we're actually going thru the bible archives of a real family. My family," she added.

He had started out on this trip feeling like two cents. Seeing Rebecca's face light up when he handed her the bible, upped the ante and bingo. Just like that, he felt like a hundred bucks.

"I love this old-fashioned handwriting but I'm going to need your help to decipher some of it, okay, senator?" she asked.

"I'll do my best. Let's see. The family history goes way back. Where do you want to start?" he sounded upbeat.

"I think," Rebecca answered, "we should start with your grandparents. I certainly want to learn about the rest of the members, but being that time is of utmost importance, maybe we could save their information for later. Of course, if you see an item of interest that may have application to our situation, by all means, go for it."

Pursuing the book for essentials, the Senator soon let out a soft whistle. "I may have something here. Look, information about my grandparents. That would make them your great grandparents."

Taking the book, Rebecca half reading aloud and half silently, learned names and dates. Important but not what she needed, he suggested she keep on reading.

"Ah, right here. Look. It lists the birth of your grandmother's first son and right here, next to it. His name is listed as Harold." Pointing to the writing in the book, Rebecca's voice escalated. "Look here." The more she found, the easier she could be heard.

"Lance look." Stretching his neck, he did the best he could. "Says this Harold died at age nine months. Another entry shows the birth and then the death of a second son, also named Harold."

"Let me see the bible for a minute, okay, Rebecca?" Lance wanted to see for himself just exactly what Rebecca had stumbled on.

"This is proof, Rebecca. I've read the entries of all thirteen sons and according to the dates, none made it past a year old." Shaking his head in uncertainty, he said, "Entries written in this family history section of the good book can't be lies and yet, this reads like something straight out of 'The Twilight Zone'."

"Quick, Lance, tell me. Does it mention how any of them died?"

"Let me see?" Double-checking, it didn't. "No. I'm afraid not, Rebecca."

"Does it say anything at all that might help us?" Rebecca, feeling more and more pangs of skepticism, pleaded.

"Sorry, Rebecca."

"Did you see the tin-type photos?" The Senator interjected the hint of slight encouragement. "Here, let me show you."

"In coffins?" Rebecca asked incredulously, "I can't believe people actually took photos of people in coffins? Why would they do such a morose thing? For God's sake, they are dead. I can't look. It's too weird and upsetting. Check it out for me, would you, Lance?"

"Sure." Checking them out, he hoped his finding would calm her or at least help her be less judgmental. "There are only a few pictures here. Maybe it became too hard for their parents to take any more."

"Now, where does this leave us, Lance? We're no closer to the solution than when we started." Discouraged, Rebecca lost her fight to hold back unwanted tears as they trickled down her cheeks.

Another shock. In the midst of the heartache, her father handed her his handkerchief and then gently put his arm around her. It felt wonderful. My father, Rebecca thought, is holding me and as she leaned into his tenderness, tears flowed and she wasn't sure why. Was she mourning the loss of the small boys or were her tears those of joy in finding her father's compassionate nature? Confused, she wiped her eyes and, until she could figure it out, decided to stay safely nestled in the crux of his caring arm.

It took enormous courage on his part but thank goodness he took the chance. Otherwise, he may have missed out on this euphoric fatherly feeling. It came to him as they rode along. He had not as yet shared his memories.

"Mrs. Miles," he was pleasantly interrupted.

"Feel free to call me Rebecca," she invited from her secure position. He smiled. "Okay. Rebecca, what I am about to tell you, I learned mostly second hand. I remember, as a child hearing people talk. Of course, I am aware of some of the facts. My grandparents lived on a poultry farm in New Jersey. That's where my mother was born and so were her baby brothers."

Rebecca's ears perked up. "You see, Rebecca," he liked saying her name, "my grandfather was a man of no scruples. My grandmother's life with him was, to say the least, difficult. I'm told he was always demanding and held much animosity toward her. He hated her for never giving him a son who lived. He blamed her for their deaths. His hostility ran deep. So deep, apparently, that he didn't give her a penny, forcing her to take in laundry. Week after week, he drank away his paycheck. My grandmother's only joy was her daughter. It was in raising my mother that her sanity was saved."

"How utterly strange and desperately sad," Rebecca commented. Then settled back eager to learn what more the Senator had to offer.

"You see, so many years ago, it was acceptable to believe in the supernatural. Superstition and fear really, went hand in hand. Evil spirits exceeding normal bounds, omens, and the like ruled the thoughts of some of even the best God-fearing people. When the babies started to die, one right after the other, it was rumored a curse hung over the heads of the household. People avoided the occupants like the plague and I understand no tears were shed for either of my grandparents upon their deaths. The townspeople were glad to be rid of the ill-fated family and the curse that went with them."

"That's horrible," Rebecca shuddered with the feeling of repugnance. "What about your poor mother, was she ostracized too?"

"No, Rebecca. She was not because she was young when she lost her parents. Alcoholism took her father first and, then within a few months, her mother died from sheer exhaustion. A distant cousin took my mother in and raised her like her own. Fortunately, that cousin lived in the city far enough away where people were less apt to know or care about the personal business of others."

As hard as she tried, Rebecca couldn't even begin to conceive of such hardships. How could any one person suffer so much? And I thought I had it bad. What my great grandmother endured is beyond comprehension.

Even after all these years, a throwback from her stay in the orphanage, she silently sent up a dart-prayer thanking the Almighty for sparing her grandmother and for getting her through her ordeal. She came close to adding, it was the least *You* could do, but, her Catholic upbringing nixed it almost before it was even a completed thought.

* * * * *

"Here we are. Just around the corner and through that gate," the Senator called their arrival to their attention. The limo driver stopped, pushed a button on the side of the brick wall, drove through the now opened gate and continued down a narrow lane.

The rain had not let up. The Senator provided Rebecca the benefit of a large, protective umbrella while regretting his inability to have provided her with a lifetime of security, minus tumultuous storms.

Walking the short distance to a peaceful area surrounded with large, oak trees, Rebecca thought, how odd the choice. Oak trees that practically live forever dwell in this land of the dead.

She didn't see them until he pointed them out to her. Then almost like a personal discovery, the inevitable presented itself. For sure enough there they were tiny headstones all in a row, almost more than she had bargained for. Nervously, Rebecca could feel every accelerated heartbeat as she fought back her apprehension.

Thirteen, she counted them. Thirteen tiny headstones in a row marking the resting place of thirteen little boys who never grew past the age of one.

Reopened wounds inflict renewed hurt. In a flash, he was at his

Rebecca's side with reassuring support. Turning to him, she whispered, "Oh, Lance, how sad."

"Sshh, Rebecca. Come on. Let the past rest. You can do this. Come on now, let's get a closer look. The Senator stood back and watched them as they approached the stones.

"Lance, look at this. The name on this stone is blurry but, on this one next to it, I can see the name clearly" Etching the letters with her fingers, she could feel the spelling of the name. It read *Harold*. Going from stone to stone, the epitaph remained the same; only the date differed.

"That's amazing, Rebecca. I'm surprised, too, at their size. The stones are smaller than I would have imagined and are in fairly good shape. I suppose being so close to the ground shields them from abusive weather conditions." Counting aloud, Lance was again amazed. "Look Rebecca. There are exactly thirteen of them. If I didn't see this for myself, I would not believe it."

The senator let them have as much time as they needed. He had done all he could as far as guiding them to the rectangular stones in memory of the little lost boys. There were two more gravesites he wanted to show them when they were ready. Although a headstone was no longer standing, he pointed out the gravesite location of the woman who had borne these little boys, and the husband who had suffered the repeated tragic loses, as well.

Leaving now, Rebecca's father reached for her hand. She let him hold it. It felt good that way to both of them. Looking him directly into his eyes, Rebecca extended her gratitude.

"Thank you for all your help, Senator," and immediately thought, idiot. You should have called him Dad.

"You are more than welcome, Rebecca. If there is any other way that I can assist you in your important endeavor, please don't hesitate to contact me. I know a lot of people. Perhaps one of them could provide you with the answers you are seeking."

Wait a dog-gone minute, she thought. Maybe I'm not an idiot, after all. His tone is ice cold. There's no mistaking it. What just happened?

Like night and day. He's all business again and, just when I felt sure he was almost human.

There was no way she could have known. He hid his true feelings too well. Meeting his daughter, seeing the tiny graves and his grandparents' grave all took their toll. Now the shell of this hard business man was shattered and he could not pick up the pieces. He could not mend his biggest mistake and it was tearing him apart.

The entire cemetery scene ripped at his heart and into the depth of his soul. Before today, he had not given much thought to the tragedy endured by his grandparents. Jolted today by the sight of all those tiny graves, shocked his mind into acknowledging the reality of the lifetime of sorrow over which his grandparents had no control. All their sons they wanted so desperately to live; died. And yet, he thought, years later, my daughter lived, and I chose to give her up for dead. The entire heavyhearted plight saddens me. Regrettably, even more so, my self-centered decision of long ago sickens me.

* * * * *

He had seen to their safe return home before heading to his New Jersey office. Just before he departed, without fanfare, he simply handed Rebecca a manila file folder. She didn't have to look into it. She knew. Stunned and, more than pleased, she tucked the highly sought-after health records under her arm for safe-keeping.

Noticing Rebecca was wearing his special necklace, the one she called purple gold, he gently touched the jewel, smiled and simply left. With that single act of endearment, and with mixed emotions, Rebecca feeling deeply moved returned her father's smile.

It was the last time Rebecca was to see her father, the distinguished Senator from New Jersey. For within two months, he was dead. The claim was death by natural causes but then, again, broken hearts don't officially get listed as cause of death.

"Rebecca," Lance spoke gently. "I'm sorry about the senator."

"It's okay, Lance. But thank you." Rebecca said gratefully for his concern as she started to clear the dinner dishes. "Are you finished here?" she asked.

"Yes. Here let me help you and then, what say we have our coffee in the rec room?"

"Sounds good." Putting the leftovers in the refrigerator, she told him of her initial reaction. "I was shocked to hear the news this afternoon. As a matter of fact, the timing was odd. I had just finished writing a letter to the Mayo Clinic and, naturally, I was thinking of the senator. I couldn't believe it. He wasn't all that old. I tried calling you as soon as I heard, but your secretary told me you were in an all day conference."

"You should have had her interrupt."

"It wasn't all that important. I just wanted you to know."

"The announcement caught me by surprise, too. I heard about it on the way home. You know, I kind of liked the old guy."

"Me, too. Wish I could say the same for my mother, though. You know, Lance, they say the people hardest to love are the ones who need it the most. I can't help it. I do feel sorry for her but, I can't go beyond that."

"Well, think about this, Rebecca. One out of two ain't bad. But what do you mean by saying the senator's death was not all that important? You really can't believe that. When he died, people lost a solid, high-ranking official, one of the few good ones left. But you, Rebecca; you lost the most. The opportunity of getting to know him better and how your father might relate to you here and now, died with him. So did his chances of ever rectifying his mistake. You know what I'm saying is true. So what made you say that?"

"It was for my protection," she answered. Then after a brief, reflective silence, she explained. "When it came to my parents, I didn't know which was worse; living in the dark or dying in the light. Then just when he started to help me decide, he died. His death cheated me, again. Now, gone forever is my childhood fantasy of a perfect father and my real one. Of even graver consequence is the demise of hope. The hope

I longed for of my father ever becoming an integral part of my life, vanished. That I will miss."

"I'm sure you will." Taking her by her hand, he repeated his suggestion. "Now, can we please go have our coffee in the rec room? I want you to talk to me, okay?"

"Okay. About what, dare I ask? Lance, you sound so serious."

"I'm not. See?" He wiggled his ears. It was a useless trick accomplished as a young boy. Rebecca giggled. "You're being silly."

"That's okay. It's good to hear you laugh again, Rebecca. Seriously now, I'm concerned about you. You've been through so much lately. Talk to me."

Of course he was right. Like a yoyo, going up and down, indeed, she was vulnerable. Just knowing how much he cared, was a big boost.

"It has been a tough day," she confided, the words catching in her throat.

"I know it has, Rebecca." Pulling her close, he whispered his assurance, "but tomorrow will be better, I know it will."

"You're right, Lance, tomorrow will be better." They sat quietly holding that thought for as long as they could. It wasn't long enough. Memories, happy and sad, flitted through her mind. "It's just that, Lance, I can't seem to really grieve and that makes me feel guilty. Then, I ask myself how can I mourn the loss of someone I never really found in the first place? I'm very confused. I just don't know how I can like and resent my father at the same time and it's doing a job on my nerves."

"I'm sure it is. That's understandable, Rebecca. You have been through a lot. Maybe your confusion is kind of a blessing in disguise. Maybe it's a way of letting you off the hook."

"I'm not sure what you mean by that."

"I mean by liking him on one hand, and resenting him on the other, you don't have to make a commitment either way. You don't have to totally like him or totally resent him at the same time. Let circumstances dictate. Whichever one works in your favor, use it."

"I'm still not getting the point, Lance. What good does this do?"

"Okay, let me explain it this way. Let's say you are having terrific thoughts about your father. Go with them. Don't let the least bit of resentment sneak into your mind and rob you of the happiness you are feeling. By the same token, if you are feeling resentment toward him, then don't let good thoughts in. Allow yourself the anger. Is that clearer now?"

"It is. I get it. It's a clever way to rid me of guilt."

"Right," Lance stressed, "and it prevents you from getting hurt. Give yourself time Rebecca, and don't be so hard on yourself. Trust me."

"I always do Lance. Thanks for standing by me throughout this stormy roller coaster ride."

"No need to thank me. Just hang in there, okay? Now, I wondered if you read the article in this evening's newspaper, per chance?"

"I didn't. What did I miss?"

"It's about your father." Picking up the newspaper, he suggested, "here, let me read this section to you. Okay?"

"Sure." Nodding, she sat back more comfortably on the sofa they shared.

"Oh, and I heard a befitting tribute to the senator's prominent standing. When it was learned that he had died, get this, Rebecca, the newspaper actually held the presses until his story made it to the front page. That really says a lot about the man. Now, listen to this." And Lance began reading the newspaper's account aloud. "*The untimely death of Darius Harden Manning, Senator of New Jersey, deprives the world of a remarkable statesman and eloquent orator.*

His persuasive voice and contagious laughter made him the center of attention in all his travels. His accomplishments for his grateful constituents will always be appreciated. It was recently learned that Senator Manning's party was backing him as their presidential candidate. He would have made an excellent president and one can only wonder the extent of his greatness, in that office, to all his fellow countrymen.

'And then, Rebecca it goes on to list his many accomplishments. I'll save them for you to read later. The point in all this, Rebecca, is that you are right in your way of thinking. You can't grieve for him because he wasn't yours to grieve. He belonged to all his people. He was your father but more so, due to circumstances being what they were, he was your senator. It may be easier for you to mourn him as such."

"You make a good point, Lance. I didn't think of it in that light but, it does make sense. Thanks for letting me lean on you, yet again."

Rolling her eyes, she said, "Seems I'm always leaning on you. Guess I always will."

"Good. Don't ever forget it." He was wearing that impish smirk of his that she so loved.

"Never," and she kissed him gently.

"Ironic, isn't it, Lance?"

"What's that?"

"The senator's ultimate ambition came so close to becoming reality. You know what?"

"What?"

"Had he been in the race, bet he would have taken the blue ribbon."

Sipping her coffee, Rebecca quietly reflected, almost, senator. Almost you made it. Just between you and me, I better understand. You did what you had to do with your life. You made your father proud. Had he lived, he would have been so pleased with your political journey. Now, your death brings an end to your book of life. It's funny how that works. It also closes that chapter of mine. Or so she thought.

* * * * *

Within a few weeks of her father's death, Rebecca the poor, little, orphan girl was destined to become wealthy beyond her wildest dreams and this, compliments of the father, who never really acknowledged her existence.

Upon his return from their joint cemetery trip, the senator had his will changed. He made sure the wording was as it should have always been. He decreed all his worldly goods to be given to his daughter. No matter that the disclosure was not made public. He had friends in high places that saw to the will's validity, and Rebecca's security, and to the confidentially for all involved.

He devoted personal attention to details guaranteeing the provisions of his will to cover essential elements. Regretting any suffering Rebecca may have endured because of him, his thoughts and actions were now solely for her benefit. Rebecca would be more than comfortable for the rest of her life.

Yet, with all his thorough and generous planning, how she wished his will had included just one more declaration. His love. His love for her declared clearly and officially, for all the world to know. Too late. It was never to be, as he was not even at liberty to reveal her name. She knew why. It was inevitable. He always was and always would be his father's obedient son.

Chapter 41

~

Too much to digest, too much yet to do, Rebecca's tired body refused to give in. She had trouble sleeping. Tossing and turning, it just wouldn't happen. Her head full of recent events, like movie reruns, the scenes kept playing over and over. When sleep of sorts did drift in, so did the same scary nightmare.

It was weird, but then that's the nature of nightmares. An evil spirit insisted on haunting her. Tonight was no different. It came accompanied by a sensation of oppressiveness and helplessness. It left poor Rebecca in such a state. Paralyzed, unable to move or fend it off, she was at its mercy.

Suddenly she found herself in that same cold darkened place, on her hands and knees, moving her hands swiftly in circles in the loosened soil of identical, miniature grave sites. Thirteen in all. She searched and searched to no avail. She found only empty graves. There was an old woman standing there who appeared to be wearing a gold neck ornament. A Lover's Knot, dully gold with a double wreath looking so much like braided hair, but it wasn't a Lover's Knot at all. No. A closer look revealed its true identity. It was a purple heart; Rebecca's purple gold and then Rebecca could hear the woman's sad petition. "Help me. Help me save them. Save my babies"… and it was always at this point Rebecca woke up in a cold sweat with her heart racing to beat the band. Thank goodness she also always awakened to Lance's strong, protective arms and reassuring voice.

"Rebecca, sshh. Quiet, now. You're okay. Having that darn nightmare again?"

"Yes. Oh, it is so real. Like I'm right there in the middle of it all, clawing in the dirt and when I awaken, I immediately check my nails half expecting to find dirt under them. Gives me shivers just thinking about it."

"I can imagine." He held her close. "You're fine now. Just lie still and try to relax. You do know this all connects with the mystery you're trying to resolve.'

"Yes," Rebecca agreed, "most likely, it does. But it scares me just the same especially that woman with the desperate look on her face. It's horrible."

"I just bet it does. But you know what I think?"

Anxious to hear his opinion, she asked, "What might that be?"

"You're not afraid of that woman or of helping her; not at all. Rebecca, you are afraid of failure. Your head is full of ideas and ways to best protect Emily. Trouble is you're not sure if any will work. You fear you might let her down. That has you scared to death. That's what I think."

Snuggling closer, she answered. "You know, Lance. I think you might just have something there, at that."

"Listen Rebecca. Here's what I would like for you to do. Put all the creepy images out of your mind. They're called nightmares, right? Well, now you are awake for the day and as far as I know there are no such things as day-mares. Tell you what," getting out of bed, he said in a strong sounding voice, "right now I need to get going for work, as much as I don't want to. But as soon as I get home, I'll help you. I promise. We'll get rid of the haunting dream, one way or another. Just hang in there, until then, okay?"

"Sounds like a plan. I'll do my best."

"In the meantime, why not take the day off? You've been through that health record file your father gave you practically every day since you got it. Give it a rest. Wait until I come home. Well, I better be on my way." Kissing the tip of her nose, he was off to work.

Window shopping is a fun way to take one's mind off of pressing problems. Rebecca pretty much spent the day in leisure, working only in terms of getting meals ready. Before she knew it, Lance had come home, the evening meal was over and now, they sat at the kitchen table working together. Dividing the file her father had given to her both looked for even the most microscopic of clues.

"Hello, what's this?" The hint of excitement in his voice led Rebecca to the note in Lance's hand. "In this small envelope here, see, there's a handwritten message."

"Funny, I didn't see that before. Let me look at it, Lance." Practically yanking it from his hands, she said anxiously, "Give it to me, please."

Her hands shaky, Rebecca removed the contents and read the note to herself. "It's from my father. Lance, maybe in his own way, he did care."

"Rebecca, unless you want me to out and out have a conniption, you better tell me what it says."

"Oh, sorry," she said, and continued to read in silence just the same.

"Rebecca," He was beginning to get annoyed. "I mean in this century."

"Oh, right. Basically," she paraphrased, "he suggests we research the work of a James Watson and a Francis Crick. He writes that these men are geniuses, the Einsteins in the work and world of DNA."

"DNA? Whoa, girl. Hold up. Don't go there. That DNA stuff is so far above the average man. It would take all of Einstein's entire brain for me to comprehend the least little portion about it and at that it still would be really ify. Clear as mud, it's that far out of my league. Who are these guys, anyway? I never even heard of them. That should tell you about the extent of my DNA knowledge."

"I haven't a clue as to who they are either, Lance. Let me see what else my father has to say about them. The note is longer than I thought. Bear with me." Fumbling and mumbling through the long explanation, Rebecca struggled in her effort to reduce it to shorter, more understandable terms. Like I know what I'm talking about, she thought.

"For starters, it says that Crick is British and Watson is American and both are remarkable scientists. Crick is an ex-physicist and Watson a former ornithology student."

"Hold up." Lance made a horizontal slashing motion over his head. "Zoom. That one went right over. What exactly does an ornithology student study?"

"The birds," she chuckled, not at his limited knowledge on the subject, but at his funny reaction. "Ornithology," she enlightened him, "Is the branch of zoology dealing with birds."

"Of course it is," he teased. "Rebecca, how do you know these things? It's like your trivial pursuit memory bank is filled with all kinds of details. You know everything. Bet you could go on a television game show and win us a fortune."

"I wouldn't count on it, especially since I'm reading the information. It's written right here. See?" Smirking, she pointed to the definition.

"Oh, a smart guy, are you? Better watch yourself, young lady." Waggling his finger, he feigned a threat and smiling suggested, "Okay, now that I'm clear on the bird thing what else should I know about those scientists?"

"It says here that together they deciphered, solved and revealed the mysterious secret of life."

"Still clear as mud and it's still making no sense to me. Rebecca, this is supposed to help us how?" His frustration was starting to show. "Exactly what the heck is this DNA that they refer to in the first place? I mean, what is it? Really?"

"I'm not sure, Lance, but don't get upset. Tell you what. Let me try to find out about it. This must be quite relevant or why else would the Senator have included this in an envelope of its own? Wait. There's more written about it. Want to hear?"

"More than ever I do, but just not tonight. This subject is way too deep. It's frying my brain. Listen, it's getting late and tomorrow is Saturday. What say we stop for now and get an early start tomorrow? We'll dig into all this when we are fresh?"

"That works for me, Lance. As anxious as I am to learn more, I have to admit it's mind-boggling and I'm tired. So we'll work on this tomorrow, all day, if need be, okay?"

"You got it."

"You coming?" Lance asked heading to the bedroom

"Just as soon as I put this folder away and turn off the lights."

In bed, he reached for her. Judging from her warm response, he knew she had, for now anyway, successfully tuned out all perplexing scientific deductions. The matter at hand, not requiring rocket scientists, was quite simple, and a lot more fun.

Chapter 42

"Got to admit, Rebecca," he moaned, "It was easier finding your parents, and that wasn't exactly a piece of cake, than it is for me to read through all this scientific jargon. These guys are such brainiacs. Not me. I'm lost."

"Lance, I know what you mean but we can't give up. Not when we're so close to finding an answer. We can find it. I know we can."

"How are we going to do that? You tell me. Then we'll both know." It took a minute before it sunk in. He was being funny.

They had gotten up early with good intentions. Then aware of this day's potential of slipping into yet another hectic day; not rushing breakfast, they sat in the kitchen savoring this quiet time for just a little longer. Recently painted, the room was inviting with the warm sun shining through the window. The walls covered in its shade of apricot, like the sky just before the fading of a brilliant sunset, were striking.

Sounds of sizzling bacon and eggs and the gurgling of freshly brewed coffee filled the room enticing them as they waited for the rewards of a good home cooked breakfast.

"Rebecca, I've been thinking," he washed down a bite of buttered toast with a swig of the hot liquid. "This DNA subject is totally beyond us. We've reached the point where we have to get help. Let's face it. We can't do anymore. It really is time to call in the big guns. We need professionals."

"You're probably right, Lance. It's just that I'm so anxious to get to the bottom of all this. Who knows how long it will take with professionals?"

"A heck of a lot less time than without them," he answered.

"Okay, let me make some phone calls. I'll start with the hospital. They will at least point us in the right direction." Emptying her cup of the last of her coffee, she couldn't resist. Opening the folder, Rebecca found the marker and took up where she had left off the night before.

"Rebecca," he softly chastised, "What are you doing?"

"It's too early for the Hospital Reference Department, so I'm just reading until they open."

"Find anything interesting?" he teased.

"Depends," keeping up with his teasing, she answered, "on your definition of interesting. All kidding aside, Lance, listen just listen, okay?" She didn't wait for his answer. Just went into sharing her find. "Those two scientists I told you about, Crick and Watson, well, according to this report they are accredited with figuring out the structure of deoxyribonucleic acid. I can see you, Lance. Stop rolling your eyes, she warned jokingly. "That's DNA. It seems that structure – a double helix can unzip, so to speak, to make copies of itself"

"Rebecca, please. It's way too early in the morning."

Before you complain, let me read what a helix is. It's interesting. It really is. A helix is any spiral as one lying in a single plane or one moving around a right circular cylinder at a constant angle, just like a screw or bolt thread does. Got it?"

"You have got to be kidding. All I've got is a headache."

"Here," Lance look," she said pointing to the diagram. "This is what it's talking about. Anyway, DNA is responsible for carrying life's hereditary information. It's what genes are made of. Listen to this. It says that just as harmless traits, like curly hair, can run in families, so also can harmful conditions. Genetic diseases can come from heredity or environment or both. "

Pausing with a frown on her face, she thought about the possibility of environment. "Lance, I may be onto something. Remember the senator mentioned his grandparents and their parents before them lived on a poultry farm in New Jersey. I've read somewhere," she gave quiet credit to the library, "that the land on which chickens live for years and years, somehow and sometimes, turn into disease bearing grounds. Maybe there's a connection. What do you think, Lance?"

"Don't know and at this rate, we're never going to find out the cause."

Lance obviously was discouraged and, like ivy covered walls, it was starting to creep into her mind, as well. Her enthusiasm was waning but she knew she had to ignore it. One had to be upbeat.

Patting him on the back, she spoke out maybe more so for her sake than for his. "Keep the faith. We'll find it."

It was his turn to feel badly. He didn't mean to bring her down. It was just so darn confusing. Even the terminology had him stymied. It may as well have been written in Sanskrit. With that Buddhist language, as foreign it was, he figured he had a better shot at it, than at this gibberish. Now for her, he read some of the information and truly tried to digest it. He read about Trisomies and Monosomics terms, described as dealing with chromosomes and multifactorial inheritance, dealing with the many factors that are involved in causing a birth defect. He read the words. He didn't comprehend. He was lost. It just didn't sink in. But he was there for her, just the same.

Chapter 43

~

Not for all the tea in China and the women who served it, would they have stopped looking. At least that's how they felt at the onset of their endeavor. Initially, attacking from all sides, they were raring to go. Now, after all this time of intense investigation, their fact-finding mission was not any closer to its conclusion.

Greedily, they devoured every morsel of information until now, when their full minds could not absorb another tidbit. Like eating ice-cream too fast, they suffered brain freeze.

Rebecca saw it coming. Tracking down her parents required mostly simple leg work. But this scientific matter was a whole new ball game. She knew they just never measured up to this complex leg of the task. How could they? They were just ordinary, worried parents. Genes, DNA, these complicated subjects certainly for them, were mysterious and way over their heads.

They went with Lance's advice now. Seeking professionals, together their trail led them off the beaten track. They traveled both on short junkets and long excursions to accommodate appointments and interviews set up with people in the medical and scientific professions, including geneticists. There was no way, of course, that they could discuss the complicated issues with the experts. Rather, Lance and Rebecca simply met and explained their mission, left copies of medical information, and then went home to nervously await findings.

Sitting in the rec room, at the end of another busy week, Lance was enjoying his wine and cheese snack. Rebecca, on the other hand, just went through the motions. Obviously, in deep thought, she missed what he was saying. He had to call her name twice before he got her attention. She saw the look on his face and she knew. Sipping his wine, he came right out with it. "Rebecca, it's time."

For weeks, she had known it was coming, still she didn't want to hear it. She wanted to cover her ears. Of course, she didn't. It didn't work that way. He talked and she heard him. It was that simple. "It's time to call it quits."

"So soon, Lance?"

"Look, Rebecca, we were not afraid to take the risks of honesty. Now, we can't be afraid to accept the results. We both know we have given this investigation our all. There's nothing more we can do. Why we even checked out that theory about chickens in New Jersey. Remember? You know we didn't find any medical evidence in the local hospitals to support that claim. Please, Rebecca. Don't look at me like that. I feel badly enough." She couldn't help it. She just wasn't sure she was ready to throw in the towel.

"Lance, I keep thinking maybe the next contact will be it."

"I know, Rebecca. But you have to admit, we have been struggling for a long time. Let's be honest. Finding a needle in a hay stack would be easier than our chances of finding this key. There's that look again, Rebecca stop, and please try to understand.

'I'm not saying the genetic problem that cheats baby boys in our family will never be resolved. Someone, somewhere, someday will find the answer. I'm saying that time is not now and is not for us. Do you agree?"

She just looked at this man who had been through just as much misery as she had, and her thoughts ran deep.

"Lance, in my heart, I know you're right. We're on the same page. It's just while my sentiment mirrors yours, our time frames are way out of sync." Gently, she took the wine glass from his hand and placed it next to hers on the coffee table. Holding his hand, she went on. "Lance, it's hard to admit defeat, especially when we're so close to possible success."

"But are we, Rebecca? That's my point and I'm tired." His admission so out of character, startled her.

"What have I done to you Lance? You bolstered me through this ordeal, always my rock and I'm afraid, all I did was sap your energy."

"Rebecca, don't think like that. You haven't done anything. It's just that I feel we've honestly come to the end of the road."

"I hear what you're saying Lance, and you're probably right. I see you are tired. Still, I just can't shake feeling if we give up now, this whole journey will have been a waste of time."

Her words, like a sword, cut him to the quick and immediately found him sitting up straight. "Don't say that, Rebecca." Somewhere from the time he urged quitting, to this moment of her expressed opportunity lost, his stamina returned. "Listen to me, Rebecca. So we floundered along the way but, we gave it our best shot. We can only do so much. Now, we have to let it go and," he added soberly, "The time spent was not wasted. It proved to be invaluable. Look what it did for our relationship. Think about the times, happy and not so happy, that we shared along the way."

Listening to him trying to better justify his point, she felt like crying. He spoke quietly.

"Rebecca, I know this is hard for you. I agree we didn't learn enough to help Emily. But, what we did learn about our sons saved us.

'Remember the doctor's first report? It claimed what happened was just a very rare coincidence. Remember, we both felt responsible. Even so, what did we immediately do? We blamed one another. You have to admit Rebecca, that's exactly what we did."

Nodding, she didn't deny the sad accusation. She couldn't. It was true.

"That dark, intimidating time almost cost us our marriage. Then slowly, as time passed lifting the heavy burden of guilt, our wounds healed, and we were able to get on with our lives. Still, when we learned you were pregnant again, we were scared. We didn't know what to expect. How we struggled with that one. Right up to Emily's first birthday we worried. That nagging fear of a repeat haunted us until after she safely passed the dreaded deadline."

"Lance, I know all that. We got to enjoy Emily and watch her grow from a toddler to a woman. I know, too, that it was in thinking about her future that compelled us to dig deeper. That thinking brought back the tragedy we had long ago put behind us."

"You're right, Rebecca. And that's exactly why we picked up where we left off. Don't you see, the journey we traveled together in search of more concrete answers, was time well spent. It was, among other benefits, therapeutic and our persistence paid off. For Heaven's sake, Rebecca, we managed to get top-notch scientists, experts in their field to analyze our case. We succeeded in tracking down vital clues to help in their studies. Remember what they concluded at the presentation of their findings?"

"Of course I do, Lance. I will never forget. They said it was a genetic flaw."

"Right and remember, too that's all they could tell us. Seriously, Rebecca, think about this. If these major league professionals cannot give us any more, who can? We keep going from one expert to another with the exact same question. No one knows the cause of this flaw."

"Lance, I'm tired, too, but don't you think we have to keep trying?"

"Rebecca. Didn't you hear what I just said? At this point, we're asking the impossible and you know it. We expect the professionals to tell us only what we want to hear. Admit it. We want a guarantee that the entire mysterious, heartbreaking problem will bypass Emily. Who are we kidding? Life doesn't hold guarantees."

The truth was out, and with it Rebecca knew they had come to the end of their quest.

"We have to let it go. But understand this, Rebecca. Just because we personally can go no farther doesn't mean the battle is over. With top-notch scientists working diligently each and every day, who knows what tomorrow holds? Remember the Greek story of Pandora's box?"

She shook her head.

"Pandora wasn't supposed to open that box Zeus gave to her under any circumstances. Remember, Rebecca, it was her curiosity that got the best of her and when she opened the box, all evil escaped and spread over the earth. It had been filled with poverty, crime, despair. Horrified, Pandora quickly shut the lid. She did so just in time to keep in one more item that was on the bottom of the box. Do you remember Rebecca, what that one last item was?"

"Hope," she answered.

"Exactly! And hope is mankind's comfort. It leads to better things. You remember the rest of the story. It's the most important part because Pandora went back and opened the box for one last time. It was a good thing she did. This time when she opened the box, out fluttered hope. And hope is still with us, Rebecca. It triumphs over tragedy. Okay, maybe we don't have the answers to our dilemma. But there's hope. So we ran into obstacles but we knew our search was going to be problematic when we started. It was a long shot; almost an impossible feat.

'We'll put it into God's hands now. That's really where it always belonged. You know what? Our quest held a handful of successes. For starters, Rebecca," he took her hand into his and looked deeply into her misty eyes, "you gained your true identity and you shared it with me."

"Yes. I'm truly pleased that I did. Confession is good for the soul."

"Well, knowing who you are must make you feel liberated."

"Oh, it does, Lance. I'm forever free from that bondage of living a lie."

"There are more successes, too, Rebecca. Not only did you find your mother, but you got to know about her life, as well. Try this one on for size. Rebecca, you got to visit with the woman who loved you enough to give you your prized possession, your purple gold."

"Yes, Lance and she loved it, too. It is a treasure."

"Think about this blessing. You had the opportunity of meeting your father and talking to him face to face in an almost impossible situation. Now, when you think about all these positive happenings, do you still think we've gained nothing for our efforts?"

"No. Lance. I knew all the pieces were there. I just never took time to fit them together. Looking at the full picture, I guess you could say while we didn't finish in first place, we earned a placement ribbon, just the same."

Smiling they were reminded of the senator. "Who knew your father would turn out to be a United States Senator? Not only that, Rebecca, had he lived, he had a good shot at becoming President. How many daughters can make that claim?"

"He was quite a man, wasn't he, Lance?" She savored the feeling of warmth.

"Most of all, Rebecca, he loved you. Both your parents did, each in their own way. For your father to remember you by leaving you everything he had Rebecca, you know he did all that he could to help ease the pain of your past. You have got to be pleased that you were able to share a part of both your parents' lives, if even for just a few days. Memories are to be treasured and hope is for lingering."

"Lance, I love the way you always make my heart smile." Leaning toward him, she kissed him tenderly.

It went quiet now, just the two of them sitting and enjoying this time together.

"Lance, will you help me explain as much as possible to Emily? She has a right to know her ancestors and what her future might hold. But, I don't think I can do it alone."

"And you won't have to. You don't have to do anything alone. We became a pair forever when we joined together in marriage and in the wages of everyday life. Just do me a favor."

"Of course, what's that?"

"Just don't underestimate Emily. I don't think she cares where or who you came from. She loves you for you. As to the future's rough spots, we'll get through them. I promise Rebecca, I'll be at your side every step of the way."

Chapter 44

~

"Emily, calm down. At this rate you'll be a wreck by your wedding day." Mother and daughter were talking on the phone. Emily was calling from the bridal shop to lament her troubles to the one who listened to her the best. Her mother had a knack for taking whatever she was told under advisement then answering after careful consideration. She never came out with a quick answer. She cared too much. With her relaxed mannerisms, she was easy to talk to. She always seemed to know just what to say to make it better. Emily surmised it was a Mom thing.

"Look, darling, don't fret over the headpiece. I'm sure the seamstress can make necessary adjustments. She'll fix it. In fact, tomorrow we can go to the shop together and see how we can get it straightened out. It sounds like a communication problem to me."

"Thanks, Mom. Then there's no sense me staying here any longer. I'm on my way."

"Okay, Emily. See you shortly." The phone call ended simultaneously.

Lance was sitting in front of the television watching a sports program. The last week or so had been tough on both Lance and Rebecca as they actually sat down and kind of mapped out how and what they would reveal to Emily.

Knowing the importance of getting Rebecca to relax, Lance interrupted his TV show.

"Rebecca, listen. It's under control. You've got to lighten up. I could cut the tension in here with a knife. I don't understand why you are so nervous. Relax. It's our daughter we'll be talking to not a stranger."

"That's just it. I think I could manage a stranger a whole lot easier, oh Lance," her voice betrayed her as her words marched out staccato fashion, "how do I tell my daughter that her mother is a fraud? She'll hate me. I just know she will."

"Then you don't know your daughter," he interjected. "Emily is mature and understanding and, above all, she dearly loves you. Like I said before, I don't think she'll care about your past in terms of your background. I really don't. If we have to worry about anything, it will be how she handles the news about the tragedy that befalls baby boys in this family. That's the real challenge."

"Lance, about that, I've been thinking. I know we discussed this issue from top to bottom and decided what course of action we will follow but, forgive me. I'm not sure it's the right way to go and I have yet another idea."

"What idea is that, Rebecca? I mean we covered them all. How can there be any left?"

"There's one we haven't discussed and it is simple enough. Just don't tell Emily any part involving the genetic flaw."

"What? Rebecca, do you realize what you are suggesting? What purpose would that serve and what brought on this sudden change of heart?"

"I've thought of it before from time to time. I just figured as long as we were searching, we would eventually find not only the cause but how to fix it. Now I know we have taken it as far as we can. It's just that I'm not seeing the benefits Emily stands to gain by knowing at this time. I mean it's not like we can change anything and short of not having children, there's nothing she can do, either. Both she and Michael are wrapped up in their wedding plans. What right do we have to shatter their dreams? Throwing a monkey-wrench into them will only cause Emily and Michael both to worry. They would live everyday with a what-if dark shadow hanging over them. I don't see the sense to it."

"I don't know about that Rebecca. I thought the reason we set out searching in the first place was to find the answers to prevent Emily from suffering."

"Exactly, and I don't think telling her will do that. We need to work to that end by taking a different direction. Lately, Lance, this nagging feeling has consumed my every thought. I'm tormented. I keep wondering what gives any of us the right to play God? When you come down to it; it really is not up to us to decide who gets to live or die. I can't shake it, Lance, I feel we should hold off telling her."

"You threw me a curve, Rebecca. I'll have to give it thought. I'm not totally sure I'm comfortable with going this way."

"Okay. Lance, how about this idea? We hold off telling her now but, not forever. If down the road, unforeseen circumstances warrant it, then we tell her the full story."

Their serious conversation that begged for a serious consideration was interrupted by a sunny voice yelling into the room.

"I'm home."

Effervescent, bubbly Emily and her special way about her that made everyone cheerful, had arrived. Whatever the bridal shop problem, it seemed to have dissipated.

"We're in here." Lance switched off the television and greeted his daughter with one of his bear hugs. Emily finally managed her release and gave her mother a kiss on the cheek. "Sorry about that panicky phone call, Mom. That woman in the shop gave me a scare. Turns out she had ordered the wrong headpiece. It's straightened out now so you won't have to go there tomorrow. But, you should have seen it. I swear, Mom, it was this big." Creating a large circle with her hands, she insisted. "It was the size of a dinner plate. It was so big that it slid over my head and, around my neck. Okay, stop smiling Mom. I tell you it wasn't funny."

"I'm sure it wasn't dear." Still smiling, she gave Emily a hug. Now, before we eat would you mind calling Michael to invite him over for dessert? Your father and I would like to talk to the both of you."

"Sure. I'll be glad to call him but what's this all about, wedding secrets?" She giggled her little girl giggle that so endeared her to her parents. Rebecca only smiled and thought oh, if only it was that easy.

Obviously planning this evening for days, Rebecca went all out. Her table was set beautifully with a floral center piece arrangement of pink and white carnations. The good china and silver made their elegant appearance as well.

Taking in its loveliness, Emily whistled and then yelled out, "Wow, this has got to be something big, all right."

Rebecca's plan to set a nice table and serve Emily's favorites was not meant as a precursor to a fantastic evening. Rather it was meant as an appeasement. A kind of peace-offering if you will, for the shocking and maybe destructive unveiling of the family Rebecca was soon to introduce. Her real family

In his usual upbeat way, Lance encouraged pleasant conversation. "So, tell us, young lady, how are the wedding plans coming along?" "Great, Dad, just great. Michael's parents have most of the seating arrangement completed for their side of the family. Now all we have to do is go over our side."

Rebecca felt chilled just hearing Emily's choice of words. Our side, she questioned silently? But, Emily dear, I don't have one. You mean your father's family, too, but I can't help feeling so left out in the cold.

"Okay," Lance quipped, "Just so I get to sit at the head table with all the action."

"No worries there, Dad. It's an automatic," Emily shot back.

Rebecca appreciated their teasing. If ever there was a time she needed humorous banter, it was now. Patting his full stomach, his mark of approval of the delicious food, he pushed his chair back from the table.

"No more. I can't eat another bite. Rebecca, you have outdone yourself. Boy, you cooked all my favorites."

"Mine, too," Emily chimed in. "Guess like father, like daughter or something like that?" Chuckling, she turned to compliment the cook. "That lemon chicken was to die for, absolutely perfect, Mom."

"To say nothing of the creamy, mashed potatoes, green bean salad and hot rolls," Lance added his two cents.

"Enough already," Rebecca laughed. "It's just dinner. It's not a Can-You-Top-This game? I'm glad you both enjoyed it. Now, let's clear the table and get dessert ready. Michael should be here shortly."

The pumpkin pie with whipped cream and hot coffee sat on the sideboard waiting to serve those who had room to indulge. His timing was perfect. The doorbell rang and there stood Michael, smiling and anxious to spend time with the love of his life, and her family, since tonight she came with the package.

"Hi, Michael," Emily greeted him at the door and they shared butterfly kisses. Anything with more energy would have to wait until they were alone.

"Come in my boy," Lance invited. "Sit here on the sofa with Emily."

"Hello, Mr. and Mrs. Miles, thanks for inviting me for dessert. I think it's the best part of the meal."

"Of course you would," Emily teased. "But I have to tell you Michael, this time you may just be right. Mom, your meal is a feast fit for a king, but your pies are to die for. Michael, the grand finale is her pumpkin pie served warm. Wait until you taste it."

Knowing full-well the significance, but not yet the consequence, of bringing her valid autobiography to light, which was exactly what she was about to do, their frivolous chit-chat was now annoying. Serving dessert slowly, Rebecca dragging her feet, delayed the inevitable for as long as she could. When Lance wiped the last smidgen of whipped cream from his lips, she knew. Everyone had finished eating and it was time to wipe her slate clean. No more stalling.

"Emily, Michael." Her tone so serious immediately erased Emily's smile and even Michael flinched a little. It gained her their undivided attention. It also gave Emily quite a start. Apprehensive now, she anticipated the worst.

"Mom, what is it? Are you or Dad sick?"

"Oh, no, dear, we are both fine. It's just that I have some important information to share with you and it's long overdue." Quiet invaded the household. Only the ticking of the living room clock could be heard, and maybe the loud heartbeat of the young, ill-at-ease couple, now straining their ears to listen intently.

"I won't keep you in suspense. I'm just going to tell it like it is and I'll answer any questions you may have, as best as I can, Okay? There's a lot to cover so I ask you to make allowances for any rambling."

"Okay, Mom. But now you're really making me nervous. What is this all about?"

"In the simplest of terms, Emily, I have a confession to make." Releasing a long, trembling sigh, determined to make amends, Rebecca began. "Emily, this is about your grandparents on my side. It is simple, really. They just never existed or at least the ones that I painted for you did not." Seeing the confused expressions, Rebecca decided a condensed version would speed up her awaited explanation for the young, anxious listeners. Details could be filled in later. "There was no war hero and my mother did not die from cancer. The truth of the matter is that, as a child, I didn't even know my parents."

Rebecca was grateful for the coffee Lance handed her. She had not asked for it. He knew her like an open book. Just with those few spoken words, she already was at the mercy of cotton-mouth. A few swallows of the hot liquid provided just enough needed lubrication to liberate her stuck words, making it easier to continue.

"You see, Emily, I was born out of wedlock and was quickly relegated to an orphanage." There, dear daughter, she thought, you have it. I have bared my soul. I have declared myself fraudulent. Pausing now, Rebecca waited for Emily to say something; anything. But Emily, wearing a perplexed express, just sat in silence. Well, Rebecca thought, since she hasn't fallen off her chair, maybe so far so good? Maybe not, and I better go on with my story before I turn chicken. "Raised by nuns, I lived there for sixteen years at which time I was transferred to a private home to help with the housework and the couple's young daughter. It was the closest thing I had to knowing home life and to call that place home was a far stretch. At least, I got to shed my uniform and attend public school. The very best outcome of that transition was at that high school I met your father."

As her nerves calmed, her voice steadied and words flowed like a swift running brook. "You know my life-long friends, Annette, Annmarie and Theresa, the ones who always send such pretty Christmas cards with catch-up notes, well their friendships were not formed in high school as you were led to believe. I grew up with them. They, too, were orphans."

Like a giant wheel, Emily's mind gyrated in circles with a series of just learned circumstances reacting one upon the other. She thought to herself, wheels of progress always demand a price. Most times it's worth it; sometimes not, and wondered the cost to her mother.

"The medals, Mom," she could sit quiet no longer, "what about all Pop-Pop's medals? I remember you even telling me the names of the actual campaigns where he earned them. What about them? They sounded so real?"

"Emily, those medals did exist. They were real. They belonged to a true hero who earned them for service above and beyond the call of duty in World War II. I stole his credentials from a library book and smuggled his list of accomplishments to be memorized and used to my advantage." Now dear daughter, she thought. Your mother has just conceded to being both a liar and a thief. Some role model! Please don't hate me.

"What about Mom-Mom," Emily questioned, "she wasn't real either?"

"No. She wasn't."

"I'm having trouble with this, Mom. Mom-Mom wasn't real?" she repeated. "What about all those nights when I was a little girl and we prayed together for her at bedtime? In fact, if memory serves me right, we prayed for both sets of grandparents. If they didn't exist, who exactly did we pray for? Gosh Mom, some nights I even fell asleep dreaming of this man in uniform just covered with shiny medals. I told my friends all about him and his bravery. Really, Mom, I don't understand. You actually lied to me. Why? How could you?"

There it is, Rebecca conceded, Emily's first accusation. It cut to the quick. Actually, both women were in pain. The daughter stung from learning the serious flaws of the mother. The mother hurt from losing the innocent trust of the daughter.

As is the case in most young daughter/mother relationships, mothers can do no wrong. Of course as age takes over, so does logic. The daughter sees Mom for what she is; human with human frailties. But there still tends to be a place for at least a partial halo. Again, with the daughter's continuing maturity, so also comes common sense. No one is perfect. But much pleasure is derived from the daughter's thinking that maybe, just maybe, her Mom is close.

There was no missing Emily's pained expression. Rebecca, stung by her conscience, sadly surmised; and to think, I didn't want her to suffer. Now, I am about to make it worse. For as difficult as this information is for Emily to digest, I know the next page from my diary of life can only inflict more torment.

Maybe Emily sensed it. "Mom, why did you wait all these years to tell me about your past? I loved your made up parents. Why didn't you just leave it at that? I mean, really, what good or need is there in revealing all this family history now?"

Why indeed? Rebecca came close to shouting it out. Love! Love is the first and foremost reason. Silently, she check-marked more reasons. Because I'm running out of time; because I must clear up this family mess to save you from lurking unknown despair; because I must clean my heart of its many years of lies. Rebecca didn't reveal her reasons but tucked them away in her mind to be explained when the time was right.

"Michael, would you mind switching places with me? I'd like to sit next to Emily."

"No, not at all, Mrs. Miles," he was only too willing to get out of the line of fire. As far as he was concerned, he had fallen into the middle of some mighty private issues. Ready or not, all this nitty-gritty, nuts and bolts type principles were now imbedded in his mind, too.

She took hold of her daughter's hand and held it tightly. "Emily, you have a right to know your true heritage. I was wrong in making you wait so long to introduce you to your real family. I'm sorry. I can't reverse my actions. But, I can and I will make sure you know the truth, and it starts now." More than a little confused, Emily sat listening with her heart as much as with her ears. "You are aware that I have no siblings. What you don't know is you have a grandmother who is very much alive. She is healthy and wealthy in her own right. Your grandfather, however, is deceased. He was a colorful man, Emily and this may come as a shock to you. It did me. Your grandfather was the well-loved Senator from New Jersey."

As a mental portrait emerged, astonished, Emily's jaw dropped open and her eyes grew as big as saucers. Skeptical, she dared to question. "For real? You don't mean Senator Manning. Do you?"

Rebecca acknowledged proudly, "One and the same. Gospel truth." She waited a moment to let this verifiable claim sink in before sharing the unfulfilled, yet exciting, prediction. "Not only that, Emily, he was most likely on his way to the presidency." This news was easy to share. Smiling, no, beaming with pride, Rebecca added. "That's a pretty good pedigree for the daughter of this orphan girl wouldn't you say?"

"Gosh, Mom, it's a great deal more than pretty good. It's fantastic."

Emily's mind was going round in circles. First to learn of the ins and outs of her family and now, to top it off that she was related to a Senator. It didn't take long and once the realization of that fact sunk in, she felt a little giddy and a whole lot proud.

Rebecca glanced over at Lance and in that split second she knew. His slight smile endorsed his answer. She knew he was in agreement with her. Now was not the time to discuss the boys. Allowing Emily time to revel in her newly found genealogy, was enough for now. Rebecca ended her confession. She just sat quietly delighting in Emily's arms tightly wrapped around her.

"I love you Mom, with or without real parents, forever."

Lance winked at his Rebecca still in Emily's embrace. She smiled and mouthed words of endearment to which he promptly gave two thumbs up.

Chapter 45

⌒

Emily and Liz

E mily loved her job and her fifth grade students. She had landed this position straight out of college. Teaching elementary social studies, her classroom decorations held a reflection of her enthusiasm.

Framed portraits of U.S. Presidents hung around the perimeter of the room as if ever vigilant over the young statesmen of tomorrow. These men had set the foundation. The future of the country was temporarily stored in the minds and hearts of these young Americans sitting in her classroom. Like sponges, they absorbed the teaching imparted; like vessels filled with knowledge to be poured out at a later date.

Flags, pennants, and banners, quiet representations of country pride gave credence to the precious quality of freedom. Banners waved of freedom of speech. Pennants reeked of liberty so often interchangeable with freedom.

Emily's interest and eagerness spilled into every nook and cranny. She taught with a passion. How lucky her students. If all teachers embraced their responsibility with only half of her enthusiasm, absenteeism would be at an all time low.

The last class dismissed, Emily filled her attaché case with papers to be graded tonight in the quiet of her living room. Work always found a way home with Emily. Teaching was, after all, at least a twelve hour position, at least in Emily's eyes. How some, not all, but there were those few of her peers, got away with doing so little, bothered her. Not from the standpoint of less work for them; more for her, but from the point of view students did not come first. In that respect, Emily felt students were being cheated.

Once home, she was grateful for leftovers from last night's baked chicken. Now it was easy. She simply prepared a light meal of a chicken salad, rolls and a cold glass of lemonade, followed by a few chocolate chip cookies which her mother had baked for her.

The food eaten, she headed for the desk and settled with the task at hand of correcting homework papers and grading recently administered tests. She was pleased. The excellent results on the students work added credence to her theory. It was simple enough. Just make learning fun, and the kids would be eager to learn.

In the middle of her thoughts, the phone rang. It was her friend and co-educator. Liz had always been in total agreement with Emily's teaching technique. In fact, she applied it to her class of third graders in the school district where she worked.

"Hello, Emily. How are you?"

"Okay and you?"

"Well, with the exception of boredom which is slowly consuming me, I'm fine. Would you believe my schedule is clear from all homework? How rare a phenomenon is that?"

"Yet, Liz, the free time kind of holds you captive," she giggled, "think about it. Listen. Why don't you come over, help me finish the little paperwork I have left to do and then we'll watch a movie or go for ice-cream or something. How's that sound?"

"Less boring by the minute. I knew I could count on you, Emily. I'm on my way but oh, what about Michael? I don't want to disrupt his plans."

"Don't worry. You won't. He's on a two day seminar and won't be back until late tomorrow night. So, get your body over here, okay?"

"You bet. Bye."

Emily missed Michael. She didn't enjoy being alone for any extended period of time and now she looked forward to her best friend's company. Like two peas in a pod, she and Liz would make excellent use of that gift of time and their gift of gab. It was nice having Liz live so close by.

"Well, that didn't take long. Come in Liz."

"So, where are the papers we need to correct?"

"You correct them, Liz and I'll grade them." It was only fair considering the responsibility of grading rested squarely on the shoulders of the teacher in charge. Liz agreed with Emily's ethics.

"Got any snacks?" Liz could never be accused of being bashful.

"Grab a lemonade, and some cookies. I'm working in here." Emily walked over to the desk. Liz, her hands filled with lemonade and cookies, followed close behind. Together, they finished sooner than expected. All papers present and accounted for were neatly tucked back into the safety of Emily's attaché case ready to leave with her in the morning. Now the time belonged to them.

"It's countdown to ice-cream time, don't you think so?" Liz asked.

"Sure. Then how about we come back and break out the Scrabble game?"

"Sounds like a plan." Emily, reminded of the many hours spent in their college dorm placing the lettered tiles in an order to produce legitimate words, and then the time spent negotiating their validity, smiled.

Tonight, with the exception of one element, the game's fixings were the same. It started out with the usual frivolity but that something missing was Emily's bubbly chatter.

"Emily, you're really quiet. What's up?"

"Nothing. I'm just not in a talkative mood."

"Or is it," Liz teased, "Because you can't stand to see me enter this three point letter score? Read it and weep, my quiet friend."

"Can't fool you, can I, Liz? You got me."

"In a cat's eye, I got you. Emily, I've known you forever and there is something definitely bothering you. Now, spit it out."

"Honestly, Liz, sometimes you can be as tactful as a sledge hammer. Okay. It's just that my Mother told me about some pretty serious family news. Secrets, really and I was unprepared. Now, I can't seem to shake the residue. A part of me is fine with it and part keeps consuming the leftovers. Maybe I'm just a glutton for punishment. I don't know."

Liz pushed the game aside. "Emily, talk to me. Maybe we can get to the bottom of what's bothering you."

"It's a long story. Besides Liz, you're never going to believe it. I'm still trying to convince myself."

"Try me," Liz persistently urged.

"Okay. But don't blame me when you hear how ludicrous this sounds. Here goes. Seems my grandparents on my Mother's side never existed. My Mother was an orphan and concocted the entire story about her youth. Slapping together all these pieces, apparently from articles she read in the library. My Mom made it all up. In fact, my real grandmother is still alive somewhere and you will never, in a hundred years, believe this." Taking a deep breath, Emily announced, "my grandfather is the late Senator Darius Harden Manning of New Jersey."

"You mean the one who died just as he was getting ready to be a presidential candidate?"

"One and the same."

"Wow! Color me impressed." Liz was all ears. "This gets better and better."

"Not for me, it doesn't," Emily interjected.

"Sorry. Go on."

"Well, Mom told me this last week and I think, I really think that I'm okay with it. I mean I love my Mother. Since the pretend grandparents were supposedly dead when I was yet a child, I don't miss them. Guess the idea of belonging is what initiated this whole plot. Anyway, Mom is Mom and I dearly love her."

"So Mrs. M. was an orphan." Liz took a second to let that bit of shocking news sink in. "Wow! How about that? At least she was honest with you. You have to admire her that. It probably took a lot of courage on her part. But, question? Why did she bother to tell you now? I mean after all those years."

"I asked the same question. I think, Liz, hearing about the Senator's death may have precipitated it. It made the headline news and the TV never let up. You know what the media's like. They went on and on all about his life and accomplishments. That's what triggered it, I think."

"Sounds plausible. Now, Emily, you say you're okay with it. So, what's the hang-up? Other than having this famous person sitting in your family tree, what's the big deal? I don't understand Emily." Emily could see from the perplexed look on Liz's face, she most assuredly did not.

"It's Michael."

"Doesn't he know?"

"Of course, he does. Honestly, sometimes Liz you can be so exasperating."

"Look, Emily, I'm trying to understand so I can help you. You don't have to snap my head off. I'm on your side, you know."

"Sorry, Liz, I really am. Believe me I'm glad you're my friend. It's just I'm on edge and I don't know what to do. Yes, Michael knows the story. That's just it. I don't know if I'm reading too much into this, but ever since he found out, he's been awfully quiet. He has not been himself. Now, I'm thinking, Liz, maybe this fake background is more than he can handle. I mean, it's one thing for me to accept this lie, but to throw it on him and his family, this late in the game, it's quite another."

"Listen, Emily. Do you hear yourself? You're not making sense. No one is asking you to accept a lie. That's over with. It's not a fake background that is being passed around. It's the real McCoy. It's the truth that is being handed out and, I might add, it's a mighty impressive one, at that."

"I hope you are right. Jeez, Liz, at one point I even considered calling off the wedding. You know Michael's much too nice a guy to hurt my feelings. So he wouldn't do it, even if he wanted to and I don't want him to feel trapped."

"Oh, no you don't Missy." Liz's eyes got as big as saucers. "That would be absolutely asinine. How selfish of you to even think that way? Besides, I already paid for my gown." Her last remark brought a smile to Emily's serious face. It was good while it lasted, but gone in a wink.

"What about children, Liz?"

"What about them? Other than I don't see any here yet?"

"I mean, do I tell them about all their grandparents, real and pretend or what?"

"Gee. Talk about putting the cart before the horse. How about getting married first? Besides, how much sleep do you think your kids will lose over this? Probably, all they'll ever want will be grandparents who smother them with kisses and candy. And as to their, hmmm, let me think, great grandparents? I somehow don't think they will be at the top of their priority list, either. Come on, Emily, you're just stressed out. Lighten up. Anyway, why not just get married and see what happens from there."

"You're probably right, Liz."

With a twinkle in her eye, Liz couldn't resist and added, "I've another solution."

"And that would be?"

"Forego the kids."

That one earned Liz a friendly punch to her arm. Smiling, Emily said, "Why Liz, you are nothing more than an imp. Now, girl for heaven's sake, let's go for a walk. The fresh air will do us both good."

Liz put her arm around Emily's shoulder and out the door they went.

Chapter 46

~

Emily and Michael

E mily was more than pleased with Michael's return. She needed
him just as much as he did her. They went out for dinner and
the ambience of a nice restaurant. Their budget did not permit
this luxury on a regular basis. Tonight was special. He shared his
excitement from the seminar. They ate expensive food and they laughed.
It felt good. Neither brought up the shadow that hung over them. It
wasn't the time or the place.

Back at her apartment, Emily sat on the couch and patted the seat next
to her. He didn't need the invitation twice and in a flash was sitting as close
to her as he could. He inhaled the sweet smell of her. Her hair, her perfume,
all intoxicating and he realized how much he loved her all over again.

"Penny?" he questioned with hopes the shadow wouldn't invade this
pleasant moment.

Reaching for his hand, Emily smiled. "I was just remembering the
time you proposed." Her voice sailed dreamily over waves of quiet and
loudness.

"Boy, I remember, too," he said. "I was scared. I didn't want you to
turn me down but you really didn't have a reason to accept me. I mean,
I'm a far cry from what you deserve."

"Michael Brian Wendell, don't' you dare talk like that. Don't you put yourself down. Ever." Her delivery was adamant.

"Okay, okay," he was both surprised and pleased.

"Anyway, Michael, I can still see that priceless look on your face."

"Yours, too, when you agreed." Laughing, they savored the memory, and topped it with a gentle kiss.

"Our wedding is going to be great. Jeez, Emily, I don't mind telling you, I'm a bit nervous. In fact, butterflies have set up house in the pit of my stomach. I can't get them to leave."

"Maybe you should up their rent."

"Oh, cute, Emily. Cute," and tickled her. She couldn't stop laughing.

"Truce, truce," she begged amid the giggling. "I'm nervous, too, you ninny. You know what? We need to get out our wedding plan book again." She was up like a shot racing to the book's location.

"Oh, no. Not that. Now, you're plain being a glutton for punishment not to mention a pain in my neck." Michael rubbed his neck feigning hardship.

"Come on. Don't be a curmudgeon," laughing she said, "Let's see how much more we have to do to get this show on the road."

"Grrrr," he responded; then teased, "You know a tub of Rocky Road would go good right about now."

"Rocky Road. Ha, ha, funny mister. For your information, this wedding is a smooth drive ahead. No rocks or even pebbles along the way, Got it?"

"Guess there goes the ice-cream." Then placating her, he agreed. "I got it."

Settling down to the serious business at hand, Michael took the floor. "Seems to me, Emily that we have done a lot, are we near the end?"

"We are, Michael."

"Whew!" Relieved, slowly and deliberately he wiped his forehead with the back of his hand.

"The seating chart seems to be the one spot that needs help. Michael, how about if you ask your parents to get cracking on where they want us to seat the last of their friends and relatives. They can't have too much more to do considering they were almost done last week. What's the hold-up? I mean, my parents' side is done." She couldn't resist adding, "Of course, it doesn't take long to seat relatives when you barely have any. Right, Michael?"

"Emily, stop it. Let it go. That kind of talk doesn't help anybody. All it really does is tear you apart. Come on, now. Look, I'll ask my folks to meet with us this weekend and I'll tell them their seating arrangements must be complete by then. You know what else?"

"What, Michael?"

"We need to put this book away. We need to talk. I mean seriously. We need to talk about what we know is bothering the both of us. We can't keep hiding our heads in the sand. Time is marching on and we had better get in step." Closing the book, he placed it on the table and then took her hands into his.

"Michael, look. We don't have answers. That subject only seems to pull at our heartstrings and we always wind up just as confused as when we started."

"We have to try anyway. Remember, Emily, if our love is being tested, we can't fail on that score."

She melted. How many times had she thanked her lucky stars for this special man who was always there for her? His shoulders board, and strong enough for him to stand on his own; were just as big for her, if needed.

They were good for each other, this young soon to marry couple. Not always in agreement, they had their share of loud discussions. Both accomplished in their education and careers, both were ready for the next step; marriage and all its trimmings.

Michael often thought of his good fortune. Emily was the person with whom he wanted to share the rest of his life. Attracted to her from the first time they met, she excited him without even trying. Never trying to change him or mold him into someone else, it seemed she loved him just the way he was. Michael knew he wasn't perfect but, with Emily, perfection was never a prerequisite. They were perfect for each other and that's what counted. They had a problem to resolve and without benefit of a crystal ball.

"Michael, I can only imagine how hard my Mother's curve ball hit you, especially since it practically knocked me out. Ever since learning the news, the both of us are guilty of sweeping it, and our feelings, under the rug. If you say it's time to talk, then that's what we'll do. Be brutally honest. I'm asking you straight out. Does this situation change our plans? Michael, do you still want to marry me?"

"Emily, of course, I do. But, being brutally honest, I'll admit at first I wasn't totally sure. I had a few doubts. Don't get me wrong. My love for you was never in question. It was my initial reaction and inability to deal with reality and, frankly, it was prejudiced."

"You lost me, Michael. Explain please."

"Okay, think about this. You know what a stickler I am for principle, right?"

"I'm with you."

"How I believe the foundation of any relationship is based on honesty."

"I know you do, and I agree."

"You see, Emily, I still believe that, but I got blindsided; caught off guard. My focus went directly to your Mother's dishonesty only."

"It caught us both off guard."

"Right, Emily. But what I didn't see at first was as plain as the nose on your face."

"What exactly was that, Michael?"

"That we were thinking too much about your Mother in terms of being dishonest, when all our thinking should have revolved around her honesty. I mean, we have to give credit where credit is due. It was tough for her to open up."

"You know Michael, you are right. We owe her that."

"I have to tell you too Emily," he smiled, "I kind of like the idea of being related to a famous person."

"Sshh..That's not for broadcasting."

"Like people would believe me, right?" he said confidently.

Chapter 47

The wedding day arrived. It was May 3, 1983, and before long, Emily was to become Mrs. Michael Brian Wendell. Together, she and Michael were soon to become one in heart, soul, and purpose.

Father Miller stood at the main altar facing the congregation and awaited the wedding party's entrance. He would officiate at the solemn Nuptial Mass with Fathers Ryan and Davis assisting.

Members of the church choir had filled the church with memorable strains of Ave Maria, and the majestic Lord's Prayer. Paschabel's Canon, Emily's very favorite, was soon to be presented by the accomplished organist on the magnificent hundred-year-old, solid brass pipe organ. The congregation awaited the harmony.

Every detail, from the placement of the huge, white, pew bows to the placement of the miniature reception hall mints, was in order, as this wedding promised to be the social event of the year.

Rebecca and Lance had dedicated their time and talent; her deceased father, his money. For his generosity, Rebecca was truly grateful to the man. Without doubt, it helped to make this wedding a picture-perfect, memorable, celebration. It was, after all, for his granddaughter. Rebecca truly felt that had he the opportunity of meeting precious Emily, he would be in total agreement that she was most deserving.

Emily had spent the night before in her old room at her parents' house. Logistically, it was the best plan. Both the rehearsal and rehearsal dinner had gone well. Now it was time to close up shop. Emily needed sleep. She would head straight for bed just after a soothing hot bath. Her bath water drawn, Emily let the bubbles cling to her body savoring the warmness of the water that helped calm her nerves. She sat still and studied the many tiny bubbles that were beginning to disappear. Soon they were none. They tempted her to analyze life by breaking it down to components as she plugged in the pieces.

Was life like this? Beginning with warmth and surrounding you with happiness which eventually dissipates leaving you cold? Shuddering, Emily physically felt chilled now as she watched the last of the bubbles ebb down the drain.

She dried herself with a soft comforting towel and slipped into her satin pajamas, fully aware of her stomach flutters. Boy, this getting married is a big deal, she thought.

At least her mother didn't nag her to eat a bedtime snack. Thank goodness for the precepts of the church. Dictating strict fast from midnight until the time of receiving communion, Emily's poor stomach wasn't threatened by too much food.

Then finally, despite pre-wedding jitters, Emily was able to sleep. It wasn't for long. Before she knew it, morning arrived and the weather was kind. The day was perfect for a wedding.

"Let's do it, Liz." The bride announced in a shaky voice.

"You got it. But Oh, Emily, first may I say, as your official maid of honor, you look absolutely divine." Liz was sincere in her assessment.

"Thanks, Liz. And as the official bride, may I say, you look terrific, too?"

In keeping with their easy-going friendship, despite butterflies, their bantering continued.

"You may. May I say, I agree? I like this pastel pink gown and get a load of this matching bolero jacket." She spun around for effect. "Good choice. But, tell me, do you think wearing a circle of daisies on my head is a tad too much? I mean, really?"

"Nah. As the one who picked it out for you, I must say it looks good and so does the matching daisy nosegay, too." The room grew quiet and Emily grew serious. "Liz, thanks for always being here for me. I know I don't tell you often enough, but I sincerely appreciate all you do."

"No need to thank me. It's my pleasure. Besides, it's a two-way street. What are friends for?"

Being careful not to wrinkle lovely materials, the forever-friend's hug that seized the moment then sent them on their way, was brief.

Emily saw the trip to the church as a blur. She simply arrived. Once there, standing in its vestibule, reality set in and it became clear. This was it.

Here we ago, she said to herself, thinking the music, that's our cue. And as Wagner's Wedding March began, the wedding party processed down the aisle.

All eyes focused on the absolutely radiant bride. Her lovely short sleeve gown, with a full ballroom skirt, had a detachable cathedral train just perfect for dancing later at the reception. The empire bodice was embroidered with lace, beads and sequins and it featured a jewel neckline. For elegance, the back had twenty-two bridal buttons.

Liz was quick to attest to the number as those tiny buttons took her forever to fasten. The back of the gown was also adorned with a large rosette bow and two long streamers, one on each side of it.

Emily's headpiece, that was now a perfect fit, was a circle of miniature pink, roses with an attached finger length veil. She carried a cascade bouquet of miniature pink roses mixed with white bridal wreath entwined with satin ribbon. But the focal point, the main stage of attraction rested at her neck.

Just before heading out to the church, helping Emily with the finishing touches, her mother had an important mission.

"Emily, you are the most beautiful bride in the world."

"Thank you, Mom," she whispered, "I love you." Both held back the tears so close to being shed.

"I have something to give you." Rebecca opened the velvet lined box.

"Oh, Mom. It's your purple gold. I couldn't. It means too much to you."

"But you Emily, you, mean more." Gulping back tears, Rebecca fastened the clasp of her prized possession on Emily and whispered, "A treasure for a treasure."

Looking into the mirror both women could clearly see, not only its shinning brilliance, but, more importantly, the reflection of love that filled the room.

As is the case in weddings, all the hours and months spent planning rush by in a flash. Emily and Michael's wedding was no different. There were no flaws. No funny stories to be laughed at years later. Everything went off without a hitch, but before Emily and Michael knew it, their perfect day had come to an end. It was time to head out on their honeymoon. It was time to head out in their married life. It was time to head out into the world.

Chapter 48

1989

"It soon will be Emily and Michael's sixth anniversary, can you believe it, Lance?"

Rebecca turned the pages, again. The wedding album, covered in leather with their names engraved in thin gold writing, had been a gift to the parents from the bride and groom years ago.

"It is hard to believe and if you don't stop that, you'll wear the pages out."

"Oh, Lance," she smiled. "What a gift this turned out to be." Like a cricket, Rebecca jumped from place to place. First she was looking and talking about some activity in the album. Next, she was talking about what might be an appropriate anniversary gift. Lance smiled. He knew her so well and almost envied her ability to handle more than one thing at a time. Obviously, when that blessing of multi-tasking was handed out, he had been passed-over.

He was pleased then, when Rebecca settled into talking about her friends of long ago whose group picture just popped up in the album as a reminder. It was easier following her when he knew what direction she was taking.

"Wasn't it wonderful that my old friends Annette, Theresa and Annmarie made it? That was one of the most precious highlights for me. When I invited them, I had no idea that they would travel so far to attend."

Staring out in space remembering the happy time, she sighed, "Wasn't it great?" Caught up in reminiscing, she wasn't expecting an answer and went right on talking. "Theresa and Andy flew in from Florida. Annmarie from Arizona, and Annette and Allen came all the way from California. Isn't it funny and terrific how both Theresa and Annette married Andy and Allen, and all were sweethearts at the orphanage? That was so long ago and here, after all those years, they're still together. It was so good seeing Annmarie again. Too bad her husband had to attend the policeman's conference. None of us have met him, but knowing Annmarie, her pick would surely be a winner."

Rebecca turned the page in the album and was treated to a photo that featured the guests dancing at the reception. It included a terrific shot of her friends.

"Lance, did you see the dance steps on that Andy? When he and Theresa danced the polka, everybody cleared the dance floor for them. Boy, Theresa matched Andy's steps to a tee. Then everybody clapped, even the bride and groom, remember?"

"I do. They did make a great dance team, Rebecca, and I'm really glad for you that you finally decided to invite your old friends. I was especially proud of you when you asked them back to the house after the reception and told them about your true identity. Every one of them embraced you. Obviously, they never cared who hung from the branches of your family tree."

"That didn't matter to them, did it?"

"Nope. But Rebecca, I have to admit they were impressed with the Senator. But then, who wouldn't be?"

She smiled and moved on. "You noticed that didn't last very long. They had so many tales to exchange about their lives and kids. It was like we never parted ways. It reminded me of long ago and the hours we spent talking and talking before lights out. They all looked good too; older but good."

"None of us are getting younger, Rebecca. That's just par for the course."

"Guess so." But she was not about to let a cloud sneak in and rain on her parade. "You know the best part, Lance?" Not waiting for an answer, she revealed her opinion. "Now that they know where we live, they plan to visit at least once a year. Of course, we'll never stop writing, either. Isn't that great?"

Lance just nodded. He knew she wasn't expecting an answer. He knew she was just caught up in her own excitement.

Chapter 49

〜

"Hurry," Emily encouraged. "It's almost time for the party. In fact, Michael, I think our folks are at the door now." Sure enough, it was the doorbell Emily heard. When Michael opened the door, he was greeted by the four eager grandparents.

"Hello, Michael, and where is our birthday boy? Where is that grandson of ours?" Rebecca asked excitedly.

"He was here a minute ago. Tommy," he yelled, "where are you? Grandma and Grandpa are here and so are Gram and Gramps. Come on out."

"Oh, let him be," Lance said, "we'll find him. In fact, if my ears don't deceive me, I think I already have."

"Michael, you didn't. And Emily, you let him?"

"Oh, no, I'm not guilty, Mother Wendell. He did that on his own. Can you imagine? Who gives their three-year-old son a drum set for his birthday?"

"Got to admit, Emily," Michael announced facetiously, "you always know where he is."

"Well, come in, everybody," Emily invited. "Just cover your ears. I promise I'll try to divert his attention ASAP."

"Thanks, dear," Rebecca shouted. "I'll help."

"Ooh, that's so much better. Listen."

"To what, Dad?" Michael asked, "I don't hear anything."

"My point, exactly, son," and he slapped his knee in amusement.

Chuckling, Emily reminded the guests of the impending changing of the guard.

"Enjoy it while you can. Jimmy will be up from his nap in two shakes of a lamb's tail and Joey will be close behind."

"Oh, my aching head," Lance holding his head, feigned a headache.

"Emily you and Michael weren't kidding when you said you wanted six kids, were you?"

"Nope. Not at all, Dad. Just think we only have three more to go."

"Michael, I think Jimmy is up. Would you please get him?"

"Let me help." Rebecca asked and was up on her way before there was an answer.

"Me, too," Michael's Mother declared. "I'm not missing out on this fun."

"Well, guess that leaves you grandfathers to give me a hand with the party. I think Emily wants all the presents to go in the wagon. It's a gift from me and Emily."

"That's a nice sized wagon, son. I remember getting one like that for you when you were about Tommy's age. Remember?"

"Sure do. I had some fun with that thing. I think if memory serves me right, I ran it into the ground."

"We'll, I'll say this. You got my money's worth out of that present. Bet Tommy does the same. Wait and see. Speaking of the little guy, here he is now."

"Hurry, get the camera, Michael. Get candid shots." Emily was almost as excited as the guest of honor.

"Light the candles, Mommy," Tommy begged.

Isn't he something?" Michael's Mom pointed out, "making sure everybody gets to join in the party? I thought surely he would run to his presents first."

"Oh," Emily smiled, "you thought he was practicing good etiquette on his own? Had you fooled! I told him that he couldn't open his presents until everybody had a piece of cake. Otherwise, none of us would get to eat."

"Emily, that's sneaky; clever, but sneaky."

"I had a good teacher, Dad." she said laughing.

"Okay, then, but Tommy gets the first piece. I bet you love chocolate cake, don't you, Tommy?"

Tommy just nodded his approval and it didn't take long until the boy was a chocolate mess and loving every morsel and minute of it. Wiped clean, he anxiously opened his birthday presents. His excitement was contagious and before long Tommy and his brothers and all the grown-ups, too, were on the floor sharing in the fun time.

"Looks like Macy's toy department in here, and you want three more?" Lance asked his daughter. "Unbelievable?"

Tommy, like the wind-up toys, was winding down. Emily recognized the signs. It was time for his nap.

"If you'll excuse us, everybody, I'm going to put this birthday boy to bed. If he doesn't get his sleep, he's a bear."

"Like his father?" Michael's mother quipped.

"Now wait just a doggone minute," Michael protested, "I'm no bear."

"Well, maybe not now but when you were little, you…"

"Whoa. Hold up, Mom," he teased, "telling tales out of school isn't fair."

Michael took Tommy from Emily's arms. "Here, I'll carry him. He's getting too big and heavy."

"First," both grandmothers commanded, "kisses all around."

✳ ✳ ✳ ✳ ✳

The party long since over; calling it a day, Lance and Rebecca were getting ready for bed. Her make-up removed, Rebecca sat at her dressing table finishing up with her nightly ritual. His routine, of course being far less involved, didn't take half as long. Already finished, he headed for bed. Attracted by her beauty, he was pleasantly waylaid.

Conscientiously brushing her hair; keeping track of the number of strokes applied, at first, she didn't see him. Then, suddenly his reflection appeared in her mirror and there he was standing behind her. Unable to resist, he swooped down, wrapped his arms around her and pressed his cheek against hers, savoring its softness. Gently he rocked side to side. Facing her in the mirror, he said grinning, "well, Grandma that was some party. Look at you. You're a Grandmother of three and still pretty as a picture."

"You're not wearing your glasses again," She gave him a little squeeze. "Furthermore," feeling a tad risqué, with a twinkle in her eye, she went on.

"Just look at you. You're a Grandpa of those same three and still a handsome flirt. Only now, you're better than ever." That said, she flashed a wink and a smile.

"Why Grandma, you make me blush. But they do say, the older you are, the better you get."

"That may well be true. But right now, this old Grandma is going to bed. I'm tired. Honestly, Lance. Those boys wore me out. I swear I don't know how Emily does it? But doesn't she just radiate? Her world revolves around those boys."

"You're right on the mark on that score. Now, come here, Rebecca." Fluffing up her pillow, he invited, "come cuddle close to me."

"Okay. I'll be there in a minute." And she was.

"There that's better now, isn't it Rebecca? You know I can't sleep without you right next to me."

"Me, too. Works both ways, you know." She assured him and they enjoyed the quiet of the night until Rebecca mentioned her predicament. "You know something Lance, as tired as my body is; my mind won't quit. All these scenarios keep popping in and out of my mind. I'm having trouble getting to sleep." Listening, he waited. But without another word, she went quiet.

"Come here," he suggested. Gently pulling her even closer, until it appeared they were hooked at the hip. "Now, tell me. Why all of a sudden so pensive? What's on your mind?" He sincerely wanted to know, thinking maybe if she opened up, then she could sleep. In fact, then they both could.

"Oh, I was just thinking about Emily and Michael and how a parent's job is never done."

"It's most certainly true in their case. Three boys keep them stepping. But you know, Rebecca, they both love kids. Want to bet they do wind up with six?"

"Oh, no, Mr., I'm not betting on a sure thing in your favor."

"So, thinking about dealing with maybe six grandkids running around, is why you can't sleep?" he asked trying to pinpoint the puzzler.

"Of course not, it's just that," Rebecca paused. Then in all seriousness asked, "Don't you ever wonder about what a bizarre and ironic turn of events our lives have taken? I mean, who could have ever guessed the way things turned out? Until I confessed to you, all my life I worried sick for fear of losing my pretend identity. It was an obsession and, I let it eat at me for too long. I was scared to death that people would find out the truth and I would be doomed. How? I don't know. But, deep down, I hated the thoughts of people turning away from me. I hated being rejected. I didn't belong. I hated the world for robbing me of a normal childhood, the luxury of a nice home and security. I truly hated being an orphan."

Lance held her and let her talk. After all the years together and in their many talks, she had never opened up to him like she was doing at this moment.

"The odd part, Lance, was that neither you nor Emily got up-tight about it. You accepted me with my hang-ups. I didn't need to worry. I'm glad too, people today are more open minded and don't look at orphans with a jaundiced eye."

"Rebecca, it's good to know where you are coming from. To be honest with you, I never could understand why you kept it hush-hush. As far as I was concerned, it was never that big of a deal. I never looked at it from your point of view but then, I never really gave orphans a lot of thought."

"Holy Hannah, Lance, I don't know where all that came from. We were talking about Emily. Now where were we?"

"I know. We'll talk about her but, first Rebecca, I want you to know how truly sorry I am that you had to hurt for so many years."

"Thank you Lance. You don't know what a comfort it is for me knowing you are always there for me."

She was eager to put her subject to rest. "Now about Emily. Talk about ironic turn of events, who would have guessed that outcome? Remember that mind boggling, scientific talk we muddled through trying to find answers to help her? I mean, what did we know about genetics? But that didn't stop us. There was a lot of confusion and arguments. Remember?"

"How could I forget? That ordeal made me feel really dumb. It was tough. But you know Rebecca, what was even worse? The agonizing time we spent coming to terms with whether or not to tell Emily and Michael what might be in store for them. Oh, the hours, we spent going over the pros and cons with a fine-tooth comb. I don't ever want to go through that kind of torment again. You know what I'm talking about."

"I do, Lance. It's etched deeply in my mind."

"Still Rebecca, I'm convinced we made the right decision. We had to tell them before they got married. They deserved to know. But that didn't make it any easier. I will never forget the look on Emily's face. It almost killed me. And Michael's reaction was one of sheer shock. He just sat there shaking his head."

"I know Lance but we agreed and still do that it was the responsible thing to do. You handled it so well. You didn't pull any punches. You told them exactly what possibilities they faced. How conditions involved, like Russian roulette, had to be lined up perfectly for them to suffer the same fate that we did. Most importantly, you told them the odds of it happening were astronomical. I remember feeling sick for both of them. We dropped the heavy weight of this burden squarely on their shoulders."

"I know, Rebecca. It was a lousy thing to spring on a happy couple. To tell them that in the future, unspeakable tragedy might attack and kill their baby boys."

"Lance, you never said that. You broke the sad news to them gently. Stop beating yourself with that one. Think about the possible consequences if you didn't tell them the truth. Just be thankful for the way everything turned out."

"I am. And I'm thankful for Emily and Michael's intelligence and perseverance."

"What do you mean?"

"Remember after the initial shock wore off, that Michael asked for the reams of scientific reports? I cringed. I mean there's a mountain of terms and phrases to make your head spin. Yet, that didn't stop him and it didn't take him as long as it did us. He shared every detail with Emily. Together, they retraced our tracks from beginning to end. They investigated to their satisfaction. Come to think of it, probably that was harder on them than on us. Theirs was about prevention, while ours was after the fact. We didn't get to call the shots but, that possibility was theirs. That's what made their decision crucial. Their hearts and minds made up, they reached their conclusion."

In their determination, with medical requirements addressed, they never had to worry. Emily never had to give birth to any of her children. It took them three years to follow their dreams. Working with the adoption agency, so far three boys were happily adopted.

Chapter 50

~

Rebecca and Lance

"Lance, it has been a long time since you and I have had a meaningful conversation and it feels good. Doesn't matter how tired I am, I think it even beats sleeping."

"It was meaningful, Rebecca, I'll say that. But it is getting late. Now just clear your mind. Close your eyes and relax. Tomorrow is another day." That said, suddenly, out of the blue, Lance nixed his own plan. "Wait a minute, Rebecca. An amazing thought just popped into my head. It can't wait and you'll never guess."

"Well, then tell me, Lance," she said intrigued and, despite his sleep-inducing suggestions, was not the least bit sleepy now.

"Your purple gold deserves celebrity status."

"What? What in the world do you mean, Lance? You know other than taking delight in seeing the pleasure Emily gets out of wearing it, I haven't thought of my precious purple gold in a long time. So tell me. What's this about celebrity status?"

"Well, think about it. It played a big role in getting us to this point. Your father's initial reaction to your claim of being his daughter almost got us both kicked out of his office. Remember how he refused to even look at your birth certificate?"

"Don't remind me."

"But then you showed him your necklace and bingo. That did the trick. He did a complete 360. You found your father and the rest is history." Lance smiled broadly in his clever deduction that, in his eyes, just couldn't wait another minute to be told.   Sharing in his infectious excitement, Rebecca answered happily. "You're right. My purple gold was always a prized possession. Until now, I just never realized the magnitude of this treasure's true value. You know what else is still kind of hard for me to believe, Lance?"

"What's that?"

"After all these years, I actually have real parents hanging on my family tree. And my father turned out to be a senator, a celebrity in his own right. Not only did this senator hold his constituents near and dear to his heart; but turns out, loved his daughter, as well."

Lying in bed close to his Rebecca, stroking her soft hair, Lance arrived at an astounding deduction. "You know Rebecca, I was just thinking. Time is flying by so fast and, before we know it, we'll have three more grandchildren." Content, he whispered. "And to think, Rebecca, we worried about creating a legacy of lost promises."